THE
SOUL of the
MATTER

A Novel

Bruce Buff

HOWARD BOOKS
AN IMPRINT OF SIMON & SCHUSTER, INC.

New York   Nashville   London   Toronto   Sydney   New Delhi

Howard Books
An Imprint of Simon & Schuster, Inc.
1230 Avenue of the Americas
New York, NY 10020

First Howard Books paperback edition July 2017

HOWARD and colophon are trademarks of Simon & Schuster, Inc.

For information about special discounts for bulk purchases, please contact Simon & Schuster Special Sales at 1-866-506-1949 or business@simonandschuster.com.

The Simon & Schuster Speakers Bureau can bring authors to your live event. For more information or to book an event, contact the Simon & Schuster Speakers Bureau at 1-866-248-3049 or visit our website at www.simonspeakers.com.

Manufactured in the United States of America

10 9 8 7 6 5 4 3 2 1

Library of Congress Cataloging-in-Publication Data is available.

ISBN 978-1-5011-4071-6
ISBN 978-1-5011-4188-1 (pbk)
ISBN 978-1-5011-4076-1 (ebook)

*To the people who give meaning to my life: my wife, Claire,
and our children, Maggie, Julia, Susanna, Timothy, and Patrick*

PART 1

Chapter 1

EARLY FALL, 1998

In the murky early years of post-Soviet Russia, a dark veil hung where once there had been an iron curtain. Within its folds lurked danger and despair, threatening anyone who became entangled with the remnants of the Soviet Union.

Through bursts of showers on a chilly, black night, Dan had driven Russian scientist Pavel Sarasov, his wife, Katya, and their six-year-old son, Mikhail, from Moscow over three hundred fifty miles of bumpy highways and rougher roads.

Five hundred feet ahead was the Ukrainian border. Hastily constructed a few years earlier, a simple building on each side of the road housed border guards, Russians on one side, Ukrainians on the other. Two lanes in each direction, with a concrete median in between, separated the structures. A tollgate blocked vehicles from passing until authorized. Moisture from the recent rain cloaked the buildings, dripping from the edges of the roof. Puddles dotted the pavement. Mist rose languidly from the ground, forming an opaque barrier through which Dan strained to see what awaited them.

Reaching the gate, Dan stopped as a car that had been cleared on the other side passed them. No other vehicles were in sight.

Dan lowered the car window and handed passports and other travel papers through the open window to the guard inside. The guard flipped through the items several times, barely looking at them. Although Dan was only on his first real assignment after field training, he knew something was amiss. The paperwork with their false identities was flawless. Had anyone doubted their authenticity, they would have examined the papers closely. Instead, the guard seemed disinterested in them and was merely stalling for time.

Apprehensive but outwardly calm, Dan glanced in the rearview mirror, and then looked ahead.

Finally, speaking in Russian, the border guard said, "Please come inside."

Replying in fluent Russian, Dan said, "Park there?" pointing to spaces beyond the gate, thinking that if they could just get to the other side, whatever came next, most of the danger would have passed.

"Leave the car and come now," the border guard commanded in a menacing voice.

Heeding the warning, Dan and the Sarasovs got out of the car. They ignored gestures from the guard for them to enter the building on the Russian side and moved toward a door on the Ukrainian side, looking over their shoulders as they walked.

It was clear that getting Pavel and his family out of Russia was going to be more difficult than it had first seemed. Pavel Sarasov was a hot commodity, and Russia was not about to let him go. The scientist was reportedly working on a program to enhance human capabilities, perhaps even radically evolve the human species. There was nothing new with that aspiration. What was different, and what the US wanted to get its hands on, was technology that could lead to the rapid sequencing *and* manipulation of the whole human genome. Nothing like it existed—or was even close to existing—anywhere else. Word in the US intelligence community was that Pavel had achieved several major advances but was hindered from further progress by the limits of Russian technology. With access to superior technologies and funding, Pavel might be able to complete his work—for US interests. The human species was on the cusp of a new future.

Acting confidently, Dan continued to guide the Sarasovs ahead, Pavel on his right, the others on his left. Pavel was mid-fifties, with graying black hair. His slim face was expressionless and tight. Behind him, Katya clasped Mikhail's small hand in hers while she brushed a shock of wavy black hair out of his eyes. She was about forty but looked older, a reflection of a childhood spent in Siberia. Mikhail, too young to understand what was going on but old enough to sense it was something big, remained quiet as his wide, brown eyes gazed up at his mother.

Before they had gone far, a man yelled out from behind them, "Halt, Dr. Sarasov, or your family will be shot, one by one!"

Turning round, they faced a man standing fifty feet away. A little over six feet, he had a stout build and rigid posture. A thick, jagged scar crossed his left eyebrow. A holstered gun was visible under his open black-leather jacket. In a loud, authoritative voice filled with arrogance, he said, "Dr. Sarasov. You are committing a grave crime by attempting to leave the country. Come back now and, *this one time,* we will overlook your transgression."

A red laser dot, meant to be seen, from the rifle of a hidden sniper appeared on Katya's right shoulder.

"Return *now*," the Russian ordered.

In a strong voice, Pavel said, "I no will longer work for people who intend to use my research as a weapon against others."

After nodding at each other, Pavel and Katya began to turn toward the Ukrainian side.

The sound of a gunshot ripped the air. Katya crumbled to the ground, holding her shoulder, but not letting out even a whimper. Ashen-faced, Pavel quickly knelt beside her and opened her coat to look at the wound. Dan bent down next to both of them. Frightened, Mikhail grabbed his mother's hand.

"She will live if she gets immediate treatment in a *Russian* hospital. The choice is yours," the Russian said to Pavel.

Whispering to Dan, Katya said, "We cannot, *will not,* go back."

"The consequences are on your shoulders," the Russian yelled.

A red dot appeared on Mikhail's forehead.

Immediately, Dan picked up the small, trembling boy and, using his own body to shield Mikhail, took a few steps toward the Ukrainian side of the border. A sharp pain ripped through the meaty part of Dan's left arm, followed by the shot's report.

"The next bullet will shatter your skull, Mr. Lawson," the Russian said in English as he began to walk toward them.

Through his pain, Dan was startled that the Russian knew who he was.

Out of the denser mist on the Ukrainian side, two vehicles materialized. Special Agent Evans, head of Dan's CIA division and also his mentor, jumped out of one car with a Ukrainian government security agent, while two other Ukrainian agents emerged from the second.

Signaling for the agents to remain behind, Evans walked over to Pavel.

Across the narrow divide, Evans and the Russian stared at each other with malice.

It was now a standoff, though Dan doubted the Ukrainian security agents would act against the Russian. But the possibility was apparently enough to deter the Russian, and his sniper, from further action.

Taking advantage of the situation, Dan carried Mikhail to the building, left him inside, and then returned to Sarasov and Evans. Blood ran down Dan's left arm. Evans glanced at it, then looked at the Russian before bending down to help Katya up with Pavel's assistance.

Again in English, the Russian said, "Your appearance doesn't change anything, Agent Evans. Pavel Sarasov will not be allowed to leave."

A red dot was now on Evans's chest, over his heart. It would be an act of extreme aggression to kill an American official on Ukrainian soil with a shot fired in Russia. Maybe it was a bluff, maybe the Russian was deadly serious. Somehow, despite the international consequences that would follow, Dan believed this Russian would, without any hesitation, do whatever he wanted.

Ignoring the threat, Evans turned and helped Katya walk toward his car.

After three steps, two shots in quick succession split the air. Katya's and Pavel's bodies slammed to the pavement.

Evans turned, drew his gun, and aimed it at the Russian, ready to pull the trigger regardless of the cost. The red dot was now on Evans's forehead. Seeing it, Dan threw himself against Evans and knocked him out of the way behind the corner of the building just before another shot rang out. When Dan peered out, the Russian was gone.

Getting to his feet, Evans rushed over to Katya and Pavel, with Dan right next to him. Katya was dead; soon Pavel would be, too.

Looking at Katya forlornly, in a thin voice, punctuated by shallow gasps, Pavel said, "I thought I had found the key to unlock the secrets of creation."

Leaning close to Pavel, Evans asked, "What key? Hang in there!"

"The Torah says that God banished humanity from Eden to keep people from the Tree of Life," Pavel continued, gasping for breath to form each word.

Turning his palms and eyes upward, as his chest heaved, Pavel said, "Maybe there is a God. Maybe He meant what He said."

And then Pavel exhaled for the last time.

Chapter 2

PRESENT DAY
MID-DECEMBER, EVENING

Dan awoke as though he had been slapped. Perspiration coated his skin. Visions of the soulless Russian at the Ukrainian border dissipated as he stared at the ceiling. All he could remember of the Russian's face was the thick scar across his left eyebrow.

The vivid memories had reemerged in his dream after all this time. Dan wondered what had triggered their recall. Pavel's and Katya's deaths had haunted him for years, but gradually, and through great effort, the memories had faded into the deep recesses of his mind. It had been a long time since he had thought about them.

Miles away, yet right next to him, Laura slept soundly. Unless things changed, *Dan* changed, she would leave. A chasm had grown between them, not because she didn't love him, but because what they once had was no longer enough, and he couldn't offer even that anymore. For reasons unknown to himself, he was becoming a shell of a person. He knew his deficiencies were their problem but there was nothing he could do about it. And he had been honest from the beginning. He didn't think himself capable of, and didn't want, a long-term commitment. In the end, nothing lasts and there was no reason to pretend otherwise. Still, he felt for her and was aware of the hole that would be left in his life once she was gone.

Unsettled, he got up, walked to the living room window, and peered out into the cold December night. Across Storrow Drive, where few cars traversed at this hour, Dan looked at the placid Charles River, with Boston to his right and Cambridge to the left.

Although the repercussions for Dan had been nowhere near as severe as for the Sarasovs, he, too, had suffered consequences. After an extensive investigation, it had been decided that Dan's unauthorized participation in a Moscow food bank while he waited to make arrangements to get the Sarasovs out, although motivated by noble intentions, had made him too visible and contributed to the failure of the mission. There was also the matter of getting too close to a woman who, they later found out, had government ties. After the Sarasovs, there were other incidents, all minor, all involving Dan taking too much risk and caring too little about his own safety in pursuit of ideals beyond his assigned mission. Even though the later assignments were all successful, and he was regarded as a talented agent, he was also considered a liability.

Throughout it all, Evans had kept a close eye on Dan, guiding him wherever he could, perhaps in gratitude for saving his life, or perhaps to make up for sending Dan out on a first mission without more support. Although Evans wasn't quite old enough to be Dan's father, at least according to present family practices, they had a bond that had evolved from stern direction to cautious oversight to mutual respect. Not that Dan didn't create challenging moments for Evans along the way.

Eventually, when Dan was on the verge of being fired for taking one too many risks, Evans had intervened and arranged Dan's transfer to a cyber-intelligence division, where he subsequently excelled. A decade later, with the expertise he had developed, Dan left to start an Internet security company, where he also prospered. A few years after that, the company was bought out, giving him the freedom to do mostly what he wanted.

Despite all his financial success, he was not a happy man. At one time, he had thought that a world based solely on science would transform humanity for the better. That belief was the last of his faiths to die.

Turning his gaze toward Cambridge, he realized why he had thought of Pavel and his family. Earlier in the day he had read an

article about ENCODE, a project to identify all the functional components of DNA. Though the author of the article didn't mean to
imply anything supernatural, he had used the phrase *Book of Life* to
describe DNA, almost the same way Pavel once implied.

Thinking of the article now also reminded Dan of his near-lifelong
friend Stephen Bishop. It had been a long time since they had spoken and longer still since it had been a good friendship.

Settling his weary body onto the couch, Dan turned on his laptop
and typed "Stephen Bishop, geneticist." A string of results, mostly
headlines from various articles, appeared: "World's Preeminent
Geneticist"; "How Long until a Nobel Prize?"; "Rock Star Scientist
Leaves Academia to Lead the Human Betterment Corporation"; "It's
Just a Matter of Time until Science Learns the Secrets of DNA"; "On
the Threshold of Genetic Breakthroughs"; "Ethical Use of Genetic
Information"; "Reading the Language of Evolution"; "Gene-Editing
the Human Species"; and "Are We Now God?"

Thinking of Pavel and his warnings, for a brief moment Dan
considered putting aside his anger and reaching out to Stephen, but
decided against it. Stephen had ignored his overtures for some time,
and Dan wasn't going to give him the chance to do it again.

If there was one thing Stephen had made clear, it was that he
could take care of himself.

Without directing any ill will his way, Dan thought people like
Stephen always believed they could handle anything, always believed
their success was due solely to themselves, always believed they deserved every good thing that came their way, until too late they realized all of that was wrong.

Chapter 3

CAMBRIDGE, MASSACHUSETTS
SAME EVENING

Stephen Bishop would soon have the power to reshape the world—for good. The universe's greatest secrets were within his reach. The conflict between science and religion would be over. Fact and reason would finally replace ignorance and dogma.

Sitting at his office desk, he marveled at the image unfolding before him. On a large monitor, a series of numbers and ratios were connected by colored lines to different parts of a mannequin view of the human body. Using the Bluetooth trackball connected to his notebook computer, he zoomed in on areas of the image, smiling as he looked at the rough features of a human being. Once the processors in the nearby data center had finished their calculations, he'd be able to examine the image in detail.

He had done it! Within his grasp was the blueprint for all life, and potentially much more.

For months, he and Alex Robertson had spent a nearly continuous stream of long nights toiling in secret, trying to crack what had to be the most extraordinary encryption ever devised. What they had encountered should have been unbreakable.

It was remarkable that, through a series of astounding discoveries, they had gotten as far as they had, only to be stymied by a final puzzle that had defied solving.

It was even more remarkable that the answer to that last obstacle had suddenly come to him this morning. Realizing the implications of what they were about to obtain, he had decided to wait until he was certain what it would reveal before sharing his breakthrough with Alex. There was no telling how Alex would react to something that would challenge his worldview so dramatically. Still, after all they had done together, he questioned his decision.

Unsettled, Stephen rose from his desk, walked to the window, and looked out into the darkness. His office was on the top floor of the ten-story Human Betterment Corporation building, on the southwest side of Cambridge, overlooking the Charles River. HBC, as it was generally known, was one of the world's leading biotech corporations, focused on understanding the human genome and developing genetic-based treatments. As its president, he was in charge of all its research, though the work he was doing with Alex was outside his HBC work and unknown to them.

Though it was after midnight, and the sky was blanketed by thick clouds, swaying street lights illuminated the patches of snow and ice scattered across the gray lawn. In the shifting light, it created the impression of turbulent waters—or of a troubled soul.

Returning to the desk, he picked up a flat, glass paperweight etched with the yin-yang symbol. In good, the seeds of evil. In evil, the seeds of good. He turned it over a few times, wondering how much more he'd have to compromise in his pursuit of knowledge and goodness.

Alex was one of his smaller concerns. Twenty minutes earlier, believing they were still a long way from cracking the code, Alex had walked into Stephen's office, pointed to the adjacent conference room, and said, "We need to talk."

Without responding, Stephen had followed Alex into the room. A long, dark oak oval table, surrounded by brown leather chairs, took up the majority of the ten- by twenty-foot area. A whiteboard covered most of one of the long walls. Alex stopped in front of it.

Alex was barely five foot seven, with a round physique, and his wavy gray hair streaked with traces of black was pulled into a small ponytail. With his baggy clothes, and a craggy face adorned with black, hornrimmed, glasses, Alex resembled a gnome. But Alex had a fearsomely sharp mind. For thirty-five years, he'd taught physics to

PhD candidates at MIT. He'd also used his exceptional mathematical skills to master advanced cryptology. Both of Alex's skill sets were indispensable to Stephen. Without them, Stephen never would have been able to crack the codes. Alex had also provided the technology to perform and protect their work.

Picking up a blue marker, Alex said, "Look. We know that a dozen complex elements form the last code," as he rapidly drew complex shapes on the white board.

"You still don't like calling them symbols."

"To be symbols, they have to be symbolic to someone or something. And since you claim the origin of most of the coded information is from DNA, and I'm not ready to accept the connotations of that, I'm not going to call them symbols."

"What's wrong with a complete understanding of science and reason that points to something much bigger than us?"

"Give me concrete proof and then ask me the question."

"Break the code and you'll have your proof. There's only about a half billion permutations. What's the big deal? Get to it," Stephen said facetiously.

"Four hundred seventy-nine million, one thousand, six hundred, to be precise. There must be something that can help us narrow down the possibilities to a manageable number."

Yes, there is, Stephen thought. And that morning, he had become the only person in the world to know it. Now he was about to decode what could be the Rosetta Stone of all of life. Only there was much more to it than that.

"With luck, we'll figure it out in the next few days, before we've moved to the new computer infrastructure," Stephen said, referring to the planned migration off HBC's network to something new Alex was setting up. While Alex's encryption had kept their work hidden from prying eyes, it wasn't strong enough to withstand a determined examination, and they couldn't keep pressing their luck. Sooner or later, some IT person or senior researcher at HBC would notice the computer activity and ask Stephen about it, drawing unwanted attention that could be problematic.

"Remember, there's at least two sets of codes to break, maybe a third if your intuition is correct," Alex said. "The number I gave you is the very low end of what we're facing."

"Relax, go home, get some rest. Something will come to us," Stephen said calmly, though inwardly he was bothered by his own words. He'd always been a straight shooter, known for his integrity. Yet his single-minded pursuit to break the codes had led him to more and more deceit, for what he told himself were good reasons.

"What's the saying? From your lips to God's ears," Alex replied.

Trying to ease the tension in the room, Stephen said, "I'm not worried about what God hears; I'm more concerned what He'll do."

"Near as I can tell," Alex said, walking out the door, "if He exists, He doesn't do much of anything."

Chapter 4

To work off frustration, Alex decided to walk down the ten flights of stairs to the service entrance instead of taking the elevator.

He had to find out what they were decoding. It didn't help that he doubted the source of their work and, by extension, Stephen. The encryption they were decoding was extraordinarily sophisticated. It was difficult for a materialist like Alex, who believed only in the natural world, to think that the coded information was based on DNA, despite what Stephen had said. And the apparent relationship of DNA's coding to the laws of physics was also hard to fathom, yet he seemed to see it himself. The implications were profound.

One of his biggest worries had always been misuse of science by big business and government. It was the reason he had joined a group of scientists and ethicists who met twice a month to discuss the use of science. Until a few months ago, it had seemed a safe thing to do.

Then Elena began attending. She had said she was an independent European journalist investigating international networks that were determined to manipulate genetic research to their advantage, regardless of its impact on others.

Curious about what she knew, Alex had gone to coffee with her after a few meetings, often in the same café, to discuss the threat they agreed unconstrained science posed to humanity. He found her thoughtful, informed, and well-intentioned. She radiated eastern European mystery and sensuality, with short, frosted blond hair, dark green eyes, and soft features layered on top of what, at times, seemed like a hard foundation. Despite his strong marriage, he was drawn to her, and she seemed to encourage and welcome the interest. It disturbed and enthralled him, though he told himself nothing would ever come of it.

Two weeks ago, she had turned the café discussions to Boston-area biotech firms, HBC in particular, saying their work was leading toward unprecedented genetic technology. She talked about Stephen, claiming that he had a myopic focus on research that others would exploit to genetically modify life in unimaginable ways.

To defend him, Alex told her that he knew a little about Stephen's work and was confident that his intentions were good and broader than she thought.

She pressed him. He told her general things—nothing about encrypted information and his efforts to help Stephen decode it. Elena said that it was clear that Alex was aiding Stephen in important ways and insisted he find out more, lest he became an unwitting tool for the very things he said he opposed.

Alarmed by her interest and pressure, he cut off contact and stopped attending meetings.

It wasn't enough.

Just that morning, Elena had shown up outside his MIT office. "I understand your confusion," she said. "You're in a tough position. You're worried about Stephen's work, yet you don't want to do anything disloyal. I can help you with that."

Without waiting for his response, she clasped his hands warmly in hers, looked deep into his eyes, and said, "Won't the peace of mind be worth it?"

With his guard momentarily down, Alex told her Stephen was about to move his work from HBC's computers to a more secure environment, leaving out his own role in the move.

The warmth in her eyes had been replaced at disconcerting speed by a steely glint. Her previously velvety voice took on an icy hardness. "The world is on the precipice of a tremendous transformation. An enormous amount rests on your willingness to do the right thing."

Then her voice turned soft again, and she said, "Don't we have the same interests?" She paused, her eyes lingering on his. "I have to go now. Find out what you can." As a warm smile crossed her face, she kissed his cheek, then turned and was gone.

Throughout the rest of the day, Alex struggled with his doubts. Thoughts of Elena elicited a mixture of caution, desire, fear, and excitement. She called several times in the afternoon, but he ignored the calls and the messages she left.

Reaching the service door now, Alex turned up his collar and put on his gloves. It would be a cold walk to his car, parked in a remote section of the lot, hidden from view. He had once thought Stephen's precautions excessive. Now he hoped they'd be enough.

Stepping outside, he was struck hard by the bitter wind.

Chapter 5

A series of sharp tones jolted Stephen. The processing of the first set of information was complete. A more detailed image of a human body was displayed on the monitor.

Collecting himself, Stephen sat back down, entered a series of commands, and kicked off the processing of a second set of data. While the computers were busy completing their work, he clicked an option on the upper right of the image labeled Time Series.

Immediately, the monitor went blank, and then a small image of a newborn appeared in the center. Gradually, the image developed and aged as it progressed from newborn to toddler, child, teenager, young adult, through middle age and then old age: a lifetime of human development compressed into a few minutes. The mesmerizing visual results weren't remarkable in and of themselves. What was incredible was the source of the information used to generate the images. They were based solely on DNA, not computer simulation. He had unlocked and translated all the information that directed human development!

Beaming, Stephen turned his attention to the horizontal slide bars on the bottom of the screen and the numbers associated with them. After changing a number connected to the figure's torso, he watched the body elongate. When he increased a different number, the head grew larger and became misshapen. Clearly, important balances needed to be maintained.

After selecting Reset, the image reverted to its original version. Stephen gradually changed a slide bar and watched the image redisplay in different proportions. The bars were master controls for the entire image. Rotating a dial backward, a result resembling a Neanderthal was displayed. Rotating the same dial further backward, after several moments, what had once appeared human now looked like an unknown type of primate.

Astounded, he wondered if he was looking at actual evolutionary history. Was it possible that every prior version of humans was still in DNA? Or was a there a master set of genes that, when combined in different ways, could generate every creature in the human evolutionary branch? Could this information be used to re-create long-lost species?

More important, what would it mean for humanity's future?

Chapter 6

Steeling himself, Alex walked out into the cold night and toward his car.

As he approached it, a familiar voice said, "I've got the solution to our problems."

Alarmed, he turned to see Elena walking toward him. She was enveloped in a white, three-quarter-length down coat that shimmered unnaturally against the night sky.

"What are you doing here?" he said with more bravado than he felt. All of a sudden, Elena seemed far more formidable than her five-foot-eight frame would indicate. A shiver, not from the cold air, coursed through his body.

Without breaking stride, Elena said, "I couldn't reach you. We have to act quickly."

"To do what?"

"Find out what Bishop is up to. He's been hiding what he's been doing from everyone, even you. Right now, he's continuing his work by himself."

"How do you know that?" Alex exclaimed, upset that it might be true.

"I work with people who can access virtually any computer system in the world," Elena said, then looked at a text message on her phone. "In fact, he's using the computers heavily at this very moment."

"If he is, it won't be for long. I have the security keys the programs need to run and they're about to time out," Alex replied. He regretted his words as soon as he had said them.

"Quickly, then, let's see what he's doing. With your help, we can do that without him knowing."

"Who are you? What do you want?" Alex asked. Was she more connected to the people she claimed to be investigating than she let on?

"The same things you do. A better society, answers to the biggest questions about life, protecting people from the rich and powerful." Elena reached him and put her right hand on his left forearm.

Alex eased slightly away, but Elena's left arm reached around Alex's waist, toward his back, heightening the mixed feelings of attraction and wariness. The latter was winning.

"Please, no one is going to hurt you. We just have to know, as do you."

Alex tried to think of something to say. He looked around, avoiding her gaze. Alone, in the far reaches of an empty parking lot, with a person he didn't trust, he felt completely exposed.

As Elena's hands started to move around him, he realized she was actually feeling for the small devices that could be used to hold security keys used to access networks and encrypt files.

He tried to pull away. Elena shifted her position and grip and Alex found himself being twisted around. A frantic effort to pull free caused him to slip on a patch of ice. His feet came out from underneath him and he slammed onto the pavement. Splinters of light and pain shot through his head. Rolling slowly to his side, he reached into his pocket, grabbed his phone, and threw it weakly toward a bunch of bushes.

He struggled to stand up and said, "The security keys are in the phone. It isn't locked. Now find out whatever you want and leave me alone."

Elena ran to the bushes and thrashed through them.

Wobbling, Alex stepped toward his car. He looked down and saw Elena's purse, picked it up, unlocked his car, and got in. His keys shook in his hands. He struggled to put them into the ignition and then started the car.

Hearing the engine rev, Elena stood up, Alex's phone in her hand. She ran to the car's driver window. Realizing Alex had her purse, she pounded on the window and yelled, "Give it back to me."

"I'm going to find out what you're really after," Alex yelled back.

"You don't know who you're dealing with," Elena said in a voice heavy with threat.

Instead of answering, Alex stomped on the gas. Wheels spinning, he accelerated toward the parking lot exit.

Her expression frozen into stone, Elena waved toward a car parked alongside the road that Alex hadn't previously noticed. Its lights flashed on as it drove toward Elena.

Alex turned left on Western Avenue and pressed down the accelerator. How could he have been so foolish? He needed to warn Stephen, but without his phone, he had no way of doing so. At least he still had the computer security keys. Reaching into his pocket, he pulled out a plastic, one-inch-long USB flash drive, containing information about Stephen's work, and a fob that displayed the constantly changing security keys used to provide secondary authentication for accessing Stephen's private computer infrastructure.

Looking back, he saw that the headlights of the car Elena had gotten into were growing alarmingly close.

Despite the frigid night, beads of perspiration formed on his forehead. He wiped them off with the back of his trembling hand. His head throbbed and he had a hard time keeping the car in a straight line.

He wasn't cut out for this.

He searched for a place where he could hide or get help, but all he saw were blurry images of industrial warehouses and business buildings, all closed.

Alex raced his car across the intersection as the traffic light turned red. Looking behind, he saw that his pursuers had run the light as well.

Realizing that he might be caught, and that he couldn't let them have access to the computers, he opened his window and started biting pieces off of the USB drive and spitting them out as he drove, then did the same with the fob.

Up ahead, he saw a ramp for Soldier's Field Road, the highway that ran along the south side of the Charles River. Alex slowed slightly to let Elena and her companion catch up to him, then slammed his brakes and turned sharply right. They shot past him, missing the entrance. Alex drove down the ramp and onto the highway, headed toward Boston. If he could just make it to the Mass Pike, he could get help at the tollbooths.

Moments later, he saw the headlights of an oncoming car. With a sickening feeling, he realized that he was headed the wrong way and wouldn't be able to get off until the next entrance. Glancing back, he saw that his pursuers had resumed the chase, also on the wrong side of the highway, and were gaining on him.

Alex was trapped. A hip-high metal fence bordered the outside lanes and left no room to pull off. He thought of stopping and making a run for it, but his pursuers were too close. They'd catch him before he got far, caged by the river on one side and the road on the other.

He switched lanes rapidly to avoid the cars coming at him, their horns blaring and tires screeching. His sweaty hands made it hard to grab the wheel. He could hear his quick, shallow breathing, compounding his fear.

Swerving to avoid a car in the inside lane, he drove left onto a short breakdown area before he had to steer quickly back onto the highway. The abrupt maneuver propelled him across the lanes. The right side of his car scraped the median's guardrails and the rebound almost pushed him back into an oncoming car in the outer lane.

He sped onward. The road dipped down below a street crossing overhead. The sharp angle and high speed caused his car to bottom out, and he almost lost control.

Up ahead, he saw an entrance ramp to the highway from an overpass that was under construction—it could be his exit. As his pursuers closed to within a few car lengths, he hoped he would reach the entrance in time. As he neared the ramp, two cars in the outside lane approached with their lights flashing and horns screaming. There was just enough of a gap between them.

Alex hit his brakes after the first car passed, sending a plume of burnt rubber from his tires into the air, crossed the lanes, and pulled onto the ramp. His pursuers were blocked by the second car and missed the turnoff.

Too late, he saw a car headed down the ramp toward him. To the left was a steep embankment that ended at a stone wall. That way meant a violent impact, maybe death. Going right would mean a chance of getting back safely onto the highway or slamming head-on into another car, likely meaning death for all. With no time to do anything else but react, he swerved left. He wasn't willing to risk other lives in an attempt to save his own. His car hit the curb, went airborne, landed on the embankment, and tumbled sideways as it slammed into the wall.

Inside the mangled, steaming wreck, Alex's battered, limp body slowly leaked life.

Through the broken window, a hand reached in and removed Elena's purse.

Chapter 7

Stephen rushed back to the monitor. The second set of results had appeared. He scanned the images. On the left side was a geometric shape consisting of nodes and connecting rods. On the far right was a series of equations. As he clicked on each node, a different equation was highlighted. Some contained values of fundamental constants of physics. Others showed unfamiliar formulas. All seemed to indicate some physical aspect or property of the universe and how they related to each other.

Of course, scientists had known for some time the incredibly precise balance of the physical constants, the relative proportions between gravitational, electromagnetic, strong nuclear, and weak nuclear forces. The smallest change in just one of these, almost to the quadrillionth decimal place, and nothing would exist. If a tape measure spanned the whole universe, twenty-eight billion light-years, and the point in front of him was the value for gravitational force, a change of just one inch in either direction would have been enough to keep the universe from forming. That's how precise things needed to be for life to exist.

Stephen was relieved when he realized Alex could help him interpret what the equations meant. That was one dilemma solved. In the morning, he'd share everything with him.

Preparing to start the last processing, he entered the necessary instructions and codes, and then initiated the command to generate what could be a third and final set of results. Their contents, if they even existed, were unknown, but their potential impact was even more astounding than the first two.

As a bell chimed in the distance, announcing the late hour, he entered commands to transfer the first and second sets of results onto his computer. He would need a lot of time, and assistance, to analyze and understand them. Tonight was for completing as much decoding as possible.

With time to kill before the final processing completed, and exhausted, he lowered his face into his hands. Slowly, he sank deeper into his chair, and his upper body slumped forward. The excitement and fatigue had become too much. Overcome, he drifted into a restless sleep.

Stephen woke with a start. He wasn't sure how long it had been since he had nodded off, but he snapped alert and looked at the computer display. An error message filled the screen, indicating that the processing had aborted. With a sly smile, Stephen realized that Alex had put a time limit on the security keys they were using to protect their work. In the morning, he'd have Alex supply the keys needed to complete the processing.

Just as he was about to shut everything down, one line appeared at the bottom of the screen. Maybe it was randomly generated from the partially completed processing, maybe not. In plain text, in language that stunned him, were two short words. He had been ready for almost anything, but not this.

PART 2

Chapter 8

Viktor Weisman had spent most of his life pursuing the power of the sun. Few people understood it as he did. None was as close to recreating it.

As Director of MIT's Plasma Science and Fusion Center, he led a team of the world's top physicists in an effort to develop fusion energy as a major power source. Unlike today's fission power plants, fusion energy promised unlimited, safe, and virtually waste-free power.

Viktor had been working on fusion research for more than fifty years. In the early days, he had shared the belief, then common among physicists, that plentiful, clean, cheap fusion energy would be a reality within a generation or two. The goal had proved far more elusive. A fusion-powered world was still decades away, and he would never live to see it. Yet even in his old age, he continued to work to ensure that the research was funded and the program unlike him wouldn't die out.

That was yesterday's world.

Ever since Stephen had approached him four months ago, he'd known that fusion power was within reach.

Now he was only weeks from realizing his lifetime goal—that and much more.

Even the sun itself seemed to realize that the chase was almost over as it darted in and out from behind the few clouds still left in the early morning sky. It amused him.

Viktor crossed the Harvard Bridge over the Charles River toward Cambridge and paused at Memorial Drive to observe people walking, running, and biking on the wide, tree-lined strip that ran between the parkway and the north bank of the river. He enjoyed watching people happy, experiencing life.

Smiling to himself, he reflected on how he had gotten to this point.

Somehow, John Welch, an up-and-coming theoretical physicist with good connections to academia, industry, and government communities, had access to research and discoveries that gave him insights apparently only few knew about. And for reasons that continued to puzzle Viktor, Stephen Bishop had introduced them and seemed to be coordinating their research.

Weeks ago, Viktor had questioned Stephen about it. Stephen had answered, "Of course I'm not involved in physics research. Because of relationships I have, I'm simply the intermediary for a number of private, leading-edge initiatives." He'd been cool and confident, and Viktor had been inclined to trust him as he continued, "Due to the wide-ranging implications, they need to understand and prove out some of the capabilities before making them public or involving others. For that, they need the use of your reactor. Knowing our relationship, and since I was already working with them on other research, they asked me to contact you, hoping that you'd be willing to work with them via me, under the necessary conditions, including keeping everything absolutely secret."

If it had been anyone but Stephen, Viktor would probably have declined to participate and not allowed the reactor to be used for his experiments. But over the years, Stephen and Viktor had become close friends, despite the differences in age and scientific fields. He had come to learn that Stephen was one of the highest-principled people there were, though whether that was a good benchmark remained to be determined.

Ultimately, though Viktor had some reservations, he had decided that he didn't want to do anything to jeopardize his position in the project. Success meant a key role in one of the most important scientific breakthroughs the world had yet seen. Fusion energy could be a near-term reality. After agreeing to Stephen's conditions, Viktor had spent months working with Welch, figuring out how to apply Stephen's astonishing physics theories and prepare for the upcoming fusion energy experiments.

Although the sunshine felt wonderful, Viktor still checked, as he often did, that his golf jacket was zipped all the way up and that his shoes were securely tied. Ever since he'd been a frail six-year-old, shivering barefoot in the camp yard, he had been obsessed with warmth.

He was a Holocaust survivor who still remembered. A minority of a minority of a minority. In 1944, his family's hiding spot in Belgium had been found, and they had been shipped off, like refuse, to Auschwitz. There they had seen things, some under the guise of medical experiments, that he could never have imagined. Whatever arguments there were for the innate goodness and dignity of man, Auschwitz had emphatically refuted them.

After the camp was liberated, Viktor made it to America with the shattered remnants of his family: his father and one of his three older brothers.

It was then that he dedicated himself to providing people with warmth in all its forms, to try to wipe out the conditions that led to evil. Science was his way to reduce suffering. If people felt secure, had what they needed, perhaps things as terrible as holocausts and world wars wouldn't happen again.

Resuming his walk, he headed to the old three-story, redbrick building on the MIT campus where Nabisco ovens used to bake cookies. Now it housed the hottest oven in the world, the superconducting Alcator-E, the world's most powerful experimental nuclear fusion reactor.

Viktor had secured its funding, headed up the research and teams that had led to its development, and controlled its use. Alcator-E was why he was still working at seventy-eight.

Entering the lab, Viktor saw Sousan Ghardi standing outside his office. Sousan led the plasma research group. Viktor was surprised to see her, as she was supposed to be taking the day off. In fact, he had been counting on it.

She was a top-notch physicist, forty-eight years old, attractive though she played it down, and was well regarded by everyone at the center. Her father had been a well-off scientist in Iran before the revolution. Afterward, he brought his family to America to give his inquisitive, rational daughter the same opportunities and intellectual freedom that had benefited him.

In America, Sousan had carved out a strong academic career, then had come to the lab ten years ago. More than just a valued coworker, she had become a good friend.

Spotting Viktor, Sousan walked briskly toward him. "Viktor, what's this I hear about experimental shots this morning?" She was referring to the term they used to describe experiments in the fusion reactor. "There's nothing on the calendar, and almost all of the staff are gone for the holiday weekend."

"Sousan, I'm glad you're here, though I hope you didn't come in just for this." Viktor forced a weary smile. "All we're doing is calibrating the measurement equipment you've seen being installed. Since the Alcator is going offline next week for six months of maintenance, it made sense to fit in whatever we could." He lied with extreme discomfort. The Friday before Memorial Day should have been the perfect opportunity for him to conduct his unusual experiments without unwanted eyes around.

"Well, *the calibrations,* as you call them, should have been added to the calendar, and the staff should have been notified in case anyone wanted to observe. And, as director of plasma research, overseeing a new reactor, I definitely should be here, and *you* know that," said Sousan.

"All the data will be available to anyone who wants to see it. Stay if you like, whatever you prefer. It looks like a great day to be outdoors. But if you're inquisitive, please stay."

Using an even voice ringing with fake pleasantness, Sousan replied, "Of *course* I'll stay. You're short-staffed, and I would love to get in a few more shots while we can." She paused, her lips pulling back into a devious smile. "By the way, the reason I'm here is to prepare for a last-minute tour I'm supposed to give shortly to students from Newton High School. It's a favor for a board member; one of the kids is her daughter. Unfortunately, since I now need to get ready for today's *opportunistic* experiments, somebody else will have to give the tour. Sorry, but I think that will have to be you."

Viktor noted the pleasure this gave her. It was well known that he didn't like giving tours.

He tried to appear sincere as he replied, "For you, Sousan, I would be happy to do it."

Viktor entered his office and found John Welch, and a pot of coffee, waiting for him.

Viktor greeted him with a thin smile. "Looks like we'll have more company than we planned on." He took off his jacket, combed his thin, gray hair, and poured himself a cup.

"It should be fine. She won't know what's really happening. The good news is that I finished setting everything up."

"Great. Let's take a look," Viktor said with palpable excitement.

Together, they walked briskly down the hall into the reactor room. It was an open space, sixty square feet, two floors high, with second-level metal walkways on the left. Various elaborate-looking pipes, wires, and devices were interspersed around the room's perimeter. All were to support the superconducting, experimental fusion reactor located in the center of the room. The Alcator-E was circular, twenty-three feet in diameter and just as tall, though it was partially recessed into the floor, with about ten feet showing. Wrapped in light-gray foam, the reactor that generated the highest temperatures and pressures on earth, outside of a hydrogen bomb, didn't look like much.

Welch walked over to a three-foot cube, black metal box set five feet back from the reactor. Fifteen others were similarly placed evenly around the reactor's perimeter. Bending down and opening the top cover, he pointed inside at the thick coils. "These will generate the pulses that will help tune the fields."

Viktor took a look at them and then pointed at the microwave generators along the outer perimeter of the reactor, eyebrows raised.

Welch nodded. "We've increased their power, altered the frequencies, and modified the operational software. We'll get more efficient results, and then, when the plasma is in the proper configuration, we'll turn on the coils, providing the compression boost and reducing the proton repulsion that'll get us a sustained fusion burn with lower input power. At least that's the theory."

"Time to find out if reality can measure up to it," Viktor said, thinking about all that was at stake if it didn't.

Chapter 9

Life has no meaning once you lose the illusion of being eternal.
—JEAN-PAUL SARTRE

Dan Lawson stared out his bedroom window at the cloudless early-morning sky and wondered why everything looked so gray and he felt so cold. It was almost summer, but all he felt was winter.

He knew that it shouldn't be this way. There were so many fun things he could be doing: wasn't that all there was to life for those fortunate enough to experience it that way? With the forecast calling for brilliant sunshine and warm temperatures, he could hang out at the Common, catch the afternoon game at Fenway, row on the Charles River, or head down to the Cape.

Instead, he sat in a chair by his bed and struggled to find a way to get going for the day before his recent turn inward consumed him and movement became impossible.

The longer he sat, the less likely he was to move. While he was out in the world, he could get around with relative ease, forget the peculiar void that he sensed in himself, act normal. But when he was alone, he withdrew within himself, with little interest in entering back into the world, as though an energy-absorbing barrier stood between him and normal life.

If this had been a few months earlier, he would already have finished a long run or a gym workout, and would feel exhilarated.

Instead, he was increasingly lethargic, finding each day more soul draining than the last.

Until recently, things had always come easily to him. The future, as far out as he ever viewed it, was promising. He was a financially secure, good-looking, forty-three-year-old, single-by-design man, simply trying to enjoy one day at a time. He lived on the top floor of the brownstone he owned, renting out the ground floor to a couple with a young child and the middle floor to a British expat over on a temporary assignment for his insurance company employer.

All Dan wanted was for life to be interesting and fun, not too challenging or stressful. He lived by the modern version of the golden rule—*You do your thing, I do mine*—and when a person could, extend a helping hand to those in need. Over time, he had learned that trying to do any more than that only led to being overwhelmed by the problems of the world, problems he could never solve.

Now, with all the energy he could muster, he looked at the emails on his smartphone.

One from two days ago stood out from the rest, annoying him.

It was from Stephen Bishop. As Stephen had progressed in his career, he'd left his past, and his friends, behind. After ignoring Dan's attempts to get in touch with him seven months ago, Dan had decided Stephen was no longer worth what to him was a one-way effort of trying to maintain a long-dying friendship. It had been time to recognize the reality that Stephen seemed to have already accepted.

Given all of that, the subject line in Stephen's email was certainly bold: "Please come to dinner at my house Friday at seven—it's important to both of us."

No explanations. No apologies. Just summoned to dinner. Though momentarily intrigued, there was no way Dan was going to accept, let alone acknowledge, the request, or the several follow-up messages Stephen had sent.

Moving on, he noticed a text message from his sister Joanna that he had somehow missed. "Hi Dan. Turns out I have to be in Boston early this morning. I'd like to stop by to say a quick hello. See you soon."

Thinking that she'd probably want to discuss his state of mind, he didn't want to respond. Things had gotten to the point where he didn't want to talk with even his sister. It bothered him that he wanted to keep his distance from her, yet his desire for isolation outweighed his willingness, his ability, to be himself.

But he knew his sister wouldn't be put off and he was forced to reply, writing back, "Just got your message. Will be great to see you. How soon?" with an attempt at light-heartedness, an act he intended to continue through her visit.

A moment later, she answered, "I'm at a shop a few blocks from you. How's twenty minutes?"

"That works. See you then."

Dan raced to clean up. He emptied the sink of dirty dishes and started the dishwasher. He took the recycling bag, overflowing with bottles, and grabbed the empty wine bottle from the countertop, and put both out on the fire escape. He gathered the clothes strewn around his bedroom and threw them into the hamper in his closet and made his bed for the first time in weeks.

Stepping back, seeing that things looked presentable, he headed into the bathroom.

At Laura's insistence, it had been restored to Victorian perfection. A claw-foot porcelain bathtub dominated the far wall, adorned above with a stained glass window. Rectangular white tiles ran four feet up every wall. To the right was a glass-enclosed, stand-alone shower with porcelain handles.

As he stepped into the shower, he remembered Laura's deep and provocative laugh, straight dark hair, and unusual warm brown eyes with glints of gold. He felt a tinge of regret over their breakup but told himself she deserved more than someone just to pass the time with.

Well, their relationship was over and done with, and there was nothing he could do about it. Looking back was a waste of time and energy. He was proud of his ability to seal off the past without having to reach closure or come to terms with whatever had transpired. He had worked hard to develop that skill.

Invigorated by water so hot that it bordered on scalding, he walked through the small alcove off his bedroom into his closet and dressed quickly. He looked closely in the mirror and was pleased to see that he still looked young for his age, with smooth skin, medium complexion, and a full head of reddish-brown hair.

Done dressing, he returned to the alcove and lowered himself onto the intricately carved wooden chair that faced the computer. On the nearby stand was the guitar he once played. Red Sox World Series ticket stubs and framed autographed album covers of Dire Straits, the Allman Brothers, and Bruce Springsteen hung on the wall. On the desktop, to the left of the computer screen, was a picture of his parents, both long gone, in their fifties. He wondered what they would have thought of his "lethargy," as he preferred to think of his present state of mind.

They probably would have said, as they had before, that his problem was that he didn't believe in God, that he lacked a real purpose in his life. To their dismay, he had discarded whatever thoughts he had of a God a long time ago. Although he once followed Catholic rituals and supposed he believed in an all-loving, all-powerful God, the teachings of his instructors did not hold up under questioning, nor to the experiences of real life.

He wondered what his parents had thought about their faith as his mother slowly, and painfully, dissipated from her cancer. There was nothing just or redemptive about it. She had been a pious, gentle woman; all she had ever done was love others. If he knew this, then surely any God would have as well and would have done something about her suffering. The answer was simple. There was no God, no ultimate purpose in life. Nothing a person did had any lasting consequences. There was no absolute moral standard by which people were judged.

Religion certainly didn't provide his father much comfort either, for it wasn't long after his wife died that he lost interest in living and one morning just didn't wake up. Although Dan missed his father, he was glad his sorrow was over and his death easy.

With his parents gone, Dan was free to discard all pretense of religion. He was now a member of the age of enlightenment, where reason ruled and there was nothing that science wouldn't eventually explain.

Any thoughts to the contrary he consistently pushed to the side. His disciplined, logical mind was one of his greatest strengths. He prided himself on being able to face honestly what very few could. Humans were simply a temporary collection of atoms subject to the laws of physics, and nothing else. Still, with no more motivation than his own desire, he did his share of good things for others. He had nothing to apologize for or regret.

Yet he still felt anxious about Joanna's visit. It was unlike her to just show up. Something must be up.

Chapter 10

Assembled in front of Viktor were eighteen high school students and their teacher, Mr. Reilly. They were in the center's media room, which was designed expressly for activities like tours and information sessions. Its walls were covered with colorful posters about fusion. On a table in the center of the room was a cutaway mock-up of the Alcator-E reactor. Off to the side was another table supporting a long, glass tube with electrodes at each end.

"I'm Dr. Weisman, and I'm pleased to be your guide this morning. I hope when you leave here, you'll have a good understanding of the importance, principles, and challenges of fusion energy," Viktor said. He looked around at the students. "I'd like to begin by having one of you explain the difference between fusion and fission energy. And I have to caution you, I pick people at random if no one volunteers to answer a question."

A tall, thin boy wearing a button-down shirt, navy-blue dress pants, and polished black shoes raised his hand. Viktor nodded and the boy answered, "Fission is when a larger atom is split into smaller atoms. Fusion is when smaller atoms are joined together to produce a larger atom. Both release large amounts of energy, though fusion produces much more and is what fuels our sun."

"Good, your answer indicates that you are in the right place. Next question. Why does fusion energy matter?"

This time a girl in skinny jeans and a fashionable shirt responded, "Fusion can produce enormous amounts of energy without generating a lot of dangerous radioactive waste, and there is an almost unlimited supply of fuel."

"Right. So why don't we have fusion power plants today? Why do we need a research facility such as this?"

This time a number of students raised their hands. The girl Viktor picked said, "You need extremely high temperatures and pressures and a way to generate power from that. No one's figured out how to do that yet."

"Mostly correct. I see Mr. Reilly has prepared you very well. As you pointed out, the difficulties in building a fusion energy plant are significant. First, we have to create the conditions necessary for fusion to occur, in a controlled manner. Second, we have to get more energy out than was used to generate the fusion. Third, we need to build a plant that can capture that energy to generate electricity. Each of these is tough, and, as much progress as we've made, there is still a long way to go. Now please turn around and face the poster with the sun on it. Can anyone tell me the conditions under which fusion takes place in the sun?"

This time, only one student raised his hand. He answered, "Fusion takes place in the core of the sun, under intense gravitational pressure, where the temperature is about fifteen million degrees Celsius."

Viktor nodded with a small smile. "Of course, we can't create pressure as intense as the core of the sun. So we need higher temperatures, in the range of one hundred million degrees. The Alcator-E is the experimental fusion reactor that does that for us." Pointing to the cutout model on the nearby table, he added, "As you can see, it is a doughnut-shaped device. Powerful, hollow magnets form a ring. Inside, magnetic fields follow the shape of the doughnut and keep the fuel in place as it is superheated and compressed. Let me show you an example of using magnets to shape a field."

Viktor pointed at the glass tube in the room and turned on a switch. "Inside this tube is ionized gas. High energy causes electrons to separate from the atoms' nuclei, thereby creating plasma, the fourth state of matter. The plasma in here is glowing pink and runs in a line, in the center of the tube, from end to end. Because the plasma consists of charged particles, we can shape it using a magnetic field." As he said this, he picked up a fist-sized magnet and pulled it along the bottom of the tube. Wherever the magnet was, the glowing plasma dipped down. He flipped the magnet over, thereby reversing the charge against the glass tube, and the plasma moved away from it. "In the Alcator reactor, we use the same principle to shape and compress the plasma."

He then gave the magnet to the students and let them play with it, watching as they tried to create interesting shapes and effects.

As they took turns with the magnet, he asked, "Why do we need such high pressures and temperatures to fuse atoms?"

A student answered, "To overcome the electromagnetic repulsion of two positively charged particles."

"You are a well-informed group of high school students."

The student smiled and then looked at Mr. Reilly.

"We spent yesterday's class preparing. We appreciate the time you are giving us and wanted to get the most out of the tour," Mr. Reilly said.

Looking at the room, Viktor said, "Very good. Then let's dispense with the simpler questions and get to more interesting ones. Once fused, why do the particles stay together?"

This time, no one rushed to answer.

Viktor said, "In the interest of time, I'll answer that. There are four fundamental forces in the universe: gravitational, electromagnetic, strong nuclear, and weak nuclear. The strong force binds particles in atomic nuclei together. It's only effective at small distances, basically the width of the nucleus of an atom, while the electromagnetic force retains its strength over very long distances. Once a force sufficient to overcome the electromagnetic repulsion has pushed two positively charged protons close enough together, they bind and release large amounts of energy. This shows the importance of how the ratio of the fundamental forces of physics determines all the behavior in the universe, even yours and mine. Now, what if the ratio of forces was just the least bit different, even less than a billionth of a billionth?"

"There would no universe at all," replied the student who had provided the last answer.

"That's right. Pretty remarkable, and fortunate, that the forces just happen to be what they need to be for us to exist."

A quiet, serious-looking boy asked, "Why are they that way? Could they someday change?"

Viktor knew this discussion could turn in the wrong direction rather quickly. He'd had many discussions with people who claimed that a creator "tuned and maintains" the forces so that life could form and exist specifically on earth, and he was determined to avoid the controversial topic. In reply, he said, "Quantum physics supports the existence of an infinite number of multiverses where, in aggregate, anything that can happen, does happen, somewhere. Accordingly, there is a universe capable of supporting our existence and we're in it."

The boy crossed his arms. "So you're saying that every time any-one, anywhere, makes a decision or does anything, a whole new universe, with all the matter and energy and history of this one, instantaneously springs into existence out of nothingness into dimen-sions that we can't perceive, a multitude of big bangs bigger than the first big bang, and that the new universes don't interact with any other universe?"

Flustered, Viktor's face tightened. "I just stated one of the more generally recognized theories. In time, it may be disproved or re-placed by another theory that better suits the data. But for now, many believe this best explains our universe."

Mr. Reilly jumped in. "Ted is something of a science prodigy and has read up on quantum physics. A little bit of knowledge can be dangerous."

"That's all right. Questioning is healthy," Viktor said through tight lips.

With a look that hinted at sarcasm, the boy said, "It would be cool if multiverses were true. Every time I'd do or not do anything, my thoughts would cause the creation of a whole new universe in which another me, with the exact same history and mind as me, would have decided to do a different thing. I'd be more powerful than God, since He only created the universe once and I get to do it over and over again."

Viktor didn't answer, so the boy continued. "And this would be happening with everyone, at all times. Not only that, but it took God six days and took so much out of Him that He had to rest a whole day and I do it instantly and feel like nothing happened."

Another boy, with a muscular build and Patriots football jersey, teased, "Come on Ted. You can't even get Alyssa to go to the prom with you, and you think your thoughts create an infinite number of invisible universes?"

Ted replied, "The good news is that in a very large number of them, she actually said yes. Too bad she didn't in this one."

An embarrassed girl who Viktor assumed was Alyssa said, "You asked better in the other universes." Several girls stifled laughs.

As Ted's mouth flew open to reply, Mr. Reilly said in a strong voice, "Cut it out, or I'll make sure no one goes to any prom, in any universe."

After everyone had quieted down, Viktor said, "All kidding aside, there is a lot we still need to find out. That's the fun thing about physics. There is always something new to learn. Now, let's go see what you came for."

Everyone followed Viktor down the hall and formed a small circle by the door to the reactor room.

Viktor began, "As you may have noticed, these concrete doors are two feet thick. They shield us from the lethal neutrons generated by the reactor. Inside the large gray foam cylinder in front of you is the Alcator-E reactor. It has superconducting magnets that produce magnetic fields two hundred thousand times stronger than Earth's. Over there are radio frequency generators where radio waves, a thousand times stronger than a radio station's, are used to heat the plasma. When we run experiments, which we call 'shots,' we heat and compress the plasma intensely for up to thirty seconds. During that period, we use as much power as the entire city of Cambridge. Of course, you can't just get that all at once from the power lines, so we build up a charge, store it in a huge flywheel, and then release it when it's needed. Before we head over to the control room, are there any questions?"

Instantly, a half dozen hands went up. Working left to right, Viktor picked one.

"What do you fuel this with?"

"Great question, and something I should have already mentioned," Viktor answered. "We use a form of hydrogen called deuterium. It has two neutrons instead of the usual one, hence the 'deu' in its name. An actual power-generating reactor would use a hydrogen mix that included tritium, which, as its name implies, has yet one more neutron. We don't use tritium here because we don't need to; it's hard to handle, and it's mildly radioactive, although it's only toxic if inhaled, and it's use is highly restricted."

"Can the reactor explode or go critical?"

"Not in any sense of a nuclear explosion. There isn't enough fuel and you can't get runaway reactions. The worst that happens is the magnetic field fails and superheated fuel hits the walls and damages them." Viktor pointed at the reactor and said, "Plus, with this, the hottest we get is seventy-five million degrees Celsius. For significant amounts of fusion, you need two hundred million degrees for a deuterium-to-deuterium reaction and one hundred million for a deuterium-to-tritium reaction."

"What happens if something does go wrong?" one student asked.

"The worst case is you can get a beam of runaway electrons that could burn through solid steel. To prevent that, we have an extinguisher that releases argon gas into the vessel if there's a problem. This would convert the energy of the electrons into photons. The resulting light would be briefly brighter than a billion lightbulbs, or the brightest beam of light that's ever existed." Pausing to let the idea sink in, Viktor then said, "Now let's head into the control room."

After entering the room, Viktor faced the tour group and said, "The actual shots follow a procedure a lot like a space launch, with people sitting at monitors as a recorded voice counts down. While the shot is underway, we can see computer-generated images of the plasma and readings. Before you know it, the shot is over, and you're getting ready for another one. Pretty impressive, isn't it? Before I conclude the tour, are there any final questions?"

One student asked, "How do you measure the plasma temperature?"

"Another good question. Obviously, there aren't any physical probes that could withstand the heat. What we do is bounce laser beams off the plasma. While this is an accurate enough technique, it takes time for the computers to process the data and give us a reading."

Mr. Reilly, stepped forward. "How far away are we from fusion energy?"

Victor sighed. "Decades. A consortium is building a prototype reactor in France called ITER. It was supposed to take ten years, but it's already been delayed. After that, it would still be a long time before we could get to the point of building commercial fusion power plants. Beyond the technical questions, it's an issue of how much we spend." He directed his attention to the students. "That brings me to a last question: how much do we spend in the US per year on fusion energy research?"

A number of students shouted out amounts ranging from one billion dollars to fifty billion dollars.

"Not even close. How about two hundred million dollars? In a country that has been energy-dependent, we spend less on this than on studying the mating habits of various animals, less than on bridges that go nowhere, and a fraction of what the President of the United States spent on his campaign."

"Isn't that because people aren't sure it can ever work?" one student asked.

"Personally, I think it is more about energy politics than anything else. After all, look at the tens of billions of dollars the government spends every year on ideas that can't possibly provide the amount of energy we need."

One student asked, "Is there anything we can do about this?"

Viktor answered, "It would help to have an informed and involved electorate." In truth, he thought the odds against that were very high. Just look at how little effort people put into understanding financial markets, government and trade deficits, and the state of education. After all, writing something witty on Facebook or Twitter already took up a lot of their time. In this willfully knowledge-limited world, emotional self-certainty was more than enough to fuel support for candidates.

"Maybe anything nuclear sounding seems like it can always go wrong," Alyssa said.

"Something can always go wrong with anything, often in unexpected ways," Viktor said.

Chapter 11

After Dan buzzed Joanna in, he poured a cup of coffee, opened a book, and placed both on the kitchen table, trying to make everything seem relaxed and natural. He opened the door and smiled as Joanna climbed the last few steps of the stairway.

Happily married for more than twenty-seven years, Joanna had two children in college and a nice income from her remarkably accomplished impressionist painting. Joanna lived on the coast of Connecticut, not far from the Rhode Island border, in Stonington, an old fishing town with classic homes and a quaint main street. She was one of the rare people actually content with life.

Although she was twelve years older, Joanna and Dan had always been close. When he was young, her steadiness and warmth had always comforted him. Though she was only ninety minutes away, Dan didn't visit her often. Not these days.

"Dan, it's great to see you," she said as she entered his apartment and hugged him. Tall and angular, she had long, light-brown hair with natural highlights framing her face. Her brown eyes sparkled.

"You, too," he replied with muted pleasure.

"The coffee smells good. Mind if I pour myself a cup?"

"I'll get it. I hope you can stay awhile," Dan said, not sure if that was what he wanted at all.

"Not long. I have to get back home. How's everything?"

"Good. Staying busy with work and other things," Dan answered, his internal alarms rising for the probing he thought he heard in her voice.

"Honestly? You don't seem to be yourself these days."

"Everything is fine. Really it is," Dan said, trying to convince them both with an almost upbeat voice as the questioning that he dreaded was materializing.

"Lately you've sounded so unhappy. I've been worried."

"Is this why you came by?" Exasperated, Dan walked to the window, quickly glanced out, then turned toward Joanna and waited for her response.

"Although I wanted to see you anyway, I need a simple, but important, favor."

Relaxing, he said, "What can I do for my favorite sister?"

"At risk of that exalted position, as your *only* sister, I would like you to hear what Stephen has to say."

So *that's* it! Stephen's recruited Joanna to plead his case, Dan thought with disdain.

Standing up, face and voice tightening, Dan said, "I have better things to do. And you don't need to get involved."

"I figured that was going to be your response." Joanna said. "Don't you know friendships like the one you two had are really hard to come by? What's he done that's so terrible? Is it worth throwing away your lifelong relationship and ignoring him when he says something is important?"

In fact, no fight had led to the split, just small disagreements here and there. They spent less and less time with each other and their interactions had become increasingly superficial, as though the illusion of a close friendship was more important than the risk of actually trying to have one.

"Maybe we weren't the friends we thought we were. Maybe we aren't who we were. People change, develop other interests."

Joanna said, "I don't know what your problem is, but get over it. You want to be by yourself, create grudges that you won't even talk about, fine. But when someone you've known your whole life, whom you've been so close with, says something is important, you do it. Stop feeling so sorry for yourself. You need to question who you're becoming."

Dan was startled. Joanna hadn't spoken to him like this since he was much younger. "It's not like he's made any effort before he suddenly realized he wanted to talk with me. And I have better things to do than to pretend something is there that isn't," Dan said.

"Like what? It seems like you are not doing much of anything these days. What's up with the sports league for the inner-city kids you were helping to run?"

"It's done for the year, at least as far as my involvement goes. Same for the high-school tutoring I was doing."

"What about the group of guys in the neighborhood you hang out with?" Joanna asked.

"We get together once in a while. There is a dinner coming up, but that's with wives and girlfriends, so I'll skip that."

"I'm seeing a pattern here, and it worries me," Joanna said.

"Oh yeah, what's that?" Dan challenged.

"You're pulling away from people. The fun things you used to do are no longer enough of a distraction. There's a void in your life you can't fill and can't look away from anymore."

"I'd ask what you think should fill what you call my void, but we both know what you'd say and that won't work for me. I know too much," Dan said.

"You need something."

"You're not my psychologist. And it's not unnatural to be a little sad now. The last of our parents' siblings just died and our ties to that generation are gone." Left unsaid was the toll that helping to take care of their uncle, their father's brother, had taken on Dan. He had spent almost every day at his uncle's house, for a month, as old age finally took him.

"I know, and you were wonderful, as you were with our parents."

"Then you can cut me some slack," Dan said, knowing that despite his denial, he did need something to anchor him. The world was shaking beneath him, seemingly ready to fall apart.

"Except for things that would be good for you. Go see Stephen. Act graciously, regardless of how difficult that may be. Find out what he needs and, afterward, if you want to, you can go your separate way again. Unfortunately, that, seems to be your approach to people these days." She walked over to Dan and gently laid her hand on his shoulder. "One day, I'm afraid you may do that to me."

"You know that would never happen. I would have to be dead."

Looking straight into his eyes, Joanna said, "I hope not. Some people die inside even though they still look alive."

"I'm all right. Really I am," Dan protested, though feeling far less sincere than his words.

"Then go to Stephen's, if for no other reason than as a favor to me," Joanna commanded.

Quietly, Dan replied, "Okay, but it's pointless."

"Well, you have nothing to lose, and you might even be pleasantly surprised. Then come visit us. It's been way too long."

"Yes, it has."

"Dan, no matter what, I'll never let you push me away."

"I said I'm not going to push anyone away!"

"Good," Joanna said. "You know you've always been a terrific person, loved by everyone, for all the right reasons. I want whatever is bothering you to pass. I want my joyful brother back, for your sake more than mine."

"I'm still here," he answered with insufficient conviction.

"I have to go now. Thanks for letting me stop by."

"You're always welcome, even when you're nagging me," Dan said, walking her to the door.

Joanna smiled, then walked down the stairs. Dan closed the door, picked up his phone, and reluctantly texted Stephen, "I'll be there."

Stephen's reply was nearly instantaneous: "Outstanding. We're looking forward to it."

Unable to avoid the day any further, he left his apartment, descended the stairs, and exited his building. Confusion ruled his mind. The sunlight stabbed at him and almost threw him back inside. He tried to open his eyes, and when he did, everything seemed shadowy. In a world full of colors, he could no longer see even black and white, only muted shades of gray.

About the only thing he was certain of was that going to Stephen's for dinner was a bad idea.

Chapter 12

Viktor walked into the control room. Everyone was already at their stations, waiting expectantly for the experiments to begin.

The room was about thirty feet wide and twice as long. On the far end were the main consoles, a double row of six large-screen monitors mounted on metal racks, filled with equipment. Large bundles of wires ran in every direction. Down the center of the room, two banks of desks and computers faced each other. More desks and computers spanned the room's perimeter.

As planned, there were fewer people than normal occupying the various stations.

Ravi Kannan sat at the X-ray monitors. Carol Williams looked over the power supply and magnetic fields. Karl Ashford checked the fuel levels. Nicco Pappas manned the computers that calculated the plasma temperatures. A few graduate students were scattered around the room. Sousan stood sentry near the main monitors, where she could view the plasma images and oversee everything and everyone, including Welch, who was standing next to her.

Viktor ran down the pre-shot checklist with everyone. The reactor room was visually inspected to ensure no one was in it and then the huge concrete and steel reactor room doors were closed. The supercooled magnets were operating within tolerances. The flywheel was fully charged, prepared to let loose a massive burst of electricity through the thick stainless steel bars that ran overhead from the generator into the reactor room.

Viktor called out, "All right, we're a go on the baseline shot," and then started the automated procedure. A computer-generated voice counted down from ten. Hydrogen gas was injected into the reactor, ionized into plasma, and prepared. If all went as planned, the shot would last fifteen seconds and then be repeated four more times, under increasingly powerful conditions. They would spend the next few days analyzing the results, preparing for the critical test next week.

The countdown reached zero and the fusion reactor ramped up. As expected, the plasma gas, racing around the inside, was visible on the monitors placed at ports around the perimeter of the massive magnets. Readings were compared to expected levels. Throughout the room, there was a deep hum and a high-pitched tone.

Fifteen seconds later, the shot was over. Viktor asked Welch, "Readings, please."

"All within tolerances," Welch answered.

"Let me know when you're ready for the next shot."

Welch directed everyone's preparations: the refueling of the reactor, building up the electrical charges, and preparing data collection. He adjusted a few of the controls, checked power levels, and then said, "All set."

Once again, Viktor started the countdown, and the shot began.

Sousan stared at the plasma image, then looked at Viktor with a puzzled expression and said, "That's odd. The plasma looks brighter than usual."

"I don't notice a difference," Viktor lied. "But just in case, Nicco, give us a temperature reading."

"In a moment. The computer is calculating it," Nicco answered.

Looking doubtful, Sousan turned to Viktor and said, "What's going on? Does the new equipment have anything to do with it? You said it was just for measurement."

Viktor ignored her questions and turned toward Nicco.

Nicco called out, "Temperature is at the top of the expected range. Sixty million degrees."

"Are you sure?" Sousan said, her face scrunched up in a quizzical expression.

And then the shot was over. Sousan glared at Viktor and Welch, then walked over to Nicco and examined his monitor. It read sixty million degrees Celsius, normal for the reactor. But it was not, in fact, a true reading. At Viktor's direction, Nicco had altered the programming so that Sousan would not see the actual, much higher, result.

Welch reviewed the other readings and said, "Everything nominal. The reactor is performing as expected."

"Okay then, everyone ready for the third shot?" said Viktor.

One by one, the scientists nodded yes.

Welch adjusted some more controls and quietly said to Viktor, "Field modulators are ready. RF has been increased with timed pulses."

"Here we go," Viktor said with a small smile as he started the countdown to the event that he expected would confirm they were on the right path.

Two seconds into the shot, Welch increased the level of one of the new controls to halfway. Instantly, the plasma contracted into a narrower band and glowed brighter, clearly indicating higher pressures and temperatures. Sousan turned to Viktor with an expression that was both startled and accusatory. The possibility of hiding the real results from her appeared lost.

Ravi announced, "X-ray emissions are up ten percent."

Viktor called out, "I need a temperature reading."

Nicco answered, "I'm working on it."

Without waiting for an answer, Welch flipped another switch and turned the knob the rest of the way. The plasma contracted further and began to pulsate irregularly.

Viktor's throat tightened. Something powerful seemed to be pressing against his forehead. The experiments were supposed to have been straightforward and low-risk. Instead, he was worried that they were jeopardizing the reactor, and perhaps more, with pressures and heat it wasn't capable of handling. A faint, disconcerting feeling came over him, tugging at the periphery of his senses. It was like nothing he had ever experienced. He almost felt detached from his body, while, at the same time, he was aware of strange sensations washing over him. He mentally probed for the source of the sensations; they seemed unrelated to the natural nervousness that sometimes accompanied running a new experiment.

"X-rays are up twenty-seven percent," Ravi called out.

Viktor yelled, "We need that temperature, now!"

Nicco worked frantically to adjust the laser calibration needed for the reading.

The plasma began to swerve slowly. Sousan yelled out, "What's going on, Viktor? Shut it down."

"Nicco!" Viktor yelled.

Carol Williams called out, "The magnets are heating up."

People looked at one another with confused and worried expressions. Viktor wondered if they were experiencing similar odd sensations. Beads of sweat formed on Nicco's forehead as he tried to get the reading. His equipment wasn't set up properly for such high temperatures.

As the plasma swerved more wildly, Sousan yelled out, "We could lose containment. Abort now!"

"Shut it down, John," Viktor ordered, then turned to Sousan and said, "We're not going to lose containment."

Welch lowered the levels, brought the reactor under control, and shut it down.

"Viktor, no more shots until you level with me and we figure out what just happened," Sousan declared.

Ignoring her, Viktor stood up to speak, but he couldn't shake the idea that some of the others had also experienced what he had but were reluctant to mention it. Composing himself, he announced to the room, "Obviously, we had unexpected results. I'm confident that was due to problems with the reactor's calibrations and they caused minor problems with the plasma's stabilization. Nothing more than that. However, until further notice, I have to insist that everyone keep this under wraps until we verify what happened. We're in the midst of a government budget cycle, and in today's sequestration environment, I don't want anything to put our funding at risk. I'm sure we'll quickly figure things out and make whatever adjustments are necessary. Meanwhile, I'm sorry for the inconvenience, but that is all I can say for now." Looking at Sousan, he added, "We'll discuss this further in my office."

Viktor walked briskly down the hall with Sousan by his side.

Looking sternly at him as she walked, Sousan said, "Viktor, it's time to cut the subterfuge. We could have damaged the reactor."

He deliberated what to tell her. It would need to be a satisfactory explanation but still withhold the essence of what was going on. On the one hand, he had promised Stephen complete secrecy except for the few people who had to be in the know. On the other hand, Sousan had seen enough to know something big was going on, and she could easily stir things up trying to find out.

Entering his office, he closed the door, sat down at his desk, and pointed to the chair across from him. Sousan slowly lowered herself into the seat, her eyes trained on Viktor.

Finally, Viktor spoke. "What I'm about to tell you has to stay between us. If you agree to that, I'll tell you what I can for now, and more later. All right?"

Sousan nodded her consent.

"I was introduced to Welch four months ago. I had reason to believe that he was involved in a privately sponsored breakthrough, collaborating with a top-secret government research program, that promised to accelerate fusion energy research. But he needed a facility like ours to test their new theories. As you know, we're an unclassified center, just like all of the other fusion research centers in the US. Yet the implications were so great that his project sponsors needed to guard the research. So, as you've probably guessed, we picked this Friday, with most of the staff out, to start the tests. Only, as you saw, we got more than we expected and were prepared to handle."

"You're not kidding. I think when we're done analyzing the data, and I do mean *we,* we'll find out the temperatures and pressures were far higher than ever achieved in a fusion reactor. How did you do it?"

"We've found a way to use quantum wave theories to help overcome proton electromagnetic repulsion." Viktor said this in a matter-of-fact voice—despite the extraordinary nature of what they were doing—in an attempt to manage Sousan's reaction.

"But that's impossible. The forces are universal constants. If they can be changed, everything collapses and there is no universe, no you, no me," Sousan said.

"You saw the same things I did. Do you have another explanation for it?" Viktor answered. "Anyway, the forces aren't changed. It's more like a deeper understanding of them can be used to affect their interactions in small, tightly controlled areas."

Hesitantly, Sousan asked, "Is there any possibility of the effects rippling outward?"

Left unspoken was that his feeling of his body detaching from all around him was more real than imagined, and that she had felt it, too.

"Absolutely not. The effects are all within the confines of our reactor," Viktor replied.

"Why didn't you include me from the beginning? You need my expertise. We've worked side by side for so long. I'm really ticked off that you didn't confide in me," Sousan said, raising her arms and shaking them forward.

"Trust had nothing to do with it. I had to agree to conditions beyond my control."

"Well, now I'll need to know everything. I'll want to see all of the research, know everyone who is involved with this," Sousan asserted.

"That's not possible. Even I don't know all of that."

"It's your reactor. Find out."

"I'll do what I can. Everything is on a need-to-know basis," Viktor said while thinking that he wanted the same answers.

"Tell whomever you have to that things have changed and that *I need to know*. For one, you'll need my help to fix the plasma turbulence. When's the next experiment?"

"Tuesday."

"Does it have to be that soon? I need time to get up to speed and analyze the data."

"We have no choice but to stick with the schedule. As you know, the reactor will be shut down for maintenance after that. If we're successful, we'll have what we need to argue for a whole new energy policy. Funds will flood in, fusion power plants will be built rapidly, dependence on foreign oil will be eliminated, fracking can be put on hold, carbon emissions will be reduced, and we'll have a green— actually, to be more accurate, less brown—America and a booming economy. So it really is a matter of national security, but not from a direct military perspective."

"I can't believe it; we could be on the verge of developing fusion energy power."

"Go home and enjoy the day. Next week will be very busy for both of us."

"I will. And thanks for the illumination," Sousan said with a smirk.

With a feigned look of disdain at the pun, Viktor waved her out of his office.

Viktor closed the door to his office, sat down at his desk, and removed the lower drawer. Taped to the bottom was a pouch. He opened it, withdrew a page, and examined what looked like a satellite image of an area of land. Scattered across it were circles of different colors and sizes. There were indeed a lot of powerful implications that could come from their work. The images he'd just viewed could dramatically alter balances of power and trigger dreadful events.

After placing the image in his jacket pocket, he sifted through a dozen other images, chose two, and put them in an envelope that he then sealed and addressed.

Replacing the drawer, Viktor put on his jacket. It was time to get real answers from Stephen. The discussion could turn out as hot as the experiments that he had just conducted. Powerful forces were building, the world was approaching another terrible juncture, and he had to make sure the right things were done.

Chapter 13

Professor Bishop, as Stephen was known to his students, sat at his office desk, located on the second floor of the Koch Building, headquarters of MIT's Department of Biology, leafing through stacks of mail and papers that had grown in his absence.

He was rarely there these days, instead spending the majority of his time at the Human Betterment Corporation headquarters, where his office had a stunning view and walls decorated with numerous awards, framed magazine covers, and other forms of recognition of his accomplishments and stature. While they didn't interest him much, they helped impress potential investors and collaborators. There was no need for that here.

As he waited for Viktor to arrive, for a conversation he wasn't looking forward to having, Stephen thought how strange it was that he felt out of place in his old, now mostly barren, office.

It had once felt as cozy as any science professor's office could have, which was good considering all the time he had spent there. Other than a small, flat-screen monitor and the papers he was disposing of, the only thing on his desk was a large picture of his wife, Nancy, hugging their nine-year-old-daughter, Ava. Looking at their picture, he regretted all the time he had spent away from them, working late nights and weekends, trying to unlock the secrets of DNA. He was fascinated by the way information from long strings of base pairs, like a four-letter alphabet—G, T, A, and C—directed the size and shape of people, determined hair color, differentiated cell development so that eyes actually saw, structured the brain so minds could think, and regulated complex protein development.

It had been an extraordinary trip of exploration that had been full of surprises. At first, the idea of sequencing the human genome—basically, reading each of the three-billion letters within the chromosomes—was something that had seemed possible only in the long-off future. Then a steady stream of progress in DNA sequencing had reduced the time needed to do this from decades to a few years. Two competing initiatives, one privately sponsored, the other government funded, both succeeded, culminating in a completely sequenced human genome in 2003. Since then, incredible advances had cut the time needed to decode DNA from years to days, and now, even to hours.

After DNA was sequenced, it was time to figure out how the genome did its thing. It was expected that he, as one of the world's top geneticists, would play a leading role in this effort.

Naturally, he should have jumped at the opportunity to lead research at a start-up biotech company with a team of his choosing, financed by one of the richest men in the world.

Nonetheless, he had repeatedly spurned HBC's numerous offers, uncomfortable with the idea of commercializing genetics. It wasn't until Ava's diagnosis that he had relented, hoping that large investments could speed the pace of discoveries, including the ones his daughter might need. He was also lured by the emerging field of gene editing. The idea of designer humans bothered him, and the only way to influence the direction of that was to be part of it.

In the beginning, it had been slow going, and frustrating. But then came the surprise of surprises, a shock so great that no one could have been prepared for it. Even now, he was amazed that he had stumbled upon it, as though he was meant to discover it, for he doubted it could be found otherwise.

He wondered where everything would lead.

Viktor's work would help answer part of that question.

So far, it had cost one person severely. According to the police report, prior to his crash, Alex had cracked his skull, most likely from a fall in the HBC parking lot. The resulting concussion had disoriented him, leading to his tragic decision to enter the highway's exit ramp.

At least that is what the report said. Stephen worried that there was more to it.

Chapter 14

His energy was all but spent and he felt already separated from the world, his nearly skeletal frame motionless under the hospital bedsheets. Slowly, he rolled his head to the right and angled it down.

Through half-opened eyes—eyes that saw the world through a gray-scale tunnel, when they saw at all—he stared at his right hand. Jaundiced, nearly translucent, paper-thin skin traced the contours of the bones of his fingers and wrist.

Incapable of yelling out loud, of any sound more than a raspy whisper, in one of the lucid moments that came but a few times a day, he shouted to himself that he was not going to die, ever.

Yet the signs on the multiphase bio-monitor were unmistakable. He observed a series of lines tracing irregular paths, each with a distinct rhythm, across the monitor's display. All were outside the normal parameters indicated on the monitor, illustrating that his body's key functions were in the throes of a final breakdown.

Time was cruelly teasing him as his was running out. His life was ending just as *The Singularity*—when technology would transform humans past the limits of their biological bodies—was on the horizon. Why should a mind like his be subject to decay when machines that humans created could go on indefinitely? Why couldn't silicon chips hold his mind until the day came when it could be replaced by something more eternal and powerful? Intelligence should be able to create something superior to that which had not been created, that had come into existence simply through random interactions.

Stuck in the present, he was fighting merely to survive.

With extreme effort, he tried to raise his hand. Initially, it only trembled. Gradually, though his elbow remained anchored to the bed, his forearm rose, his wrist hanging limply. With his forearm nearly at its apex, he struggled to lift his hand and reach the bio-monitor.

His outstretched finger almost touched the device, only inches short. Straining, he tried to get closer by rolling his body, but despite the strenuous effort that was reflected on the bio-monitor, he could not budge.

He concentrated all his will on the small gap left between his forefinger and the bio-monitor's controls.

Electric shocks began to course through his body. The room's lights flickered. A surge of visible energy jumped from his finger to the monitor's surface. He felt his essence begin to leave his body. The monitor's display began to dance with unfamiliar images.

Suddenly, darkness came, followed by a brilliant flash. Fully conscious, his mind once again vibrant, he was aware that he no longer inhabited his lifeless body but yet was still alive.

A startling realization overcame him. He was now one with a machine.

Sarastro woke with a start. He almost never dreamed. Yet, for the past three nights, he'd had the same one of his corporal death and the metamorphosis of his mind into a machine.

He was not superstitious, but he nonetheless thought the dream had meaning.

Time indeed was running out, and things were headed in the wrong direction. The diagnosis was absolute: without an extraordinary medical breakthrough, he would be dead within three years.

At first, he had sought a cure. But then something with even more promise seemed possible. That something could provide true immortality *and* power.

Devastatingly, however, and without warning, the scientific breakthroughs that could save him, that seemed so imminent, were not materializing as they should have been. Something was amiss. People who were supposed to be committed to the project's success were not delivering.

He would rectify that.

He hadn't overcome all that he had, fought tooth and nail each step of the way through darkness so deep that it caused even the strongest hearts to tremble, to get to the pinnacle that he had, to just go meekly into the void, subdued by nothing more than time and decay.

Sarastro, leader of The Commission, had no intention of dying, of dissipating until the weakest of breezes could destroy his form. It wouldn't be enough for the heavens to remember him, to scream his magnificence. He intended to *become* the heavens, to provide the light to which others flocked, to create a haven for them within the eternal world he'd shape.

Yet here he was, he of all people, almost shuddering from a dream of mortality. On the verge of immortality, a convergence of consciousness with the eternal on the horizon, and yet fear and doubt had crept in.

Without question, it was time to act.

Chapter 15

Viktor marched into Stephen's office and flung himself down in the chair across from him. Perspiration dotted Viktor's partially flushed, sun-worn face.

"I expect Welch called and told you about the results of our little preliminary experiment," Viktor said with irritation that bordered on indictment.

"He said that it was a success, though not without the expected rough spots."

"That's one way of putting it. Another is that we came close to severely damaging the reactor, alarmed a few of our staff, and raised a red flag to someone we were trying to keep in the dark. Other than that, it definitely was a resounding success," Viktor said sarcastically.

"What I heard was that you validated the theories, collected the data you needed, and that you're in a good position for next week's tests. I'd say that's pretty good for a first run."

"Aren't you concerned about what news of our work could unleash?"

"Of course I am, Viktor. But from what I understand, there wasn't much for people to put together. And you told them this was just an issue with calibrating a new reactor," said Stephen. "So what's really bothering you? You didn't charge over here just to talk about things I know you can easily handle yourself."

Narrowing his eyes, Viktor said, "I need real answers. The ambiguous ones you've given before won't do any longer. We *all* have a lot of skin in this game and I'd like to keep mine from getting burned."

Stephen clasped his hands behind his head while leaning back in his chair. He had good reasons for withholding information from Viktor. Until Stephen knew all that he was dealing with, he had to limit what people knew to the barest minimum, and sometimes what they had been told wasn't completely true.

Welch was one of the few who knew more, most of it true. Stephen had met Welch through Alex. After Alex's death, Stephen had shared some of the physics insights with Welch.

Welch was a good choice because he knew the latest research, both public and classified, and had access to equipment to test aspects of the theories in small ways without attracting attention. At times this included unauthorized use of top-secret government facilities. Another thing was that Stephen knew from discussions they'd previously had that Welch believed that the universe was the work of divine providence. Stephen used this to both interest Welch and ensure his confidentiality by telling him that Stephen and Alex had been working together on the relationship between the laws of physics and the origin of human life.

For now, the less Viktor knew, the better. Still, Stephen had to tell Viktor something more now to satisfy him for a while longer.

Straightening, Stephen said, "Viktor, have you ever thought that maybe, given all your concerns, we're protecting *you*?"

"I don't care about protection. I want to make sure everything we do is for the right purpose. You haven't lived through the things I have, where scientific advances were used to destroy and subjugate. The world was the emigration of a few scientists away from being dominated by an atomic-armed Nazi Germany," Viktor said emphatically.

"It's exactly because of things you experienced that I hold back some information for now. We need a little more time," Stephen said. It was a plea as much as a statement of fact. "I will tell you one thing that I haven't before. The connection between physics and biology may be closer than you think. It looks like certain properties of matter predispose the formation of life. Understand one well and you understand the other better. The symmetry in physical laws is somehow related to the organization of life. Your tests will help prove some of this. That's part of the reason I'm involved."

Viktor sat silently for a few minutes, lost in thought, and then said, "In some ways, that's not surprising. I've often speculated about the incredible odds involved in evolution and have never been satisfied with the idea of an overwhelming large universe, or an infinite number of multiverses, as an answer, despite what the math says is possible. But it's all the more reason that I need to know what's going on."

"When the time's right, I promise that you'll receive all the information and assurances you need, from as high an authority as you could want."

"I'm going to hold you to that," said Viktor. "And remember, I value truth, not authority."

"Don't worry, you'll be satisfied."

"What do we do about computer security in the interim? The lab's servers aren't capable of protecting the data, and things could easily get hot in more ways than one after next week's experiments," Viktor stated.

"I'm taking care of that tonight," said Stephen.

"With your not-so-friendly friend Dan, the guy you keep trying to get in touch with? Is he even up for this? Can't we get someone else?"

"He's one of the best and, once he's on board, we can depend on him without question." Stephen looked away into the distance.

After a long pause, Viktor said, "Your silence doesn't inspire confidence."

Stephen replied, "Dan *is* the right guy for us. For a good part of his career, he worked in a government intelligence agency as one of its top data encryption and computer security experts. We need both of these capabilities to protect our work."

"I hope you're right about Dan. Take a look at this," Viktor said. He pulled an 8½-by-11-inch image from his jacket pocket, unfolded it, and placed it on the desk between them. On it, lines indicated the major geographic features and borders of the United States. Different-sized colored circles were dispersed over the area.

Stephen sat straight up as though a massive electric shock had just traveled through his spine, grabbed the image, and said, "Is this what I think it is?"

"Absolutely. The circles indicate the type, quantity, and location of all significant amounts of nuclear material within the geographic area of the image."

"Then what the hell are you doing carrying this around?" Stephen said loudly. "Don't you have any idea what certain countries would do to get hold of images like this, what they'd do with them? You know what could happen."

"Sure I do."

"How did you generate them?"

"You're not the only one with clever ideas. All I did was tap into and adapt technologies that were already in place, plus borrowed equipment from a few labs. Anyway, I'll tell you my secrets when you tell me yours."

"You know I could cut you out of this program anytime I want. Welch works with me," Stephen answered with more than a little threat in his voice.

"You can relax. Welch knows how I created the images. And we're a long way from being able to generate global images. These are only proof-of-concepts."

After a brief pause, Viktor added, "Stephen, we've known each other a long time, and I have a great respect for you, but are you sure you're not in over your head?"

"I'm handling things just fine, thanks."

After another period of silence, Viktor said, "It really is incredible what we're doing. Who would have thought we'd get so close to understanding the foundations of physical laws and use that knowledge to generate fusion power, and eventually way more than that?"

Stephen answered, "Sometimes I wonder if we should even be doing these things."

"The simple fact is that you can't hold back progress. Someone else would eventually make the same discoveries, so it might as well be us," Viktor said.

"I'm not so sure we should have discovered what we did," Stephen replied. He wondered about the price that might have to be paid for the privilege of being the pioneers and for seeing what he had. In the Old Testament, anyone who gazed at God died.

"There's no point in second-guessing the inevitable. All we can do now is secure the findings and do the best we can with them. I look forward to the day when we can work on this with a full team and I have the answers to all my questions."

"Be careful what you ask for. Some questions are better left unanswered, perhaps even yours. Reality may not be what we think it is. You could be in for big surprises."

"Reality is clear enough to me. It's what exists physically. Anything else is mysticism."

Smiling wryly, Stephen said, "You're a good scientist, Viktor."

"Well, this good scientist had better return to his office. I'll talk to you later and get ready for the grand finale of our universe-changing experiments. Do you want to be there?" Viktor said jovially.

"No, thanks. I don't want to have to explain my presence. And as long as I don't see a big cloud or feel any tremors emanating from your lab, I'll know it went fine."

As Viktor walked back to his lab, he worried that the Stephen he had known for more than a decade was changing. The world was much closer to a destiny-altering transformation than anyone knew.

After looking around to make sure no one was nearby, he pulled out the envelope he had prepared earlier and dropped it into the mailbox on the corner.

Stephen swung his chair around and sat facing the window, staring out into the bright morning sky, mentally going over his conversation with Viktor. They would have to be careful indeed.

He didn't really understand how he had gotten to this frontier and where it would lead. All he knew for certain was that, despite what he had told Viktor, the things he was working with were definitely more than he was prepared to handle. He prayed that he wouldn't mess up. As long as he could keep things under wraps, he would be in control.

Finally focusing on the view outside, Stephen realized that the vibrant blue sky looked wonderful. It was a great day, and he was looking forward to the walk back to his laboratory.

Chapter 16

Driving had a calming effect on Dan, particularly in nice weather. The evening was warm and he had the top down. Wind rippled through his hair and massaged his scalp. The sound and vibration of the rumbling engine gave him a sense of power and vitality. The sun had reached the point in its daily transit where it was low enough for rich colors to emerge from the landscape but still high enough to avoid unpleasant glare. He pulled into the street and headed to the Mass Pike, where he carefully merged into the lingering rush-hour and holiday traffic. He figured it would take about twenty minutes to reach Stephen's.

He felt relaxed for the first time all day. He'd deal with whatever would transpire at dinner. He'd listen politely, not show any anger or weakness, then be done with it. Indifference would be a far more powerful rebuke than anger.

He thought back to when he had first met Stephen. Dan's family had moved from Brooklyn to Hopkinton, outside of Boston. It was the summer right after sixth grade. He was an eleven-year-old city kid moving to the suburbs. A bunch of boys were playing baseball in a field. Dan stood off to the side, watching, until Stephen spotted him and yelled out, "Don't just stand there. Grab a bat and take a swing." They quickly became good friends, though that never prevented Stephen from teasing Dan from time to time about how Dan had stood still, too shy to join in on his own.

Later they attended Holy Trinity High School, run by Franciscan Brothers. Competitive in a friendly way, they pushed each other to excel, getting top grades, leading teams to victory, dating nice girls.

They had a wide circle of friends, though Dan and Stephen had remained the closest. They even shared families, treated by each other's as their own.

They both wound up at MIT, partly by design, partly by chance. Once there, they left high school, including whatever religion they once had, behind. The Brothers at Holy Trinity had been good, but despite trying their best, couldn't pass on a lasting faith. As the school motto said, the truth would set them free—and it had, just not the way the Brothers had thought it would.

Reaching his exit, Dan headed south on Centre Street, a mostly residential area, until it hit Beacon Street. The intersection was Newton's main square and commercial area. The town had excellent schools, good neighborhoods, and was close to Stephen's office.

He thought of Stephen living there, with an extraordinary career to go along with his lovely wife and beautiful daughter, and wondered who could have a better life.

Apparently, it was so good, there was no room for Dan in it. As resentment started to rise, he caught himself.

The reality was they had been drifting apart for a long time. There was no big issue. Just distance. As Dan's recent struggles had increased, his anger at Stephen was fueled mostly by what he felt they had lost more than anything else, and what that had once meant to him. It was time to get over it and not blame Stephen. It didn't mean he had to like Stephen, but it sure meant he didn't have to resent or be mad at him.

Reaching Stephen's neighborhood, Dan turned onto The Ledges Road, named so because the houses sat on a high rock ridge that backed up to Beacon Street. The area was secluded. Everything was in full bloom. As he parked in front of Stephen's house, a flood of memories came to him; all the barbecues and parties, the quiet get-togethers they'd had. It was a good-sized, well-landscaped, two-story, Tudor-style home that had beige stucco siding and brown wood trim. On each side of the central entrance, symmetrical wings extended outward.

Before he could ring the bell, Nancy Bishop opened the door, engulfed him with an embrace, and gave him a kiss on the cheek. "I'm so glad you're here."

Nancy's warmth made him aware of the void in himself while momentarily filling it. He said, "It's great to see you. I'm looking forward to one of your delicious dinners."

Smiling, she took him by the arm and led him inside. Above them was a magnificent chandelier that illuminated her and the large central hall with a comforting glow. It cast dancing shadows from the banisters of the wide circular staircase, directly across from the front door, that led to the second floor.

She was tall, with a lean but toned body, silky brown hair and sparkling hazel eyes. She radiated affection and caring, none of it artificial or put on. She had the rare ability to be distantly refined, totally self-possessed, and yet immediately present and accessible, all at the same time.

"Nancy, you're still the most genuine and gracious person I've ever known. And you always look wonderful, never more so than now."

Nancy smiled and said, "You're too kind, but I'll take the compliment. Why don't we go into the study and catch up? Something urgent came up for Stephen, but he'll be right with us."

Dan followed her into the room on the right of the hall. They sat down in wing-back chairs facing each other, talking about their families, laughing about things they remembered.

After a few minutes, Nancy said, "I have to apologize. I won't be able to stay for dinner. Ava's undergoing routine tests to make sure everything is still good and I'm spending the night with her. But I promise we'll have you over again real soon so we can all have dinner together."

"Tests for what?" Dan said hesitantly.

"You didn't hear?" Nancy asked.

"Stephen and I haven't spoken in a long time. Is Ava all right?" Dan asked.

"She's fine now, thank God. Last Christmas, Ava was diagnosed with leukemia. Fortunately, it was caught early and quickly treatable. Today is her one-month checkup since she was declared in remission."

The room tilted on Dan. An innocent child having to experience what she had. He couldn't imagine what it had been like for all of them. To potentially lose a child—he couldn't fathom it. Dan replied solemnly, "I'm so sorry. That must have been awful and scary. I wished I could have helped." He didn't know what else to say. What can you say to a parent that offered any wisdom or provided any comfort? All you could do is be there for them. He hadn't been and felt selfish that he was upset about being denied the chance.

"We tried keeping it to ourselves. While she was in treatment, our focus was solely on her. For some reason I thought you heard afterward. We didn't mean anything by it."

"I understand. You had a lot to deal with. All that matters is that she is fine now."

"She had fantastic care. Her doctor was incredible, looking after Ava as if she were her own."

"It's wonderful you were able to find such outstanding care."

"Yes, it was. But enough of Ava's illness. How have you been? I feel terrible that we haven't seen you in so long. We're definitely going to change that," Nancy said with another warm smile.

"I'm good. Just taking my time before I figure out what adventure to tackle next."

Before Nancy replied, Stephen entered, carrying a beer. He walked over to Dan and eagerly shook his hand, saying, "It's fantastic to see you. Thanks for coming. I suspect it wasn't at the top of the list of things you thought you'd do when you woke up this morning, but I'm pretty sure you'll be glad you did once we discuss what I have in mind. But we can save that for after dinner. For now, how about a beer?"

Stephen acted confident and comfortable. He still had an athletic build, though he didn't appear to be in quite his usual shape. There were touches of gray in his mostly black hair, and his hairline was slightly receding. He wore silver wire-frame glasses. Overall, he looked dignified and serious. Not much different than when Dan last saw him, though perhaps wearier.

Dan took the beer, and said with slight reserve, "Few days turn out the way I think they will. But I am glad that I'm here. Thanks for the invite."

"I'm hoping this is the first of many visits," Stephen said.

Nancy looked at her watch and said to Stephen, "I should be going."

"I'll walk you to the car," Stephen said.

As Nancy and Stephen left, Nancy looked over her shoulder and said, "Hopefully Stephen is good enough company that we'll see you again sooner than you might think."

The words sounded mysterious, almost haunting.

As he took a big swig of his beer, Dan wondered if what he had referred to as his next adventure might turn out to be much more than he could have anticipated. Nancy and Stephen seemed like they were doing all they could to draw him in.

Chapter 17

Sitting in her living room on the thirtieth floor of the high-rise apartment building, Sousan sipped a bourbon, looking out at the Boston skyline.

She had hoped the day would never have come where she'd be pressed to fulfill the dreaded terms of the agreement that had allowed her family to emigrate from Iran.

For more than three decades, Sousan had lived a secular life devoted to science. It provided all the meaning and fulfillment that she had sought, free of the religious passions and restrictions that engulfed her homeland.

In part a form of rebellion against male domination in her old society, in part due to her dedication to her work, as well as a reflection of her discomfort with trusting close, personal relationships, she had never married.

Even though she tried to be as much of an American as anyone, she still felt like an outsider, as though people couldn't get past her background.

Viktor was one of the few she was completely comfortable with, whom she let her guard down around, whom she felt a genuine connection with. Until today, she had always believed he felt the same about her.

That illusion had been shattered by his excluding her from what had to be the most important research they would ever conduct and his subsequent lies. It left her feeling bitter.

She swallowed the remaining third of the glass of bourbon and refilled it.

In spite of it all, she didn't want to place the call that was expected of her. She was an American. There were people she cared about here, even if some had let her down.

She debated what to do. Place the call and hopefully be done with it. Or ignore it and hope they'd never find out her involvement; claim, not entirely incorrectly, that she had been kept in the dark. Or tell Viktor and ask for his assistance.

None of the options was satisfactory.

Her handlers would eventually find out and extract a penalty. If it was just her, she could deal with that. But she still had relatives back in Iran to be concerned about.

Resentful at her situation, anger at Viktor's deceit took over and helped her make the decision.

Walking over to the filing cabinet in her closet, she opened a lockbox in the top drawer. Removing a disposable cell phone and an untraceable calling card, she dialed the number she memorized long ago.

After a few rings, a man answered, "Name."

"Cybil from Project Icarus."

"You're breaking protocols. Are you secure?"

She answered, "There have been major developments. Put him on the line."

Chapter 18

Dan looked around the study. It was Stephen's sanctuary, his favorite place to relax, think, have a drink, or share a moment with friends.

The room was rectangular and spacious. A long expanse of large windows covered the length of the front side of the room, from knee high almost all the way up to the ceiling. A bench at the base of the windows also spanned the length of the room. The wall opposite consisted of white-painted cabinets from the floor to waist height, with bookshelves on top extending to the ceiling. French doors that opened onto an outside patio filled the wall opposite the study's entrance. Right inside the entrance was a large mahogany rolltop desk that Stephen had inherited from his grandfather. In the center of the desk, recessed into the back, was a flat-screen monitor. On it, a screensaver drew images of vividly colored, repeating shapes. Some looked lifelike. Near the center of the room was a grand piano that Stephen often liked to play.

Dan looked at the bookshelves and saw many of the types of books he would expect to see in Stephen's study. Most focused on biology, evolution, or the human genome. Stephen was an ardent supporter of evolution and Dan knew that Stephen would be scornful and dismissive of the views of the "semi-intelligent" design fringe that believed evolution was directed by God, though they refuse to say it was God they were talking about. A few of the books were written by Stephen and covered complex topics on genetic mechanisms.

The center shelves were filled with pictures. Properly displayed in the middle were Nancy's and Stephen's wedding pictures. Dan had been the best man and appeared in some of the shots. There were also pictures of Stephen's daughter, Ava, at various ages. She had golden-blond hair and looked angelic, with a radiant smile capable of melting any heart.

Moving on to the shelves on the right side of the wall, still close to the center, were books on American history, various world civilizations, and a few on the power of myth. Dan was bemused to see the next books. They were on the topic of "the mystery of consciousness," something he thought was more about the vast complexity of the brain than about any real mystery, except to the superstitious religious seeking a reason to believe in souls.

Finally, on the far right, was a smaller set of books on spiritual matters. Although Stephen was a serious agnostic with a sound, scientific, analytical, and rational mind, it wouldn't be surprising if even he had faltered in the face of the unbearable and sought the comfort of the fanciful to get him through tough times. Dan looked closer. If all the books were all like the first book on the shelf, *Why Do Bad Things Happen to Good People?*, with the concept of a nebulous, weak, and not really relevant God, that would have made sense. But there were also traditionally oriented religious books: *The Problem of Pain*, *Making Sense Out of Suffering*, and *Miracles*. The first was considered a classic by those futilely trying to reconcile suffering and religion; the second was written by a Boston College professor and the third by a more recent, evangelical author.

The title of the next book, *Lost in the Cosmos: The Last Self-Help Book*, seemed like something he could get into. He'd had enough of self-help and therapy and looked forward to anything that could put an end to that. The back cover read, "Why is it that the more we know about the world the less we know about human nature?"

Dan opened it and read, "Are you a self in search of yourself?" He flipped to a different page as quickly as he could and saw, "Can you explain why it is that there are, at last count, sixteen schools of psychotherapy with sixteen theories of the personality and its disorders and that patients treated in one school seem to do as well or as badly as patients treated in any other—while there is only one generally accepted theory of the cause and cure of pneumococcal pneumonia and only one generally accepted theory of the orbits of the planets and the gravitational attraction of our galaxy and the galaxy M31 in Andromeda?" There were also questions about apparently dislocated selves that hit too close to home, disturbing him.

Dan put the book back just as Stephen returned carrying his own half-full beer.

"I'm sorry about the news about Ava," Stephen said. "For some reason, I thought you knew. I apologize for not talking directly with you about it."

"I know it must have been hard for all of you. You know I would have done anything you asked."

"I know. But Nancy and I were struggling with so much, lots of things were complicated, and we just wanted to keep things as simple as possible. And you and I had our own issues and I didn't want to use Ava's illness to overcome them. Had things gotten worse, I definitely would have reached out."

"I'm extremely glad she's fine. She's a tough, wonderful little kid. But as a condition of me hearing you out tonight, and whatever that may subsequently entail, as I know something is coming, you have to agree to never exclude me from something like this again. I can stay out of the way or do whatever you want, but you have to tell me."

"That's a fair condition. So, do you want to hear what I have to say?

"It had better be interesting."

"It is. Look, I know we . . . *I* . . . haven't been the friend I should have been. And I admit I'm reaching out to you in need. But that doesn't mean we shouldn't try to improve things."

Dan was becoming open to the possibilities, though they had a long way to go to be genuine friends again, if that was even possible. But *friendly* might be enough.

"That's fine. Ava's illness aside, I get the feeling that I'm about to be set up."

"I'm just using skills you taught me."

"They were meant for meeting ladies, not for manipulating supposed friends."

"How can it be manipulating when you know what I'm doing?" Stephen said as he shrugged with feigned innocence.

Playing along, Dan answered in mock offense, "I want to remind you that I'm not easy. I need to be well fed, and it'll take more than one beer."

"Easy is the last thing anyone would ever consider you," Stephen quickly answered.

"Careful! I haven't heard what you have to say. It might not be as convincing as you think."

"It will be."

"Not so fast. One of my other conditions is that I have to see Ava before I do anything."

"Now you're ruining things. As part of my devious scheme, I had planned on convincing you to drive me to the hospital tomorrow morning to pick up Ava and then drive down with me to the Cape, where Nancy and Ava would join us. And here you are insisting on something like it before I even have to ask."

"What about the interesting part?"

"That's a piece of cake. We'll talk about that soon. The only problem for me is that I had planned on having to do all sorts of things to coerce you into doing what I wanted. I feel let down. You *are* easy after all."

"Actually, I feel like I'm getting pulled into something I know nothing about, that could be risky, all in the name of a questionable friendship," Dan said with a sarcastic edge in his voice.

Stephen quickly replied, "Taking risks on the behalf of others is part of life. Now, how about we cook up some nice rib eye steaks and have another beer? As I recall, you have a certain fondness for both, in sometimes unhealthy quantities."

"I'll agree to that. And, by the way, according to your wife, I look pretty good, so it can't be that bad for me."

"Enough about how my wife thinks you're attractive. Let's go."

Dan followed Stephen through the kitchen and onto the back deck, where a plate of steaks and vegetables were on the side tray of a hot charcoal grill. Dan picked two beers out of a nearby cooler. While the food cooked, they reminisced.

Finishing his second beer, Dan asked, "In your well-thought-out schemes, how can I have more beers and get home safely?"

"Oh, that's easy. You take a car service. I have the number here. Then tomorrow, I drive your car to the hospital. You walk there. Together we pick up Ava and bring her back here. Then we'll drive down to the Cape in your car. Nancy and Ava will follow after Ava's piano lesson. It's all part of the plan."

"You really do intend to take me for a ride, literally and figuratively," Dan said while questioning whether he was setting himself up for a big fall by buying into Stephen's plans.

"It'll be good for you."

"I'm wondering if you're confusing my interests with your own."

"Don't worry, I know the difference. In this case, our interests overlap."

"You'll have to prove that," Dan said with more meaning than he had intended.

Stephen shot Dan a look, then said, "The steaks are done. Let's sit down." Savoring the juicy, flavorful meat, they ate in reflective silence, pausing only to sip from their beers.

After they cleaned up, Stephen said, "I want to show you something you'll appreciate. I recently added a theater system to the house. Come on downstairs. Then we can talk about what I'm dragging you into."

Dan followed Stephen down the stairs, into the finished basement, past the pool table, and into the theater room. It was done well. There were four rows of six seats, with a middle aisle, facing a large screen. Sound-damping tiles covered the walls and ceilings.

Stephen picked up the remote control and turned to Dan. "So what do you think?"

"Impressive, though I thought you were too practical for something like this."

"How about some music?" Stephen pressed a few buttons and Renaissance's "Ashes Are Burning" started playing as colorful visual effects of lines, circles, starbursts, and other images appeared on the screen.

Dan said, "Nice job."

"It is pretty good, though I didn't build this room for entertainment."

"What do you mean?" Dan asked.

"It's actually—and this may seem strange at first—my only secure site for talking and working. The room is surrounded by double walls with sound, vibration, and electromagnetic damping. The only wires into the room are the electrical and the cable, and they're electronically scrubbed to make sure nothing is transmitted out over them. For extra security, I have battery power, so when I flip a switch, the room is completely isolated. The air vents are also isolated. With your background, I thought you would appreciate this."

"I do." Dan hesitated, frowned, and then said, "Are you in danger?"

Chapter 19

The man, esteemed within influential circles throughout the world and known within The Commission as Sarastro, entered his private study. The room was modest in size for a man of his means and it was paneled with ornate walnut woodwork. Heavy green curtains parted just enough to let slivers of light enter the room. Marble squares formed a black and white checkerboard pattern on the floor.

The Commission itself was composed of a select group of like-minded people from top leadership positions in important institutions throughout the world, whether government, academia, business—even religious organizations. They thought of themselves as enlightened, powerful, and entitled, though compassionate and magnanimous. Their mission was to direct humanity for the good of all, provide for those who could contribute, and in time gently weed out those whose existence was a burden even to themselves, all the while ensuring humanity's future, and The Commission's members' positions within it, as humanity was transformed from a flawed, mortal existence to immortality and prosperity. No more would humans be limited by mere biology.

Walking over to a small rolltop desk by a closed door, Sarastro opened the top left drawer, placed his right hand on a small touch screen, and said, "Identity: Sarastro. Command: Access communications room."

A magnetic lock released, and a hidden door in the nearby wall opened a few inches, revealing a six- by nine-foot room with bare white walls and a large flat-screen monitor mounted opposite the door. Sarastro entered the room and the door closed firmly behind him. A single desk with a keyboard, touch pad, and microphone faced the monitor.

Sarastro sat in the chair, placed his hand on the touchpad, and issued a series of commands. Six squares appeared on the monitor, each displaying the face of another member of The Commission's nucleus. Together, the people in the nucleus directed The Commission's activities without the rest of The Commission being aware of how they, like the rest of humanity, were being directed.

Although the seven members were supposed to be equals, in actuality, Sarastro worked quietly behind the scenes as the effective, but unrecognized, leader. When the time was right, he would assert his authority and assume his rightful role as the supreme among the elite.

The nucleus was assembled to discuss the serious matter of Dr. Stephen Bishop. Unbeknownst to Stephen, The Commission had manipulated its connections to people within HBC, and its relationships with other scientific researchers, to ensure his placement at the company. When Stephen's daughter had been diagnosed with leukemia, a highly fortuitous event from The Commission's point of view, Stephen had sought help in developing experimental treatment and getting around FDA authorization.

A Commission intermediary, from outside HBC, contacted Stephen. In exchange for help researching and developing experimental medicine, Stephen had agreed to share all of his research—only now, it was clear that Stephen had not kept his side of the bargain. Something had to be done about that, not just for The Commission's benefit, but for Sarastro's. Unbeknownst to The Commission, he had been recently diagnosed with a progressive neuromuscular disease. His mind would remain intact as his body became useless, an unfit vessel for him. The disease might progress slowly and it might not. He couldn't afford to take the chance.

Speaking first, Sarastro said in low voice, "As you all know from the report that was sent to each of you beforehand, by all indications, Dr. Bishop has achieved incredible breakthroughs in decoding DNA and its relationship to human development. None of the information he's uncovered about it, however, is stored at HBC." Sarastro stopped speaking to let others take the discussion in the direction he wanted it to go anyway.

A well-known health and spiritual figure spoke. " How can that be?"

A top US government official said, "You have the report. He's done it, and we don't know how or where. This is a big risk. And now that he's resumed contact with Dan Lawson, a cybersecurity expert, it appears that Bishop has no intention of providing us with anything of value. We might not be able to get it from him."

Then a Chinese leader, the only person who inspired any trepidation in Sarastro, quietly added, "This cannot be allowed to continue. Effective action must be taken immediately. We cannot have any more mistakes." The last statement was a rebuke at the failed attempt to compromise Alex Robertson and subsequent efforts to monitor Stephen.

"Steps are already underway," Sarastro assured him. "A series of events will make the cost of noncooperation and the extent of our power increasingly clear to Stephen Bishop. We will make plain to him the benefit of being a member in good standing of The Commission— an invitation we will extend and ensure he accepts. At the right time, I will reveal myself to him and confirm his compliance."

The one woman among the seven said, "Are you sure it is wise to reveal yourself? I think that is a matter for us to discuss and decide. Preserving our anonymity is critical."

"The shock of my identity will destroy his defenses and convince him of the futility of trying anything else. I will ensure he is beholden to us," Sarastro said.

After a few minutes of discussion, the Chinese official said, "We will give this plan one week to succeed. If it does not, I am prepared to provide an environment more hospitable for Dr. Bishop's research and cooperation."

Everyone nodded their consent, though moving Stephen Bishop to China would be the last thing Sarastro would allow.

Stephen's research would help Sarastro realize his ultimate ambitions, including being one of the first to achieve immortality through the merging of man and machine. Nothing would stand in the way of that.

Chapter 20

hope I'm not in danger," Stephen said, in response to Dan's question. "But I have pretty good reasons to take these precautions." He gestured around the home theater. "Before I get into that, though, I need to bring you up to speed on my work on the human genome. As you probably know, the genome was completely sequenced thirteen years ago."

Dan nodded. Most people who followed science were familiar with that.

"That was the easy part," Stephen continued. "The hard part is figuring out how it all works—what's the actual language of the genetic code, how it interacts with the rest of the cell, and, most important, how it makes a person a person."

"When we started sequencing DNA, geneticists had expected to find over one hundred thousand genes. As the sequencing progressed, geneticists lowered their estimates to thirty thousand, then actually found only twenty thousand, an unexpectedly low number for an organism as complex as a human being."

"Does that mean individual genes do more than originally thought?" Dan asked.

"Some very much so, but that has big implications that I'll get to shortly."

"In the end, will it matter much if there are one hundred thousand genes or ten thousand genes with ten times the expected information?" Dan asked. "The total DNA in genes is the same."

"Actually, there is a lot less useful DNA than expected. Of the three billion DNA base pairs in the genome, a significant portion of them had been assumed to be junk left over from evolution, though now far less than we had once thought. Regardless, a large part of the known, useful genome controls how chromosones are utilized, such as indicating where genes stop and start, turning them on and off, correcting for informational errors and many other genome regulatory functions. There really isn't much left over after all of this."

Stephen paused, then added, "So while people talk about the incredible amount of information in the genome, it's a lot more complicated to direct human development than we had once thought. When you start with three billion base pairs, you would think that would be plenty for all the information you need. After all, most of the hundreds of different cell types have the same proteins and structures in common."

"Yes, I've read a decent bit about it," said Dan.

"Well, it turns out that it's not that simple. What gets tricky is that many of these cells, such as those that pertain to the brain organization and the shape of the human body, have information that is specific only to them. For us to see and think, many of the individual neurons have to be 'pre-wired' to each other in a precise way and that requires instructions on how to do it. Likewise, if observable behavior is as strongly influenced by genetics as many assert, then there also has to be a lot of hardwiring, and that, too, requires an enormous amount of genetic information."

"Even though it's the same cell types that get used over and over?"

Stephen nodded. "Absolutely. For the body, and the organs within it, to grow into the shape that it has, there has to be exact, cell-specific information on how cells divide and communicate. That means that the information for this also has to be in the genome. All of a sudden, we're not sure how this is done. There are way more things that need individual instructions than there are base pairs of DNA, even if every one of them is useful for human development, which they are not. Three billion isn't that big a number when you're dealing with thirty-seven trillion cells in the human body, one hundred billion neurons in the brain, each with up to a thousand synapses with other neurons, and one hundred million photoreceptors in each eye."

"In other words, there is a huge gap between how much useful DNA exists and how much appears to be needed."

"Exactly. Even if just ten percent of human cells require targeted instructions, that is over one thousand times more instructions than we have of base pairs of DNA. And when you factor in that it probably takes multiple base pairs for a single instruction, and factor out the non-instructional DNA, it's clear there aren't remotely enough base pairs for human development to be based on direct linear translation from genome to organism function."

"Can you say that in regular language to make sure I understand?"

"Sure. I'll give you an analogy," Stephen said. "In a recipe, each instruction results in one or two things happening, such as mixing one set of ingredients. If that was the case with the genome, then we are missing an enormous amount of information as the number of possible instructions is far less than the number of specific outcomes, e.g., a cell divides a certain way at a certain point in time, needed to get us. For our 'recipe,' the ratio of instructions needed versus the amount of useful, informational, DNA is at least several thousand to one."

Incredulous, Dan asked, "Are you saying that there is some sort of non-DNA genome information that hasn't yet been found?"

"No. The solution to what otherwise seems like too little DNA came with the idea that the translation is not always direct, that there are algorithms—"

"Mathematical?" Dan asked, immediately thinking of the connotations.

"Sort of like equations or minicomputer programs. They turn a small amount of DNA into a much larger number of instructions," Stephen said. "This really shouldn't be surprising, as body symmetry—how the left and right sides of creatures are mirror images—can only come about if they are developed off the same set of instructions." Stephen sounded just like the college professor he once was.

Dan paused, thought a bit, then asked: "What type of algorithms could account for these things?"

"Right on. Watch this." With the remote in his hand, Stephen proceeded to show a series of amazingly complex images. They were all based on the image Dan had seen on the screensaver upstairs.

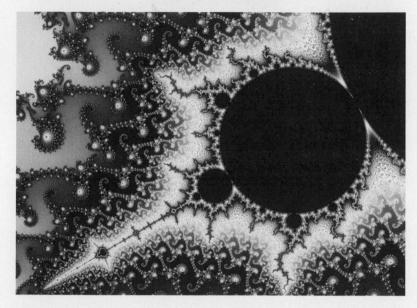

"Dan, each of the images you just saw was produced by iterations of the exact same, simple equation, otherwise known as the Mandelbrot fractal set. You've heard of it?" He scribbled a formula down and showed it to Dan:

$$Z_{n+1} = Z_n^2 + C$$

"Yes."

"Then you know that though there are only three parts in the equation, they can produce an infinite amount of detailed instructions."

"You don't mean to say that something like this equation is encoded in our DNA?" Dan asked, questioning how something that implied programmed-in-processing, and therefore a programmer, could be incorporated into the cell of every living organism.

"Well, some type of algorithmic processing is definitely needed. The Mandelbrot equation is an example of just one possible type. Does this make sense to you?"

"It's logical based on the numbers you've stated, but it's astounding."

"It gets even better. There are things called epi-markers, also known as epigenetics, which act like external switches that activate and deactivate different genes to produce different results from the same set of DNA. These also influence what gets passed from one generation to the next. Some appear to be impacted by what an organism experiences, thinks, and feels. So there must be some mechanism that controls the link between the mind and how specific epigenetic switches are set. The specificity of the mechanisms must be incredible."

"That's just natural selection, isn't it?" Dan asked. He was trying to nail down where this was headed, worried that in fact that wasn't what Stephen meant.

"Sure, if the mind is strictly biology based. But we don't know that. In fact, physics can't even propose how the mind can do what it does. At least not yet. Perhaps the soul isn't dead. Who knows? Even *you* may have one!"

"Very funny. But seriously, you haven't become one of those anti-science, antievolution fanatics who thinks everything is designed into us, have you?"

"Relax. I'm only a scientist searching for knowledge."

"Good. Because I don't want our first real discussion in over a year to wander into the territory of religious fundamentalism and creationism in the guise of science."

"Religion doesn't drive my science. I simply go where evidence and reason leads me."

"Why haven't I read anything about genetic algorithms or missing DNA? Based on what you said, it seems like the type of thing lots of geneticists would know and write about."

"That's a discussion for another night. The short answer is, they should be, but they either aren't asking the obvious questions or choose not to state what they know."

"It still sounds like you're questioning evolution."

"I'm not saying that evolution didn't happen. I *am* saying that there may have been different mechanisms for it other than the strict Darwinist view of evolution via an accumulation of random mutations and natural selection. There are gaps that need to be filled with processes and causes. Anyway, what makes you so confident, and *so obviously happy,* in thinking physical matter is all there is?" Stephen asked. "Surely you know that means no free will, no objective morality, no meaning or purpose to life, no value to loving or being loved?"

Yes, he did know that all too well. But he was not prepared to engage in the subject that had already been causing him so much trouble. Instead, Dan asked, "What about the spiritually oriented books I saw upstairs? Is your work causing you to become religious again?" He left out any mention of the role Ava's illness could have played.

"I was headed down that path anyway. You might want to rethink it yourself."

"I know you're too smart to have asked me here to discuss science and religion. Let's cut to the chase. What do you need my help with?"

"Be patient. I'm almost there. While researching algorithm translation mechanisms, we quickly found unexpected things. Once I realized where it could lead, but before I had any major breakthroughs, I took the research offline, to be worked on in secret only by a small, trusted team, while I went through the motions at work." Stephen paused.

Straightening up, Dan asked, "Why did you do that?"

"I was afraid of the power of what we would find. And I was right. We discovered multiple segments of unusually encoded DNA, each with a different algorithm and, for lack of a better description, translation codes. Six months ago, I broke two sets of algorithms and translation codes and thought I might be on the verge of a third. What the two revealed was beyond anything I could have imagined, with implications well beyond biology."

"You mean you've decoded the genome and now know everything about human development?" Dan said, trying to figure out what Stephen meant.

"Yes and no. I did break the code, but it will take a long time to figure it all out. What I do know is that there are amazing possibilities, including some that scare the hell out of me. In the wrong hands, they could do terrible things. Beyond that I'm not able to say right now, though convince me your head is on straight, that I can still count on you like I used to, and I'll tell you everything very soon."

"Well, you're going to have to do that if I'm going to help you. Though you still haven't told me what you need from me. And my head is fine, whatever you may think of it," Dan said, standing up to stretch and then sitting back down, as he tried to process what he was hearing. "But okay, for now, the biggest questions I have are why are you hiding things from HBC? Why did you think you had to build this room in your own home?"

"Imagine having all the knowledge of human biology at your fingertips, knowing how to engineer life and knowing what makes a person a person. That also means having the knowledge to alter virtually anything about people. I need to find some way to protect its use before allowing anyone else to get anywhere near it. Scientists in several countries are already experimenting with altering the genome. While I have no concerns about HBC in general, once they're involved, I'd lose control of the research, so I'd no longer be able to direct how it would be used. I have too much responsibility to do that. In a scary development, right after my breakthrough five months ago, one of my close collaborators, Alex Robertson—you've met him a few times— died under questionable circumstances."

After a pause, Dan said, "I'm sorry. That must be very hard on his family and on you."

"It was and is."

"So where do I come in, and why was a physicist involved?"

"Glad you're still as sharp as ever. Alex was helping me with the encryption to protect our work—one of his areas of expertise. I need someone I can trust absolutely, to replace him. That's you. I need your help in setting up a secure, confidential computer network for me. I also need you to help me with something else Alex and I were working on. As I said a moment ago, we broke, or more accurately, decoded, two complete sets of information. The night of the biggest breakthroughs, after Alex had gone home, the security keys he was using to protect our work timed out and the processing stopped before I could find out if there was actually a third set of coded information. I don't have the technical ability to set up the computer environment and resume processing and haven't found anyone I trust enough to help me do it. With your knowledge of computers, mathematics, and code breaking, I'm hoping you can help me continue the processing and see if there is something there. If it's anything like I think, it has great potential to change the world."

"Guess I really should've found out what you wanted before I said yes."

"You would've done it anyway."

"Probably. Why are you trusting me with all of this?" Dan said, amazed by Stephen's claims. Could they possibly be true?

"Because you're very good at what you do, and I have complete faith that no matter how angry or anything else you become, you will never let me or my family down," Stephen said, while thinking *And because I really need help and have nowhere else to turn.*

"Are you sure you're not already compromised?"

Stephen turned solemn and pensive, looked away, cleared his throat, and said, "There's nothing for anyone to find. We don't use HBC computers since Alex died. Most of my team's security is sneaker-net, stand-alone, air-gapped computers and local encryption. We should be fine. Still, if you can, I'd like you to see if my computer activity is being tracked or anything's been hacked."

"You know, if you are being observed, wouldn't people already know you've reached out to me? After all, you used an email to get me here tonight," Dan asked.

"I don't think everything I do is being tracked. Nonetheless, I brought you here as an old friend. That won't look strange. It will make sense for you to visit Ava in the hospital and come to the Cape. All of our activities upstairs were in the open. Down here, we're secure. I apologize for asking all of this of you, but I really don't have any better options. And you really are good at your work."

"Don't worry about it. And you needn't flatter me," Dan said, then spoke at length about how he would set up the secure computers and networks. Most of what he needed was already in place and he'd be able to show it to Stephen at the Cape.

After Dan was done describing it, he asked, "I love the Cape, so I don't need an excuse to go there. But why do you want me to go with you tomorrow?"

"There are some files at the Marine Biological Laboratory I need your help with and they aren't accessible remotely. It won't take long."

"Good, because I'd rather spend my time on many other things whenever I'm there."

"There will be plenty of time for that," Stephen said, then stood up and walked toward the door. "As for now, how about a game of pool? I can probably beat you these days."

"Don't count on it. But first, another beer. That will be the price of your futile attempt."

"Another is well worth the pleasure of teaching you the first of many important lessons, humility. Just to let you know, while you were always better at the angles, I can handle rebounds better and shoot straighter."

"Very funny, and dead wrong, especially from someone who's at risk from his own hubris," Dan said. "Near as I can tell, you've been playing every possible angle recently. But then again, aren't politics and angles challenging in the supposedly objective world of academic science? Anyway, it's time to put up or shut up."

"My thoughts exactly."

Stephen walked upstairs to get the beers while Dan racked the balls. As they started the game, "Question" by the Moody Blues played in the background. Dan hummed along with the words, *Why do we never get an answer, when we're knocking at the door?*

After the words *a thousand million questions*, Stephen said, "Be careful what you ask for. We have a long way to go, and what we find could change how you think about the world."

"Trust me. I could use a break from the way I've been feeling," Dan said. If what Stephen had told him was true, there really might be some answers out there to the things that had been bothering him. Whether Dan would like the answers would be another thing. But just the thought that they could exist was already changing his mood.

The song continued: *To learn as we grow old, the secrets of our soul.*

After they played a couple of overly competitive games that they split, they returned to the study and talked some more.

Finally, just as Dan was getting up to leave, Stephen went over to the piano and started playing Springsteen's "Thunder Road." Dan came over and they sang together in low voices, not quite in harmony and barely on pitch. When they had finished, Stephen looked up and said, "It might have been twenty-five years since we've done that."

"Our voices haven't improved, and they weren't great to begin with."

"Thanks a lot. Now get out of here before one of us changes our mind about tomorrow. We've got a lot to do."

Dan handed his car keys to Stephen and said, "It'll be nice to see Ava and spend time at the Cape."

"Good night," Stephen said.

Walking outside, Dan got into the backseat of the waiting car. As it drove off, he was energized. He felt his blood pulse through his body. A veil was lifting. Everything looked so colorful, even in the dark. The night was fragrant and full of sound. His buoyed spirit, however, was tempered by the knowledge of Ava's past illness and Stephen's concerns. As long as there was any possibility of helping Ava or finding answers to the questions he now knew he needed to consider, Dan would do everything he possibly could to help.

Chapter 21

Dan hated hospitals. They reminded him of mortality, illness, and dissolution. Though it was justifiably recognized as an outstanding medical center, Boston Children's Hospital could often do nothing but provide temporary relief or a slight extension of life for a child. That was just the nature of things. One more indication of the pointlessness of life. Not good. Not evil. It just was, though that provided no meaningful answers and certainly no solace.

Yet, for many, it was unquestionably a place of hope. That was what was on Dan's mind when he had woken this morning. Though he had slept much better than he had in a long time, the old doubts were nagging him again. Still, the possibility for hope, and the desire to see Ava, helped him focus outside of himself today and provided an energy he hadn't felt in a long time.

Now he was waiting in the hospital lobby to meet Stephen and Ava. Stephen had arrived earlier, in Dan's car, and was now with Ava. Nancy had gone home to get some rest. Dan and Stephen would drop Ava off with her mother and then head down to the Cape. Nancy and Ava would follow shortly thereafter.

Dan was early, since it had taken less time than he thought to walk the two miles to the hospital, despite the fact that he carried a large gym bag filled with his weekend clothes.

At 10 a.m. Stephen strode into the lobby. He looked at Dan's gym bag and said, "I'm happy to see that you're still game. Wasn't sure what you'd be thinking after you had time to sleep on things."

"Can't say that I didn't have second thoughts . . . then thirds . . . then fourths. Luckily for you, I couldn't find a way to back out and still see Ava. And there's the little matter of getting my car back. Pretty clever of you." He smiled at his old friend. "So, how is Ava?"

"She's great. Handled the tests wonderfully. Although we don't have all the results, everything looks really good. Let's go and get her out of here," Stephen said cheerily.

Dan followed Stephen down the hallway and into Ava's room. It was a private room, in a wing of the hospital for children with less severe ailments. Next to her bed was a fully extended lounge chair, where Nancy had slept the previous evening.

The room was empty. A note rested on top of the pillow. Stephen picked it up, smiled, and said, "Ava went to visit some of the other kids. She'll be back in a few minutes."

"You said Ava is doing well. Why did she have to stay overnight?"

"Some of the tests require special preparation, and if you group them together properly, you can get them done quicker and easier, even if it does require an overnight stay. Ava's physician, Dr. Alighieri, has been outstanding through all of this. She helped us with the scheduling, and now we can enjoy the weekend."

After a pause, Dan asked, "Can your work help the children here?"

"That's part of what I'm striving for. It's also part of the reason why I need your help."

"You know I could never say no to anything that would help with this."

"That's one of the exceptional things about you. You really should remind yourself of that from time to time."

Dan was looking out the window at the increasingly overcast sky when Ava came bounding in and lit everything up, as though the full force of the sun was focused on the room. Seeing him, she let out little sounds of happiness. He turned in time to catch her as she jumped into his arms. It had been well over a year since they had last seen each other, and she was still as warm to him as ever. Her blue eyes beamed into his as he held her. Long, light-brown hair, the color of vibrant summer wheat, hung around her shoulders. She felt solid, healthy, not frail. And he felt whole with his arms wrapped around her.

When he finally put her down, she went over to her father, who was talking to a young woman dressed in casual clothes. There was something odd about the woman, though Dan couldn't put a finger on what.

As Dan walked over, Stephen turned and said, "Dan, this is Dr. Alighieri. She was tremendous throughout Ava's illness."

As she turned toward him, Dan extended his hand and said, "Pleased to meet you." He was surprised how young she was—probably in her early thirties—yet she carried herself with the complete assurance of someone with a lifetime of experience and certainty in everything around her.

Dr. Alighieri faced Dan directly. Her dark-blue eyes, the color of the early-evening sky when the stars first appear, seemed to reach through his. Jet-black, shoulder-length hair framed an interesting face, but all Dan could think about was his increasing discomfort, uncertain of whether he was being drawn to or repelled by her. He almost started to turn away and withdraw his hand, but before he could do so, she grabbed his arm and said, "I've heard so much about you. I'm glad we finally get to meet."

He didn't move until she released him, then mumbled, "Thank you for all you did for Ava. She's really special."

Looking at him quizzically, Dr. Alighieri replied, "They all are. Especially her."

Perplexed by the odd interaction, Stephen said to Dan, "Why don't we get the car, and Ava and Dr. Alighieri can meet us out front?"

On the way down the elevator, Stephen asked, "What was that about?"

"There was something disconcerting about her. My instincts were blaring alarms."

"What kind of nonsense is that? Dr. Alighieri used cutting-edge medicine, and provided around-the-clock care. She gave everything of herself to help Ava, was even organizing trials in case we needed to try new medicines, and you let a funny feeling get to you? What type of alarms do you think you were hearing? Your vanishing sanity?"

"I appreciate what she did. Something just didn't feel right about her, there was definitely something odd and unsettling."

"Given how your life's going lately, the last thing you should trust is your instincts."

"I'd be careful. Those are the same instincts that are telling me to help you."

"Maybe they need to be recalibrated for different circumstances."

"Perhaps. Nonetheless."

"Get over it. I know Trish Alighieri really, really well. She did incredible things for Ava. Perhaps just think of that," Stephen answered in an sharp-edged voice.

"I'm sorry I upset you. Maybe it's just my state of mind," Dan said, while thinking he knew what he knew, even in his present, less than optimal, state.

"Your car is just to the left of the front door. Why don't you pull it up while I wait for Ava?" Stephen suggested while handing Dan the keys, still sounding a bit annoyed. "By the way: Trish is going to be at the Cape for the afternoon. She is going to help out a doctor at Falmouth Hospital and visit a patient."

Dan couldn't decide whether he was pleased or annoyed by the news.

Chapter 22

Dan stood in Stephen's front yard waiting to leave for the Cape. The drive back from the hospital had been mostly silent, the atmosphere tense.

The sky was overcast, like his mood had once again become.

Thinking back to his meeting with Ava's doctor, Dan was surprised that Stephen was so offended by his reaction. At worst, it was nothing more than awkwardness. He felt indignant at Stephen's response and questioned his decision to help him.

Anger and resentment began to occupy his mind. He felt himself being dragged toward the same dark places that he had been pulled toward in recent weeks. The only thing that kept him from seeing what was there was the dread that he might not be able to return, that what had been him would be gone, replaced by a shell. But he was weakening, and the assaults on his resistance were becoming more frequent—almost voices—and harder to overcome. A climactic battle was coming, and he feared its outcome. Everywhere he turned, he saw pointlessness and futility. Everything was a lie.

He began walking toward his car, tempted to get in and drive home.

As he passed a thick-trunked tree in the middle of the front yard, he was so wrapped up in his inner thoughts that he didn't notice the tip of a sneaker sticking out at the base of the tree. Too late, he heard a *whump* and instinctively started to go into a tuck position. Something hard, smooth, and damp slammed into his cheek and he fell to the ground. A weight pounced on his chest and he heard high-pitched laughter. Looking up, he saw Ava's beaming face above him.

"You used to be quicker than that." Laughing, Ava added, "I'm sorry the ball hit you in the face. I was aiming for your body but you ducked. Are you all right?"

Dan blinked several times as his vision cleared and the dark thoughts vanished, replaced by gradual warmth. He was not too far gone to appreciate the joy of children, especially this one, and their naïve optimism. It gave him something to hold on to.

After a moment, he smiled and said, "If you weren't such an angel, I'd say you were being devilish. Of course you know I allowed you to do this."

"You're not kidding anyone. You didn't even know where I was. I kicked the ball pretty hard, didn't I?"

"You sure did. Must have been practicing a lot since the last time I saw you; maybe even taking steroids to get stronger."

Ava gave him a weird look, and he realized she probably didn't even know what steroids were. But then Ava slapped his chest and said, "Tag! You're it," and sprinted off.

Dan chased her around bushes, trees, and other obstacles. While he was faster, she was quick, short, and more nimble, changing directions in a flash or ducking under most of his attempts to tag her. They did this for several rounds, alternately tagging each other and running off. Dan slipped on the damp grass a few times, streaking his jeans in the process. The exertion felt good. Ava's laughter and squeals felt better. He was no longer aware of his earlier, dismal thoughts.

Then Ava ran to the soccer ball and launched another shot at him. Alert this time, he caught it and handed it back to her as she hugged him around his waist.

Dan said, "You weren't going to get me twice like that, even though you are smarter than the average bear."

Looking perplexed, Ava replied, "Who said bears are smart?"

Laughing, Dan answered, "You need to watch *The Yogi Bear Show*."

"Is he that guy in the commercial with the talking duck?"

"Yogi Bear, not Yogi Berra! Man, kids today really are missing out on the good things. We're going to have to watch old cartoons together this weekend."

Before Ava could reply, the front door opened, and Nancy appeared in the doorway and called out, "Okay you two, time to cut it out. Ava, come on in and take a shower. Dan, Stephen will be out in a minute." Ava walked into the house. Nancy smiled, winked at Dan, then went back inside, closing the door behind her.

While waiting, Dan tried juggling the soccer ball. Although the sky was still overcast, he felt sunny. He couldn't put his finger on it, but he felt that the dark places were no longer a threat. He was not going to vanish into an abyss.

Leaning back against the tree from which Ava had sprung, he filled his lungs with the late-spring air. This far north, plants bloomed late, especially after a cold spring like this year's. While the lilacs were almost past peak, and the lavender was just emerging, they still scented the air. The rhododendrons had yet to put on their show. He marveled at the beauty of the world. With the darkness pushed back, the tension was gone as well, and he felt a pleasant, relaxed tiredness that reflected the sleep he still needed to catch up on.

His brief rest was interrupted by Stephen striding out of the house carrying his suitcase and computer bag. Smiling at Dan, he said, "Don't tell me a little girl just out of the hospital wore you out that quickly?"

"She's pretty athletic. Obviously takes after her mother."

Dan wondered whether Stephen's friendliness was real or feigned. How could he put their disagreements behind him so easily?

Together they walked to the car. Dan turned to Stephen, tossed him the keys, and said, "Since I'm such a tired old man, you'd better drive."

Looking surprised, Stephen said, "Now that's a first. How do I merit such an honor?" Dan almost never let anyone drive his cars. He was known for needing to feel in control.

"You don't. I need to rest since I was up most of the night getting stuff ready for you, " Dan replied, exaggerating his lack of sleep. But he was tired, thought he could nap, and wanted to take advantage of it while he could. The respite from his restlessness might prove brief.

Stephen's eyes widened, belying his characteristic calm. "Did you finish figuring out my cyber-security setup already?"

"I just need to show you how to use it once we get to the Cape. *And* I need to decide how much to charge you," Dan said in jest and with a broad smile.

"We can discuss that so-called fee later," Stephen replied as they got into the car. "If this is all it took, I need to get you out more."

"As I said yesterday, make things interesting enough and I might be game."

"Now it's your turn to be careful what you ask for."

"I can handle it."

"I wasn't so sure of that when I saw my daughter getting the better of you."

Remembering the morning, Dan straightened up and asked, "Is Ava really okay?"

"She's fine, thank God."

Dan thought, *For what, not being as cruel as usual?*

As the car accelerated onto the road, Dan drifted off, hoping for reasons to believe in a better life.

Chapter 23

The midday sunlight bounced off the vigorous chop, spraying dancing patches of white light across the walls of the second floor study that overlooked the beach. A brisk sea breeze easily penetrated the screened windows, filling the room with marine-scented air that infused Dan's lungs and invigorated him. In the distance, Martha's Vineyard's contours were clearly visible, while closer to shore, a regatta of sailboats from nearby Falmouth Harbor erased a winter's worth of creases from their sails as their crews competed to reach the next mark.

After a ninety-minute drive that seemed far shorter, Dan was in Stephen's summer home.

With Stephen standing nearby, Dan opened an old brown Coach satchel, pulled out a metal-cased laptop and flip-style cell phone, and placed both on the desk that faced the windows and the water. As Stephen reached for the computer, Dan said, "Remember, this is a two-way street. In exchange for what I'm doing, you're going to tell me everything about your work. With the risks I'm taking, I have a right to know."

Stephen answered, "Agreed. But after a major experiment on Tuesday. I'll know a lot more myself then."

"Why not tell me now?"

"We're just getting comfortable with each other again. I need to reestablish my credibility with you before I explain some remarkable things, and having the evidence from the experiment will be helpful. Also, to be honest, I want to know more about your state of mind."

"Fine. Keep in mind that my security requires dual keys to access it. I provide one for accessing the servers and you pick another for encrypting your directories. Without mine, which I can change anytime, you can't do anything," Dan replied.

"I guess that makes us partners."

"I suppose, except at the moment, I'm the one at legal risk with the technology I'm giving you."

"Then why are you doing this?"

"Based on what you've told me, you need the best tools to protect your work. I'm the only one who can get you them. Plus, perhaps I think I'm too clever to be caught, or in my state of mind I don't care much about what happens, or maybe I just like the idea of putting you at risk with me," Dan said with a half-smile.

"I like the first reason more than the last three," Stephen said.

"They're a package deal. Anyway, for starters, the computer and cell phone are both as secure as any device of their kind in the world. No one, not even the government, should be able to get data off this computer without your consent. The cell phone has a special secure channel that cannot be hacked, tapped, or listened in on. It's a flip phone because it's a more secure interface and was easier for me to obtain. I have a secure smartphone, and we can use them to communicate with each other. There are two other important parts of the setup. The first is encryption—how we prevent unauthorized people from reading whatever you're working on or storing. The second is network masking—how we prevent people from monitoring your communications, or in fact even knowing that you are communicating, whether with another person or with remote servers. You'll need help with both of these. As I'm sure you know, encryption is a series of steps that translates comprehensible data into apparently random gibberish. The trick to it is to set up sufficiently complex translation steps and the key that determines how those steps operate. The longer the key, the more difficult it is for someone to crack the code and access whatever it is you have encrypted. Got it?"

"Yes."

"Good. The next part of this is the masking. If people don't know you've stored anything, they can't find it and try to decode it. However, in today's day and age, almost anything can be monitored.

Network sniffers, hacking into Web servers, wireless snooping, really any technology you can imagine can be used to monitor electronic communications."

"Your old colleagues in the government have made this abundantly clear. What can we do about it?"

"The trick is misdirection, masking, and physical separation. If you break things into enough pieces, send them to lots of different directions, make it seem like they're something else, and have them appear to jump out of the network only to reappear in a disconnected point that's off the monitored grid, then you stand a pretty good chance of being unobservable. And that's really important, because what can't be decrypted today might be easily decoded in the future with much faster computers."

"Where are the computers you're using? And where's the data storage?"

"All over the place. Mostly cloud-based. Some privately hosted."

"I'm impressed. I knew I asked the right person for this."

"Don't forget, there's significant risk to both of us. You'll be in possession of classified capabilities, and I'll have broken federal laws in giving them to you. We could be charged with serious criminal offenses."

"I'd be happy if that's our biggest risk," Stephen said.

"They're not our only computer risks."

"What do you mean?"

"Watch what I found out a little while ago," Dan said, then opened his computer.

After a few moments a network diagram with a lot of dots and lines connecting them appeared. One green dot near the center had a green circle around it. A little to the right side of it, a blue dot had a blue circle around it.

Dan pointed to the green dot and said, "That dot represents the internet gateway for your network at HBC. The blue dot represents the remote server I'm using. Watch what happens when I initiate a transmission that appears to try and hack in to HBC." Dan entered a few commands. A line between Dan's server and the HBC gateway pulsed briefly. Immediately afterward, a line pulsed from HBC to a dot on the far left. Then several lines from the far left pulsed briefly to the blue dot that Dan had initiated the original command from. Periodically, the pulses repeated.

"See that? My attempt to probe HBC triggered a reaction from a monitoring layer outside of HBC to other servers that then sought to probe me. Of course, I let them see my server, or at least what they think is my server."

"So HBC has good security and is trying to track you down. Why is that a bad thing?"

"It's not that simple. Now watch this." Dan entered a few more commands, and lines pulsed from his server to the servers that had sought him. Rapidly, a myriad of lines pulsed from the left of the screen and seemed to besiege his server, trying to find a path from that location to the computer in front of him and their location. "What you're watching is a widespread cyber attack that has figured out my server is a dummy server and is trying to find us. They won't succeed, at least not today. I've terminated all connections. What's particularly interesting is the origin of the attacks and the HBC monitors." Dan hit a function key and a map was superimposed over the network diagram. The far left of the screen was all within China. "Do you want to explain to me why a large number of Chinese hackers, which is what these network addresses belong to, have to do with HBC, and why such sophisticated technology is being used to monitor your company? While Chinese hackers are commonplace, they usually try to break into things, not keep others out."

Stephen got up, walked to the window, looked at the water, and said quietly, "I can't answer that."

"You can't or won't?" Dan demanded.

"Can't. Though maybe you can help me find out," Stephen challenged.

"You're going to have to let me," Dan replied.

Stephen looked back at computer screen as a large number of lines pulsed all over in an ongoing attempt to find them. He nodded, then said, "How are you able to find all of this out without being observed yourself?"

"I made sure that I initiated my probing using proxy servers that are set up specially to capture and transmit this information without being monitored themselves. I also used a 'ghosted' server for my communications. It seems physically real, in a specific location, when in fact it's not. A non-network relay, untraceable unless you know where to physically look for it, routes communications to my computer here."

"Impressive. Why do you have this setup?"

"I got bored with my agency work and wanted an anonymous way of operating."

"Can you find out what's going on with those other computers?"

"I can try. Watch this," Dan said, entering a few commands.

Moments later, the screen pulsed with lines flashing from the China-based networks to a new dot on the map.

Dan pointed to it. "Do you know where that is?"

Looking at the superimposed map, Stephen said, "It's near DC."

"It's actually a secret computer facility for the NSA. By now, alarms are going off and they are going to do everything they can to find out the source of the attacks and deal with them. They'll do our work for us, without even knowing it."

"You like playing with fire."

"The heat reminds me I'm alive."

"Get too close to it and that won't be a question you'll be able to ask again."

"How did you get involved with an outfit like HBC?" Dan asked.

"They had been pursuing me for a while, but I wasn't interested. Then I had Ava's genome tested for predispositions for a set of inheritable diseases that new tests could detect. Ava's showed the potential to develop a nasty form of leukemia. I decided to join HBC to find a treatment for it in the event she might need it. Our research also looks at the possibility of gene editing, and I want to know where that is going and what I can do to help direct its ethical use. Shortly after I joined HBC is when I discovered the DNA coding, and I formed a small team, with Alex, to try to decode it. After Alex died, I put the decoding on hold and focused on understanding what I already had. Soon thereafter, Ava did actually develop leukemia, but not as nasty a type as we first feared."

"Did your work identify a cure?" Dan asked.

"No, that was going to take a long time. So I had to search for existing, cutting-edge treatments. Some seemed promising but couldn't be developed quickly enough in the US. Another organization found foreign corporations that could speed up development. Trish—I mean Dr. Alighieri—was setting up trials at her hospital to test current treatments and prepare for foreign ones, should they become available. But, unexpectedly, a conventional treatment was quickly effective."

"What organization was helping you find new treatments?"

"I can't tell you yet. Maybe soon."

"Stephen, it sounds like you're the pushing the envelope big-time, with questionable people. You really should let me help you further."

"I will, when I know I won't jeopardize you."

"That sounds ominous."

"It's nothing too serious. I'm just being cautious."

Before they could say anything else, they heard a car drive up. Looking out the front window, Dan saw Nancy, Ava, and Trish get out of the car. Ava looked up and waved to them as Nancy and Trish carried their bags up the steps of the house.

Seeing the awkward look on Dan's face, Stephen said, "Don't worry. She's not staying long."

"I can handle it."

Stephen turned to look out the window to the beach beyond, and said in a wonder-filled voice, "Imagine what it would mean if finding out everything there is to know about DNA, including its origin, revealed everything there is to know about science and the universe."

"I think that would explain your need for security. It would also beg an enormous number of big questions," Dan answered, questioning how what Stephen said could be true.

"That's right."

Dan decided to change the subject until Stephen was ready to share more. "So the genetic code is really a code, like a computer programming language."

"Exactly," Stephen said.

"And once it's fully understood, along with all cell processes, then scientists, if they have the right tools, will be able to change anything they want—whether it's something simple like making people bigger, stronger, and faster, or creating a whole new species."

"Well yes, though there is an enormous amount of complexity that needs to be understood well beyond just the DNA sequence," Stephen replied.

"And this is where you come in. You're trying to figure all of this out."

"You're making me feel like I'm being interviewed. But yes."

"That's an awful lot of power for scientists. Who will make sure they make the right decisions, do the right things? What about whatever you're doing?" Dan asked.

"These types of questions are what the whole field of bioethics is about. The president has chartered a committee to look at these issues."

"I've seen the list of its members. An unelected, eclectic bunch that meets four times a year is going to decide this for us? I don't think so. I think it's more likely that a lot of scientists will do whatever they want, whether they have the right to or not."

"Now you're into the territory of what makes anything right or wrong," Stephen said.

"I'm an expert programmer. I'm very familiar with targeted cyber attacks that, in effect, aren't all that different from biological viruses. So I have to ask, what's to stop someone from designing viruses that target portions of the population by specific traits? Could someone go after something as simple as hair color, or even just a specific individual, based on their sequenced DNA?"

"Nothing but time. After all, look how common and cheap DNA sequencing has become. It might be near impossible to stop the development of designer viruses unless the first to master the technology somehow finds a way to control all of it."

"That's all very scary," Dan replied.

"Unless, of course, there are other limitations we're not aware of. I think there may be some. That is part of what you're going to help me with."

"To overcome them?"

"No, to make sure they are *not* overcome."

They both stood in silence, taking in the beautiful morning and the water. Several minutes passed before Stephen said, "I have an interesting scientific question for you. What do you think would happen if DNA didn't use compression to store information, and didn't use algorithmic processing to direct biological processes?"

"Either there would have to be a lot more of it, or there would be a lot less information," Dan replied.

"Let's say there had to be several orders of magnitude—more DNA than known in human cells. Then what? It's simple, obvious stuff. Nothing you need to know much about biochemistry to understand."

"Well, DNA would take up a lot more space, probably requiring a larger nucleus, maybe a much larger cell," Dan said, intrigued by the implications.

"How would that impact us physically?" Stephen said.

"I see the professor is leading his students," Dan said with a smile. "Well, for one, it would change the ratio of surface area to volume, adversely affecting critically important membrane processes and increasing the pressure on the cell membrane."

"Exactly. The larger volume would impact the overall ability of the cell to function, making it harder to transport molecules, maybe slowing down metabolism. *And*, this is a beautiful part, unless DNA replication was greatly speeded up—remember, DNA already copies three thousand base pairs per minute per replication site—the gestation period of offspring would exceed the maternal life span. The mother would be dead before the child was born! And to replicate even at present speeds, there has to be an incredible assembly line of correct nucleotides lined up, ready to be linked into new DNA strands, and energy sources to fuel the separation of the original DNA duplex to form individual templates for the synethesis of new strands. It's just amazing. And if that isn't enough to fathom, think about this: if cells were much larger, they'd have to either have more rigid cell walls, making them unable to move, or they'd be prone to rupturing. That would make life as we know it impossible. Darn good thing that compressed information just happened to be there, right from the beginning, with a means to translate and express it," Stephen said triumphantly.

"You know, you keep doing the same thing to me, teasing me with these extraordinary speculations that nobody but you seems to know. It's getting really frustrating. Why haven't I heard any of this from other sources?"

"Groupthink to the extreme, lots of microfocus on just pieces of the puzzle, and an orthodoxy that tries to suppress anything that could have metaphysical implications. Oh, and a desire for academic prestige over truth."

"Anything else?" Dan said facetiously.

"Well, since you asked."

"I was just being polite," Dan said with feigned exasperation.

"What if decoded DNA doesn't explain how the mind works? What if, in fact, it shows something like the brain being the motherboard to the soul's CPU?"

"You have evidence for this?" Dan said in a sharp, intense, voice, as the battle that had been reignited within him between meaninglessness and meaning came to the fore.

"No, but I'll know soon. DNA has to contain the blueprint for whatever the brain does, or does not, do, including whether it is self-contained or works with something else."

"You know you keep blowing my mind, whatever it is made of."

"Then it's a good thing that it's so resilient."

"That is a recent development that I don't want to jeopardize," Dan said.

After another period of quiet, during which big cumulous clouds cast passing shadows between moments of brilliant sunshine, Dan said, "I don't get it. You claim that you've found things encoded in DNA that reveal more than biology, that also mean they are there by intent. Why would a God do such a thing?"

"Whatever the reason, it probably wouldn't be dropped there by accident. It's safe to say it would probably be for a greater purpose."

At first pensive, then turning jovial, Dan said, "If you had the means to do it, what type of life-form would you design?"

Smiling broadly, looking at a woman sunning herself on the sand,

Stephen answered mischievously, "I can think of a lot of wonderful ideas, but it depends if I want my wife to kill me or not."

Laughing, thinking of the possibilities of enhanced humans or designed species, Dan responded, "Then do it for me. Design the perfect woman for me, as the price of my help."

"What if I think, as a form of natural selection, that you shouldn't reproduce?"

"I might agree with you but insist you try anyway. Besides, wasn't complete sexual freedom, the fruits of a godless process if not world, one of the benefits of Darwinism that its early supporters liked best?" Dan said.

"Ah, rights without obligations. An interesting conundrum."

"You mean like me having a purpose and plan in mind about whether I should be allowed to reproduce?"

"You get it after all."

"Nah, I just know how to play word games."

"At least you think so."

"You know, seriously, either you really do have the incredible things you're implying or you're snowing me big-time, using knowledge of my present weaknesses, to get what you want."

"What do you think? You know me."

"I'll think about it and let you know."

Stephen laughed. "I'm sure you will. Now, how about we get the Marine Biological Laboratory stuff out of the way and then we'll have the rest of the day to relax."

Smiling, Dan said, "Geez, so much for time to think about things."

"This is a small thing. And you're a quick thinker anyway."

"All right. I'll see what I can figure out during my run afterward."

"Good idea."

Words no longer needed, they let the refreshing sea breeze gently ripple through the window and over them.

It was one of those days that, in retrospect, seemed way too calm for what lay ahead.

Chapter 24

From his office at the Marine Biological Laboratory's Genetics Research Center, Stephen had a panoramic view. The top floor of the hilltop building offered unobstructed sight to the beaches on his left, the water and the Vineyard in the center, and to his right, the Nobska lighthouse, the outskirts of Woods Hole, and its harbor,. Nonetheless, when he was focused on his work, as he was now, the views might as well have been cinder-block walls for all it mattered to Stephen.

This building was just one of the many, scattered throughout the small village of Woods Hole, that together formed a renowned international center for research and education in the biological and earth sciences.

Woods Hole itself—while it still had the appearance of a quaint fishing village—was actually now a major scientific research center. Beyond the world-renowned Oceanographic Research Institute, where Robert Ballard, who found the *Titanic*, was based, Woods Hole was home to a branch of the US National Geographic Survey and was also a meeting center for the National Academy of Sciences. On a per capita basis, depending on the time of year, Woods Hole might have more Noble Laureates than anywhere else in the world.

Stephen felt fortunate that he was able work so close to his childhood vacation home. Some things, through no planning or action, just happen to turn out well. Before Ava fell ill, his whole life had seemed that way. Even through the illness, the best possible outcomes happened. Sometimes he wondered, why him? Why should chance favor him so much and so many others suffered?

Now he wondered if he was overdrawn in the account of good

fortune and it was time for fate to collect on a long-overdue debt. Perhaps, with Dan's help, he'd be able to forestall any reckoning just long enough.

Despite the numerous times he'd visited the Cape, this was the first Dan had been to Stephen's Woods Hole office. There wouldn't be time for a tour of the facilities.

Stephen was seated at his desk. After logging on to the MBL network, he stood up and gestured for Dan to sit down at the computer.

"What exactly do you want me to do?" Dan asked.

"I'd like to protect files here until I can get home and upload other files into the secure sites you set up. Then I'd like to permanently delete the files here."

"What about backups? Will we have to find and delete them too?"

"I've excluded the file directories from the backup service. That's why I have copies in multiple sites. They back each other up without winding up elsewhere via backups or disaster-recovery procedures."

Dan placed his hand on his chin and thought for a few moments. "I presume you don't want anyone to know we've done this."

"That's right."

"Then we shouldn't use your account. We don't want anything traceable back to you, and your account probably doesn't have the administrative privileges we'll need anyway," Dan said.

"Can you do something?"

"Probably."

"You don't lack for confidence."

"This is based on experience, not vanity. Trust me, there are far more vulnerabilities in major enterprises than you'd ever want to know. It will take years to mitigate most of them, presuming they are willing to sacrifice current earnings to do it."

"You're scaring me again."

"It's not me you should be afraid of."

"I know, but that doesn't help."

"Is there a kitchen or pantry nearby?"

"You're hungry now? We don't have much time. Octavio Romanov may stop by. He's been pressuring me to attend a National Academy of Science gala that's nearby this weekend."

"HBC's chairman?"

"That's right."

Dan didn't have time to worry about why Stephen's boss might be dropping in. He needed to get working. "No, I'm not hungry, but a pantry is usually an innocuous location for me to work, and they can have some of the more vulnerable network access points."

"Follow me. It's around the corner," Stephen said.

Inside a small kitchenette, Dan sat at a small table with Stephen next to him.

He had been typing commands on his computer at a furious pace for fifteen minutes while automated programs ran in the background.

Stopping, he leaned back. "I now have all the access we need."

"How did you do that so fast? MBL has a very secure infrastructure."

"That's what they all say, though few do."

"I'm not a tech guy, but I'd like to know how you did it by just plugging into the telephone jack."

"First I tried the wireless network. It was well done, which isn't surprising, since that's the first place companies secure to prevent outside intrusions. Fortunately, this is a voice-over-IP telephone, meaning it's connected to the overall MBL computer network. As is often the case, the voice network does not have the same local area network access controls as the rest of the network. Once I got on there, I needed an authorized identity to look around. Using an insufficiently protected Microsoft directory, I obtained anonymous credentials from your log-on, elevated their privileges to overall network administrative authority, and then mapped the network. Later, I'll set up a secure, hidden VPN so you can connect remotely and delete what you need to, once I install the commands for that."

"I hope financial institutions are protected better than this."

"I wouldn't bet on it."

Stephen sighed. "I think I'm going to buy gold coins,"

"What's the name of the directories of the files you want protected?"

"They are all in a directory I named Adirondacks."

Dan replied mockingly, "Oh that's clever. I'm sure no one would ever associate that server with you, given the cabin you own in that region. What's your password? Something unhackable, such as Nancy?"

"You really are a hard case, aren't you? How about lightening up a little?"

"Fine. Now enter a long phrase as your encryption key. I won't look. Not that I couldn't be recording all of your keystrokes. But for the record, I'm not."

Dan passed his laptop computer to Stephen, who had a scornful look on his face.

After typing about twenty characters, he passed the computer back to Dan and said, "Done."

"This may take a while, depending on the size of the files," Dan said.

Twenty-five minutes later, the processing stopped.

"I'll install the secure VPN now, then the delete command that you will be able to execute from anywhere, and we'll be done."

Before Stephen could reply, his phone buzzed, indicating that he had received a text. "Octavio Romanov is here early and on the way up. We have to finish now," he exclaimed.

"I don't have time to install the VPN."

"What about the delete command?"

"Almost done."

"Meet me back in my office. That's where Octavio will go first."

Dan entered Stephen's office barely a minute before Octavio did.

The media's pictures and videos didn't do the man justice. He was immaculately dressed in a seersucker suit and moved with apparently effortless ease. He had a full shock of gray hair that reflected his years but belied his vigor, and he emanated power and authority, yet somehow hinted that there was much more to be called on if needed. Despite his considerable abilities and position, he was known for his reserved demeanor and respectful interactions. He was so strong and confident that he had no need of standing above anyone else.

Dan had read that at a young age, Octoavio had emigrated from an eastern European country and arrived penniless in America with his family. He excelled at everything he did, quickly amassing a small fortune on Wall Street that he turned into a much larger fortune in international finance, including currency trading. Nary a rumor or inkling of scandal or poor behavior accompanied his rise. A solid family man, he had a long marriage to his childhood sweetheart, who had passed away a few years earlier. After a period of grieving, he had dedicated himself to philanthropy and science with the aim of improving the human condition. It was in this capacity that he had founded HBC and was now the chairman of the corporation whose research Stephen Bishop led. Given all of this, it was remarkable that he apparently had no escort, no security with him in the building, just a limo and a driver out front.

Quickly taking in the room, Octavio noted Dan with the slightest of raised eyebrows, smiled fully and warmly at Stephen, and then said, "Stephen, my excellent lab director, I was hoping you'd be gone by now. Then we could have arranged to have a pleasant drink somewhere before I have to head over to the boring reception whose invitation you've turned down, leaving me to fend for myself."

"You unduly flatter me. I'm quite certain there are many more interesting people than me at the foundation's party. In fact, if I'm not careful, you might meet fascinating Nobel Prize winners and decide to replace me."

"Nonsense. I'd take you over any of them. Your research is extraordinary. But just what are you doing here on a day like this?"

"I need to apologize for my poor manners in not introducing my childhood friend, Dan Lawson. Dan has been joining my family on the Cape for as long as I can remember, and after a few years' hiatus, he's staying with us this weekend. He wanted to see my office. He's part of the reason I had to decline your invitation to the barbecue."

"Welcome, Mr. Lawson. Anyone whom Stephen has been friends with so long must be someone of great character. If there is an opportunity, I'd enjoy having a cocktail with both of you. Alas, it apparently can't be this weekend. I'm sorry that Stephen has dragged you here on a day with weather as beautiful as this."

Before Stephen could reply further, Dan answered, "I've always wanted to see his office. We're only taking a quick look and then getting back to the beach. The view out the windows is just as spectacular as he said."

"Yes it is. What do you do, Mr. Lawson?"

"I'm a computer network consultant," Dan said, providing the least amount of information he could.

"Well, if you know anything about IT security, I may need your help. HBC's Information Security Officer tells me that we recently experienced a series of cyber attacks. We've had no luck tracking them down. In today's world, you can't be too secure."

"I'm afraid that's all too common these days."

"I'll have Stephen give me your information. For now, I must be off. Let me know the next time you're here. I'd love to have both of you join me on my yacht for cocktails. It's berthed at Woods Hole and I always enjoy visitors."

Stephen said, "I'll definitely do that. Thank you."

With that, they shook hands and walked out together.

After Octavio drove off, Stephen said, "We'll have to finish up some other time. Though he's not someone I'm worried about, there's no need to raise suspicions."

"Are you still going to Falmouth Hospital to meet up with Dr. Alighieri?"

"You can call her Trish, and yes I am."

"What is she doing there?"

"Trish is checking in on a patient. Ava is with her, too. They became friends when Ava was sick. I also want to see how the girl is doing and say hello to her parents."

Somberly, Dan said, "I hope things turn out well for her."

"So far, so good."

"That's great. You don't mind that I go for a run from here while you do that?"

"No. I'll take your extra clothes back."

"Thank you."

"See you at the house."

Chapter 25

Dan was lying in the hammock near the water when Dr. Alighieri returned from Falmouth Hospital, saying the young patient was doing very well.

After Trish entered the house, Stephen came over to Dan and said, "How was your run?"

"Felt great. I ran on the bike path into Woods Hole, then back along the Falmouth Road Race course to the finish line, and then back here."

"Twelve miles. Not bad for an old, out-of-shape man."

"I'm neither, though I could really use some hydration and carbohydrates. Perhaps at the same time."

"Beer isn't good for you at this time of day," Stephen said teasingly.

"Then a large glass of iced tea, followed by a beer, would be perfect," Dan replied.

"Most of the time, I like playing the role of gracious host. Of course, there are always exceptions," Stephen said.

"I appreciate your hospitality. Some music would be nice, too."

"That will be later, at Liam's."

"That's worth waiting for," Dan said.

"It looks like it is not an either-or situation," Stephen said as patio speakers began to play music from the Martha's Vineyard radio station, WMVY, and Nancy and Trish walked out carrying several beers. Ava ran out behind them, hurried over to the hammock, and jumped on it opposite Dan.

"Hey, squirt," Dan said to Ava. Trish handed him a beer then sat down on a deck chair next to Nancy and Stephen.

"You're in my hammock," Ava said.

"Thank you for sharing it with me."

To avoid awkwardness and seem friendly, though he still felt uneasy, he glanced over at Trish. "It seems like everyone is having a nice, relaxing day."

Trish nodded and said, "Not a care in the world."

"That used to be how I felt until it seemed I'd never feel that way again. I'm glad I was wrong," Dan found himself shocked to say. He was uncomfortable with what he'd spontaneously revealed with a frankness that was completely uncharacteristic for him. There was definitely something odd about Trish Alighieri, and it brought out something strange in him as well. He wasn't sure what to think about it.

"I love hearing you say you're wrong," Stephen said, a huge smile crossing his face.

"That's because you have to say it so often to me," Dan jousted back.

"And here I thought you were getting over your delusions."

"Have they always spoken to each other like that?" Trish said to Nancy.

"Always," Nancy said with mock resignation.

"It's amazing they're still friends."

"Amazing indeed," Nancy answered.

Trish turned to Dan. "How long have you known each other?"

"Stephen since we were eleven. I met Nancy early in college. After quickly realizing she had better taste in men than me, I introduced her to Stephen, for which they are still insufficiently grateful," Dan said.

"Trust me, I am extremely grateful, in both regards," Nancy said, laughing.

"I left out that there was a gap in between when I met Nancy and when I introduced her to Stephen. I liked having my bachelor friend and knew, once they met, that would be it for him," Dan said.

"You have good insight into people," Trish said.

"Except himself," Stephen said.

"That hardly makes me unique. I believe we took a philosophy class that asserted that the one thing we truly couldn't know is ourselves," Dan said.

Stephen chuckled. "You've made an art form of that."

"Despite what these guys are saying, Dan was a remarkable guy back then, and not bad now, either," Nancy said. "A near autodidactic, quick mind, and kind heart. We met at a big-brother and big-sister organization."

"That's a pretty good thing for a college guy to be doing," Trish said.

"Someone told me that was the place to met soft-hearted college women with poor judgment in men," Dan said.

"Fortunately for me, there was a limit to Nancy's soft-heartedness," Stephen said.

"Actually, she was saving it for those more in need," Dan said.

"Where are you sleeping tonight?" Stephen said, smiling.

"I meant the child services organizations she still helps run. That takes both a tough and tender heart. Puts us both to shame," Dan said.

"I'm not sure I like being an observer as you two talk about me," Nancy joked.

"I'll change the subject then," Dan said. "Trish, what do you think about scientists' someday being able to engineer life?"

Neither of the women seemed bothered by the abrupt change in topic.

"It's scary but seems unavoidable," Trish answered reservedly.

"So's death," Dan replied.

"Maybe not, if I'm really successful," Stephen said.

"I haven't yet met anyone I think should be immortal, except your wife and daughter," Dan answered.

"Good answer," Trish added.

Looking at Stephen, Dan said, "Given what appears to be your renewed religious beliefs, at least as the books in your study and conversation the other night seem to indicate, which include God mixing up speech to keep humans from building a tower that could reach him and expelling Adam and Eve from the Garden of Eden to keep them from eating from the Tree of Life, aren't you afraid of what might come of your attempts to read what some would call God's handwriting? God, if he exists, might not like it."

"This is the second time you've told me this," Stephen said.

"When was the first?"

"When you told me about what happened with Pavel Sarasov. His words have rung in my ears for years, and the papers of his you gave me helped trigger part of my work," Stephen answered.

Touching the scar on his arm, a remnant of the tragic night with the Sarasovs, Dan said, "I think I am going to have to learn a lot more, about a lot of things. I've always liked thinking that coincidences are a matter of odds and opportunity. What if there is more to it?"

"Then there might be a plan for you," Stephen said.

"If so, it would help if whoever did the planning did a better job of it."

"How do you know what you're experiencing isn't best for you?"

"If that's true, I need a new way of thinking about things."

"Exactly. I've got books inside that might interest you."

"Can I take them with me when I go back to Boston? I think I need Liam's first."

Stephen laughed. "You might need Liam's afterward."

Chapter 26

Dan and Stephen had started patronizing Liam Maguire's, a restaurant and Irish pub, when it first opened in the early nineties. They had spent many a night there since then, downing pints, listening to music, and occasionally singing along, badly, to traditional Irish tunes.

On this evening, the restaurant was filled with patrons of all ages. The rectangular main dining area occupied most of the space. A bar ran the length of one side, while a small platform, just big enough for three performers, served as a stage on the other side. Irish music memorabilia and framed sayings were scattered along the cream-colored walls. A clock by the bar counted down the days, hours, and minutes to St. Patrick's Day. Banjos and guitars hung at the back of the stage. An autographed picture of Tommy Makem hung nearby, paying homage to the Irish bard, one of the godfathers of Irish music.

Dan and Stephen sat off to the right of the stage and were nearing the end of their first beer. As they had walked the half mile from the house, they weren't about to hold themselves to a strict limit, though their pace and limit these days were, wisely, slower and lower than in their youth.

Dan looked across the small table at Stephen, who was staring off into space with his chin resting on his open hand. "What's up with you? I'm supposed to be the one with the questionable state of mind."

"I'm just trying to make sense of a few things," Stephen replied pensively.

"Now you *do* sound like me. Don't forget you promised explanations. They'd better be compelling. If I don't like what I hear, my skills could just as easily make your life miserable as help you," Dan said with a smile.

"You don't need technology to make people miserable," Stephen answered wryly. "Anyway, I'll tell you soon enough. First I have a question for you. I need you to answer it seriously. As someone who doesn't believe in God, tell me how you, in the role of God, would prevent human suffering. Would you stop all suffering? Only the most severe? Or only what you considered unjustified? And, as a formerly well-educated Catholic school student, explain to me how your answer relates to the meaning of life and happiness. How would you explain to someone that their request for a miracle would not be granted but someone else's would?"

"What's this got to do with your work? I don't think this is the time or place for a discussion of this nature, even if I was willing to have it—which I'm not," Dan answered, doing his best not to show his annoyance.

"Humor me for a minute. It's relevant. If something had happened to Ava today, maybe a car swerved into her when she was riding her bike, how should we view it? Should God's hidden hand have prevented it? And if so, what does that mean for all the times God does nothing to prevent tragedies?"

"You're asking an atheist to provide a satisfactory theological explanation of a God's powers and actions. If I could do that, I probably wouldn't be an atheist."

"Fine. But if someone is going to use what he thinks God should have done as an argument against his existence, as you have, don't you think it makes sense to have an idea of how that person thinks things *should* work? Or is finding easy objections enough to satisfy your inquires without trying to provide the hard answers? Your approach provides no answers, no meaning, only excuses."

"Why are you pushing this?" Dan replied, his irritation starting to show. "I can't answer what is fundamentally a nonsensical question. And I thought we're trying to be on good terms again."

"Here's the thing, and it's relevant: maybe you've never tried because you worry you might not like the answer. I need you to be open to big possibilities, wherever they lead. In the end, I believe my work will yield insights about God and human destiny. Are you able to accept that God might exist? That is why I am asking you these questions."

"Only with irrefutable proof."

"That's quite a presumption."

"About what?"

"That God has to prove his existence to you according to your criteria. Isn't it possible that there is sufficient indication for those open to him? Where's the scientific proof that God has to provide you with scientific proof?"

"We live in the world governed by science and reason. All I see from religion is irrationality and the harm it inflicts. Asking people to believe, and the 'right beliefs' at that, absent of proof, would be unfair to us and not worthy of a God," Dan said with conviction.

"Unless doing so would get in the way of something more important. Or if what you're asking for isn't as necessary as you think it is."

"Who's being presumptuous now?" Dan replied.

"How about this? Can you put aside emotion and your convictions, as repugnant as you find religion, and just pretend that you're willing to accept the possibility that God might exist?"

"I'll pretend I don't know better. But you need to be open to the idea that you may be fundamentally wrong."

"I'll do what I can given my numerous limitations," Stephen said with a bemused expression. "Before this is all over, I'm sure I'll be humbled hugely many times."

"Now that is something worth sticking around to see," Dan said with a restrained but friendly smile. "But enough of the abstract and hypothetical. What have you got to say? What insights has your work in biology given you about philosophical questions no one else in human history has been able to solve?"

Stephen placed his elbows on the table, leaned forward, combed his fingers through his hair, then took a deep breath. "I'll get to the point—and it does involve way, way more than biology." He paused and looked over his shoulder at the room.

"You can speak freely as long as you're not too loud and you angle your face toward the wall. I don't see anyone we need to be worried about," Dan said, looking at his tablet on the table in front of him.

"I'd feel more confident about that if you could tear your eyes from your tablet and actually seem like you were aware of your surroundings."

"Relax. I've got everything under control. Take a look." Dan pushed his tablet over to Stephen. On the screen were eight sections of video displaying different camera views of the interior and exterior of Liam's. "I linked into these before dinner. Since we've arrived, I've toyed around with the idea of hacking into cell phones of people sitting near us to get views from their cameras. Instead, I just ran profiles on them. Run of the mill people, like you and me. Satisfied?"

"You know, you really are a scary guy."

"You need to keep that in mind from time to time," Dan said with a slight grin.

"It never leaves my mind," Stephen said, smiling in return. Turning serious, he continued, "All right then. I hope you're ready for this. Six months ago, I was working with Alex Robertson to decode the human genome. As I said before, this wasn't a simple code in the sense of understanding the basic syntax of a rudimentary language or learning how DNA makes a person. Incorporated into our DNA is a highly encrypted, symbolic code, with *purposeful intent,* that if it wasn't for extraordinarily unlikely chance events, should have never been broken, *could never have been broken.* If you believe only one thing I have or ever will tell you, you must believe this."

Despite a room full of happy people talking loudly to one another, Dan heard nothing but the reverberations of Stephen's voice. His words were easy to understand, but the statements were near impossible to fathom. Symbolic code with intent had profound implications for human origin. It pointed at the existence of the Being Whom, if he existed, Dan had viewed far more as nemesis than as benevolent and loving Creator.

Continuing, Stephen said, "Do you understand what I'm saying to you? Symbolic coding. You know what that means? Intent of some sort has to be behind its origin. Do you believe me?"

After a deep gulp of Guinness, Dan said, "I'm pretty sure *you* believe what you're telling me. Beyond that, I'll have to see the en-crypted code for myself."

"I figured nothing less would do for you. After Tuesday, you can have access to everything. No secrets. Other than me, you'll be the only one to know everything. You can wait three days, can't you?"

"With mind-blowing claims like yours, it won't be easy. Why not now?

"I figure our conversation will be a lot easier if I have more proof of the nature you say you require. And there is more that I need to know before then."

"How can what you're saying be true? You know far better than almost anyone else the foundations it would shake," Dan said.

"I can only think of three possibilities for the existence of the symbolic coding, though that doesn't mean there aren't more. First, of course, is the obvious one: God created it and us. Second is Fran-cis Crick's: An alien race created DNA and, by extension, us. Third is natural teleology: something in nature leads to a tendency for the universe to produce certain outcomes though no specific being or intelligence is behind it. Any of these would be profound. The first two require a source for their own existence. But whatever the code's origin, it exists."

In his mind, Dan searched through all possibilities, including the thought that Stephen might be misleading him for purposes still un-known. Speaking with forced confidence, he said, "I hope you're not trying to pull a fast one on me, creating confusion while you get what you want, then blowing me off later. After all, I now control your se-curity."

"There are some things you can't fake, and after you've seen what I have, you'll know this is one of them. It feels like looking into the heart of creation. I bet it rocks your world just as much as mine, doesn't it?"

"You're asking me to absorb and accept a lot. Surely you know it's an extraordinary thing to ask of anyone, especially me. Isn't there *any-thing* else you can share now?"

After a long pause, Stephen smiled slyly then said, "A bit more should be fine. As I said before, there are two, maybe three, sets of coded information—but they are very different. The first is related to human biology. Think of it as both a blueprint for life and a description of human design. The second, well, that indicates information on the physical universe," Stephen said, pausing for full effect. "Beyond indications of how things operate in the physical world, there appears to be a relationship between quantum physics, which explains how everything works at the subatomic level, and cell function regulation. In a way, that makes lots of sense because there is too much going on that needs to be well coordinated, without other means to do so. Purely biochemical means may not be enough. Oddest of all is what should be an inherent contradiction, that each person consists of a 'quantum unity' and that this helped shape evolution. We're both a large collection of parts and a whole, simultaneously. Have you ever wondered how a multitude of separate atoms, consisting only of objective states, such as the direction of the spin of an electron, could produce whole subjective experiences such as you looking at, and hearing, me, all of me, at the same time?"

No, Dan had in fact never thought about the basis of human consciousness. It was shocking to think that his very self, at any moment, might be more than physical matter. Determined to retain his poise, he asked, "How did you find a relationship between DNA and physics? That's an incredible connection."

"It is. Alex found it after I saw symmetry in the DNA patterns once they were converted into symbolic code. He saw something very similar to the symmetry in the equations that physicists use to explain the behavior of the material world. It seems like the fabric of the universe is set up to guide the formation of life."

"I really do need to see this."

"You will."

"And the third set?" Dan asked.

"I'm not sure, but if you can believe it, the little I saw was more startling than what was in the first two sets. Maybe there is no more to it. But if so, it could relate to the origin of the universe, our ultimate destiny, and how I should use the other information. Everything is all so bizarre. It's as though I specifically was meant to find it; that I'm being trusted to use the knowledge for great good. And yet, I've learned things that I feel I have no right to know and shouldn't play around with. I don't know which is true and need your help finding out. I am keeping everything as secret as I can because I don't know if there is a third set and what could be in it."

Once again, Dan couldn't help but question Stephen's extraordinary claims. But with nothing to go on until Stephen showed him more, all he could say was, "I don't understand. I thought you had already broken the codes."

"I had. As I said, it was through extraordinary circumstances. I had been working late at night with Alex for a long time. One day, things just came to me. I don't know if you heard this before, but Dr. Charles Townes, the Nobel Prize–winning inventor of the maser, which led to the laser, has described his scientific breakthroughs as being like religious revelations. Well, it was like a revelation for me, too. I was incredulous and overjoyed as I viewed parts of the first two sets of decoded information. Before the processing completed to produce what could have been a third set of information, it timed out. Alex had set a 'time to live' on the security keys used to encrypt our work. That restricted how long it could run until he renewed the keys. Unfortunately, he had gone home and crashed on the way. There was nothing further I could do. I need you to look at what he had done and figure out how to get it going again. I only saw the smallest bit of what could be a third set. What I think I saw indicated that if there is anything there, it is critical for knowing how I should use what I already have. I'm hoping you can find something on the laptop I used that night to help figure out how to set up what's needed to resume processing."

"You can bet I'll do everything I can to see anything of the nature you've described." Dan paused before adding, "What about consciousness? How does that relate to what you described as a 'quantum unity'?"

"Now you're getting to the heart of things. I need to do more research into that. If I'm right, I'll have found proof of the human soul, yours included."

"Depending on the path I'm on, that might not be good news," Dan answered. He knew it was a flip response, but things had gone beyond the believable.

"Finding out what you're made of might help you with your path," Stephen answered.

Dan laughed, surprisingly relaxed, pleased at the prospects ahead of him, and said, "Well, I can't imagine you proposing anything more dramatic or intriguing. You know you didn't need to say anything as extraordinary as this. Despite our recent differences, I would have provided you the security you requested, and recovered your lost data, just for the personal satisfaction of having done so and the desire to spend time with Ava. Though, obviously, I would have extracted what I could along the way."

"It's remarkable how little you've changed," Stephen said.

Dan finished his pint. "If what you're saying about your discoveries is right, this is for all the marbles of every game worth playing."

"I'm glad you finally understand," Stephen said.

"The stakes you've laid out are pretty darn high," Dan answered. He didn't have any idea what to believe. The claims were too incredible. Stephen was either onto what he said he was, or was dangerously deluded.

"They always are, for anything really worth doing," Stephen replied.

"Yeah, well, I'm afraid that once we're done, I'll either have lost all possibility of something to believe in—including you—or I'll find stark answers that require hard choices."

"That's life for you. Only two possibilities. Either everything matters or nothing does. No in-between. Few people recognize that. Even atheists rarely acknowledge that no God means no morality."

"Sometimes I wish you'd stick with science and leave the deep thoughts to the philosophers. The ability to conduct experiments and analyze quantitative data is not the same as the ability to reason."

"You're right."

"Now, *that* is something I've waited a long time to hear," Dan exclaimed.

"I'm sure you'll never tire of it," Stephen joked.

Laughing, raising their glasses toward each other, they listened as the musicians began playing "Roddy McCorley," about the rebellion of 1798. Liam Maguire's warm, rich baritone voice, accompanied by a skillfully played guitar, filled the restaurant.

O see the fleet-foot host of men, who march with faces drawn,
From farmstead and from fishers' cot, along the banks of Ban;
They come with vengeance in their eyes. Too late! Too late are they,
For young Roddy McCorley goes to die on the bridge of Toome today.

Talking quietly below the music, Stephen said, "I always loved this song, long before I understood where the event it was based on ultimately led. It's extraordinary how seemingly remote things may be connected."

"What do you mean?"

"Well, the Irish Rebellion of 1798 led to the dissolution of the Irish government and the incorporation of their one hundred votes into the English Parliament. This was meant to quell Ireland's drive for independence. Instead, the Irish became the swing votes in the English Parliament. In order to stay in power, in the late eighteen hundreds, the British prime minister agreed to Irish Home Rule in exchange for Irish votes. Before Home Rule could be implemented, in 1912, many British were actively arming the Northern Irish Protestants in preparation for a civil war against what would have been the future Irish government. This led Germany to believe that England would not interfere on the Continent, being preoccupied with Ireland. They were wrong, and it contributed to the start of World War I. And without the First World War, Hitler doesn't come to power and the Germans have the scientists and the time to develop the atomic bomb. A strong, nuclear-armed, Germany is then free to assert itself against the world. To sum it up, without the rebellion of 1798, Germany rules the world, with many of the attitudes it had at the time."

Stephen continues, "The idea I'm exploring is whether God directs events that shape history over long periods of time. Does He paint with long, faint, brushstrokes that are only visible from a great distance, with eyes sharp enough to see them, to keep history on track? So, in the end, while our sufferings matter greatly to Him, they are not the last word, something greater is at stake."

Dan took a moment to reply. "Haven't you already stretched well beyond the limit of what I can contemplate for one evening without sounding like you think you can read the mind of whatever God might—and I emphasize might—exist?"

"Just giving you hints to the question you wouldn't attempt answering earlier."

"What you have to show me better be really good to make me put up with all of this."

"There is an important, practical, aspect to this. What are we meant to do with whatever I've discovered? How could it impact humanity? It's a heck of a responsibility."

"If what you've said is true, it certainly would be."

A couple of hours later, Dan and Stephen started walking back to Stephen's house. It was a moonless, cloudless night. The few streetlights were spaced far apart, serving more as distant beacons than as guidance for where to place their feet. In the dim spaces between the lights, the Milky Way stood out clearly from the rest of the dark sky.

Halfway home, Stephen said, "I've always enjoyed looking at the constellations. I wonder how they looked to the ancients."

"They change over time, but slowly," Dan answered.

"I need to remember that. You know, it's amazing just how finely tuned everything is for the universe to even exist—even more so for us."

"Well, with an infinite number of universes, at least one should be like this."

"You know, the belief in the existence of multiverses is an act of faith based on the idea that whatever can be represented by mathematics should in fact exist."

"I guess you're not going to let up," said Dan.

"I'm sorry, but when you think you start to see things as they really are, you can't stop seeing things as they really are," Stephen said jovially.

"That's an addiction I've tried to avoid."

"And look where that got you. Anyway, it's quite a journey we're about to embark on."

"I prefer a sojourn," Dan replied.

"That's not what the songs on your main playlist tell me. One word sums them up. Plaintive. Sorry, I looked. You're searching just like the rest of us."

"Remember listening to our first Genesis song, 'Watchers of the Skies'? That's what I think of on a night like this," Dan said.

"I remember listening to that when we were out on the lake late at night. The Adirondacks are great. We *really* need to get up there again," Stephen said.

"We were naïve. I wish we could have stayed that way," Dan said wistfully.

"As we both now know, you can't stay naïve when you start to understand that life either does or doesn't have ultimate meaning."

"Either possibility is staggering," Dan said with a touch of wonder in his voice.

"You're staggering."

"I know."

"Ah, once again, the beginning of wisdom," Stephen said.

"You're way too repetitive. You should hire a speechwriter."

"I'm done talking for tonight."

"Thank God for small favors!" Dan answered.

Chapter 27

Sousan's instructions from her foreign handlers at Project Icarus were clear-cut: get the fusion reaction information; make sure the reactor is damaged beyond repair; and incriminate her fellow researchers so that they would be lucky to stay out of jail, let alone be able to conduct further research. Since she had been kept in the dark by Viktor, she could claim that she was duped and, as she'd be the only "innocent" director left, she'd be appointed to run the lab.

The plan she'd come up with was to substitute a mix of tritium and deuterium for pure deuterium in the last of the planned experiments. A "deteriorating condition, present but undetected for years," would prevent the abort button from working. This would cause a higher-yield reaction, generating enough heat to destroy the reactor, while leading to a minor release of radioactive tritium—a major breach of atomic energy regulations—and the lab's shutdown.

In the subsequent investigation, the cause would appear to be a loading error by a worker whom the investigators would be unable to find. More damning would be the determination of lax oversight and controls, poor procedures, inadequate record keeping, and reckless actions. Of course, she would provide manufactured evidence claiming that she had been reporting these shortcomings for years but had been ignored, bolstering the case for her appointment as the new head of the lab. If he was lucky, Viktor would only be forced to retire, though he could easily face more severe consequences. Welsh would be finished, and if she had her way, would face jail time.

All in all, a simple, effective, and wonderful plan.

Sousan went to the loading dock and opened the doors for the delivery truck. No ordinary truck, it carried the deuterium. Unbeknownst to Viktor, this time it also carried the highly restricted and controlled tritium. The men on the truck were also not ordinary deliverymen. Like Sousan, they were agents of a foreign interest.

During the course of the delivery, they'd make adjustments to the reactor's fuel delivery system. When the time was right, Sousan would instruct the reactor systems to supplement the deuterium with tritium. The resulting reaction would produce more heat than the reactor could handle, damaging it, potentially beyond repair, setting the project back by years, enough time to give her sponsors time to make their moves.

Satisfied with the progress of the agents, Sousan returned to the lab. As soon as she was gone, the men made additional adjustments to the fuel systems and disabled more of the reactor's safety mechanisms. Whether Sousan survived or not was of no consequence to their sponsors. In fact, it would better if she did not. One less loose end that could become entangled.

Chapter 28

The last rays of the sun had departed some time ago, and what little dusk left wasn't far behind. Only the barest hints of wintergreen lingered on the horizon, visible to Stephen only because he was on the top floor of the HBC building. To the east, most of the sky was already black with the last remainders of light about to be extinguished.

It wouldn't be much longer until the experiments. They would prove that what he had decoded with Alex was valid, as well as show what it ultimately meant. Fusion power, as important as it was, was only an afterthought. The more important part was validating the relationship between the physical laws of the universe and the organization of biological life.

If things went as expected, his already difficult task of being the guardian of all the knowledge he possessed would become exponentially more difficult. Too much power and responsibility for him to handle. Not enough wisdom.

Nonetheless, he'd have to press ahead. Over the last few days, he'd come to realize that the path humanity was on would be its end if it didn't change soon. But misusing what was in his possession could also mean the end of humanity. Given all of this, he was surprisingly calm. He felt he was being guided, and as long as he didn't let his own failings get in the way, he'd make the right decisions.

The thought sent a strange shiver through him. He wondered if it was the same sensation Viktor had told him he'd felt during the first round of experiments. The odd thing was that Viktor said he had felt it from the outside and inside, as though something was reaching into him and pulling at his soul, which was a remarkable statement, since Viktor did not believe in the soul in the literal, nonmaterial sense.

Stephen dismissed the feeling of the strange shiver. Given what he was facing, there would certainly be a lot more sensations, some decidedly unpleasant, in the months and years to come.

For now, he wanted to appreciate joy whenever he could. Energy independence, from unlimited, clean sources was important, but it was one small, modest step in the transformation that he knew was to come. After fusion, there would be many more physics breakthroughs. The proving out and applying what he had was relatively straightforward for the right people, though the impact would be great. But this was small compared to the biology side, his area of expertise. Even with the complete set of decoded information, biology required understanding the behavior of an enormous number of elements with complex behaviors within an even more complex system. And then there was the question of cellular regulatory mechanisms. Were some based on more than physical matter? How did this relate to the soul? What made a person a whole being?

He still hoped that there was a third set of information and that it would provide the guidance he needed, though he feared what it might also reveal.

Throughout his life, he had often lived by the principles "Don't ask a question unless you want to hear the answer," and "It's easier to ask forgiveness than permission." Seeing a third set of information might violate both those principles and place him in a position where a lot would have to be sacrificed.

He was thankful Dan was helping him. After the past weekend, he knew, as he had hoped, that he could depend on him. The value of close friendship wasn't in liking the same things or always getting along, but in the willingness and appreciation of doing whatever was needed to truly help the other, and liking the person despite differences. He was grateful to have that again with Dan and pleased that they were back on a decent path.

The days since the Cape had been good for their friendship. Dan had continued to provide more computer security support, showing him how to organize and store his information. Though pressed for time, they had gotten together a few times as well.

As promised, soon Stephen would share everything with him. He knew Dan would eventually come around and see things in the right light. They would be in this together, and Stephen would value Dan's perspective. Together, they'd figure out the future.

Stephen decided that the one mistake he wasn't going to make again was to think that he alone always knew what was best. He would make sure to trust those that he should.

Chapter 29

Viktor's nose stung from the fumes of the cleaning fluid and markers. The whiteboard, wiped clear fifteen minutes ago, was again covered with colored numbers, Greek letters, and squiggly lines. The symbols were grouped into four separate sections, depicting each of the experiments they planned to conduct in a half-hour.

Welch stood off to the side, reviewing what he had written. Viktor, Nicco, and Sousan sat at the large oval table opposite the board. All stared silently ahead, eyes focused on the parameters of the experiments.

After a short period, Viktor said, "So that's it. Four short steps to achieve what decades of international scientific research couldn't."

Even now, Viktor could hardly believe it. It was as though instead of sailing across the ocean in three frail ships, hoping to find a shorter passage to India, Columbus had been given a way to travel back and forth instantaneously. He almost felt cheated out of the coming accomplishments, except that he would be able to ensure the spoils went to good use. Still, he felt uneasy.

Sousan looked up from her notes on her tablet and said, "Do you want to push the envelope a little further? I'm confident that, with the adjustments we've made, we can control the plasma."

Welch replied, "First of all, this is the most heat we can subject the reactor to in this period of time. Second, if it works as I expect it will, it's all the proof we'll need. If it doesn't work, then we'll need time to figure out more adjustments and try again tomorrow, before the reactor is shut down. But I'm confident it'll work."

Viktor answered, "Well, it better. At my age, I'm not sure how much more my overstressed old heart can take. After it does work, whatever comes next, even if it's my last heartbeat, will be worth it."

"I prefer you stick around. There will be lots to do after this," Welch said, finally smiling. Turning toward Nicco and Sousan, he added, "Are you two clear on everything?"

Nicco said, "Got it. The first shot will be a standard calibration. Nothing special there. The second will prove out the balance between our new field effect and the electromagnetic repulsion. The third will be a longer period test of this balance, under a variety of different combinations. The fourth will be a short burst of high-yield fusion."

"That's right. Together, they'll demonstrate that fusion energy is now a reality," Welch answered.

Even though she had been briefed over the last few days, what Sousan was taking in still felt like too much, too soon. "Once word gets out, how are we going to handle the fallout? Sorry, poor choice of words; I mean peoples' reactions. How are we going to handle it?"

Viktor said, "One step at a time. Let's make sure of what we've got before we worry about whom we tell and when. We can all keep quiet until then, *right*?"

Sousan glanced at Welch, and then looked away from him. She didn't want anyone to notice her contempt and anger. Where did he get off acting so superior and cocky? The breakthroughs clearly weren't his. It was part of an act that Viktor and Welch were performing to distract people from realizing that it was really Viktor's work, based on his discoveries and secret government programs he wasn't disclosing. She was not going to be deceived by Welch's arrogance and Viktor's assertions. At first, she'd been disappointed and hurt by Viktor's deception and exclusion of her; he had been her friend and mentor, a righteous man who had suffered much in life and still viewed all people as worthy human beings. Now she realized that it had all been an act, that he had used her all these years.

At first she hadn't wanted to believe that, despite what her handlers had told her. They were trying to compel her to take the steps she was about to take, steps she'd at first thought were wrong. She now saw the truth of what they had told her.

Fusion energy would be used to repress her people and plunge them back into economic hardship. It was a plot to drive down the value of oil, to weaken Muslim countries, to prop up the illegitimate Jewish regime in Palestine, and it was work against Allah.

She was disappointed in herself for not seeing this sooner, for repressing her Islamic identity and adopting a secular view of the world, just for meager success as a scientist. It had all been an illusion. Seeing the hardship that the Western world caused her people, and listening to the holy words of her handlers, had made all this clear.

She was glad that she had a way to atone for her transgressions. Yet, as she prepared to execute the computer commands that would activate the sabotage, she hesitated. The odd sensations she had experienced while the experiment was going on last Friday had unsettled her, made her feel uncertain about the path she had chosen. She worried that her decisions posed a risk to her well-being, but these feelings had passed.

Then her eye caught Welch and Viktor talking quietly, no doubt conspiring about some further slight. Without hesitation, she initiated the commands.

The plan was perfect, and everyone would get their rightful due, including her.

Viktor stood at the main console and watched Welch complete the preparations. Minutes away from the momentous events, he was surprised that he felt so calm.

While he was disappointed that Stephen wasn't there to see it, Viktor understood. Stephen's presence could only raise questions about his connection to the research and the experiments.

Viktor scanned the room one more time and saw Nicco repeatedly running the temperature and spectrometer analysis programs on an empty and dormant reactor. He was consistently getting readings that confirmed the obvious: nothing was going on. Sousan was on the opposite end of the room, away from the main console, and close to the door, calmly poised to monitor the plasma. Her steely resolve was complemented by her normal standoffishness and determination.

Welch was on the last item of the pre-experiment checklist. He exhaled slowly, smiled, and said to Viktor, "Ready to do the honors?"

Almost instantly, Viktor's muscles tightened and his pulse jumped, even though this first experiment was only a standard calibration exercise. After taking a steady, deep breath so no one would notice his excitement, he said, "Okay. Here we go. Round One is starting." With that, he pressed the button that started the sequence. The computer-generated voice counted down, 10, 9, . . . 3, 2, 1. The screens lit up with the bright plasma, the readings registered on the monitors, and in a few brief seconds, the shot was over.

Immediately, Welch called out, "Everyone, please confirm readings were within the expected ranges." As he looked at each person in turn, they called out the results. Everything was as it ought to have been.

Glancing at Viktor, Welsh added, "Now onto the fun stuff. But just a little at a time." He turned to the room and said, "Let's review the procedures as indicated on the program monitor. After the fuel is loaded, and the magnetic field has pressurized the plasma, the quantum field generator will fire a short burst that will reduce the apparent electromagnetic repulsion of the nuclei and cause the plasma to compress further. Everyone ready?"

After his colleagues called out that they were, Welch initiated the program and started the countdown. As before, the plasma formed a bright circular ring within the reactor. Then the quantum field kicked in and the plasma shrank into a narrower and brighter band.

Viktor felt the same faint unease he had experienced in the first round of tests. It was hard to place. Looking around the room, he couldn't determine if others were experiencing similar feelings, though there was no natural reason why they should be.

Meanwhile, the experiment had ended, and Welch once again confirmed that the readings for the shot were within the expected ranges. He fed the readings into a computer program that analyzed them to produce slightly modified parameters for the third experiment. This is where things would get really interesting: demonstrating a mastery of the forces that governed subatomic behavior and fusion reactions.

Repeating the previous procedures, Welch loaded the program and reviewed the steps with everyone. With a slight nod, Viktor indicated it was time to start the third experimental shot.

This time, a progression of quantum and magnetic field combinations would control and manipulate the plasma under different conditions. Unlike the earlier experiments, which had lasted five to ten seconds, this would last twenty-five. It would demonstrate that they knew enough about the physics to control fusion and produce significantly more energy than was consumed. The key had been the discovery of how to reduce momentarily the repulsion of atomic nuclei, the alteration of the forces that held the universe together. He was glad it could only be done on a small scale, with no possibility of a chain reaction, otherwise the consequences would be quite severe and irreversible.

Once again, the computer-generated voice counted down to the start of the shot. The first result visible on the monitors was a wide, diffuse band of plasma. At intervals of five seconds, the band constricted as the quantum field was applied and then expanded as the field was reduced. It was almost like tones on a music scale that got progressively higher. The band widened, but not as much as the prior iteration, then it contracted quicker and more intensely than before. They were pushing the boundaries of how much they could compress and control the plasma without actually producing high-yield fusion.

The scientists around the room looked amazed by what they saw. Blazingly hot plasma, compressed into a tighter band than they had ever seen, seemed to jump in and out as the band expanded and contracted. Each time it rapidly contracted to a narrower band, they flinched, half expecting intense combustion and a powerful fusion reaction. Nervously, they looked back and forth between their instruments and the monitors. Viktor felt a combination of awe and joy that was washed over by the waves of the odd sensations, both physical and mental, that seemed to pulse with the plasma.

Finally, after twenty-five seconds, the experiment was over. Welch gathered the readings and strutted over to Viktor, who patted him on the back. They were ready for the final step. He was almost amused by how well it had worked. Several people were visibly excited, and Sousan looked stunned. Then he reminded himself that it was too soon for self-congratulations and that the source of their imminent triumph was not solely the fruits of his labors.

Excited by the success of the experiments, Welch wanted to push the envelope. They wouldn't get another chance for many months and, by then, he didn't know where things would stand with the fusion center. He wanted to repeat the last experiments with a lot more plasma in the reactor, for a longer duration. That would demonstrate, almost at the conditions needed for commercial operations, that high compression and control could be achieved at low power, using today's engineering. The ramifications for people throughout the world would be incredible.

After conferring with Welch, Viktor announced, "The outstanding results of the first three experiments have given us the confidence to perform an additional experiment. We're going to repeat the last shot with double the fuel in the reactor for a total duration of thirty seconds. This will demonstrate our capabilities at almost commercial levels. Then we'll continue with the original fourth test, the final fusion reaction. After that, well, it'll be a new world for us, and we'll have to celebrate appropriately. I don't know about the rest of you, but I feel like consuming some fusion cuisine accompanied by the right fluid dynamics."

The groans at his bad pun notwithstanding, Viktor saw a lot of excited faces. He was surprised to see Sousan, who had been on her way over to him, turn and rush back to her station.

He wondered if there was something wrong. Before he could check, Welch had started the automated countdown.

Sousan didn't know what to do. The tritium was supposed to be for the last shot. Now it would be used in this shot, only at much higher fuel levels. In the few seconds she had as the countdown commenced, she tried to figure what would happen as a result of the change. Would the excess fuel prevent the fusion reaction, or would something far more dangerous occur? Should she stop the countdown, and reveal herself and the plan, to avoid a potentially catastrophic reaction from harming the others?

Angry, she thought that whatever happened, it was Viktor's fault. He should have respected her.

As before, the experiment started with a wide band of plasma. It was immediately apparent that something was very different from the prior experiment; something more than just a denser plasma from the higher fuel levels. The readings were elevated well beyond expectations.

Viktor shouted out to Nicco, "Something's way off. What do the instruments show?"

Nicco's face was tense. He answered, "I don't know yet, but something is definitely . . . wait . . ." His voice changed from confusion to alarm. "This can't be. Oh . . . no . . . There's tritium in the plasma. It looks optimized for a reaction. How in the world . . . ?"

Before Nicco could finish, Viktor slammed his hand down on the abort button. It had no effect. He tried it again, and still nothing changed.

Welch yelled, "We have to shut down immediately!"

"I can't!" Viktor shouted. He knew what would happen if they couldn't stop this. There would be a full fusion reaction and more heat than anything the reactor, or any of them, would be able to withstand."

Desperate, Viktor yelled to Sousan, "Cut the power to the reactor!" This would severely damage the walls of the vessel and release radioactive tritium, but at least everything else would be spared.

Sousan screamed back, "The controls aren't responding!"

As she said this, the plasma compressed sharply in the first of the three planned sequences. Someone yelled out, "We've got big problems. The X-ray emissions are way off the charts. Full fusion is taking place."

Viktor felt the odd sensations again, only this time they were much stronger. Once again it felt like something was pulling at him from the outside, as though his soul was being torn violently from his body. The bewildered and frightened expressions on the staff's faces told him they felt the same sensations. It was no illusion. Some unanticipated effect of the fusion, or perhaps of the quantum manipulation of what was supposed to be fixed forces of nature, was making them feel as though their existence was slipping away, as though the fabric of space was dissolving.

At the ten-second mark, as programmed, the plasma compression decreased, and the feelings vanished.

Welch yelled out to everyone, "Do whatever you can to stop this. Don't worry about anything else. Just do it now!"

People immediately tried different computer commands, searched for the right wires to pull, or switches to trigger, all to no avail.

Nicco cried out, "I'll try and reach the main power supply." It was a floor below, just outside the reactor room. He'd have to race down a short hall, down a flight of stairs, and then down another short hall. Then he'd have to unlock the power closet and trip the large switch—no easy task. All in as little as ten seconds, certainly no more than twenty-five. In desperation, he ran out of the room, his feet sliding on the polished stone floor.

Sousan ran out after him, but then headed the opposite way. Viktor was surprised by her reaction. She was heading for the door. He had thought she was stronger than that. But then, you really never know about people until they are tested.

At the fifteen-second mark, the plasma contracted again, further this time. The greater intensity caused stronger feelings of pulling him toward something that he began to fear greatly. Some of the people in the room doubled over from what he now knew were similar effects. Having already withstood extraordinary terror in the camps, he stoically accepted whatever was coming.

After five more seconds the plasma expanded and the sensations dissipated. In the background, he heard the stairway door swing shut. Nicco was down the stairs. There was a chance he could cut the power before the last plasma compression.

Otherwise, in five to ten seconds, the experiment would likely yield the largest man-made fusion reaction ever outside of an atomic bomb—one neither the reactor nor they would survive. With a detached sense of irony, he thought that perhaps it wasn't a good idea to fool around with the fundamental forces of nature.

In what he knew were his last moments, Viktor understood that someone had sabotaged the experiment, loaded the wrong fuel, disabled the abort button, and cut off every other means to stop it. Deep down, he knew it had been Sousan. There was nothing that could be done. Grim, he realized that their work would not, by itself, help lead to a peaceful world free of strife and suffering. Technology was not the problem, nor the answer. A little thing like human nature stood in the way, and that couldn't be reengineered.

Twenty-three seconds. Two more until the last plasma pulse would begin.

With the little time left, he felt a desire that was as powerful as the strongest prayer. He liked the idea that it was the power of the sun, and not the slow decomposition of organic matter, that would claim his body. He thought of his family and wanted them to remember him well, not be distraught at how he'd died.

Twenty-five seconds. He put his arm around Welch's shoulders and looked at the monitor in time to see the last plasma compression vanish into a blinding flash. As the containment vessel failed, a beam of electrons broke free from the reactor's magnetic field and cut through the magnets and the roof of building, headed skyward. Argon gas was released in the reactor room and turned the electrons into the brightest beam of light ever seen on Earth. In his last instant, Viktor was aware of a powerful rumble and intense sound. Before the furious forces reached his body, he imagined that he felt his soul release, and then the shock of complete serenity.

Lives were extinguished as the building was engulfed in a violent explosion of heat and flames. Fire leapt hundreds of feet upward until settling into a seething cauldron several stories high.

Chapter 30

Stephen gazed out from his office, across the river, toward the fusion center. Of course, with all the other buildings in the way, he could not see it. Still, he believed he could feel its presence. As much as he wanted to be with Viktor tonight, they both had thought it best that Stephen stay away, not do anything that might attract additional attention. There would be plenty of time later for his participation.

Right now, Viktor was in the midst of the experiments that would prove the validity and value of Stephen's discoveries. This one was just one of many revelations to come. It happened to be easier to test and had more practical, immediate value than the others. Along with the imaging technology they were developing, the results of these experiments could change the direction of the world and prevent precipitous conflicts—so long as the same tools didn't ignite disastrous conflicts before then.

It was more power than one person should possess, and there was a lot more to come. But at least he would use it for benevolent purposes and try to thwart people from ever using it against others.

Then he would be onto the more challenging technology. Complex biological systems, even when you knew how they were supposed to work, were difficult to understand and modify at anything above the level of individual molecular reactions or simple gene substitution. Still, in time, he and his team would figure it all out.

Once the experiments were completed, he would receive a message telling him what he needed to know. Until then, there was nothing for him to do but wait patiently.

Standing at the window, he had thought himself relaxed. His aching hands told him otherwise. He unclasped them from a rigid grip and was surprised to see how sweaty they were.

He turned from the window to get a napkin from his desk and was startled by what felt like a pat on his back. It was just like a gesture Viktor would occasionally make.

Stephen jumped and turned around in time to see an enormously bright ray of light flash skyward and then vanish. It was followed by something far more ominous. The succeeding explosion illuminated the surrounding area before settling into steady, unearthly flames. An instant later he heard a deathly rumble.

He needed no explanation. Despite the assurances he had received that nothing of this nature could happen, it had.

Air was sucked out of his lungs, as if from an enormous shock wave, and he fell to his knees. He gasped for breath. The air seemed impossibly hot, even though its temperature had not actually changed, and the windows were intact.

A voice in his head cried out *What have I done*? First Alex, now this. Why did others have to pay the price for his hubris and ambition?

Trying to get to his feet, he struggled to grasp the window ledge with his sweaty hands. They slipped repeatedly until he was finally able to stand on wobbly legs.

He looked out the window to face what he had helped wrought. He could see that the blast had thrown the city into turmoil. Cars were stopped everywhere he looked. The sinister glow of the orange and crimson flames reflected off the low cloud cover, casting an eerie glow on the entire city.

He wondered if this foreshadowed that what he had sought to prevent would nonetheless be unleashed.

Though he knew nothing could be done, he had to get over to what remained of the fusion laboratory. He changed into a pair of running sneakers that he kept in his office, picked up the cell phone Dan had given him, and rushed out of the building.

Chapter 31

S ousan was almost a block away from the center, running as fast as she could, when the blast knocked her to the ground. It was accompanied by an intense wave of heat that burned the exposed parts of her neck and arms. The back of her lab coat caught fire, and she rolled to put it out. Her hair was a singed tangle. Small bits of debris rained down, pelting her body.

Stunned more by the deaths of her coworkers than by her injuries, she crawled a few yards until she was able to stand. The palms of her hands stung from the exposed, raw skin that remained after the surface had been scraped off along the pavement when she fell.

She felt shattered in body and spirit as she stumbled away from what had been her place of work, her real home, for the last sixteen years.

Although she had always known there would be a debt to pay for her parents' being allowed to immigrate to America, she had thought she would only be called on to pass along information that could do no real harm. Even then, if Viktor had properly respected her, she wouldn't have said anything. That was what she had told herself when asked to sabotage the experiments.

But this—this chaos she'd barely escaped, which had killed her coworkers—this wasn't part of the plan. No one could have known this would happen. It wasn't her fault.

She knew she would be called on to answer difficult questions if she was seen, so she walked hurriedly along the sides of the buildings, trying to slip away unnoticed. With the building destroyed, there was nothing to place her at the site unless she was spotted now. She would stay out of the range of security cameras and hide her face.

Dozens of people were charging past her toward the remains of the building, their attention focused on the blaze. She was practically invisible in the shadows. The sirens of approaching rescue vehicles blared. The reflections of the flames performed an evil dance on the windows of the buildings around her.

She turned to look at the building one last time and stared at the raging inferno. The little that was left burned violently, the blaze forming cathedrals of destruction whose spires rose and fell. Thick, black smoke emanated from the fire and strangled the night sky. The flames crackled like whips striking flesh. Wretched smells filled the air, carried by an unnatural breeze.

It all felt like hell.

As her senses regained their awareness, her injuries began to scream. But she couldn't seek treatment from any conventional medical facility. That would require explanations she couldn't give. She'd have to obtain treatment elsewhere.

There was only one thing to do. Get far, far away. Find a safe haven.

Now with the streets filling up with every imaginable official vehicle, and authorities guiding people away from the site, she disappeared into the crowd.

Chapter 32

Stephen half walked, half jogged, onto the Western Avenue Bridge toward the fusion center. His legs felt like they were trying to churn uphill through waist-deep snow.

His right foot caught on a patch of crumbled pavement and he stumbled forward. Tripping, he started to fall, and then awkwardly regained his balance. The sharp movement launched the cell phone Dan had given him out of his shirt pocket and across the sidewalk into the street. He scrambled along the ground, searching for it, and found it on the grate of a storm drain, tilted on edge, nearly through the metal slot. Carefully retrieving it, he put it in his pants pocket.

Looking ahead, he could see that the blaze had spread. A bright orange-crimson glow spread out like the top slice of a sphere, like an aberrant sunset portending a dreadful night.

Even though it was late in the evening, and traffic hadn't been too heavy, activities were at a near standstill. Police were directing traffic—mostly stopping it—so that rescue vehicles could get to the scene. Drivers on the bridge, with nothing to do but wait, got out of their cars and looked toward the conflagration, clogging the pedestrian path.

As Stephen resumed his trek, easing through gaps between people, sidestepping past those blocking his path, he heard car radios tuned to news stations stating that the explosion and fire were being treated as a potential terrorist attack. Speculation ran rampant. To the best of the announcers' knowledge, it seemed unlikely that the fusion center, given its unclassified, basic research function, would have been the target of any interests that had the capability to cause an incident like this. Yet there was nothing in the lab that apparently could have caused the blast, either. There was some talk that perhaps the Novartis Institute for Biological Research, across the street, was the actual target, and that the perpetrators had hit the wrong building. Meanwhile, comprehensive emergency security measures were kicking in citywide, and everything was being affected.

Stephen steadily made his way through all this across the last mile to what was left of the fusion center. Along the way, he tried to spot security cameras and stay out of their field of vision.

Thoughts jumbled in his head. Foremost was grief over the un-doubted loss of his friend and his associates. What could have happened?

He would see what he could, then he would head to his MIT office and figure out what to do next.

Finally across the bridge, he tried to make his way down Massachusetts Avenue, but the police had cordoned that off. They were walking around with bullhorns telling the gathering crowds to go to their homes and clear the area.

Seeking a better view, Stephen climbed onto a base of a light pole and looked down the street. All he could see were fire and police vehicles and the reflections of the flames that bounced off the exteriors of the buildings.

He had to find a way to get closer. It had been only twenty minutes since the blast, and there were not yet enough police around to control and handle everything. Stephen took off in a moderate jog down side streets until he found a passageway between two buildings that was unguarded. He traversed its short length and stepped out into the middle of the scene.

To his right, the ring of police was keeping the crowds at bay. In front of him, firemen were consumed with attacking the fire. With responders still arriving, no one was paying attention to a lone person standing with his back against the wall of an unaffected building.

The heat was too intense for him to stand there long. The acrid air burned his nostrils and throat. The blast had set everything within a row of buildings on fire. The fusion center itself was flattened, and nothing recognizable remained. There was just a hole where it used to be and flames that looked like they sprang from a sulfurous pit.

What looked like more than a hundred firefighters bravely fought to keep the flames on the lab side of the street from jumping to the other, but the heat kept pushing them back. More vehicles arrived, and helicopters began dropping fire-extinguishing chemicals from above.

Through all of this, Stephen kept staring, focusing on what to do while fighting off sorrow and guilt.

More police arrived, accompanied by even more serious-looking personnel wearing jackets that said Homeland Security and FBI. One or two glanced his way.

It was time to go.

He started to head back out the way he had slipped in, but now the outer edge of that path was secured by police. Stephen came up with the best ruse he could. He walked up to one officer and said that he was an off-duty early responder and had been sent back out by the commander to get into proper equipment to assist with the rest of the operation.

The policeman just nodded, and Stephen walked out, slipping between all the people, as he started to make his way across campus to his MIT office. He was careful to avoid security cameras, hoping none would get a clear shot of his face.

With a heavy heart and burdened mind, he knew it was time to ditch his plan. He had to come up with one capable of dealing with what he now faced.

For that, he definitely needed Dan's help.

Chapter 33

For the last three days, Dan had been engrossed in researching evolution, biology, and genetics. It wasn't something a novice could master, but he thought that he could learn enough to judge the plausibility of Stephen's claims.

The good thing was that his studies were occupying his mind, drawing him further out of himself. He was able to enjoy the possibilities the study provided. He was more energized and far less melancholy. He was even having fun once in a while.

The Cape trip had been especially fun. He thought back to the morning after Liam's, when he'd had the best breakfast he'd had in a long time. It was just the four of them—Dan, Stephen, Nancy, and Ava. Trish had left the night before. Nancy had prepared corn beef hash, breakfast sausages, and eggs over easy.

Stephen had loaded him up with a bunch of books—Francis Collins's *Language of God*, Stephen Barr's *Modern Physics and Ancient Faith*, Stephen Meyer's *Signature in the Cell*, Ken Miller's *Darwin's God*, Wesley Smith's *The War on Humans*—all attempts to reconcile science, faith, and humanity. Now he was so absorbed with what he was reading that he was only faintly aware of the distant sirens.

Eventually, the sound grew so loud that he was unable to ignore the sirens shrieking down Storrow Drive. Turning away from his computer screen, he wondered what could be going on. He didn't have to speculate long. He left his secluded alcove and entered his darkened bedroom, where he was confronted by reflections of light from a ghastly fire, bouncing off his walls. Rushing to the window, he immediately saw the smoke and flames across the river. They were originating from somewhere on the western side of the MIT campus. The light radiated off the clouds and the river, creating a confluence of chaotic images.

He turned the TV to a news station and cranked the volume way up, then went to his computer to open the local Boston news website. Both the television and internet had disturbing images of a block of buildings fully engulfed in a raging fire. The early reports stated that an explosion of surprising force at MIT's Plasma Science and Fusion Center had unleashed an intense fire that quickly spread. There were also unconfirmed reports that the explosion had been preceded by a narrow beam of light that had pierced the night sky. A leak from an unnamed government official claimed that traces of a radioactive substance, tritium, had been detected, and the area was cordoned off. While the cause was unknown, terrorism was a distinct possibility, and the city was being locked down until more was known about the incident.

Dan recalled Stephen's relationship with Viktor Weisman, director of the fusion center. It had caught his attention when he noticed that the source of some of the files being moved onto his secure computer environment emanated from the very location that had just been leveled. Suspicious, he had penetrated the lab's computer network and made copies of all of the original, unencrypted files. He didn't intend to make the same mistake that he had made with Stephen—allowing him to copy files onto his computer environment without his being able to view them.

He hoped that the explosion wasn't the result of Stephen's planned big test and that Stephen had been nowhere near the site. Dan placed calls to Stephen's office and regular cell phone, as well as the modified cell phone he had given him, but all went to voice mail.

Increasingly concerned, he initiated a tracing program on his own specialized cell phone, and it showed Dan exactly where Stephen's special cell phone was right now. Time stamps indicated when Stephen had passed different points between HBC and the MIT fusion lab. Relieved, Dan realized that Stephen had been at HBC at the time of blast and was now in motion.

After unsuccessfully trying to reach Stephen again, Dan decided to use the tracking program to meet up with him.

Looking outside, Dan saw that police had closed off Storrow Drive to all but official vehicles, and side streets were clogged with traffic. So many people had gone outside to have a look at what was going on that the sidewalks were filling up as well. He couldn't drive or bike over. Public transportation was also a no-go. The only way to get to Stephen was by foot. Dan laced on his running sneakers and pulled a cap low over his forehead. With his heart already pounding and blood racing, he charged out the door and down the steps.

Immediately, he smelled the burning odor. It had drifted the short distance across the river and pervaded the air. Ahead, he could see the flashing lights of the rescue vehicles on the Harvard Bridge. He doubted he would be allowed to cross that way. He'd have to take the longer route by first heading east, then go over the Longfellow Bridge and head west toward MIT and Stephen. That would double the distance he'd have to cover to almost two and a half miles. Fighting through the crowds, it would take Dan about twenty-five minutes to get to Stephen, as long as Stephen didn't go too far.

As Dan started half-jogging, he saw crowds of people looking from the riverbank to the direction of the fire. Some cars had radios tuned to news stations. He could hear the announcers saying that firefighters had prevented the blaze from spreading any further but had a long way to go before they could bring it under control.

Dan weaved left and right, trying to avoid the crowds, but it wasn't easy. In the darkness punctuated by vehicle headlights, the people were invisible until he almost collided with them. More than once, people yelled at him to watch where he was going.

Every few minutes, he stopped to call Stephen's special cell phone. Each time it went straight to voice mail. Still, presuming Stephen was with his cell phone, he could see that he was moving toward his MIT biology office.

Finally, Dan crossed over the Longfellow Bridge. Soon he'd intersect with Stephen, or at least his phone, find out what had happened, and then they could plot a way forward.

Chapter 34

WASHINGTON, DC

Special Agent Evans worked his way down a hallway he thought he'd never see again. He was in the area of the building that housed some of the most important and sensitive operations of the Department of Homeland Security. After a decade of service to the agency, preceded by twenty-five years in a different agency gathering foreign intelligence, he had put in his resignation and was now counting down the weeks until his retirement. He was the longest tenured, most experienced, most decorated African American agent in the US intelligence community. It was time to move on, and he was supposed to have been taken off all active assignments.

Half an hour earlier, he had been at home, reading a mindless novel, sitting quietly next to his wife, practicing for a relaxed lifestyle. Determined to concentrate on the new life ahead of him, he had ignored the first rings of his agency-issued cell phone. As much as he had wanted to, he couldn't ignore the subsequent calls. Reluctantly, and with a measure of alarm, he had agreed to come in right away.

The drive in had been quick but long enough for him to hear radio reports. What he heard sounded catastrophic for those on-site when the blast occurred, and disruptive to the Boston area, but didn't seem like anything that would require pulling him in from near retirement. While they had to check out all possibilities, terrorism seemed unlikely for a blast of this nature, and other agents ought to have been able to handle the investigation.

Entering the executive director's conference room, Evans saw that the room was full, save one chair. The executive director, his chief of staff, several of Evans's counterparts, and finally, the head of Homeland Security himself, Secretary Robbins, were all there. The executive director motioned Evans toward the empty chair. Sitting down, Evans glanced at the folder in front of him on the table, labeled "Cambridge Incident."

"Now that we're all here," the ED said, "We can brief everyone and give you your assignments. But first, Secretary Robbins will address you. Mr. Secretary."

"This is a matter of utmost national security. I've just come from a briefing with the President. This is what we know at this time. At 21:03 hours, in an experimental MIT fusion reactor that was supposed to lack the ability to generate a fusion reaction, a significant fusion event did, in fact, take place, resulting in the destruction of the site, a to-be-determined number of lives lost, and an intense blaze. Satellite spectral analysis indicates that despite being under tight federal controls, and against regulations, tritium was present in the reactor. Just preceding the event, an extraordinarily bright beam of light emanated skyward from the lab. According to our experts, this was indicative of a beam of electrons that had burned through the reactor, triggering the release of argon gas and subsequent conversion of high energy into light. Please take a look at the images in front of you for a few moments."

Big questions formed in Agent Evans's mind, probably the same ones running through everyone else's. Was the fusion event, as it was referred to, an accident? How did tritium get there? Was this the result of an unknown government black project? Were scientists at MIT secretly developing technology and lost control of it? The images were astonishing, showing in time series a normal-looking site, the light beam, and then the progressive explosion. Data reports indicated estimates of the amount of fusion energy, the presence of tritium, the rate at which it dispersed, and the force of the blast. These were not the results of a low-profile research program.

After a few minutes, Secretary Robbins continued, "As you would expect, a number of important countries, both allies and not, have collected similar information. The State Department's phones have been ringing off the hook. Some countries have accused the US of running a secret weapons program. They are most alarmed by the notion of us running a fusion power program of that scale and want to know how we'd put that power to use. Concerns about space-based lasers and other missile defense systems, in gross violation of treaties, have been expressed in the strongest terms. We've assured the countries that the US is doing nothing of the sort and that we are as surprised as they are by what has transpired, and that it in fact might be a radical escalation of terrorism. They have not found these statements compelling and are very upset."

One of the agents in the room spoke up: "Can't we just stonewall, say it was the result of a structural failure of defective magnets?"

"Tritium just doesn't wind up in the wrong place. Heretofore unachievable fusion power just doesn't happen from conducting innocuous tests. And to address the unasked question in the strongest terms possible, the US government was not conducting a black or any other type of program at MIT. We are as mystified by this as you are. That cannot remain the case. The president has authorized whatever measures are necessary to get to the bottom of this. Time is of the essence. So is discretion. Everything else is unimportant. Mr. Director, toward these ends, would you please continue?"

"You have been selected, based on your backgrounds and exemplary work, to lead this effort in your respective areas. You are to dedicate one hundred percent of your time to this, regardless of whatever else you were working on, whatever other obligations you once thought you had, whatever you thought of your status." The executive director turned toward Agent Evans for the last statement. "Everyone on board with this," he said, expressed as a statement of fact and not a question that invited an answer.

Everyone nodded their consent. Evans realized that an investigation of this nature would take way more than the few weeks he had left before his retirement. While he resented the typical Agency heavy-handedness, he also felt a sense of duty, as well as curiosity to find out what had taken place.

"Good. Now, let's get going, we're already late. Each of you has a packet with a room number. Please head there for additional briefings and your specific instructions. Any questions?"

Based on the news reports he'd heard, Evans asked, "Why has this been described as a possible terrorist act? They wouldn't have capabilities to generate small-scale fusion reactions."

Before the ED could answer, Secretary Robbins put out his hand. "You are correct. We do not think this was the result of a terrorist act. Nonetheless, we are not going to announce to the general population that a fusion reaction took place within the confines of the Boston metropolitan area, and without the US government's knowledge. Furthermore, the city's treating it like a potential terrorist act is beneficial to our efforts to identify and bring in anyone associated with this, while slowing down, and helping to track, any activity of 'concerned' foreign governments."

"Got it," Evans replied.

"Any more questions?" Robbins asked. "Good. Each of you is to proceed immediately to the room written on your packet. Get to it!"

As people filed out, Evans noted that his packet did not have a room number.

He looked at Robbins, who said, "That's right. You're to remain here. You'll be getting your instructions straight from us, then heading immediately to Boston. You'll be there in two hours. And if you find yourself short-staffed, you can even draft your old protégé. I wonder what the hell he's been up to?"

That would be last thing Evans would do, and the ED knew that. He was done placing himself in jeopardy because of Dan Lawson.

Chapter 35

The crowds had thinned as Stephen walked away from the fire. He was in the main academic part of the campus. Departmental buildings, multiple stories high, lined each side of the road.

He glanced back several times and thought he saw two people taking a similar path, walking close to buildings, mostly out of sight. He stepped off to the side and waited for their approach, with no plan or means to defend himself if they confronted him. His eyes twitched as he tried to see into the shadows. No one came. If anyone had been following him, they were no longer visible.

Wiping drops of perspiration off his brow, he resumed his walk, picked up the pace, and quickly covered the last few blocks to his office. He fumbled for his security card, swiped it along the reader, and entered the building, looking back one last time as the door shut.

Outside, the orange and brown flames found cracks between the buildings, trees, and other structures that stood as insufficient barriers to the shafts of eerie light.

Stephen entered his office without turning on the lights. Although that would have banished the sickly reflections from the fire, it would have also announced his presence and left him blind to what was going on outside.

He had pushed things far enough for now. It was time to put everything on hold and regroup from a better position. While the results were terrible, there was no doubt that the information he possessed had led to the generation of tremendous power. That was worth something. Although he had just begun to scratch the surface of what he could do with the biology information, it would soon yield valuable results that could be put to good use. The only thing holding him back was seeing if there was indeed a third set of information.

He grabbed a bottle of water from the small refrigerator under his desk, sat down, and turned on his computer. He tilted his head back, closed his mouth around the opening, and squeezed the bottle, using the water pressure to force open his constricted throat.

Computer ready, he opened up a browser window containing a montage of security camera images from in and around the biology building. He leaned closer, as if that would let him peer into the depths and around the corners. Everything looked as it should.

Then he used Dan's secure websites to notify the remaining members of his secret team to lie low and break off contact until he reached out to them, probably in several weeks. Except for one, to whom Stephen referred as Galileo, none was as high within the team, nor knew as much, as Welch. They had all worked only on small pieces without knowing what anyone else was doing, even who the others were, or what it all meant in aggregate. As for Galileo, he was Stephen's right-hand man in the genetics and biology areas. Nervous about recent events, Stephen had already sent him underground to await further instructions.

Next, using a protocol Dan had established with him, Stephen changed the access keys on all of his secure sites, save for one server. It no longer existed, destroyed with the rest of the equipment at the fusion center. He hoped that its backup was current and had all the data needed to reconstruct what had happened. Corrections needed to be made. The explosion was a costly interruption, not a permanent breach, except for those who had died.

Stephen let his mind wander while he caught his breath. He suddenly realized that he hadn't called Nancy to let her know he was safe—not that she should have expected otherwise. After that, he'd contact Dan and get going on whatever they'd have to do next.

He used his office phone to dial home. Nancy picked up after one ring, saying, "Oh, Stephen, thank God. I kept worrying when I couldn't reach you. And then I saw on the news what happened at Viktor's lab. Is he safe? Where are you?"

"Slow down . . . I'm at MIT, and I'm very sorry I didn't call sooner. I saw the explosion from my HBC office window and just reacted. It was terrible. I'm pretty sure Viktor was working there when it happened. When I couldn't reach him, I ran over, but I forgot to call you. It took a long time to get there. Looking at the scene, I think he's gone."

After a gasp and deep silence that was filled with emotion, Nancy spoke. "I'm so sorry, Stephen. His poor family. You must feel awful, too. I wish you were home now. Everything in Boston is a mess. How will you get here?"

"I think the main roadways within the city are closed off. I'll walk back to my HBC office, get my car, and get onto the Mass Pike headed away from the city. Unless traffic is much worse than I think, I should be home in about an hour. How's Ava? I need a big hug from you both."

"Ava's fine. I sent her to bed a few minutes ago. We've been watching the news together. That's a big fire. The firefighters have been lucky to keep it from spreading."

"The TV can't do it justice. It looks and smells like something out of a medieval depiction of hell."

"Come home."

"I'm on my way."

"I love you."

"Love you, too."

After he hung up, Stephen had one more call to place. It was time to share everything with Dan. He tried to use the cell phone Dan had given him, and he was upset to see that it had broken when it fell out of his pocket when he was crossing the bridge earlier. The screen and keyboard were cracked. The display was black, and the only button that seemed to work was the speed dial for his voice mail. He thought of using his office phone but knew that was a bad idea.

While he tried to figure out how to reach Dan, Stephen clicked back to the montage of security images. Of the twelve video feeds, eleven showed the glow of the fire reflecting on its surroundings. But the view of the front door looked exactly as it would on any other night. Where was the light from the fire?

He realized that a prerecorded feed had been substituted for the live one.

He tried to see what was going on near the front entrance, by sliding along his office walls and stretching to glance out the window, but he wasn't at the right angle to see anything without exposing himself. Once again, his hands began to sweat. He had to reach Dan.

He decided on a two-pronged approach. First he wrote an ordinary email on his computer to Dan's regular account: "Terrible explosion and fire at MIT. May have lost a good friend. Thankful for our friendship. Heading home. Stay safe, my friend!"

Then he pressed the only button on the cell phone Dan had given him that still worked, his own voice mail, and left a message in his own in-box. Hopefully, it was something he'd left for himself, and Dan would never need to hear it. But if not, it would be a secure message that Dan would eventually retrieve, knowing that Stephen could not.

Time to go. He turned off his computer, took deep breaths, silently prayed *May I return home safely,* then walked toward the back exit. Cautiously, he opened the door, looked around as best he could without exposing himself, and launched himself out of the building, prepared to take off in a sprint.

As he did, a man grabbed Stephen's arm and a mountain of muscle stepped in front of him.

The man holding his arm said, "Whoa, what's the hurry? The fire will die out soon. You don't want the same to happen to you, do you?"

"What do you want?" Stephen said in a voice that sounded far braver then he felt.

"Our employer is a chessmaster. He likes to make sure all of his pieces are following his strategy. You're to come with us so the king can see what his bishop has been up to," the man said, chuckling at his witticism.

"There are a lot of people around. You don't want a scene."

"Nor do you. Take a look at this." With that, the muscleman produced a tablet. On it was video of Stephen's house, focused on Ava's window. "And if that isn't persuasive enough, remember that two knights always defeat a lone bishop. As your colleague found out six months ago, it doesn't pay to try to run away. The outcome can be much worse than the alternative."

Stunned with the truth of what he had always feared—that Alex's crash wasn't an accident—Stephen realized that things were beyond anything he could handle.

With one man in front of him and another behind, Stephen started walking toward a panel truck parked in the biology building's back lot. The first man opened the rear doors and gestured for Stephen to get in. Stephen and the two men stepped inside and closed the doors. There was a small window in the front through which Stephen could see only a little of what was ahead. Directed by an unseen driver, the vehicle drove off slowly through the thinning crowds and traffic, toward Boston and an uncertain future.

Chapter 36

Dan reached the other side of the bridge and had less than a quarter mile to go. Acrid smoke from the fire had drifted all the way over, and periodically he got strong whiffs that made him recoil.

A ping from the Bluetooth earbud in his right ear notified him of an email from Stephen. Although the message indicated that Stephen was not in danger, Dan wanted to talk with him to be sure. A glance at his phone's screen showed that Stephen's cell phone was in the MIT biology building. Dan sprinted the short distance remaining. All the office lights were out. If Stephen was there, he was in the dark.

Again Dan tried calling Stephen. Again the call went unanswered.

Meanwhile, police were directing the few stragglers in the area to go home and get off the streets. One policeman approached Dan and motioned for him to move on. Dan pointed at Stephen's building, made as though he was getting out keys, and walked to the front door.

The policeman nodded and walked on.

Dan knocked progressively louder on the glass doors until he was pounding on them. No response. Increasingly concerned, he walked around the outside of the building to see if he could find a way in. He reached the back corner just in time to catch a glimpse of someone who looked liked Stephen, being escorted by two men into the back of a panel truck.

Dan yelled and sprinted after the truck as it pulled out. Within moments, it was gone.

Out of breath, Dan stopped, slapped his hands on his thighs, and bent over, breathing heavily. He pulled out his phone. The dot that represented Stephen, or at least the cell phone Dan had given him, crossed into Boston, headed south on I-93, and toward the tunnels that ran underneath the city.

Then signal from the phone was lost.

He waited a few minutes for the vehicle to leave the tunnel and for the signal to reappear, but nothing showed up. He didn't know what that meant. Was the phone destroyed, or was the signal masked?

Dan looked for a taxi, but there were none to be found.

Jogging slowly into East Cambridge, he came across a teenage boy sitting on an old, beat-up, ten-speed Schwinn bicycle. Dan paid him eighty dollars for it and rode off toward Boston and along the path that the truck had traveled.

Chapter 37

D r. Bishop, thank you so kindly for joining us. Momentous events today, don't you think? Even life-altering for some, and perhaps world-changing for many," said a voice from the shadows that Stephen recognized.

Stephen yelled out, "Reveal yourself!"

"You have known me for a long time in one capacity, but I have another identity. You may have heard of The Commission. I am one of its leaders, known to them as Sarastro, and will be dealing with you now in that capacity."

Even after a day of incredible and terrible events, Stephen was stunned anew, learning of the person's alternate identity and the organization he belonged to. Gathering himself, he said, "I suppose I should have suspected something."

"Then you also recognize the seriousness of the predicament and my disappointment in you."

Silence descended as Stephen reflected upon his dilemma. He was in a huge basement of an old building that was part of a run-down industrial complex that was being torn down to make way for an upscale development. Since the completion of the Big Dig, the area was considered attractive and trendy.

The basement was empty save for the chair he was sitting in, the small table to the side of it, some scattered debris on the floor, the two men and one woman who had escorted him down, and the man who referred to himself now as Sarastro. The lone light was aimed at Stephen's face, mostly blinding him while providing limited illumination of the surrounding area. The driver of the truck that had brought him there was outside, presumably keeping watch.

Before Stephen had been placed in the chair and the light turned on him, he had been able to make out wood bracing on the far wall and an open window next to it. His first impulse had been to make a run for it, but he realized he would be overtaken.

He blinked against the painful light and searched for the face that belonged to the voice. All he could make out was the familiar silhouette of Sarastro standing off to the side, while the one who looked like he was in charge of the muscle side of things stood in front of Stephen.

Stephen was dazed by the turn of events and knew he had strong reason to fear what was coming. Yet doing anything drastic would be counterproductive for Sarastro and his team. They needed Stephen's willing cooperation. Still, there was no telling what people who considered themselves beyond all norms would do. Perhaps it had been a mistake to expect rational behavior. Surely by the looks of things, he'd overestimated his advantage and underestimated the potential outcomes. Nonetheless, he'd have to pose as though he had leverage over them without being forced to turn over what he knew he could not. Grimly, he realized that the belief in control of one's life was an illusion that almost everyone held until it was shattered.

Acting indignant, Stephen said in a firm, determined voice, "Why have you brought me here this way?"

"I see we have your attention. Good! We want you to understand the gravity of the situation and what we're prepared to do to protect our interests. A more 'polite' approach might have left you thinking you have other options than full cooperation."

"I have acted as we've agreed. You have no cause to think otherwise," Stephen answered, knowing that it was false, but hoping they had no evidence to the contrary.

"I'm afraid that is where we disagree. My colleagues and I aren't sure of the details, but we believe you are connected to what happened at the MIT fusion center tonight. Not only that, but you've been conducting your research in secret, withholding important information from us. You can imagine our confusion, curiosity, and disappointment, especially after all we have done for you and were still prepared to do for your daughter, Ava," Sarastro said.

"That's ridiculous. My genetic research has nothing to do with fusion, or, for that matter, anything to do with physics."

"Is it really? As far-fetched as it *should* seem, we think you've made incredible scientific connections we need to know about. But no matter. We will find out shortly. Would it surprise you to learn that we know about all of your meetings with the regrettably late Dr. Viktor Weisman?"

"So what? I've been friends with him for over ten years."

"Yes, we know that. But as the explosion at the fusion research center demonstrated dramatically, something changed decisively."

"Yes, I lost a good friend. A number of other good people died, and the center was destroyed, too."

"*Stephen!* We know the fundamentals of what happened. Disappointingly, you have left out critical details. A powerful fusion reaction took place in a reactor that should not have been able to produce it. Satellites from numerous countries picked up all the requisite signatures. At this very instant, world powers are mobilizing to find out what happened and to get hold of the technology that made it possible. We are going to beat them to it. Before anyone else figures out the link between you and Dr. Weisman, we're going to know everything you know, about all your research, all your relationships, anything you've exchanged with others and all that you possess. That is the easy part. The more difficult part is doing it in such a way that your work continues, with your effective cooperation *and* well-being. Your responses and evasiveness are not encouraging," said Sarastro.

"I've held up my end of the agreement. In return, you spy on and threaten me?"

"We're prepared to do a lot more than that." Turning to his men, Sarastro said, "Sergei, show Dr. Bishop the contents of the bag." The man nearest the table picked out and slowly organized the contents of the bag on top of the table. There were various medical instruments, some long-handled and blunt, some sharper.

Stephen's insides twisted.

"With what you know of me, do you really think this is necessary? I don't have whatever you're after. And if you even think of using these on me, all bets are off," Stephen said defiantly.

"You're the one who will determine what is required, including whether these are used on you or someone close to you as you watch. Normally, we use more subtle methods, but events are rapidly overtaking all of us, thanks to you and your collaborators. You must know that we *will* get what we're after. Things are too important not to use all means necessary. And rest assured, we will." Continuing, Sarastro said, "I hope that we don't have to use these devices. They'd leave marks that would invite questions that are best avoided, especially while we think that you can still be useful to us. But make no mistake about it, you should do everything within your power to maintain the high expectations we have in the value of you and your work. Without our belief in that, your prospects would be nonexistent."

"What happened to your oath to use technology to make a better world?"

"I'm honoring it. There are far more important things at stake than a few individuals."

"What about your soul? In the end, that's all you've got," Stephen said in a low, gentle voice.

Laughing with scorn, Sarastro said, "Despite your display of piety and concern, in the end, when push comes to shove, your own actions are based strictly on worldly interests. But don't worry. I do have much higher aspirations than a simple, temporal destiny."

Picking up Stephen's damaged cell phone, Sarastro tried different buttons. Then he said, "You need to be more careful with phones that are old enough to be relics. What a shame about the broken display and jammed keys. But wait—I think the speed dial works. Let's try number two."

Placing his hand over the mouthpiece, Sarastro turned to Stephen and said, "It's your wife. I'm afraid I can't tell her when you'll be home. Unless you change your attitude, this may take a while." Then Sarastro hung up.

Unnerved by the voiceless call from Stephen's cell phone, that she had been unable to return, Nancy tried to come up with a reasonable explanation for why Stephen wasn't home yet. If something had come up, he should have communicated that to her. Perhaps the cell phone network was overwhelmed by people trying to contact their loved ones. Or maybe it was blocked for law enforcement reasons. Perhaps traffic outside the city was worse than it looked on the navigator maps she'd checked online. Still, he would have found a way to let her know. His dependable, sure way of handling things was one of the things that had first attracted her to him. All she could do was watch the news reports, showing the fire being brought under control, while she prayed nervously.

Desperate for answers, she called Dan.

Dan biked over the I-93 bridge in between the car lanes. Traffic was crawling as people tried to get through the security and chaos.

When he reached the central Boston side, a call rang through on his regular smart phone. It was Nancy. He was glad that he had turned off location tracking and was spoofing the cell phone tower, otherwise it could later be used to track his whereabouts.

"Dan, do you know where Stephen is?" Nancy said anxiously. "He was supposed to be home already. I just got a call from his new cell phone number, only no one was on the line, and I couldn't reach him when I called back."

Dan tried to reassure her, despite his own doubts. "I'm sure he's fine. The fire's made everything crazy. He's probably trying to make his way home and for some reason his phone isn't working." The good news was that Stephen's special cell phone had placed a call and therefore was in signal range again. He looked quickly down at his special cell phone's display and Dan saw that the blinking red dot had reappeared. He knew he had to get there as quick as he could. "Let me get back to you. I'll check into it right away."

"Thank you, Dan. I know it's not rational, but I have this terrible feeling."

"I understand. A lot of people are shaken right now. Try not to worry too much. I'll call you when I know something."

"I really appreciate it. And take care of yourself, too."

"Don't worry about me. I'll call back soon. 'Bye," Dan said, rushing off the phone before she could answer. He zoomed in on Stephen's cell phone's location. It was in a remote area of the last remnants of the Big Dig.

He was ten minutes by bike from Stephen's location. What could he, one unarmed man, do once he got there? The heck with the consequences. He wasn't going to chance losing his once-again good friend.

Using another one of his phone's special features, Dan placed an untraceable call to 911, with a voice-altering filter, telling the operator that he saw a panel truck, loaded with large propane tanks, driving toward the Ted Williams tunnel. It had stopped at a nearby abandoned building on Haul Road and people were loading things into it. They looked like they were getting ready to leave and the only main road they could take headed toward the tunnel.

That would definitely get a big response.

"You were behind Alex's death."

"I think you should focus on your own interests," Sarastro said. Opening a small case, he pulled out two vials of blood from a refrigerated box. "See these?"

Holding up one vial in his right hand, he said, "This contains the last of the healthy marrow that is the perfect match for your adorable Ava, should it ever be necessary. Let's hope it's not." Glaring at Stephen's wide-open eyes, Sarastro put the vial back in the box. His expression turning sinister, he grabbed the other vial and said, "This contains her tainted blood, rampant with leukemia. You'll notice that the vial is half full. You might want to consider where the other half is and how it could be used, if it hasn't already been. As I'm sure you know, relapses are much more difficult to treat. And of course there is the matter of the treatment we were helping develop and obtain. Fortunately, it wasn't needed for your daughter, at least not yet."

Stephen yelled, "You leave Ava out of this! She's an innocent child. What do you think you'll gain by harming her? Not what you think you will."

"Really? We've already been successful. Our lab work led you to believe she was predisposed to leukemia and got you to start the research we wanted conducted. When we realized you were keeping the research secret, and our attempts to influence Alex Robertson, which you forced on us, failed, we injected Ava with a form of leukemia that we knew was easily treatable but you did not, due to more clever lab work on our part. After all, we didn't want grieving to get in the way of your effectiveness. But it was enough for you to be open to our overtures, and did lead to our agreement to help you search for the treatment you thought you needed. Only you consider yourself more clever than you are and now we are forced by this evening's events to take more drastic measures."

Raising the first vial of blood over his head, Sarastro threw it down, smashing it on the ground. "By the way: the reason it was a perfect match was that it came from her, before she became ill. Now we're all at the point of no return."

Face warped with rage and fear, Stephen spat out, "You're a monster."

"Why? Because we are willing to do what's needed to benefit the world as a whole? It's a rather simple equation. Recognize that one life is just one and many are many. Perhaps what happens to your child could yield discoveries that would benefit thousands of others. Why should they suffer because of your selfishness? But don't worry, we have no interest in harming her. You are the one with the power to ensure your daughter's well-being, and that of others, by simply honoring your agreement and sharing your work, and everything else, with us, tonight. Your fate and theirs is in your hands. All we want is to ensure the science is developed and used for as widespread a benefit as possible. Why object to something that would help humans flourish? I am being completely honest with our intent. I just have the courage to follow it to its logical conclusion. You don't."

"I told you, I have withheld nothing," Stephen shouted, desperate to protect others but unwilling to place the power of what he had discovered in the hands of such people.

"Unfortunately, I don't believe that. I wish I could, but then that would make me a fool. I hate fools, and no one is going to treat me like one. While I'm normally patient and forgiving, you are close to leaving me no choice but to act with extreme measures."

"I have, and will, continue to honor our agreement. I can show you once I'm back at HBC," Stephen asserted.

"Tell us what you know about Viktor Weisman's work," Sarastro said.

"I only know what everyone else does. There is nothing more I can tell you."

"Where are you keeping your real work records?"

"At HBC, of course."

"Fortunately for your daughter—for now—we don't have the time it would take to let a reoccurrence of leukemia run its course and ensure your cooperation in exchange for the experimental treatment it would require."

"I will prove to you that I have not withheld anything of value," Stephen asserted, thinking that perhaps just giving them the raw data translated into the symbolic code, without the means to decode it, would be enough to hold them at bay for a while.

"We don't have time for more deceit." Gesturing to the two men standing next to Stephen, Sarastro said, "Inject Dr. Bishop."

The two men grabbed Stephen, and, while holding him down, injected him with a syringe of clear liquid.

"Don't worry," Sarastro said, noticeably more relaxed. "It's only a solution to help you be more thoughtful and forthright, freeing you from whatever worries are impeding your normally sound and well-intentioned judgment. In a few minutes, you'll be your old collaborative self and, if you're lucky, we will not require any additional means to motivate you. Then, if I like what you have to say, you can assume a proper role within our organization. Or *not*," Sarastro said with an accent on the last word that left no doubt that the latter would not lead to a good outcome for Stephen.

Dan pedaled furiously the last mile to reach the site where he thought Stephen was being held. He hadn't heard or seen police vehicles headed toward there. With a grim realization, he realized that he'd probably have to deal with the situation himself, and without any weapons. The police had to be getting a flood of calls from frightened people all across the city, and his call would have to wait its turn.

The injection was just beginning to take effect when the driver of the panel truck burst into the room, saying his police headquarters contact said police were headed their way in response to a report of a truck carrying a large explosive device targeted for the tunnel. They had only a few minutes before they arrived.

Despite the forces about to descend on them, a still-calm Sarastro pointed to two of the men and said, "Move everything into the cars. Then set the truck on fire." Walking slowly up the steps, he said, "Sergei and Elena, escort Dr. Bishop up the steps."

As they approached, Stephen reached down and grabbed a piece of loose wood and, with all the strength he had left, slammed Sergei over the head, knocking him to the ground. Elena rushed to help Sergei, but he was unable to stand.

Stephen grabbed his phone and took off toward the far end of the basement, hoping to climb out of the opening he had seen earlier. His legs were rubbery, and his vision shifted as he half ran, half jogged, toward a shaft of dim light.

Behind him, he heard yells and stumbling footsteps approaching him.

Reaching the end of the basement, Stephen saw wood scaffolding bracing a rickety part of the wall. There was a small window near the top. He grabbed the windowsill and tried to pull himself up, his feet flailing against the concrete wall as he struggled. With the drug kicking in, his legs grew increasingly weak, and he fell to the ground, panting. He got up and again tried jumping while grabbing at the window. Falling once more, he hit the floor with a gasp and the room began to spin. As he landed, his phone fell out of his pocket.

At what sounded like the other end of the basement, he heard more loud voices racing his way. If he didn't get out now, that'd be it. He had one chance left.

Looking at the unsteady wall and scaffolding, he threw his phone out the window and then began to climb up the wood bracing, trying to get high enough to slide out the opening. As he climbed, he became groggier. Near the top, he reached for the window, but he couldn't quite grab it. He lost his balance, fell backward, and lunged at a piece of scaffolding. It came free. The scaffolding collapsed, as did the cinder blocks and bricks it had been supporting.

Stephen landed headfirst and hard on the concrete floor. The remnants of the wall landed on top of him, leaving only his head and right arm free of debris. His breath eased out of him as he scrawled in the dust with his right hand.

Stephen was dead when one of the men and Elena reached his body. They shined a flashlight on Stephen's face, felt for a pulse, and knew he was gone. Sarastro screamed at them over the radio for their incompetence and told them to get out before he had them shot and left behind. In their haste to leave, they missed what Stephen had written in the dust.

Dan pulled up as two large sedans raced away, spinning wheels and kicking up a cloud of dirt. A fire burned in the panel truck—it had to be the one he'd seen earlier. Though he couldn't see into the sedan, he thought, actually hoped, that Stephen was alive in one of the cars.

Looking at his cell phone tracker again, he saw that the phone he had given Stephen was still here. Either his abductors had left Stephen, or they had taken Stephen but left the phone behind. Neither possibility was good.

Dan ran around the building, calling out, "Stephen! Stephen, it's Dan!" Reaching the back, he saw the collapsed basement retaining wall. He walked cautiously toward the ten-foot-wide jumble of dirt and bricks that sloped from outside the building down into the base-ment. Beyond the top of the pile, still outside the building, Dan saw Stephen's cell phone on the ground and picked it up. It looked dam-aged. He peered down the debris into the basement and barely made out a head and arm sticking out from the rubble. Heart sinking, Dan jumped down. It was Stephen. He felt for a pulse. Finding none, he cradled Stephen's head, and then let out an angry, bitter yell.

No one was safe. No one was spared, especially the good.

Sitting there, he held Stephen as though he could hang on to his warmth.

Soon he heard sirens approaching. Using his cell phone as a light source, he looked around quickly. Stephen's finger was pointing at writing in the dust of the basement floor. He'd drawn a lowercase *i*, followed by a question mark, then two lines that almost formed the symbol for "less than": *i*? <

Had Stephen left him one last message? Dan took a picture of it with his phone and then erased it with his sneaker. With both cell phones in his pocket, Dan jumped and pulled himself through an adjacent casement window at the top of a still-intact section of the basement wall, then wiped where his hands had touched.

After one last look back at the friend who had been with him at every important moment of his life, he turned and left. He walked the bicycle across the building's lot, crossed the street, sat down out of sight of the arriving forces, and lowered his head into his hands.

From within his heart he heard the question *Why?*

It was a question that presumed there was something that could provide an answer. But answers could only come from a source that hadn't provided any evidence of its existence. Still, Dan knew that, beaten down though he was, and stripped bare of the insulation of everyday life, the desire for an answer pervaded him.

Something had made Stephen think he had proof of God's existence, that the universe ultimately made sense. That same something probably cost Stephen his life.

Dan would find whatever Stephen had found. He would help Nancy and Ava with their grief. He would avenge Stephen's death. He would find a way to finish Stephen's work. And finally, if he found anything like a God actually existed, Dan would demand an answer to the question of why the good, the innocent, and the weak suffer, while evil prospers. Why would a God be invisible and absent at the moments of people's greatest need?

The flashing lights Dan saw approaching would be there in moments, and with them, officials who'd want answers to different questions which he wasn't ready to provide. Dan walked his bicycle away from the area, mounted it, and started toward home. There, he'd await the anguished call from Nancy and pretend that he didn't already know what he had seen firsthand. Otherwise, he'd have to explain to her and the police how he had found Stephen. He had to avoid scrutiny if he was going to keep his vows to Stephen and find out what had happened.

There was going to be hell to pay, and he was going to make sure someone did just that.

PART 3

Chapter 38

Dan took off his socks, put them inside his pants pocket, and walked up the front steps of his building. A half mile back, after wiping the bicycle for fingerprints, he had discarded it in a trash bin. A storm drain held his sneakers before their eventual journey downstream. He was getting rid of anything that could link him to the scene of Stephen's death.

With heavy legs and a heavier heart, he entered his apartment, took off his clothes, and threw them in the washer.

After putting on his bathrobe, he looked out the window and across the river at the waning smoke and lingering glow that were all that was left from the diminishing flames.

If it hadn't happened already, Nancy would soon receive the call that would suck out a large part of what had made her world joyful and real. Of course, she'd go on, especially with Ava to raise. But when you believe, as Nancy and Stephen had, that two could become one, it's pretty hard to be a whole when part of it is taken away. What remains remembers what it had been.

Turning on the TV, Dan saw more news reports on the explosion. The cause was unknown and, though it had not yet been completely discounted, earlier fears of a terrorist attack appeared unfounded. The security measures put in place were expected to subside over the next day. The low levels of radiation, apparently from tritium, had dissipated and were not a threat. Loss of life couldn't be verified until the fire had been put out and remains located. As of now, eight people were believed missing.

He turned off the TV and slammed down the remote. Yanking the vacuum out of the closet, in violent strokes he cleaned the area he had trod on since returning. Afterward he emptied the contents of the vacuum canister out of his living room window. He took off his bathrobe, placed it in the washing machine with his other clothes, and started it up. He sat down with just a towel wrapped around his waist and looked at the washer aimlessly. He realized that he was no more in control of his life than the clothes within the machine, tossed and tumbled from side to side.

After a few minutes, the resolutions he had made when he found Stephen intensified. Dan would find and deal with whoever had abducted Stephen. Dan finally had an absolute purpose.

He'd also be there for Nancy. For that, he'd better shower so he could be ready when the dreaded call inevitably came.

Too soon, his cell phone rang. He stepped out of the shower without toweling off and he answered, droplets falling off his body as energy drained out of him as well.

"Dan . . . Stephen's . . . dead," Nancy said haltingly through stifled sobs.

Though he already knew, hearing it spoken hit him anew. Even though he'd had time to think of what he'd say, all he could force out through his tightly strained throat was "How? How can that be?"

"Some sort of accident. The police will be here soon. Could you please come over? I know it's late, but I can't face this alone," Nancy cried.

"I'll be right there," Dan answered. He tried to find words to comfort her, but couldn't through his own grief.

In a quieter voice, Nancy said, "Thank you. I'm so lost. There's more that I'll tell you when you get here."

"I'm leaving now," Dan said.

What more there could be?

Chapter 39

A line of police cars, lights flashing low, filled the street in front of the Bishops' house.

As Dan walked with labored steps toward the front door, one of the police officers moved into his path. The officer started to speak, but Dan said, "I'm a friend of the family. Mrs. Bishop asked me to come here."

"Who are you?" the officer asked.

"Dan Lawson. I've known Stephen Bishop for thirty years," Dan replied, refusing to use the past tense.

"Come with me," the officer said as he turned and walked up the front steps, Dan close behind. Entering the house, the officer motioned for Dan to stop as the officer headed into the study. After a moment, the officer returned, then led Dan in.

In the study, Nancy sat rigidly on the wingback chair next to the piano, drawn but composed. Several police officers of varying ranks, milled around. Dan felt the eyes of the police officers on him, probably wondering why Nancy had called him for comfort and aid instead of a girlfriend or a relative. He, too, had wondered until remembering that Stephen's parents lived hours away, and that he was the person who had been closest to Stephen—at least for most of his life—and was one of the people to see him most recently. The last part would interest investigators.

Nancy stood up as Dan walked over to her. They hugged, though he knew there was nothing he could do that would provide her mean-ingful comfort or assuage his own grief. Releasing her, Dan said, "Nancy, I'm so sorry. I'll do whatever I can for you and Ava." He was also thinking about how he would begin the journey he was about to undertake: to find out and finish whatever Stephen had started, and to hold accountable those whose actions had led to Stephen's death. For now, that would require keeping everything close to the vest, cer-tainly not letting Nancy or anyone else know what Stephen had told him or what he had been doing to help him. No one could know that he had found Stephen's body.

With a smile, taut as a thin steel cable holding a great weight, Nancy replied, "Thank you. I'm sure Stephen knows and appreciates that."

Also present, not past, tense. But Nancy's faith led her to believe that Stephen still existed and undoubtedly was in his God's care. Putting aside his own sorrows, resentments, and questions, Dan briefly wished he could believe that himself, even if only for tempo-rary comfort.

"Is Ava asleep? How is she taking it?" Dan asked.

"She's at a sleepover at a friend's house and doesn't know yet. I've spoken to the parents, and I'll get Ava early in the morning, before she hears the news from anyone else. I dread it. Stephen and Ava were so close."

Emotion almost overcoming him, Dan breathed deeply, swal-lowed, and said, "Whatever you need, just ask." Memories of Stephen buried under the rubble kept intruding on his thoughts, making it hard to concentrate.

"Being here now is a huge help," Nancy said, motioning for him to sit on the piano bench, next to her chair. She looked at the lead in-vestigator and said, in her proper manner, "Lieutenant Slawski, could you please repeat what you told me? I'd like Dan to hear it, and I'm afraid I haven't been able to grasp all of it."

Dan listened as the lieutenant told him what he already knew. Hearing about how the officers found Stephen alone, crumpled under debris, only made the hurt Dan was feeling more real. The of-ficers explained that the situation would be suspicious under normal circumstances, because of the footprints surrounding Stephen's body and the fact that the ground had been rubbed near Stephen's right hand. Given the explosion at MIT and the phone call that led the police to the building and the burning truck, it was now being considered even more suspicious.

Ghostly pale, Nancy was frozen in position. Dan resisted the urge to give her hand a reassuring squeeze. Instead, he went to get her a glass of water.

The lieutenant asked Nancy if she felt up to answering some questions. Haltingly, she said, "Yes" and took a sip of the water.

A series of short questions followed. Nancy answered:

"I have no idea why Stephen was in that area. He had no interests there."

"I last spoke to Stephen about an hour after the explosion. He called me from his MIT office and said he was okay and would be home soon. He sounded upset."

"His friend Viktor Weisman, director of the fusion center, might have been killed in the fire."

The policemen straightened up when they heard Stephen had known Viktor. Dan, too, wanted to know more about the connection, though he had more reason, and perhaps means, to do so. Somewhere buried in his servers might be the answer.

"Mrs. Bishop, please tell us about your husband's relationship with Dr. Weisman."

"There's not much to say. They met over a decade ago at an MIT golf outing and have been friends ever since. That poor man was a concentration camp survivor. Other than mutual respect, they had no professional relationship. Physics and biology rarely cross paths, especially genomics and fusion energy research."

After taking time to read through his notes, the lieutenant said to Dan, "You mind if Sergeant Olsen asks you a few questions in the other room? We'd like to finish up for now and let Mrs. Bishop rest."

Dan followed Sergeant Olsen into the kitchen, where Dan provided quick answers to rapid-fire questions.

"I've been friends with Stephen for over thirty years, and we just had a nice weekend on the Cape with his family. Everything was fine. He didn't have enemies or problems with people."

"I know very little about Stephen's work, save for the fact that it involves genetics."

"I had only met Viktor Weisman once, briefly, years ago."

It makes no sense that Stephen was in that area, especially since he had just been in his MIT biology office."

Stephen has no enemies."

"I watched the fire across the river through my window and on TV. At one point, I walked across the street to the river and then partway over the bridge, but that was it."

"I no longer work in the intelligence community. I am now an independent computer security consultant. No, that is not another name for a professional hacker."

"I have no involvement with Stephen's work."

"I have no idea who called in the tip."

"Of course, I'll answer whatever other questions you might have anytime you want."

A little while later, the police left, saying they'd be in touch.

Looking exhausted and drained, Nancy asked Dan to stay over and sleep on the couch downstairs so that she wouldn't have to be alone in the house until her parents arrived in the morning. She then rose to get ready for a night that was sure to be without rest.

Before she left the room, Nancy pushed a hidden latch, and what had looked like a fixed panel in the cabinet opened. Reaching in, she retrieved three Moleskine books and the laptop Dan had given Stephen, then said, "Stephen kept handwritten journals. I'd like you to look through them. Neither one of us was completely honest with the police tonight. There *was* something unusual with Stephen's work. I'm not sure what it was, but I need to know if it played a role in his death and what he'd want done now. Look around as much as you want before anyone else does." Nancy said, then handed Dan an index card with usernames and passwords for all the computers in the house. Then she looked knowingly into Dan's eyes, turned, and slowly trod up the stairs. Dan sat down and started paging through the journals, wondering what he'd find.

Chapter 40

Dan had been at his computer ever since he'd returned from Nancy's, and it was now mid-morning. Without the passcodes Stephen had used to encode his work on Dan's cloud-based servers, no one would be able to access Stephen's work, ever. All of Dan's attempts to find or guess the passcodes had been futile. And there was nothing on the encoded laptop he had given Stephen in Falmouth.

The only things Dan had been able to access were the data and programs he had copied from the MIT fusion lab two days ago, the day before the explosion. They would undoubtedly be extremely important to many interests, not least of which were US security agencies, but only if they knew about their existence. So far they were of no value to Dan. He had no idea what he was looking at. Even the best fusion energy researchers in the world might not be able to understand what they meant. The text documents used symbols, words, and involved science far beyond Dan's understanding. Programs were grouped with hundreds of large data files, probably fusion test results and the programs used to analyze them. There were dozens of images of experimental conditions, but they, too, meant nothing to Dan. Finally, in a different set of file directories, were satellite images of areas of the US with colored circles, of different sizes, scattered across them.

At some point he'd get help from trusted experts who could figure out what he was looking at. Now wasn't the time for that. There was too much else that he needed to understand first.

Dan thought about the videos recorded by security cameras along the path Stephen had last traveled. While Dan was confident he could find and access most of the video libraries, he was reluctant to try, concerned that he would attract attention from security programs that might be active while the investigation into Stephen's death was underway. He also worried that he might show up in one, despite the precautions he had taken.

Sore from the hours he had spent sitting working on the computer, Dan stood up to stretch, letting out loud groans.

During the night, he had been too agitated to sleep except in brief, fitful intervals. The few times he had lain down and tried to sleep, images of Stephen buried under the stone had troubled his mind. Dan had spent most of the time copying and going through Stephen's home computers and files. There was nothing of value to be found, as Stephen had cleared off the computers, per Dan's instructions days earlier.

At first light, Dan had cooked Nancy breakfast. It was still on her plate, cold and barely touched, an hour later, when her parents arrived. After a short period of mourning with them, Dan left before Ava came home. Although he would have stayed if he could have helped, he was relived that he didn't have to witness Ava's reaction to the news and her subsequent grief. Few things impacted a child's present and future as much as the loss of a parent.

On his drive home, Dan had listened to the news. The fire had not been extinguished until 4 a.m., and eight people were presumed dead. The cause of the blast was unknown, though it was far more powerful than anything of ordinary origin. While not yet ruled out, earlier reports of a terrorist attack were considered unlikely. There was no mention of Stephen.

Since finding Stephen, Dan had kept questioning himself. Was he to blame because he hadn't helped Stephen earlier? Had his attempt to check out Stephen's HBC work triggered something? If he had noticed the fire earlier, could he have gotten to Stephen right after the explosion, perhaps in time to have helped?

Whatever answers there were, Dan knew what the future held: he had work to do. People were going to be held accountable, and whatever Stephen had died for would be seen through to its end.

Still agitated, Dan jumped up and grabbed the bar mounted on the doorway. He did pull-ups until his muscles burned and he couldn't hold on any longer. Then he did squats until he couldn't rise. Anger alternated with sorrow. He repeated the exercises.

Somewhere between an up and a down, Dan remembered that one of the things Stephen had wanted him to do was re-create Alex's computer setup and see if there was a third set of information. If Dan could find the computer Stephen had used that night, perhaps he could do that and find *everything* Stephen had done. But he had no idea where to look for it. And there was still the not improbable possibility that Stephen was mistaken or misleading him about what he had really discovered.

At a dead end, exhausted, Dan fell flat back on his couch and resumed looking through Stephen's journals. They went back two years and had lots of notes, mostly of a personal nature, including the struggle Stephen had undergone with Ava's illness. Though it would take Dan a while to get through the journals, so far nothing stood out. That changed when he turned the page: at the top were two quotes, reflecting diametrically opposed camps. Dan knew both well. The first was from the Book of Genesis.

The Lord God formed man out of the dust of the ground and blew into his nostrils the breath of life, and the man became a living being.

The next quote was from Richard Dawkins.

The universe we observe has precisely the properties we should expect if there is, at bottom, no design, no purpose, no evil, no good, nothing but blind, pitiless indifference.

The quotes made Dan wonder whether Stephen, too, despite his recently revived religious beliefs, had the same doubts as Dan. Perhaps Ava's illness had proven too much, challenged his views. Perhaps once she had recovered, in an attempt to regain his faith, Stephen had sought scientific proof for God's existence.

One thing was certain. One of the quotes was true and the other was not, and the differences meant everything.

While the world was no different than what he'd thought it was days earlier, he knew he was changing. Instead of withdrawing, he was full of fight and resolve, determined to find the truth, wherever it lay. Truth was the first step in holding someone, or something, accountable.

Looking at the table next to him, Dan picked up the cell phone he had given Stephen. The display and keyboard were broken, though Dan was able to press the 1 key, which connected him to Stephen's voice mail. Dan tried the password he had given Stephen. It still worked.

Dan sat up, pressed the phone against his ears, and from the grave, Stephen's voice spoke. "Dan, if you're hearing this, I got myself in way too deep. I don't have time to explain. Look to be contacted by a person going by the name Galileo. The two of you will figure out what to do with what I've started. I can't say more now. I'm sorry for getting you into this, but I've seen God's handwriting on each of us, you have to believe that. I thought I was meant to find it. Maybe I shouldn't have, but I did. If for some reason I'm not there for them, please look out for Nancy and Ava. And please forgive me. You've been a great friend. Thank you."

Dan didn't move. Everything went quiet. Thunder rose in his ears, then went silent again. His skin tingled.

Dan couldn't believe that what Stephen had said about God's handwriting could be true, but Dan knew Stephen had believed it. What could that say about Stephen's state of mind? What he had gotten himself involved with? Stephen had been under tremendous stress and in some way had messed up big-time. And who was Galileo?

Chapter 41

Day 8
Friday Evening

Dan and his sister sat together in the third row of seats in the funeral home room that held Stephen's remains. The viewing room consisted of two sides, and the movable partition that normally separated them had been retracted. As large as the area was, it was packed, and a long line of mourners stretched from the casket, along the extended wall, down the hall, and out the door. Stephen had earned the respect and affection of a great number of people, from many walks of life. Each approached the casket with solemn reverence, then either knelt and said a silent prayer or stood and reflected in their own way. After that, they approached Nancy and offered their condolences, which she graciously accepted, fully composed.

Breaking a long stretch of silence between them, Joanna said to Dan, "I don't know how Nancy's doing it. I'd collapse after just a few minutes." They had been there since the viewing had started at 2 p.m., watching people say their goodbyes to Stephen and pay their respects to Nancy.

"You'd find a way to handle it, just as she is doing. You both have a steadfast sense of duty and reservoirs of strength as deep as oceans," Dan responded weakly, his earlier resolve weakened by where he was and by reemergent doubts. Change wasn't going to be simple or painless.

"You make it sound easy and natural, like we're just born that way."

"I don't know where it comes from, only that I could use some of it."

"Dan, a good part of it comes from focusing on others and not so much yourself, seeing what you can do for them rather then your own problems."

"Right now, I'm going to do everything I can for Nancy and Ava," Dan answered, coming to realize that what he had let himself become over the years was wrong and that he wasn't going to be that way any longer.

"I know. You've been great," Joanna said as she tightly grasped his hand in hers.

"The one thing I can't help them with is any reassurance about Stephen's fate. In my little time with him recently, I had started to consider that there might be more to this life than I had thought. I almost wanted to find reasons to think that there is joy at the end, that perhaps we really don't lose the people we've loved, that we'll reunite elsewhere. But then things like this only lead me to doubt again, reminding me that religion is just wish fulfillment against our fear of an immense void of nothingness."

Joanna put her arm around Dan, squeezed tightly, and said, "Well, at least you're finally opening up. You might find that more helpful than pretending everything is fine. Questioning is a good start. Keep at it. You may still be surprised where you wind up."

"I don't have a choice. There's a lot I need to find out about Stephen's death, for Nancy's and Ava's sake."

"Not everything has an answer. Anyway, aren't you glad that you were able to patch things up with Stephen?"

"Yes, that was good. Now I have to make good on a few other things," Dan said firmly. The truth was that he felt myriad emotions; the only things keeping him going were his own returning sense of purpose and the significance of what Stephen had asked of him.

Sensing what Dan had implied, Joanna looked at him sternly. "You be careful and let the police do their job. I don't ever want to attend a wake for you."

"I've got a pretty good feeling that I'm going to be around a lot longer than a number of people would like." Despite what Joanna said, they both knew that he would do anything but leave this just to the police. There was nothing like giving a person who lived with a big hole in his life, with his capabilities and experience, who felt he had nothing to lose, the motivation and reason to do something important for people he cared about.

With nothing more to say on the matter, they resumed sitting in silence.

Dan thought back to Stephen's message. Who was Galileo, and how would Dan find him? He wondered about the significance of the name and whether it was a reference to the religious persecution the real Galileo had faced for his scientific discoveries. Or was it more general than that? Was it a reference to orthodoxy in general? Dan had no idea anymore what had been real, what had been misdirection, and what might have been delusion on Stephen's part.

Dan scanned the room and saw Ava coming in with Dr. Alighieri. He felt he should go over and see how Ava was doing but was reluctant to do so, remembering his uneasy feelings and interactions with Dr. Alighieri. Instead, he looked over to Nancy, who nodded toward Ava. Though hesitant, he nonetheless got up and walked over to her.

This time, when Dr. Alighieri looked at him, he didn't feel as disturbed as he had before, though he still felt a sense of unease mixed with a desire to know more about her.

Whatever he was experiencing was interrupted when Ava grabbed his hand. Dan picked her up, and she put her head down on his shoulder. "How are you, sweetie?" Dan said softly.

In a quivering voice, Ava said, "I miss Daddy. I want Mommy and me to be in heaven with him."

"I hope not yet, Ava. So many people would miss you and all the special things you have left to do," Dan said, giving her a gentle kiss on her cheek.

He looked over at Dr. Alighieri, who said, "She's very brave. And lucky to have you."

"Thank you for taking care of her so well," Dan found himself saying with an earnestness that surprised him.

She didn't acknowledge his gratitude but said, "How are you doing? I know what a strong and long friendship you and Stephen had shared," and gently placed her fingers on Dan's wrist.

Still holding Ava, Dan placed his cheek against hers. "It will always hurt, but you cherish what you had and honor it by continuing to live." As he said this, something calming and healing seemed to come through Dr. Alighieri's touch, as though something was acting through her yet also was of her. She didn't seem aware of it, as though the extraordinary was totally natural to her. Once again, Dan wanted to turn away, only this time it was because whatever she could do to comfort people made him aware of how damaged he was. He was ashamed by his vulnerability and a neediness that he wasn't normally aware of, one that he felt was unmanly to allow or acknowledge.

"Those are wise words. And please call me Trish," she answered, finally removing her hand.

Before Dan could answer, the room stirred. Octavio Romanov had entered after the line had almost dispersed. As he neared Stephen's casket, Nancy moved toward him and gave him a formal hug. After a few quiet words, he sat down in the front row, but not before giving Dan a long glance.

As HBC's chairman, Octavio was not a passive investor, and the name Human Betterment Corporation was not a marketing gimmick. Octavio meant every word of it. Recruiting Stephen to lead HBC's genome-based research and product development had been the cornerstone of his efforts. No doubt Stephen's death had been a huge blow to Octavio on many levels.

Responding to what he thought was Nancy's cue, Dan gave Ava back to Dr. Alghieri and walked toward Octavio. On the way, Dan had to get around a priest who was making his way to the other side of the room. Dan was annoyed by the priest's careless navigation.

Reaching Octavio, Dan began to reintroduce himself when Romanov said, "Dan Lawson, isn't it? Stephen's death is a terrible tragedy. What a loss for his family and the world. He had so much yet to give to it."

"Yes, it is. I sure wish I knew what he was doing in that area of town or what could have happened to him," Dan said, hoping it would prod Octavio to share anything he might know about Stephen's professional relationships that could shed light on what he had been doing.

Without hesitation, Octavio answered, "Nor do I. I thought you might have an idea, but I see that you are as confused by it as I am. I'm sure we'll know soon enough, but whatever the answer is, it won't help his family. That is something I hope to be able to do."

"Of course I'll be doing the same," Dan said.

Octavio turned his head toward Stephen's body. "Good, good. Now, this might be an awkward time to talk about this, but I've been thinking about our earlier conversation, and I'd like to engage your services to assess my corporation's computer security and the attempted breaches. I can't help but speculate if there was any connection between them and what happened to Stephen. He told me you were the best at cybersecurity, and I'm not confident the police are equipped to deal with it."

For a brief moment, Dan considered the request. It would get him inside HBC and an opportunity to see what was going on there, and also give him cover to search for the cyber agents who had monitored the HBC network. Yet Stephen had made it clear he wasn't doing his DNA decoding work there. And working there would limit what Dan could do, while potentially exposing him as well.

"Let me think about it. Honestly, I'm sure I can recommend more capable people to do the work, but let me get back to you. For now, I want to focus on Stephen's family."

"Of course, but keep in mind that time is precious; the longer we wait, the less likely it will be that we'll find something useful."

"I agree. I'll get back to you in a few days," Dan answered, thinking Octavio wasn't the type of person you closed the door on.

"Good. Now I must go. I do not want to be a distraction, with all that Nancy has to deal with."

"I understand," Dan said.

It was now 9 p.m., time for the final prayers. It would be the last time Dan would see Stephen's face. He walked over to Nancy, who was talking with Stephen's parents. They greeted him tenderly, as they had earlier in the day, and then Nancy said, "We've been talk-

ing about it, and we'd like you to say the first reading at the funeral
tomorrow. We can pick it together."

Despite his discomfort, there was only one answer: "I would be
honored to do it."

Stephen's mother said, "Thank you. Stephen would have appreciated it." Looking across the room, she added, "And I'm so glad Kevin
Collins was able to make it. With his responsibilities, I wasn't sure
he'd be able to get here. Did you two have a chance to catch up?"

Dan was confused. He hadn't seen Kevin, hadn't even thought of
him in years. In high school, Kevin had been good friends with Dan
and Stephen. He was always more of an instigator than Dan and
Stephen, the one mostly likely to stir things up just to see what could
happen, the first to pull a risky prank. But the biggest shock Kevin
had up his sleeve was graduating with top honors from the Air Force
Academy and becoming a pilot. After that, he pursued a military career that took him across the world and away from old friends. Dan
hadn't heard anything about him in over a dozen years.

"When was he here? I never saw him," a still surprised Dan asked.

"He got here a few minutes ago," Nancy said.

Confused, Dan looked across the room. "I still don't see him.
What's he wearing?"

Nancy replied, "Black, with a white collar, of course. Even though
he has a high position in the Church in Rome, even before Francis,
he always wanted to dress more humbly."

Dan's already shocked systems were rattled further. With disbelief, he looked at the priest standing nearby and saw his face for the
first time. Sure enough, an older and more worn Kevin Collins looked
back at him.

Dan said, "Kevin? You—a priest? How? When?"

Grabbing Dan's hand, shaking it, then nodding toward Stephen's
casket, Kevin said, "You holding up okay?"

"It's devastating," Dan said.

"It's hard to believe this will be the last time the three of us will be
together in this life."

"As much as I'd like to right now, I don't believe in an afterlife.

You didn't once, either. What happened?" Dan replied politely, staring at Kevin's clerical collar, bewildered.

"I have to say the closing prayers now. How about dinner afterward?"

"I don't have much of an appetite, but I'll join you," Dan said.

"Good." With that Kevin stood next to Stephen's casket, looked at the room, blessed himself and Stephen's remains, then started reading from the Bible.

All Dan could think about was the surprises that kept coming and he wondered what possibly could be next.

Chapter 42

They sat in a dimly lit wood booth in a small, mostly empty, restaurant. Dan was drinking an India pale ale, while Kevin sipped from a glass of cabernet.

They had already exhausted basic small talk and were now sitting in silence. Perhaps Kevin was reluctant to say anything more, or perhaps it was his training in hearing confessions that told him to listen, but he seemed to be waiting for Dan to reveal something meaningful first.

It wasn't as though Dan lacked for things to say or ask. And the clerical collar wasn't an impediment. Dan was just worn out and felt like he was being beaten back down just as he had pulled himself off the canvas.

Finally breaking the quiet, Dan asked, "Were you in touch with Stephen much since college? He didn't mention you in our last talks."

"Not for a while. I had fallen off the beaten path for a long time, and when I reemerged, my new life was focused around contemplation and solitude. Once I reentered the everyday world, we did touch base every now and then."

"Falling off the beaten path is an interesting way of putting going from an Air Force pilot to a priest. It's going to be hard for me to call you Father Kevin."

"Actually, I go by Father Michael now. I wanted a completely fresh start and, to prepare for what I expected to face, I picked Michael as my new name. It's not a common practice, except for the Pope, but it's done."

"What made you change?" Dan asked. Whatever had happened to the man now known as Father Michael, it must have been traumatic.

"A lot. As you probably recall, I was a rather adventurous, worldly young man."

"I'd say that you made the pre-conversion Augustine seem like an Eagle Scout," Dan said with a smile that had a hint of a smirk.

"Thanks for the flattering reminder. As I recall, you weren't much different."

"Yes, but I didn't become a priest," Dan retorted.

"You're still young. No telling what you may become."

"There are some things I'd bet everything against."

"Perhaps. Still, it may not be wise to take too strong a stand. You may neither know nor understand your adversary nor what you are wagering," Kevin replied.

"I know myself and what's real," Dan replied.

"Do you?" Kevin said in a calm, knowing, soft voice.

"Weren't you supposed to be telling me about yourself? After that we can talk about me, if that's what you really want to do," Dan said, irritated.

"As you wish. Despite my behavior as a young man, I was accepted to the Academy. I studied hard, and I was happy in my service and sure of my mission. Then I flew a number of sorties in Serbia and Kosovo. One of my missiles went astray and killed innocent villagers. It was a malfunction, nothing I caused, but still I felt incredible guilt. I couldn't sleep. My flying became erratic. I was grounded, spent a lot of time with the chaplain, and then received an early honorable discharge. Still disturbed about what I had done, I volunteered for the Peace Corps. First I went to Kosovo to try to make amends. I lived quietly among people of the Islamic faith. Then I went to places in Africa where the poverty and conditions are like nothing you can imagine. The brutality of warring factions was worse than anything I had seen: young children taken and turned into vengeful creatures, people slaughtered like animals. God seemed completely absent. Then I met missionaries serving the destitute without regard for their own safety. The charity and love they demonstrated were inspiring, and somehow they were happy in the midst of all of this. After a few months there, I felt an incredible choice presented to me. I was being called. It seemed to me that God's will was clear. There was only one thing that I needed to do: decide whether I would heed the call or not. I did, and it brought me the peace and humanity I had desperately sought. I started learning how to forgive and how to accept forgiveness, how to suffer and sacrifice, how to humbly serve others. Few things are more powerful and yet more difficult to achieve than these, especially forgiveness."

Dan thought that he, too, would have struggled mightily with the enormous guilt from killing innocent people, especially children. He was sorry for Kevin and hoped that becoming Father Michael had helped him with the guilt.

"While I *am* very sorry about what happened to you, I'm surprised that becoming a priest in a religion with so many troubles is that helpful," Dan said, then wondered whether he had said too much to someone he hadn't seen in so long and didn't expect to see much of again.

"Yes, there are problems in the Church, and part of my job is to help deal with them. Because of my background, I've became what's known as a 'Vatican fixer,' sent to deal with pressing issues whatever, and wherever, they may be. What people don't realize is that the Church is not an organization with strong management oversight and control; certainly it issues edicts, but it lacks knowledge and power over local affairs and clergy. I'm helping to bridge that gap."

"You make it sound like you're the head of the Church's Special Forces unit. Is that what you became a priest to do, cover up its problems?"

"I don't cover up; I deal with and fix them," Father Michael said, with a flash of anger. "And that is only part of my job. I also lead ecumenical missions, reaching out to other faiths. And who are you to judge me? What authority do you appeal to in your life?"

"I prefer being an atheist with no authority rather than someone who causes suffering in the name of religion."

"I know lots of atheists who are great people. There is no doubt they do wonderful things for others without being told to do so by any religion. And I agree that lots of supposedly religious people use religion as a shield to justify themselves and harm others. The question isn't whether a person can be good without religion, but can they be good without God? It isn't the same thing." He took a sip of his wine. "Why are you so antagonistic toward religion, anyway?"

"I don't like the idea that others think religion gives them authority over me," Dan said. He had considered sharing his own spiritual struggles, but he wasn't sure where those were headed and wasn't ready to talk about them yet.

"Yeah, I get that. Not that some atheists' claims aren't a form of authority over others. But let's save the philosophical discussions for another day. We haven't seen each other in a very long time, and I'd like this to be nice enough so that we want to get together again, under much happier circumstances." Father Michael smiled then raised his glass, as if making a toast.

Dan raised his beer bottle and clinked it lightly against the wineglass. "That's a good idea. As you can probably tell, I have *things*—I won't call them issues—that I'm working through, and on top of them, Stephen's death has been a real blow."

Father Michael nodded wanly as dinner arrived.

After discussing and laughing over days gone by and adventures they'd since had, and catching up on goings-on with each other's families, Dan asked, "Do you know much about Stephen's work?"

"Only what was public knowledge. I read about it with interest, but we rarely talked about it. It was well over my head, though I found what little I did understand fascinating."

"You two kept enough in touch to fly over once you heard he'd died? Or did you happen to be here?"

"Nancy contacted me, and I came right away."

"You're concelebrating the funeral Mass, I presume."

"Of course."

"When did you last talk with him?" Dan asked.

"Several months ago. It was brief. Mostly about faith and science."

"What about faith and science? That's not been one of the Church's strong points," Dan said. Was Father Michael's statement an allusion to Galileo?

"Nothing that would be surprising to you. Just the age-old questions of the boundaries and relationship between them. He did mention that you two were estranged. What happened?"

Dan's expression of discomfort alone was enough to signal to Father Michael that Dan wasn't ready to talk about that. Quickly changing the subject, Father Michael asked, "How about you? What do you know about Stephen's work?"

"Not much, though I know he thought it would shed insight into human origin and what he considered God's role in that. Quite frankly, it concerned me, and made me think that he was having trouble reconciling science and religion. He also seemed to have been getting spiritual guidance. Do you know anything about that?" Dan was probing for any hint, as unlikely as he thought it was, due to the lack of his science background, that the man now known as Father Michael might be Stephen's Galileo.

"You know you can't ask a priest what someone confides in them," Father Michael said, smiling. Was he intentionally obscuring the important difference between regular conversation and the confessional? "Still, I will say that, outwardly, Stephen didn't seem to be spiritually troubled."

"I'm trying to help Nancy through this. Let me know if you think of something that could be useful. Stephen's death is mysterious, and helping to clear that up would surely help her," Dan said.

"Definitely. Why don't you come see me sometime in Rome?"

"Thanks, but I think I'll have a lot to do here for a long time."

"I could give you a great tour, show you things the public doesn't get to see."

Dan studied him. Was he offering more than he seemed to be? Did the secret of Galileo lay in Rome? But just as Dan was about to ask, Father Michael reached out toward the waiter and signaled for the check. "Tomorrow is going to be a tough day, and it's best we try to get some rest tonight."

"Yes, and I still have to prepare to give a reading," Dan said. He insisted on paying the check, and as they left, Dan thought he'd better keep an eye on Father Michael. There was much more than met the eye there. Who knew what his experiences had done to him and what side of the Galileo equation he was really on?

Chapter 43

*R*emember, man, you are dust and unto dust you shall return," said Father Michael, standing graveside at the head of Stephen's casket. People stood rows deep in all directions.

The sky was blue, the mourners subdued. The air was unusually crisp. On the grounds of the cemetery, the sounds of everyday life were too remote to be heard. Everything felt deadened.

Dan had awoken with the emptiness that had plagued him until recently. He fought it off by focusing on the vows he had made when he had found Stephen's body. And there were other people to care for. He had to concentrate on these things.

As Father Michael continued with the rite, Dan looked discreetly at the mourners for any sign of the mysterious Galileo. Up the hill, Dan saw a white van with a small antennae dish on top. One government authority or another was checking out the mourners, while using their visible presence as low-level security. It also confirmed that, as he expected, more than the police were now involved.

Soon enough, the authorities would complete their preliminary investigations. Before then, Dan knew, more substantial agencies than the regular police would question him at length about the connections between Viktor, Stephen, and himself. Already his mind was trying to anticipate lines of questioning and how he would respond.

Dan's focus snapped back on the funeral when Father Michael

made the sign of the cross. Nancy and Ava each placed a single
flower on the coffin; Stephen's parents did the same. Dan followed,
looking hard at the highly polished walnut coffin, thinking, *Is this
really it?*

They all stood there until everyone who had a flower had placed
it. Trish placed hers last.

The service concluded, Nancy and Ava, along with Stephen's
parents, walked toward the limo awaiting them. A small group, Dan
included, would soon gather at the Bishop house for a small meal and
subdued talk.

As Dan turned to walk toward his car, Father Michael put his
hand on Dan's arm and said, "You did an excellent job with the reading. I don't think I ever heard anyone read that passage with as much
feeling and desire. I believe your prayer will be answered."

Nancy and Dan had picked the reading together, from Ecclesiastes: *There is an appointed time for everything, and a time for every
affair under the heavens. A time to give birth, and a time to die; a time
to plant, a time to uproot the plant. A time to kill, and a time to heal; a
time to tear down, and a time to build up. A time to weep, and a time to
laugh; a time to mourn, and a time to dance.*

Dan stared at Father Michael and said, "I don't pray. I read it for
Nancy."

"I heard a heart searching for an answer that would make things
right."

"Kevin, I think everyone is searching today, including you. No one
likes to think that 'the fate of the sons of men and the fate of beasts
is the same; as one dies, so dies the other. They all have the same
breath, and man has no advantage over the beasts; for all is vanity,' as
all of this shows," Dan answered while sweeping his arm across the
vista of the cemetery.

Father Michael replied, "You remember your Ecclesiastes well.
•What about 'Sorrow is better than laughter. When the face is sad, the
heart grows wise'?"

"Then why are so few wise? Why is wisdom better than happiness?" Dan said quietly.

"You know what I would say to that. But not today. What are you going to do now?"

"I have a lot to make good on."

"I know you will," Father Michael replied.

"Now, that is an act of extreme faith."

"Don't be so hard on yourself," Father Michael said, extending his hand.

After shaking hands, Dan headed toward his car. He briefly considered walking up the hill to the van, check out its occupants, and get the preliminary discussions out of the way.

He decided against it. Now was the time for action. Dan had to get to Stephen's work before others did.

Chapter 44

Agent Evans surveyed the region around the blackened, flattened remnants of MIT's Plasma Science and Fusion Center. Buildings that had once flanked the sides of the center were now charred hulks. Dozens of personnel from various government agencies were carefully sorting and cataloging the debris. Vehicles from the FBI, the atomic energy commission, other unnamed national agencies, police department, and city morgue were scattered about. Medical examiners stood among the wreckage, listless. All that remained of those caught in the blast were scorched bone fragments, and it would take a long time to find them.

Walking within the path that had been cleared, Agent Evans approached three men in white environmental suits standing on a pile of masonry and twisted metal where the entrance to the reactor room had once stood. A large tent had been erected over the reactor area. An armband on one of the men identified him as Brooker, the ranking FBI agent on-site and leader of the forensic efforts.

"What have you found?" Evans asked.

"The National Laboratory folks are working on it. They're set up inside that black trailer over there. Come on, I'll introduce you," Brooker replied.

Evans spoke as they walked. "Whatever happened here stirred up a big-time hornets' nest. The Chinese, Russians, and many others, including key allies, have accused us of running a secret weapons program in violation of every imaginable treaty agreement, and putting our own citizens at risk to do it."

"Did we?" Brooker asked.

"Emphatically no, that's what I've been told by people who ought to know."

"Which doesn't answer the question of whether you believe them. How big of an issue is this?" asked Brooker.

"Big enough that you need to treat this as the biggest thing you've ever done. But it can't look that way. We need our visible actions to align with official statements that this was merely a research experiment gone unexpectedly bad once tritium was accidentally used."

Brooker walked up the trailer steps. "Let's see what the geeks have to say."

They stepped inside, and Agent Evans was greeted by a large security officer who checked his identification and clearance. The trailer was fifty feet long and twelve feet wide. There were no windows. A long desktop extended the length of the trailer behind the driver's seat. Semicircular couches with tables in the middle and pull-out beds lined the other side. Numerous computers and scientific instruments were mounted about the desktop.

Four scientists, three men and one woman, were working in a cluster in the center. A dozen additional scientists were working outside at the blast site.

Brooker introduced Evans to the scientists, explaining that Evans was leading the local investigation for the government, reporting directly to the director of Homeland Security.

Evans started by saying, "I'm not a scientist. I'm not going to pretend to be one. What I need to find out, as quickly as possible, is what caused the explosion and whether there is any evidence of foreign activity, tampering, or other action that could have deliberately caused it. Now, let's start with what you know."

The lead scientist, a thirtysomething woman with her auburn hair pulled back into a bun, said, "As designed, nothing in the center had the capability to produce the power, heat, and atomic signatures that were observed. The reactor's size and fuel, along with the limitations of its magnetic fields, meant it was capable only of low-energy experiments. It was also designed so that if it lost plasma containment, the reactions stopped. An explosion, of any magnitude, should have been impossible."

"But something did explode. So what happened?"

A second scientist, a thin, middle-aged man in poorly fitting clothes, said, "As you probably know, immediately before the explosion, one of our satellites detected an intensely bright beam of light bursting skyward for a fraction of a second. During the explosion, satellite readings, along with recordings taken at the scene, indicated the presence of a significant percentage of tritium. They also recorded a high number of particles and energy consistent with a much larger amount of fuel than the reactor should have been able to operate with."

Evans interrupted, "So what does all of this mean?"

The lead scientist jumped in, explaining, "It means that the mixture and amount of fuel was capable of producing the heat of the blast; however, the reactor should never have been fueled that way, and especially, tritium would never be permitted here. More significantly, the reactor wasn't physically capable of compressing this mixture enough to generate the fusion that actually took place. Finally, once fusion started, it should have damaged the reactor and stopped the reaction rather than ignite."

"The blackened hole out there says someone did figure out how to make the reactor to do it, at least once. Find out how."

The lead scientist replied tersely, "Agent Evans, I don't think you appreciate what we're saying about the science involved. The magnets did not have the power or strength to compress that fuel mixture anywhere near the degree needed. They would have had to have been forty times the size they were, and would have needed far more energy than was available in this city, even if materials with sufficient strength existed. According to the known laws of physics, the reaction that occurred was not possible with this reactor, or any other in existence."

"Well, that leaves just two possibilities: either your understanding of what occurred is wrong, or people in the fusion center figured out more than you know about physics. Now, how are you planning to find out which it is? The president is anxious to know."

"So are we. That is going to be difficult. All the labs records and computers were destroyed. Off-site computer backups don't contain anything related to this. The only things that stand out are what little is left of sixteen unusual metal boxes and coils that were arrayed around the outside of the reactor. Given their condition, we haven't been able to determine their purpose or operation. Maybe further analysis of the satellite recordings will help us. It would also be helpful if your agents can find backup copies of the computer files that the lab's scientists were using to operate their experiments and store their results. Without them, we may be at a dead end."

"We've been working hard on that, without much luck. It seems Viktor Weisman, in his last days, suddenly went to great lengths to protect the secrecy of his work," Evans answered.

"What about the tritium? Can you find out how that got here?" asked the lead scientist.

"It was reported stolen from another facility. The people who delivered it here have disappeared," Evans responded. How could they have so little to go on?

"Looks like you know just as much and as little as we do."

"The difference is that I'm not supposed to know the science."

"Without further information on what they did, what breakthrough they achieved, it will be impossible to figure out what happened," the scientist said.

"Keep at it. The hell pit outside is proof enough that there is an answer somewhere. We need to find it, fast, before others do," Evans said.

As he finished, the trailer door opened, and a security guard handed Evans a sealed packet. He opened it and saw pictures, taken by security cameras near the site of the explosion, of a woman who looked like she had been injured in the blast. The caption read *Sousan Ghardi* and identified her as a senior director of the fusion center. She was of Iranian origin, and the accompanying sheet had additional information about her background. An all-points bulletin was out on her, though the big fear was that she had already fled the country and might even be in Iran.

A second set of time-stamped pictures showed Stephen Bishop, taken by security cameras, along the route he had taken from his HBC office, to the fusion center, to his MIT office. Most were grainy. One showed Stephen being directed into a brown panel truck at the back of the Koch Building. The same type of truck that someone called in a terrorist tip on; the one that led the police to the scene of Stephen's death. Who did that, and why?

Evans didn't know what Stephen had to do with anything, but he had to have some connection. He was a friend of Dr. Weisman, and they had spent a lot of time together recently. Stephen had also been friends with Alex Robertson, whose death months earlier appeared suspicious to Evans's investigators when they looked into Stephen's associates. It was too much of a coincidence that both Weisman and Robertson were physicists who knew Stephen and that all three were now dead.

And then there was Dan Lawson, the only one who knew Stephen well, who also had spent time with him recently, and who was still alive. It was near time for Evans to have a frank conversation with his former protégé.

Chapter 45

This was probably Dan's last visit to Stephen's HBC office. He was there with Nancy to pick out whatever personal effects she wanted. Everything else would be discarded or left with HBC. In a little over twenty minutes, she had put tags on a few items and put others in a box for delivery to her home. It was hard to remove traces of Stephen from where he should have been but wasn't. Others could do that later, out of her sight.

Dan was also there looking for any leads to Galileo or the symbol Stephen had drawn. Nancy sat in Stephen's chair, looking around the room, as Stephen must often have done. Dan stood behind her, with his back to the window.

Octavio Romanov walked in. Putting his hand on Nancy's shoulder, he said sympathetically, "I'm sorry things were so disturbed in here. The government investigators went through everything before taking Stephen's computer and papers with them. It seems they are straining to connect him with the explosion across the river. They're grasping at straws, but that is what government types do. They would be better served trying to learn something of merit without causing you more pain."

In a weak voice strained with resignation, Nancy replied, "I don't care what they go through. They'll find that he had no connection to the explosion despite their barely concealed attempt to link him to it. He wasn't guilty of anything, he was the victim. You know how much Stephen valued his honor and reputation."

Octavio said, "Indeed I do. And they are well deserved. That's what attracted me to him in the first place. Our loss can't compare to yours, but is also deep. When I think about all the people he could have helped through the work he had yet to complete . . . Still, I think what he did achieve here was far greater than we've yet absorbed. Over the years ahead, the advancements that will come from it will be substantial."

Dan wasn't sure, but he thought Octavio might have glanced at him out of the corner of his eye as he finished speaking to Nancy about advancements to come. Paranoia was a hard trait to shake, especially when it had once been important in surviving as a field agent.

Nancy answered, "Thank you, and I hope so."

Dan remembered that Stephen had said that his main breakthrough had occurred in the adjoining conference room. Dan entered it, stood by the table, and faced the clean whiteboard.

Octavio followed him in and said, "Tell me, Mr. Lawson, what do you see?"

"What do you mean? The board is blank."

"I think you have the gift of great sight. That you can see what others cannot. Perhaps not right away, but in time."

"If I do, it's deserting me now."

"I'll get to the point. The government agents have confirmed what my information technology staff had previously told me. HBC has been under a sustained attack from hackers in China. No one has been able to locate the source, nor determine if we've been compromised and identify what may have been stolen. From what Stephen told me, and what I consider the exceptional instincts that have gotten me to where I am, I think you might be able to track down what's transpired. I'm going to do what I almost never do; make an offer a second time. I'll pay you far more than you can get for your services elsewhere. Perhaps you'll even find an important clue about happened to Stephen."

Dan didn't answer right away. Uncertain of Octavio and his intent, not sure whether he was being tested, he again wanted to show the proper consideration that the offer merited.

"From what I understand, corporate espionage is a costly and widespread Chinese and Russian activity that the US government has not been able to stop. What makes this different, and why do you think I can do more than has been done?"

"I question how much attention the investigators are paying to my requests. They doubt the potential connection between the cyber attacks and Stephen's death and are not putting enough effort into pursuing them. Then there was what I described to you upon our first meeting. An unusual pattern of computer network activity took place before Stephen's death. I think you have the capabilities to look into this properly, especially with your connections."

"I think you overestimate me."

Giving Dan a look that suggested suspicion, Octavio added, "Why wouldn't you give this a try?"

Dan answered, "I seriously doubt that I can find out anything that isn't already known. But I will consider your offer once I help Nancy settle things. *That's* my priority now. Meanwhile, if it's all right with you, I will talk to some of my old colleagues, and, unofficially, find out how this is being treated by government cybersecurity investigators. I'll also give you the names of companies that can assist you."

"That would be an acceptable beginning. It would be a shame if Stephen's legacy were tainted and his contributions lost."

Resisting what felt like bait, Dan said, "I'm sure we will find a way to preserve both."

"There is one more thing I'm disturbed about," Octavio continued. "I haven't been able to locate one of Stephen's outside collaborators. He abruptly left his position at The Broad Institute, a genome research enterprise here in Cambridge, several months ago. He also worked on Koch Industry–funded initiatives via MIT after working for us for a short period. His name is Sam Abrams, and I'm concerned about his safety. If you encounter him, please let him know that I'd like to help him with any trouble he may be in."

"Stephen never mentioned him to me, but if I run into him, I'll be sure to pass on your message," Dan answered. If a man with Octavio's resources couldn't find Sam Abrams, it was unlikely he could.

Octavio put his hand on Dan's back and shepherded him back into Stephen's office. Nancy was talking in quiet tones on her cell phone.

Hanging up, she said to Dan, "That was a government investigator. He wants to meet us at Stephen's MIT office in fifteen minutes. He's sent a car for us."

Octavio said, "Dan, it appears that your services are in demand by another party, one that carries far more weight than I do."

Dan nodded. Perhaps this was the start of finding out what had happened. Then he could start doing something about it.

Chapter 46

The black government sedan dropped them off in front of MIT's Koch Building. A government agent awaiting their arrival opened the car door for Nancy.

Dan exited on his own, careful not to show much interest in the area. Still, his jaw clenched as they were escorted to the building's back entrance, next to where Stephen had been taken. He wondered why they weren't using the front entrance. Was it a test to see how he reacted?

Dan and Nancy followed the agent up a flight of stairs and toward Stephen's office. Yellow police tape hung limply from both sides of the door.

A man sat at Stephen's desk, his head bent, sheets of paper on the desktop. Without looking up, the agent said, "Please have a seat, Mrs. Bishop." He then raised his head and looked hard at Dan. Agent Evans said, "Lawson, you remain standing."

Dan stiffened, and with a half-smile said, "What happened to the retirement age?"

"The younger folks couldn't do the job," Evans said.

Dan shot back, "The older folks couldn't teach what the prior generation taught them."

"I hear you've had a rough patch the last few months."

"Good news really does travel fast," Dan fired back.

"What was the problem?" Evans stated more than questioned, as though he knew.

"Just needed to find something to do. Got plenty now."

Nancy's head swiveled back and forth as the two spoke.

Agent Evans looked at Nancy and said, "Lawson was one of my first pupils. A penchant for misplaced idealism and disregard for risk landed him a desk job."

"I thought it was a lack of intelligence in the intelligence section that led to my transfer."

Sternly, Agent Evans said, "I hope you're using your intelligence now." Turning his attention back to Nancy, Evans continued, "Mrs. Bishop, we have more information on Dr. Bishop's movements. I'd like to see if either of you can shed light on them."

Nancy nodded slowly and said, "Anything to find out what happened to Stephen."

"Thank you. I'll keep to the main points. The Friday of Memorial Day weekend, Viktor Weisman visited your husband in this office. Over the next several days, Dr. Bishop and Dr. Weisman communicated with each other multiple times. Tuesday night, Dr. Weisman and seven others were working at his research center. The explosion that took place was visible from Dr. Bishop's HBC office. Dr. Bishop headed over to the site. Security cameras show him crossing the bridge, dropping something and picking it up, then arriving on the scene of the raging fire, in the cordoned-off area, and then heading over here."

Nancy interrupted. "I'm confused about the continued attempts to link Stephen's death to the explosion and Viktor Weisman. They were just friends. Of course he would go to the site to see what happened and check if Viktor was safe."

Looking to deflect the line of questioning, Dan broke in and said, "In the intelligence community, nothing that has the remotest appearance of a connection to something else is ever considered a coincidence, regardless of evidence. Even when a theory is dismissed, someone is always ready to revive it. Except when it matters—then it's ignored."

Evans shot an irritated look at Dan. "I'm sorry, Mrs. Bishop, but I have to ask these questions. We have a very serious ongoing situation. Can we continue?"

Nancy said, "Yes. Whatever he did, I'm confident Stephen only acted appropriately."

Picking up where he left off, Evans said, "A short distance from the site of the explosion, security video show two men appearing to follow Dr. Bishop while attempting, but not completely succeeding, to stay out of range of the cameras. At some point, Dr. Bishop seemed to become suspicious. Once inside this office, he called you using this phone. Right after that, Dr. Bishop left this building using the back exit. Two men appeared to surprise Dr. Bishop and escorted him into the back of a brown panel truck, similar to a UPS vehicle."

Nancy gasped. Evans stopped to give her a glass of water and time to absorb the revelation that her husband had most likely been abducted. Dan wondered if any of the security cameras had picked him up outside the building, despite his own precautions.

After Nancy sipped the water, she asked, "Have you identified the two men?"

"We're working on it. From here, Dr. Bishop was driven to the site where his body was found. Shortly thereafter, someone placed a call to 911 reporting a suspicious truck with propane tanks inside it at the same site. The call was meant to generate an emergency response to the scene as quickly as possible, perhaps with the intent to get Stephen out safely. Video shows the presence of other vehicles at the site as well. All except the panel truck left in a hurry right after the call went out over the police radios. An examination of the site indicates that Dr. Bishop ran from one location in the basement of the building to the spot where he was found. Footprints indicate that he had jumped several times at nearby windows. It looks like he was trying to escape when the scaffolding broke loose and parts of the damaged foundation fell on him."

Dan watched Nancy steel herself and take another sip of water while Evans waited. Little of this was new to Dan. He was waiting for Evans to say something that would be hard for Dan to explain—perhaps that a security camera had an image of him from somewhere he had been that night. Dan knew something was coming.

Continuing, Evans said, "Constructing this timeline was straightforward, though it took time to examine the video and other records. But we're still left with many questions. Lawson, what do you think they are?"

"Aren't they obvious?" Dan answered, recognizing that his answers would be assessed for signs of information he hadn't shared as well as his earnestness to help.

"Probably, but with your knowledge of Dr. Bishop, you might be able to shed better light on what transpired," Evans replied matter-of-factly.

"Well, then, who followed Stephen and why? Did Stephen know them? Did they abduct him, or did he go willingly? What took place in the building's basement? Why did they leave without Stephen? Was he dead or dying before they left?" At the last words, Dan's voice lowered, then he said, "And of course, who placed the call to 911, and why?"

"That's right. Let's start with the last one. What can you tell me about that, Lawson?"

"Nothing. Got anything on the other missing pieces?" Dan replied. Nancy looked at him.

"Mrs. Bishop, what about you? Do you have any idea who might have placed the call? Records indicate you spoke with Dan Lawson around the same time."

"That's not new information. I told the police in the very beginning that I had called Dan when I became worried about Stephen. I don't know who placed the 911 call," Nancy answered, her voice choked with tears.

Dan walked over and put his arm around her. He looked at Evans and asked, "What more do you need from her?"

"We'd like her to take a good look around and see if anything's missing or there's anything unusual."

Composing herself, Nancy said, "That's fine. I can do that."

"Thank you," Evans said, getting up and walking toward the door, a stack of papers in his hand. Looking back over his shoulder, he said, "Lawson, let's give Mrs. Bishop her privacy as she looks through Dr. Bishop's office."

Dan followed him into an adjoining room.

Evans pulled several pages from the stack he was carrying, and handed them to Dan. They were pictures of a woman, stooped in pain, outside the burning fusion center. Pointing at an enlarged image of her head, Evans asked, "Do you recognize her?"

"No. Who is she?"

"Sousan Ghardi, an Iranian-born scientist. She was a director at the lab and, as far as we know, the only survivor of the blast."

"Why *are* you trying to connect Stephen to this?"

"Too many coincidences and a worsening situation. The lab explosion is causing serious international problems. High-yield fusion took place in a reactor that wasn't supposed to be capable of it. Fuel was used that shouldn't have been. This was a civilian program gone rogue. We don't know how they did it. Our adversaries think that the US pulled a fast one with a new weapons program and got caught. Tensions are dangerously high and getting worse. Spooks and goons are running rampant. Middle Eastern countries feel threatened by a new power program that could kill world oil dependency. All of this is off-the-record and not to be shared with anyone."

"I take it you think this Sousan Ghardi played a role in this?"

"It's one of our stronger hypotheses. It would help a whole lot if we could ask her about it."

Evans handed Dan another picture and said, "At a different location, we got a good shot of someone we think was near the scene at the time of Stephen Bishop's death. You recognize him, don't you?"

It was a solid, hard-looking man, possibly with eastern European features. His face was fuzzy, though the image was sharp enough to show a prominent scar. Before Dan could look closer, Evans said solemnly, "We crossed paths with him early in your career. He's known internationally as Sergei."

With a shocking flash of recognition, Dan involuntarily reached for the scar on his left arm, recalling the KGB agent, the pleasure he took in killing Pavel and Katya Sarasov. That night, Sergei had the coldest look Dan had ever seen.

"Yeah, it's the same guy," Evans said. "You got anything we can use to nail him?"

"No, but you can bet I'll be looking. He's another one who has got a lot to answer for," Dan said sharply, still determined to keep Stephen's work out of Evans's reach.

"Stay out of this unless you want to wind up like your friend. Sergei is not someone you mess with and survive, especially twice," Evans warned.

"Don't forget, I bailed you out of a few jams, including that night," Dan remarked.

"It's gratitude for that, and probably misplaced trust, that keeps me from letting others in my agency have their shot at you now. Make sure you don't do anything that makes either of us regret that."

Briefly, Dan considered telling Evans what he knew, but Dan was sure Stephen had died trying to protect the secrecy of his work. Dan had an obligation to fulfill, and it began with finding Galileo.

Before Dan could reply, Nancy walked in said, "Nothing seems amiss, Agent Evans. Stephen didn't spend much time here after he took the HBC position."

"Thank you, Mrs. Bishop. Lawson, I'm sure we'll be touch."

That they would be, soon, and asking tougher questions, Dan thought.

Chapter 47

DAY 11
EARLY MONDAY MORNING

Dan arrived at the Bishops' house as the sun was rising above the treetops, replacing the shortening shadows with its bright light.

Inside the house, a curtain of darkness was descending. Dan heard Nancy's deep sobs in the study. She looked up from the window seat and tried to speak as Dan entered the room. Her lips moved in only small, quivering contortions.

Dr. Alighieri was there with her arm around Nancy's sagging shoulders. For the first time, Dan looked at Trish without feeling dissociated, like there was something that had shifted reality around her. Instead, she looked like her substance had changed and she was no different from anyone else—just as ordinary, just as broken, as Nancy. There were tears at the corners of her eyes, and sadness had cast its pall on her as well.

With slow movements, Trish walked over to Dan and whispered near his ear, "Ava's cancer has returned. It shouldn't have, but it did, appearing unnaturally fast in her bloodstream. She's in the hospital now. We don't know. We just don't know." He could tell that Ava was not merely another patient for her.

His body went cold. He couldn't hear anything. Color went out of his vision.

After a moment, Dan gathered himself, sat down next to Nancy, and put both arms around her. She tilted her head against the left side of his chest, as though his heartbeat could compensate for the life she felt draining out of her world.

In a few minutes, exhausted by the effects of her sobbing, she breathed regularly, sat up with stoic posture, and wiped the last tears away.

Trish's eyes alternated slowly between Nancy and Dan.

After taking and holding a deep breath, Nancy said, "Dan, the last time Ava was sick, Stephen was working on getting a treatment that was a potential miracle cure, in case all else failed. We were lucky and didn't need it then. We may now. Stephen and I need you to find it for our daughter's sake. You were a good field agent once, and I'm sure you know people who can help. I don't know how much more Ava can suffer, or what I'll do if she doesn't get better. Will you help us?"

Again, Nancy spoke of Stephen in the present tense, as though he still existed. Whether or not that was true, Dan now had another obligation to fulfill, another answer to find. For a long time, his life hadn't felt valuable or important. Even though that had only started to change, he was completely willing to sacrifice everything for Nancy and Ava. That purpose, that intent—even if it was solely temporal and transitory—filled him with more determination and energy than he had ever had before. He would not allow fear and despair to drag him down, nor keep him from what he needed to do.

"Of course, I'll start immediately," Dan said, thinking of the organization that Stephen had mentioned was helping with foreign development of potential treatments.

"Thank you."

"What do I need to do? Contact places that might have it?"

"Trish has already done that. None of them know about it, including HBC. I don't know how to say this, though I don't think it will be a much of a surprise to you, but Stephen was involved with non-conventional researchers. He wouldn't tell me more. One of them must know something about the treatment."

Without acknowledging what he knew, Dan asked, "Where should I look and how will I recognize it?"

"I don't know." She sighed. "Perhaps something in Stephen's journals will guide you. Talk to his associates. Maybe someone at the National Institutes of Health will know something. Keep in touch with HBC. They're still looking. Or maybe you have other information sources that can be helpful," Nancy said, referring to his intelligence sources. "And Trish will help, too. She was working with Stephen to set up trials to test the treatment once he got it. She may be able to recognize it. "

Dan thought of Stephen's work and the information he was trying to decode. He wondered what Nancy knew about that. He was also mulling over what he had read in Stephen's journals, the places he'd have to visit trying to find Galileo, the chances he would have to take, his past discomfort with Trish.

Turning toward Trish, Dan said, "Thank you, but I work better alone. I have unconventional methods and need to be able to move fast. Besides, you'll obviously have to stay at the hospital and take care of Ava. When I find it, I'll get it to you right away."

As Trish started to reply, Nancy interrupted and said, "Dan, your chances of success are far greater with her than without. She knows Ava's cancer, has research experience, and can evaluate medical information. You can't do any of that. And she can supervise Ava's treatment from anywhere, at any time."

Too true, Dan thought. For some reason, Dan had felt Galileo would provide him with whatever missing information Dan needed to access Stephen's work and whatever could come from that, including a treatment. But he couldn't count on passively waiting for someone who might or might not appear, whenever that might be. Or if, in the end, this Galileo would know anything about the treatment Ava needed.

"What about your hospital responsibilities?" Dan said to Trish.

"I'm on sabbatical for the summer. Years of nonstop, intense learning followed by a practice in pediatric oncology takes its toll."

"It will probably involve traveling and meeting with unusual people and organizations." Thinking of Sergei, and others, Dan added, "And it may get intense at times."

"I climb rock walls," Trish replied with a stone face.

Nancy added, "Good. You'll need those skills working with Dan."

The words sounded to Dan like echoes of Stephen.

"One more thing," Dan added. "I'm going to clear my friend's name."

"I know you will. The best friendships, like yours, transcend death," Nancy said as she stood up and gave Dan a hug.

"Let's continue this conversation later, after I've had time to think," Dan said as he headed toward the basement. Nancy and Trish followed as he walked downstairs and into the theater room.

Chapter 48

Using the tools of his former trade, Dan completed an electronic sweep of the theater room. With what had transpired, it was reasonable to think one of the agencies and operatives that was investigating Stephen's death might have placed a bug.

Satisfied that everything was clean, Dan closed the door and sat down facing Nancy and Trish. Nancy was as composed as she could manage, though the edges of her body seemed to sag. Trish looked ready for action.

Looking at Trish, Dan asked, "How will you be able to recognize the treatment Stephen spoke of, even if we're lucky enough to find it?"

"To prepare for potential medical trials, Stephen told me enough about its characteristics that I'll be able to review and evaluate its possible effectiveness. Apparently, it's only been tried a few times in confidential, unauthorized trials in other countries where US scientists don't have access."

Dan replied, "Do you know where he expected to get the treatment from?"

"No. He said he was pulling a lot of strings, and it might come back on the people helping him if they knew. I accepted that," Trish answered.

"As well you should have," Nancy said, with enough hesitation and waver in her voice that Dan could tell she was trying to convince herself of this as well.

Trish asked Dan, "Do you know anything about who outside of HBC Stephen was working with?" Her narrowed eyes took hold of Dan and briefly gave him the same probing feeling as when they had first met. He shrugged off the invasive sensation as he thought of what to say.

He surprised himself with a more direct answer than he had intended. "Stephen told me that he had found information in DNA that could transform our knowledge of life. He didn't say what it was and I haven't seen it. He told me that someone outside of HBC may contact me about Stephen's work. I have no idea who, when, or where." Looking at Trish, he continued. "A little while ago, I thought that could have been you, but now I know that it isn't."

He paused to gauge their reactions. Nancy had a knowing look, with an upturned eyebrow that hinted that she was aware that he knew more than he was telling. He couldn't read Trish; her face was serious but betrayed nothing. Though he had said it wasn't her, he wasn't certain. He'd keep a close watch on her for any clues.

Going on, Dan said, "I've been trying to find his other work files, without success. If there was something at HBC, no one has mentioned it, and I think we would know by now. The only other thing we have to go on is his journals—and Trish, don't tell anyone I have them or they could be taken. I've read parts and found indications of Stephen's progress at different points, though the journals don't describe anything in detail. One thing that does stand out is that about fifteen months ago, Stephen visited a series of places that appear linked to whatever breakthrough he thought he had made. They're all over the country, but one is right here in Boston. Unless anyone has better ideas, I plan to start by visiting the Harvard Museum of Natural History's evolution exhibit later this morning."

Nancy's eyes narrowed. "I don't understand what that would have to do with modern medical treatment."

"Nor do I," said Trish.

"Well, it's nearby, we have to start somewhere, and it seemed to have had a big impact on him. Perhaps someone there hooked Stephen up with someone else," Dan said. While Ava's well-being was his top interest, he also wanted to find out what Stephen had decoded and how he had done it. Perhaps the places he'd visit would be helpful with that, and maybe Galileo would be at one of them.

"What are the other places?" Trish asked.

"One is the Salk Institute in San Diego. They are a worldwide leader in biological research, so that makes sense. A few places are obscure conference centers that Stephen just called. Others are the types of research centers you'd expect him to work with. Another is the Discovery Institute, headquarters of what's referred to as the intelligent design movement. They are not a serious scientific center. I don't know what Stephen could have wanted with them. But perhaps they referred Stephen to one of the nearby research centers."

Nancy said, "You plan on visiting all of them?"

Dan said, "I'll start with the ones that seem to have the strongest connections to what we are looking for or that seemed to have made a significant impact on Stephen. Going in person will be important for getting their attention and assessing their reactions."

Standing up, Dan said to Trish, "If you're coming, let's get started. We have a lot of ground to cover."

"I can grab my things in a few minutes," Trish answered.

"If I'm going to be successful, I'm going to have to try to get into Stephen's head, find out what he was thinking. That will require understanding the impact of his religious views on his actions, and it won't be easy for me. I'll need all the help from you that I can get," Dan said to Nancy.

"If anyone can do it, you can," Nancy said.

"I don't know about that, but I'll give it everything," Dan answered.

As he turned to leave, Nancy hugged him and whispered, "Stephen trusted you for a reason. I'm sure you'll find out why."

Chapter 49

"Tell me again why we're here," Trish asked, standing beneath a whale skeleton suspended from the ceiling.

"Well, according to Darwin and everything in this exhibition hall, we're the result of an accumulation of a very large number of very small, successful genetic changes over very long periods of time, filtered by natural selection that happens to align with what's beneficial and, without any evidence to the contrary, is purposeless and unguided. If all of this is true, there is no 'why'; only 'how' has relevance," Dan replied matter-of-factly.

They were inside the great mammal hall within the Harvard Museum of Natural History. Skeletons filled the lower level of the long, rectangular room. A second-level balcony, containing displays of birds, ran along the room's perimeter, leaving space for the whale skeleton. Other halls featured arthropods, dinosaurs, flowers, and minerals. One hall focused on the animals and plants that Darwin studied when developing his theory of evolution.

At this time of day, few other people were present. In the quiet of the hall, Dan reconsidered his answer to Trish. At first, he had thought of saying *Damned if I know, Didn't think about it for most of my life,* or *That's what I'm trying to find out,* but they were flip answers that the Dan he now wanted to leave behind would have given. Instead, he had chosen a response that, while arguably truthful, was a diversion from what she had asked.

Without saying anything, Trish tilted her head sideways and gave him a look that said she was disappointed.

Dan would have preferred an angry look rather than one that left him nothing to react to other than his own behavior.

"Okay, I'm sorry. The truth is pretty much what I said earlier. Somewhere along the line, Stephen collaborated on his work with someone outside of HBC. I think that person may have the information we need. I don't know anything more than that, so I'm checking out places mentioned in Stephen's journals. They're long shots and could all be a waste of time. You might want to reconsider your decision."

As he said this, Dan felt an odd combination of wishing Trish would stay back and hoping she'd insist on coming along. He didn't want to endanger anyone in case Stephen's abductors came looking for him, but there was a presence around Trish that he now wanted to understand instead of avoid.

"Nancy asked me to go with you, so that is what I'm going to do," Trish said with finality.

"If that's what you think is best."

"It is. Now, who are we here to meet and why?" Trish said quietly but firmly.

"The director of the evolution exhibit. He was here when Stephen had a discussion with Claudine Rudner, a renowned biology professor and vigorous defender of Darwinian evolution. Something they discussed influenced Stephen's thinking and set him out on a direction that altered his research. Neither the director nor Rudner is a medical researcher, so the only thing Stephen could have gotten out of the discussion is other contacts."

"And you got all of this from Stephen's journals?" Trish asked.

"Yes."

"I'd like to see them. I'll be more help if I know what we're looking for. There's also a chance I might see something that seemed insignificant to you that may mean something to me."

"Sure, after I'm done scanning them. I can't carry them around," Dan said. He didn't want to give the journals to anyone until he knew more about Stephen's work and had found Galileo.

"Why don't you give me one while you go through the others? That'll speed things up."

"They need to be kept secure. Other than Nancy, no one knows they exist. If government investigators find out, they'll take them," Dan said.

"Keeping them secure is a good idea, given we were followed here," Trish said nonchalantly.

Dan was surprised, as he thought the car that had trailed them, containing what looked like two government types, had done a decent job of staying out of sight. He had spotted it, but he was trained to do so. Laughing, he said, "I'm impressed. What tipped you off?"

"A dark sedan made an unusual series of turns and parked farther away from the entrance than needed. The men in the car are dressed like the investigators that were in the Bishops' house once when I was there."

"You have sharp eyes," Dan said.

"I've always had strong vision," Trish said. Dan tried to figure out whether she meant more than mere sight, or was it just the way she said things?

Dan smiled and looked at his watch. "We should head over to the director's office."

As they started to walk, Trish asked, "What are your thoughts on evolution?"

"When I was younger, I accepted it without thinking much about it or understanding its implications. After all, what effect did it have on my day-to-day living? Later, when I had stopped believing in dogmatic religion and applied more critical thinking, I realized evolution was incompatible with a theistic god, the only answer that could make sense to me. Given the evidence on hand for one and not the other, I completed my journey to atheism."

"I'm not religious, but it seems like you hit an intellectual dead end," Trish said. "Why couldn't a God have directed evolution without it being visible, or just start it and let it run its course? Just because things change over time doesn't mean God doesn't exist. "

Dan knew he had to back up. "The abbreviated phrase 'evolution' is misused and misunderstood. It should go by the full name of how it is intended and used today: materialistic, neo-Darwinian evolution. No one is arguing over whether things change. The argument is over what causes the changes and whether final intent is involved. But, to answer your question, you can't have a materialistic process governed only by the inviolable laws of science and a deity who created everything from the beginning according to explicit intent, unless each and every molecule in the whole universe was arranged so specifically, from the big bang onward, that uninterrupted *natural* processes led to our specifically intended existence, without any apparent divine intervention. We're talking the ultimate stacked deck of cards of unimaginable complexity.

"However, via quantum mechanics and probabilities, science rejects this idea as too extraordinary, except for all but the most fervent believers. Now, of course a God could have intervened throughout an evolutionary process in an undetectable manner, but we couldn't tell and that would not be strictly natural selection. Since science says natural mechanisms are sufficient to explain how we got here, a God did not intervene. So it's either strictly Darwinian evolution or God, not both. And if it's Darwinian evolution, the existence of a God would be of no consequence to us."

"You know a lot more than most people."

"Stephen gave me a lot to read."

"What did he think?"

"That the complexity of the human genome argues against unguided evolution, that the genome manifests divine intent," answered Dan.

"And what do you think now?"

"I don't know. I've seen no reason to believe in God or evidence of His benevolent work. Yet there are things I can't explain, and I've found atheism, taken to its logical conclusion, unlivable. That doesn't mean it's false, only that I've found it wanting. Forced by circumstances, and Stephen, I now intend to find truth wherever it leads. I've got a long ways to go and have a lot to learn," Dan was surprised to hear himself say.

"That's unexpectedly humble of you. And humility is the first fruit of wisdom."

"Thanks, I seem to be hearing that a lot these days. But humility only matters if wisdom matters, which it does only if we matter and there is a God that matters, meaning unguided Darwinian evolution is wrong, and we are more than just matter."

"It's impressive that you are willing to consider that you have been fundamentally wrong about something really important about you and life. Few people can do that."

"Most people are too focused on today, or carry too much baggage, to consider anything different than their unexamined beliefs. Until very recently, that was me," Dan said, soulfully, unable to stop sadness in his own life, Stephen's death, and Ava's illness, from breaking the surface of his stoicism. Continuing, Dan said, "I didn't mean to say all of this. We have more important things to do."

"It's fine. It's better to feel too much than too little."

Dan didn't know how to respond to Trish's comment, so he changed the subject. "What do you think about Darwinian evolution?"

"Like the younger you, I never questioned or truly understood it. It was simply an interesting fact that had no impact on me. I already felt the worth of each person—in your words, that everything does matter. That's been enough for me. What I haven't understood, perhaps, is how things tie together. Like you, I hope to learn," Trish explained. She paused. "Stephen really set that out in front of both of us, didn't he?"

"Yes, he did," Dan answered, wondering if it was just Stephen, or if somehow Stephen was right about things being orchestrated in ways beyond normal visibility.

"For now, let's focus on Ava. We may find that other stuff is wrapped up in it, but we can deal with it then," Dan said. He hoped they would indeed find much more.

"Sounds like a plan," Trish said with an enthusiasm that Dan found heartening.

They had now arrived in the evolution gallery and were headed to the director's office. As they walked through the gallery, Dan stopped at an animated exhibit called *Tree of Life,* showing the evolutionary branches and the ancestry and relationships of major species over the course of hundreds of millions of years. Dan was amazed that scientists had been able to construct it. He examined the exhibit closely, looking for anything like the symbol Stephen had drawn in the dirt.

"It's remarkable," Trish said.

"I have to say that under different circumstances, I'd get a kick out of being in Cambridge, between Oxford and Divinity Streets, discussing Darwinism. Rather fitting, all things considered," Dan said.

Dan had decided to approach the museum's director using a ruse of Stephen's having authored a book. "Thank you for meeting with us on such short notice, Dr. Erving. As I said when we spoke earlier, Stephen Bishop was writing a book on the origin of the human genome. Given the way today's media work, the book's sales prospects, and therefore its benefit to Stephen's survivors and other interested parties, are improved by a quick publication." He shrugged apologetically. "One of his chapters that was not finished pertained to a meeting that took place here fifteen months ago with Dr. Bishop, yourself, and biologist Claudine Rudner. It had a big impact on Dr. Bishop and is prominently featured in his book. It speaks admiringly about you and this museum. Do you recall the meeting?"

"Tragic death, Dr. Bishop's. What a terrible loss. I'm honored to hear that he wrote well of us," Dr. Erving said with obvious pride and importance. "And it was a memorable meeting. Hard to forget, really. I don't think Dr. Rudner enjoyed it by the end, though. And I had my own doubts about some of the things being said."

"From Stephen's notes, it appears the focus was gene encoding and expression."

"That's right. Dr. Bishop wanted to discuss the evolutionary mechanisms and implications for the processes by which the DNA template controls biological processes. At this point in our understanding of the origin of life, there can be an apparent 'chicken or the egg'–type problem."

"Can you please explain that?" Dan said.

"As Dr. Bishop said, it's hard to envision the processes whereby DNA, or even just self-replicating RNA, that have no informational meaning by themselves, consisting of seemingly random strings of text from a four-letter base-pair alphabet, independently came together with mechanisms that could turn sections of those strings of letters into something that biochemical processes, which also came about independently, can use to create living species. Of course, we'll understand this eventually. Right now our knowledge of it is in its infancy."

Interrupting, Trish said, "The chicken and egg part is how can code for something that doesn't exist come into being before that thing exists, or that thing come into existence before the code that will be subsequently used to create it, exists?"

Dan was impressed by her quick mind, but, given her occupational success, that shouldn't have been a surprise.

Dr. Erving continued, "It's an *apparent* chicken-or-the-egg problem. Anyway, there are two main concerns that people raise. The first is all the elements needed to make an organism, such as the different components of cells, developing independently and then coming together at once to create that first organism. Of course, that still leaves the question of how those first components developed when there was no means of replication, and therefore no natural selection. The second concern is how all the elements needed for the first life would have had to develop incrementally together. The challenge here is needing a combination of a large number of elements, that had no previous functions, just assembling themselves into a functioning whole, that can self-replicate, and then change incrementally, radically, over time without breaking what first worked."

"It makes the Darwinian evolution of species look like a trivial exercise," Trish said.

"Ultimately, it's a question of the law of large numbers; get enough chance occurrences and anything can happen. Get a universe full of a huge number of planets, and life was inevitable," Dr. Erving said.

"Wow. I never knew this. It's incredible stuff. All I read in the press is about the origin of a few organic molecules, and everything just follows from that," Dan said, downplaying the knowledge he had recently developed and his own beliefs.

Dr. Erving said, "Journalists are writing for the masses and tend to simplify things."

"Still, it's a big challenge to our understanding of how we got here. Could it lead to the idea that the Darwinian view of human origin is incomplete?" Dan said.

"It's just a gap in our knowledge, not an actual finding that contradicts anything. There are a number of major origin-of-life initiatives working to figure this out now. We have a big one here at Harvard—not that creationists wouldn't try to exploit the gap of what we currently can explain. Which is why we don't talk about it."

"So how did Stephen's discussion with Rudner go? I'm looking to fill in gaps in the notes pertaining to what Stephen called algorithmic genetic expression. Was that discussed?" Dan asked.

"Yes, that was at the heart of what became a contentious discussion. But it started quietly at first. Stephen asked how there were moments in evolutionary history where large numbers of new species and body plans seemed to appear spontaneously at the same time, in potential conflict with evolutionary theory, according to which mutations accumulate gradually and species change slowly. In other words, evolution is supposed to be extraordinarily slow, yet there are periods where a large number of things happened very, very fast, at least in relation to the evolutionary time scale. The most prominent of these spurts is the Cambrian explosion. Dr. Rudner responded that the Cambrian explosion was probably preceded by a long history of evolving organisms that did not fossilize."

"What about where the fossil record shows there was very little change in species over long periods of time and then all of a sudden new species arose, some seemingly without transitional species? Dr. Bishop referred to this in his notes," Dan said.

"Dr. Rudner explained to Dr. Bishop that species, in a stable environment, don't change much over time. But when something in the environment changes that creates a distinct advantage for features that present species don't have or can't fully exploit, new species will quickly arise with those features to occupy the new niches," Dr. Erving answered.

"This implies that the rate of beneficial genetic mutations is, relatively speaking, always very fast, but that natural selection kills off mutations before they can take hold when there is no niche to fill. It also means there should be a decent number of transitional species in the fossil records. Have either of these been observed?" Dan asked.

"The lack of transitional fossils is indicative of periods of fast evolution. Fossilization is a very-low-probability occurrence, since organisms have to die in an environment that preserves their bodies long enough for sediments to encase them and minerals to be absorbed into the remnants of the bodies. You need a very large number of members of a species, over a long period of time, to get just one fossil," Dr. Erving responded.

"So what you're saying is that evolution happen so fast, that even though there were other fossils from the same period, there were too few of the transition species to have left *any* fossils. The biggest activity happens off-camera, so to speak," Dan offered. Seeing the director visibly tense by how he explicitly stated things, potentially exposing issues with Darwinian theory, Dan added, "I'm not taking a position, just repeating what I think you're saying. Evolution in actuality is always a fast process held in check most of the time. Is the rate of observed genetic mutations fast enough to support the implied speed of overall rate of species mutations?"

"They clearly have to be fast enough. Further research will show that they are."

"Actually, doesn't present research show that error correction mechanisms *prevent* mutations, greatly slowing down the possible rate of evolution? Was that when Dr. Bishop mentioned potential alternative evolutionary mechanisms? Did that cause things to get heated with Dr. Rudner?"

Dr. Erving stood up and began to pace.

"Summarizing for the sake of brevity, Dr. Bishop presented his theory that a complex algorithm was involved in expressing DNA and claimed that it was consistent with the idea of punctuated equilibrium and convergent evolution. He even thought it could explain it, because the changes of what he called a few bits of input information, processed by the existing mechanisms, would lead to parallel and fast evolutionary changes without the need for a large number of gradual changes, as you noted. Dr. Rudner was stunned."

Waving his arms for effect, he continued, "Then the wheels almost came off when Dr. Bishop asked Dr. Rudner about the potential implications of what looked like a program with input variables whereby changes to the variables seem to happen in a coordinated fashion across species. Although he seemed to be basing it on data, I have to say Dr. Bishop took positions that I thought were out of the mainstream. Things were veering into the realm of faith rather than science, injecting design intent and interaction into a godless, I mean unguided, process. Despite that, I enjoyed the conversation and let it go on, as much to watch Dr. Rudner's reactions as anything else. Stephen was cornering Dr. Rudner, really needling her in a way I hadn't seen anyone do before. I thought it was long overdue. I have to admit that I liked that."

Dan said, "Dr. Rudner is well known for her scientific knowledge and beliefs about evolution. Why did you enjoy Stephen challenging her? Don't you share those beliefs?"

"Quite simply, Dr. Rudner takes positions that are inherently contradictory to virtually everyone but herself. She tries to have it both ways and plays to whatever audience she is in front of. She claims that God created evolution but then that God left evolution alone to create us, unintended; that God's intent was no intent other than evolutionary processes. She'll testify in court against intelligent design while debating atheists about the existence of the Judeo-Christian God. It seems like she is saying that God exists but didn't do anything and didn't leave any traces if He did. She's one of the few I know of who argues that position. I don't believe in God, don't know much about Judaism or Christianity, but I don't see how you can believe God exists but didn't explicitly want humans to exist and didn't arrange for that outcome."

"It is rather hard to say that we evolved unguided from apes yet are afflicted with original sin of our own collective making," Dan said.

"You would think so."

"Still, isn't Dr. Rudner popular in the evolution community, even referring to well-known atheists as her good friends—not that they say the same in return?" Dan was glad he had done his homework.

Dr. Erving said, "People in that community tolerate her because she serves a purpose in making evolution palatable to the religious. She's the nose of the camel in the tent. Once Darwinian evolution is fully understood and accepted, religion will be relegated to private faith, and eventually educated into extinction, like all other unfit characteristics of a species. It's already happening. I'm not quite so intolerant as to say that it has to happen, but it will."

The conversation had gone in a different direction than Dan had anticipated. Whether it was what had transpired between Stephen and Rudner, or just his own interests, they had spent a lot more time talking about the validity of Darwinian evolution than about what they had come to find out. He needed to pull the conversation back on track. They were there to find out anything related to a treatment for Ava, and he had to focus on that, though Stephen's other interests likely were related to it.

"How angry did they get? Did you think the conflict might escalate at some point?" Dan asked.

"At points, I had concerns, but no, it didn't get out of control. Is this what you're researching for the book?" asked Dr. Erving with skepticism.

"A part of it. Stephen's notes do indicate the broad outlines of what you described. We're also looking for a collaborator Dr. Bishop worked with on what he referred to as the DNA algorithm, or any research that might use that to understand and treat diseases. Is there any possibility Dr. Rudner may have been of some help in that area? I know that would be a long shot, as it seems she may have viewed Stephen as the equivalent of the Catholic Church trying to repress the scientific truth of the earth orbiting the sun." Dan worried that his attempt to ferret out Stephen's Galileo was too obvious, but Dr. Erving laughed.

"I'm pretty sure they didn't collaborate on anything after that discussion. It ended shortly after that, and not on warm terms."

Trish asked, "Did Stephen mention how his research could be used to develop new medical treatments?"

"No. I'm an evolutionary scientist working in a museum. It's not something people would normally discuss with me," Dr. Erving answered.

"One last question," Dan said. "For the layperson, what's the strongest evidence for Darwinian evolution?"

"That's easy: common descent, geographic distribution, speciation, and natural selection. We see the evidence all around us." Dr. Erving said confidently.

"Are these inconsistent with or at odds with a God-directed evolution?" Trish asked.

"On the surface, it's not inconsistent. But if a God directed it, the design would have been better and more tailored to individual species. There would be no need for common descent you see here," Dr. Erving said, pointing all around the hall. "And while that's not a scientific argument, there is also the issue that there is no proof for God's existence, but plenty of evidence of the harm of religion, including a poorly written Bible. This leaves natural, material means as the best explanation." Dr. Erving replied.

Dan was incredulous. "So you're saying that if God did exist, He would have done a better job and wouldn't have reused designs?" he said, his voice coming out a bit louder than he intended. "And therefore, because that isn't the case, He can't exist? Wouldn't assuming how a God should have designed everything require knowing for what *purpose* a God would create us? We don't even know how to feed people living next door to us, though that should be easy, and we think we know what a God should have done! That's quite a theological argument you are making about science."

As the words came out of his mouth, Dan realized that much of his life had been based on what he thought a God should or should not have done, if such a being in fact existed.

Visibly agitated, Dr. Erving exclaimed, "Good day, Mr. Lawson. I would like to see Dr. Bishop's manuscript before anything about this center is published."

"Certainly, but it needs to be edited first. I'll pass along your request to the estate's agent," Dan replied.

Halfway down the staircase to the first floor, Trish said to Dan, "How did that conversation turn so fast? Did you need to challenge him so harshly? He probably felt mocked."

"Necessary? No. Appropriate? Yes."

"It's a shame how much talking about evolution upsets people," Trish said.

"No matter what most people say, the strong reaction is not because of what they learn about science." Dan said. He spoke from experience on this. "It's what they want to believe about the way they want to live that gets them so riled up."

As they left the evolution gallery, Dan said, "Let's go out the side door. I want to walk by the car that was following us and say hello to the agents inside."

"You really think that's a good idea?"

"I just want to let them know that we appreciate their service. My old mentor Agent Evans is being overprotective. Those guys aren't following us to find out what we're doing. They're there to keep me from doing anything they consider risky and to keep others away from us. If Evans really thought we were connected to what happened to Stephen, or the explosion at the lab, we wouldn't be able to travel so freely and we wouldn't see our followers so easily."

"How is bothering them going to improve our chances?"

"I can skip it if it's a problem for you."

"Please do. It's pointless antagonism that could backfire," Trish said, heading for the front door. "Come on. Where to now?"

"First the hospital to see Ava, then on to San Diego. We have a promising appointment there," Dan said with a trace of optimism.

"I like how you seem to believe we'll find what we're looking for," Trish said.

"I really believe it. And I think it will be very interesting when we do."

Chapter 50

Ava sat in the orthopedic recliner in her hospital room. She was dressed in regular clothes and reading a book, and she smiled when Dan and Trish walked into the room.

"What are you reading there, squirt?" Dan asked.

"*A Wrinkle in Time*. Daddy gave it to me last week," Ava replied, her voice wavering.

Dan thought of taking the book from her, knowing it was about a young girl whose scientist father returns after a mysterious disappearance, but then thought better of it.

Trish squatted down next to the chair, combed her fingers through Ava's hair, and kissed her cheek. "Keep your chin up, and we'll get you better again, just like last time. How are you?"

"I get tired and achy. How long will it take to fix me?" Ava asked. Her complexion was pallid.

Dan wondered if treatment had already started to drain her.

Trish hugged Ava's head, then placed her hand on Ava's shoulder and stared into her eyes. Everything seemed to get quiet. Ava's eyes were locked in place, focused on Trish, and seemed to twinkle lightly. Something seemed to pass between Trish and Ava that Dan felt excluded from.

Dan remembered why they were there and pulled his thoughts back. He had to deal with reality, not indulge a childlike wish for a mystical existence that would cure all ills. Evidence to the contrary sat in rooms all around them.

Looking at his watch, Dan said to Trish, "We need to go."

"Where are you going? When will you be back?" Ava asked plaintively.

Trish replied, "To visit places where they may have some special medicine for you."

"Where's your mother?" Dan asked Ava.

"Right here," Nancy replied, walking into the room, followed by a doctor.

His thinning hair was silver, not gray, and he wore black-rimmed glasses. Trish walked over to him, and they discussed Ava's chart in hushed tones in a far corner of the room.

Motioning to the door, Trish said to Dan, "Ready?"

Dan nodded, and they both gave Nancy and Ava hugs.

In the hall, Trish said, "The cancer is remarkably aggressive, hard to treat, and progressing rapidly. I've never seen anything like it. If Stephen had an answer, we need to find it quickly."

"Isn't there something else you can do?"

"We're doing the standard typing of the cancer cells and matching it against potential treatments. We'll try something based on the results."

"What about clinical trials of new treatments?"

"Ava's type of cancer doesn't qualify for them," Trish said quietly.

"Does Nancy know how it looks?"

"Yes. She's so strong. After body blows that would knock down elephants, she gets back up and marches onward."

"Every time I begin to hope that there is an answer that explains all, I see more senseless suffering. How do you manage it?"

"I find joy in what happiness I can bring others, even if the effect is temporary or the end is not good," Trish said. She paused, then said, "Excuse me for a minute. I want to check on a few of my patients before we leave."

With that, Trish walked down the hall. Dan followed along, staying outside the rooms, though noticing how Trish greeted each patient and her demeanor going in and out of each room. He marveled at the warmth and strength that radiated from her.

When she was finished, Trish grabbed Dan by the arm and started to walk toward the exit.

After a few steps, almost sounding angry, Dan said, "I don't understand how people can see all of this and still believe in a loving God."

She asked, "Why does suffering make you hostile? Is believing there is no answer better than the possibility of an answer you don't like?"

He started, "It began with Grace—" Then he stopped himself.

"I'm not Christian, but I thought grace was supposed to make things better." Seeing Dan withdraw, she didn't push him for an answer, not yet at least.

"Grace was someone I once knew."

"What happened?"

"Some other day," Dan said stoically. "Time to focus on Ava. That's the only answer I'm interested in now."

Chapter 51

As Dan and Trish approached the security screening checkpoint at Logan Airport, Evans emerged from off to the side. "I know what you're up to, Lawson, and advise you to reconsider," he said sternly. "Your friend's dead, his daughter is sick, you want to help, and there's a good dose of revenge thrown in—I get it. But a bunch of people have already paid the ultimate price for being in over their heads. You don't need to be one of them. And you don't need to put others at risk with your reckless exploits."

With a look of exasperation, Dan said, "Thanks for your concern. But, if this helps to allay your fears, we're not doing anything more *reckless* than looking for medical treatments for Stephen's daughter."

"You know what your psychological profile looks like these days? It wasn't great to begin with and has gotten worse," Evans said. He looked at Trish, letting her know what she was getting herself in for with Dan.

"Is the investigation into the MIT explosion going so slowly that you have time to worry about what we're doing?" Dan asked.

"I'm still not buying all the coincidences," Evans said sharply.

"I can't help that." Dan took a step toward the security line, hoping Evans wasn't going to pull the plug on his plans.

Evans started to step into Dan's path.

Trish walked up to Evans, locked her eyes on him, and said, "Agent Evans, we're going to the Salk Institute, and anywhere else we need to, in search for whatever Ava Bishop needs. That's it. Now, can we please catch our flight?"

Evans hesitated. He looked off-balance and seemed not to know what to say.

Slowly yielding, he said to Dan, "On the condition you keep me informed of your whereabouts."

"Won't you know without us telling you?" Dan said.

"Yes. But check in regularly anyway. You know the protocol. And here's my contact information." Evans handed both Dan and Trish his business card. "And Lawson, at least make an attempt at pretending to be a team player. Things are heating up, and you need someone watching your back."

Dan sat in the aisle seat, Trish asleep at the window, an empty seat between them. The flight had been smooth, but a third of the way to San Diego, a minor burst of turbulence shook the plane. Trish stirred from her nap, then looked at Dan working on his computer. "What are you doing?"

"Just catching up on a few things," said Dan.

Trish reached over and put her hand on his forearm, once again looking right into him, and said, "We're in this together. We need to trust each other."

As before, her touch had more impact than her words. It was the oddest thing.

Until recently, he didn't have much awareness of why he thought what he did, why he acted the way he did, why he felt what he did. Like most people, he didn't spend much time analyzing himself. He was not a weak, sensitive, "new-age" man. No one would ever have thought that about him. Yet lately he was developing too much awareness of what he was thinking and feeling, was way too *present to himself*. It felt odd and unnatural. He wanted to push the rising awareness back down but feared he'd lose the opportunity that he was being presented to find his way out of his emotional descent. The idea that something was being presented to him *in reality* went against his view of the world.

Trish's hand made him recall how, when he was younger, a woman's touch triggered a desire for affection and warmth. Later, it made him feel appreciated in a vain way, then became something he avoided unless a necessary part of a physical relationship, until finally it was something that repulsed him, as if a hint of intimacy would shatter him. *Who thought all these things about themselves?* Why was he viewing himself as such an abstraction? But now it was different. Trish's touch pulled him back into the world and grabbed him. He didn't want it to stop, but wasn't going to acknowledge its effect.

Dan nodded. "It has to stay between us."

He motioned for her to move closer, and Trish unbuckled her seat belt, raised the armrest, and shifted to the seat next to Dan.

Dan was cautious. He typed rather than spoke.

I helped Stephen encrypt his work. I have copies of many of his files, including some on this computer, but do not have the keys to decode them. The encryption cannot be broken in a thousand lifetimes with today's technology. I have to find the phrase that Stephen used as the encryption key. I'm trying things from Stephen's journals. I know he would have left a clue for me somewhere. I haven't been able to find it.

After reading the message, Trish whispered, "How can I help?"

Think of anything Stephen may have said to you that was unusual or that seemed intended for you to notice.

She leaned closer and said in his ear, "Isn't it risky having the files on your computer?"

The computer uses encrypted flash memory. If someone attempts to get at the computer or files, I have triggers that will erase all of them, with no possibility of recovery. It is one hundred percent safe and secure.

Taking the keyboard, Trish typed, *What about the journals? When can I see them?*

Dan took the keyboard back and wrote *When we get back* and then shut the cover. All of a sudden, he wondered if his diminished state of mind had once again caused him to be easily manipulated and to share more than he should have.

He decided to turn to small talk. That was much safer. "Tell me about your background. What makes you believe what you do?"

"I don't know. I go with what feels natural. My parents didn't try to instill any particular beliefs in me. My mother is French Protestant and my father is an Italian Jew. Both are agnostic. They're reformed hippies from the early seventies who went mainstream in their occupations but never really gave up their contrary personalities, though they did mellow. I think the two things I got from them are a lack of anger and a desire to make a difference."

"That's an interesting background. Have you been in therapy long?" Dan said with a playful smile.

"What are you searching for?" Trish replied.

"You mean other than the few small things I mentioned earlier, such as a cure for Ava, finding out what happened to Stephen, and recovering his work?"

"Yes, bigger than all those things."

"I'm looking for answers that matter. Something that tells me life is more than what it seems. Is that what you meant?" Dan said.

"About what I expected."

"Well, that's a remarkable expectation. Now, how about you?"

"Not sure. I think I'm looking for a question."

"I've got plenty of those. Probably not the one you're looking for."

"Time will tell," Trish answered and then looked out the window.

It took Dan a few moments to realize that she was lost in her own thoughts. Suddenly tired, he put his head back and closed his eyes. He hoped that they both found all they were looking for, including whatever awaited them at the Salk Institute.

Chapter 52

He had seen pictures of the Salk Institute, but its beauty, perched on cliffs bordering the surf below, still surprised Dan. Stunning architecture wasn't something he normally associated with a major scientific research center.

The Salk Institute for Biological Studies had been established by Jonas Salk, lead developer of the vaccine that ended the scourge of polio in 1955. The Institute opened in 1963 in La Jolla, California, outside San Diego. The complex was designed by Louis Kahn, known for his innovative designs. Two long buildings opposed each other across a rectangular plaza bisected by a narrow channel of water that was aligned with the sunrise and sunset at the equinoxes.

The buildings had six floors, two of which were belowground though illuminated with light wells. In the fifty years since its completion, the complex's architectural accomplishments were well recognized.

The institute's scientific stature and achievements greatly outshone even the architecture. With over eight hundred researchers in over sixty research groups spanning the biological sciences, the institute was one of the top biomedical research centers in the world.

The overall impression the institute gave was of majesty and goodness, and it boosted Dan's hope of finding a treatment for Ava inside. It was also a decent location for potentially encountering Galileo and then accessing Stephen's work one way or another. With a spring in their steps, Dan and Trish entered the institute.

"Thank you for seeing us on such short notice," Trish said to Dr. Chamberlain, president of the Salk Institute. They were inside his well-appointed office, with striking views in almost every direction.

"Not at all, Dr. Alighieri. We're happy to meet with a colleague of Dr. Bishop's who's trying to continue his research. He was a giant in the genomics field, and it was our great regret that we couldn't recruit him ourselves," said Dr. Chamberlain, gesturing to chairs in front of his desk.

As Dr. Chamberlain turned to walk around his desk to his chair, Trish glared at Dan. She had not been pleased when Dan introduced her as someone involved in pediatric cancer research who had been collaborating with Stephen in his genomic-based treatment research at HBC. Both were deep areas of interest to the Salk Institute, so Dan knew it would get them in the door, but she had been angry about the lie.

After they all sat down, Dr. Chamberlain said, "Dr. Bishop's loss will be felt by many. We'll do anything we can to help."

Hearing the words again about Stephen's loss, the once sharp blade of sorrow, since dulled by too many thrusts, entered Dan again, but not as deeply. The pain felt abstract, as though he knew it was happening but its impact was lessening. It bothered him to think that someday it wouldn't hurt enough.

Trish paused, as if she too felt something at hearing the words. Then she said, "Thank you. Regrettably, I had started working with Dr. Bishop only recently. There are a few pieces missing in our knowledge of his research, and we're hoping someone here may have collaborated with him and can help us fill in the gaps."

"What specifically are you looking for? To the best of my knowledge, no one here was working with Dr. Bishop," Dr. Chamberlain replied.

"Genetically repairing and reprogramming a leukemia patient's own stem cells to produce healthy bone marrow," Trish replied, using a story she had worked out with Dan based on conversations both had had with Stephen that made it almost true, at least true enough for her not to feel bad saying it.

"Yes, that would be a wonderful treatment. Dr. Bishop did talk with Dr. Marc Senter about it. Dr. Senter leads our efforts in both the genomics and cancer research areas. Over fifty percent of our research is focused on cancer. They had a memorable discussion," Dr. Chamberlain said with a you-had-to-see-it-to-believe-it look. "I've already given him a heads-up that you'd probably want to talk with him. We can walk over to his office. It's nearby."

Inside Dr. Senter's office, after introductions, including respectful acknowledgments about Stephen's death, Trish began. "Dr. Bishop was working on a leukemia treatment for patients with highly sensitive immune systems. I believe, but am not sure, that it was for patients who required treatment with only their own cells, whose weakened condition from prior treatments also meant they could not withstand aggressive treatments. He might have been pursuing a treatment whereby a patient's own stem cells were extracted and then genetically corrected."

"This is the objective of a lot of researchers these days," Dr. Chamberlain said.

"Yes. The idea is that the corrected cells would be used to generate sufficient quantities of healthy bone marrow cells in preparation for the patient. Meanwhile, the patient's own immune system cells would be programmed to eradicate the patient's faulty bone marrow stem cells. Both the now-healthy marrow and the programmed immune cells would be injected into the patient, where they would simultaneously destroy and replace diseased cells with healthy ones—without any side effects or need for further treatment," Trish said.

"It will be wonderful when such a treatment can be provided to all patients, for all types of cancers."

"It would be a one hundred percent cure, without any threat to the patient or traumatic side effects. Almost anyone could sustain this treatment. Did you discuss this with Stephen, Dr. Senter?"

Dr. Senter took a slow, deep breath before he answered. "Yes, we had discussed this conceptually. While the treatment makes sense, and there is a lot of research showing promise in these areas, we have a tremendously long way to go before anyone will be able to try anything like this. Perhaps others researchers are closer, but that would be remarkable news to us. Frankly, I'm astounded to hear that Dr. Bishop may have already been piloting this—it would be highly unorthodox if he was."

Dan's heart sank. But perhaps Senter could still point them in the right direction or help them find Galileo, whether Senter was aware of the treatment or not. The institute was large, and any type of research could be going on there without others being aware of it.

"Is any of this being researched somewhere else that you know of?" Dan asked.

"Although initial research is being conducted today, here and elsewhere, as far as I know— and I'm well connected to research in *all* of the relevant areas—nothing is close to a pilot. In particular, we need a much better understanding of the genome so we can correct defective . . . programming," Senter said, with a noticeable pause before *programming,* and a glance at Chamberlain.

Trish said, "What were the discussions with Dr. Bishop like?" She sounded as disappointed as Dan felt.

"We met with several of our leading genome and cancer researchers. The discussion began innocuously enough, and initially covered the areas you described, though in more detail. People found the ideas stimulating and exciting. Then Dr. Bishop started to veer off in a direction that some found disturbing," Senter said, looking back and forth between Dan and Trish, seemingly assessing whether their sympathies aligned with Stephen's views, which some of the institute researchers had found troubling. Senter continued cautiously, "We were fine with exploring the idea of genome expression and the possibility of algorithmic-like processing. It was when Dr. Bishop implied that algorithmic genome expression begged the question of the manner of its origin. He asked about its impact on genetic mutations producing beneficial adaptations, as opposed to destructive malfunctions, and that's when the wheels came off. I'm afraid that, at that point, the discussions ended quickly, and poorly. We tried to return the topic back to understanding the genome, but that discussion was limited and the air strained. The meeting concluded shortly thereafter."

"I don't understand. It was acceptable to say that algorithmic processing may be involved in genetic expression, but not to discuss the implications? You folks understand DNA as well as anyone in the world. What do you think the implications are?" Dan said, channeling his disappointment into aggression.

With a sigh, Chamberlain said, "The implications of what Stephen was presenting were too much for most people in the room; though he never came out as a creationist, he was headed in that direction."

"Did Stephen actually say anything about God, a creator, or spirituality?" Trish asked.

"It wasn't necessary. He implied it when he said that DNA had no direct information content without something preexisting to interpret it; that an algorithm had to take a small amount of DNA to generate a large amount of instructions; that these instructions then needed a mechanism to direct biological development; and that all these things had to be present independently, from the beginning, for life to have formed. He entered the realm of intelligent design, and all bets were off. We're a science center, not an institution for faith-based, antiscience ideas."

Dan decided to ignore the temptation to explore Senter's definition of antiscience, because he was still holding out hope they'd find something helpful at the institute. Instead, he asked, "What happened next?"

"One of our researchers directed Dr. Bishop to the Crick-Jacobs Center. It's part of the institute. I'm sure you're familiar with Francis Crick, codiscoverer of the double-helix structure of DNA. He also believed that DNA was too complex to have evolved unaided. In his view it's alien in origin."

"So it's not acceptable to leave open the possibility of God, but it's okay to attribute everything to aliens," Trish said mildly. "Who created them?"

"Dr. Alighieri, attributing human origin to aliens is not what people in this institute ascribe to. I was simply recapping what took place that day."

"I'm sorry we've veered off topic ourselves. Let's get back to the science, which is solely where our interests lie," Dan said while looking at Trish, pleased that she picked up the cue and nodded her head in agreement. "Is there anyone else we can talk with about research they may have participated in, or know of, with Dr. Bishop? Even someone who was once involved with the institute but fell off the beaten path?"

"We had limited contact with Dr. Bishop. I know none of the people he met that day have collaborated on research with him," Senter said with an edge to his voice.

"Do you think it's worth our time checking out the Crick-Jacobs Center?" Dan asked.

"Different research areas. Can't see it helping you. But it's an impressive center. You've come this far so, if you have the time, it's worth visiting," Chamberlain said.

"Before we head over there, does this mean anything to either of you?" Dan asked, showing them a display on his smartphone of the characters of the symbol Stephen had drawn.

"Looks like an equation of sorts. No idea what for," Chamberlain said.

"Likewise," said Senter.

"Thanks anyway," Dan replied.

The Crick-Jacobs Center for Theoretical and Computational Biology housed a vast array of interdisciplinary research into the functioning of the human brain.

It was a short walk from Senter's office. Stepping into the plaza, Dan scanned the surroundings. All he saw were people moving in a casual but purposeful manner, all seemingly oblivious to him.

With a puzzled expression, Trish asked, "What does the Crick-Jacobs Center have to do with finding a treatment for Ava?"

"Probably very little. But Stephen, knowing my beliefs and state of mind, had made it a point to tell me that he was going to prove to me that I had a soul, that I was more than physical matter. He also wrote about consciousness in his journal. While we're here, it seems like a good opportunity to find out more about those things. And perhaps someone here will know about others who worked with Stephen."

"Sounds intriguing, especially the part about your having soul," Trish said, barely suppressing her amusement.

He thought of correcting Trish's usage of "soul," but then realized that she knew exactly what she was saying.

They looked toward the Pacific as they approached the Crick-Jacobs Center's main entrance, but a flash of reflected sunlight caught Dan's eyes. He turned and saw two figures, too far away for him to see clearly, wearing dark clothes that seemed out of place in the California sunshine. One of the figures lowered his hands from his face, then placed his right hand behind his back along with whatever he was holding. Dan was left with the feeling that the person was holding binoculars that had been used to view him. He proceeded with almost no reaction, giving no indication he was concerned about anything. Dan held the door for Trish as she entered the building.

"Welcome to our Center. I understand you only have a short time. We have a quick video that will give an overview of the Center's mission and work. After that, I can answer whatever questions you have."

"That would be very helpful," Trish said with a warm smile that the director appeared to appreciate.

Sitting down in the media center, they watched a ten-minute video that explained that the center was dedicated to understanding how all the different parts of the brain work together to produce behavior and cognition. Most of the video presented illustrations and images of current research. None of it explained how the brain actually worked. Brain research was still in its infancy.

After the video ended, Dan asked, "This center is focused solely on the operations of the brain?"

"Yes. We look at things from the molecular level to the systems level and try to understand how that gives rise to behavior. We also work with another branch of the institute, that's focused on visual perception, the most complex of the senses. Once that is understood, the rest of the senses should fall into place."

"And then comes cognition," Dan added.

"That's right. But we're a long way off and need better tools. Right now, we've only been able to see rudimentary activity at the neuron level. Watch this," the director said. "What you're seeing are individual neurons firing in response to visual stimuli showing the locations in the brain associated with the corresponding mental processes. It's quite exciting, actually."

"What did Dr. Bishop think when he saw this?" Dan asked.

"Like you, he was only here briefly. He had one interest. I remember it because of the conversation I heard he had before he came by and because of the discomfort the topic seemed to give those he discussed it with. He wanted to know what we thought about the basis of consciousness. We actually have a good understanding of it. Francis Crick wrote a book on it called *The Astonishing Hypothesis*. Basically, it's about how quantum mechanics effects inside neurons generate consciousness."

"You've proven this?" Trish asked.

"Not yet, but it's only a matter of time. Almost all scientists in this field recognize that discrete, individual particles consisting only of objective states, such as the spin of an electron, cannot, by themselves, generate whole, subjective experiences. There has to be something that ties the individual states and processing together. The only thing that can do that is quantum mechanics–based. In time, we'll be able to demonstrate the scientific basis for it."

"You mean since there is no soul, no immaterial mind, the cause must be material, and you just have to keep looking to find it," Dan said, remembering what Stephen had written in his journals.

"Absolutely correct. No spiritualism to fill temporary gaps in scientific knowledge. Only natural causes for natural effects," said the director emphatically.

"Which means all we are is just biological robots with the illusion of meaning, purpose, love, free will, morality, and intrinsic value," Dan added.

The director shifted in his seat. "I wouldn't say it that way, but yes, in the end we're temporary collections of atoms."

Dan restrained himself and didn't ask the director what he thought as he kissed his *biological robot offspring* good night. Was the love he felt for them an illusion to be overcome? Instead, he pointed at the poster on the wall for a conference held in 2006 called Beyond Belief: Science, Religion, Reason and Survival. Dan asked, "What was that about?"

With obvious pride the director said, "The conference was organized in response to the Templeton Foundation's efforts to merge science and religion. We weren't trying to fund scientists to say mean things about religion, but wanted to make sure all study is focused on scientific learning."

"And since religion is neither science nor worthwhile learning, it must be kept out of the sphere of all research that aspires to have anything to say about the universe and life. Science can't appear to give any legitimacy to religious belief," Dan said, playing along.

"Well, since you put it that way, yes," the director said.

"And who were the main participants in this conference?" Dan asked, knowing full well from Stephen's journals.

"Richard Dawkins, Sam Harris, Michael Shermer, Francisco Ayala—" the director began before Dan interrupted.

"Isn't Ayala the ex-priest who said God couldn't have created humans, as that would make Him responsible for human suffering, and that would be blasphemy?" Dan said.

"That's right. He's a remarkable evolutionary biologist."

"I thought the object was to keep religious views out of science. Sounds like he's using his understanding of theology, such that it is, to make scientific conclusions." As the director's face turned a shade of red, Dan added, "I'm greatly impressed by your research. I certainly don't want to give the impression that I think there is some ghost inside the skull doing all the work."

Relaxing a little, the director said, "That's good to hear. In some quarters, the things we don't yet know about consciousness are being used as a weapon against science. Even the NYU philosopher Thomas Nagel, who's an atheist, has asserted that Darwinian evolution can't explain the origin of consciousness. Of course, we're able to refute the arguments in his book, but damage is done when his antiscience assertions receive any press."

Dan looked down at Stephen's notes, which were stored on his tablet. "Well, it's a good thing he didn't say that until science has proven how consciousness works, what's called natural selection is arguably intelligent selection and evolution is not a process based strictly on physical matter, that in fact it leaves room for a God to operate. Now, that would have been really upsetting," Dan said. His tone was serious enough, so as to not insult the director, but still left room for doubt for his actual intent.

The director cleared his throat and he stood to guide Dan and Trish toward the door. "I hope I've given you a good appreciation for our center. If there is anything else you'd like to know, just call me. I'll be happy to help." It didn't sound like he meant it.

Once they were out of the director's hearing, Trish said, "You continue to argue against the position you say you hold. Why is that?"

"I don't like intellectual dishonesty. It means that either they don't want to acknowledge the weakness in their views or that they don't trust the public to come to the right conclusions about any current gaps in knowledge."

"So you're antagonistic against people who hold similar views just because of the way they represent them, not because you disagree with them?" Trish said.

Dan didn't have an answer.

"Perhaps you're not being intellectually honest about what you truly believe," Trish said.

"The problem is that I understand what materialism is, don't like its implications, but don't believe in God as the alternative."

"You sound like you're at risk for finding out you have meaning."

"What about you? Do you believe it is better to believe in life having meaning, to be wonderful to people, be personally happy, yet believe there is no spiritual basis for it? Do you think a God would provide all of this and then expect nothing in return? Or do you think

that at a minimum, he wouldn't require us to recognize what would
have to be our true nature and relationship to him?

"No."

"Exactly. Now you understand my dilemma."

"Anger isn't the best response to it," Trish said.

"I'm trying," Dan answered.

"Yes, you most certainly are," Trish said, patting Dan twice on his
shoulder. He stopped to look at her, a wide smile crossing his face,
and then he grabbed the hand that had patted him and said, "You
should be proud of me."

"Why's that?" Trish.

"I didn't ask the director what makes the natural sciences so
natural."

"I'm amazed at your restraint," Trish said facetiously, then withdrew her hand.

As they walked back to Dr. Chamberlain's office, another flash of
light caught Dan's eye. He turned and saw a figure that seemed to
linger just long enough to be deliberately seen before withdrawing
behind a corner of a building and out of sight. Before they left, Dan
planned to check it out.

Trish noticed his unease, and said, "Overall, a disappointing day.
I thought this place held real promise. I doubt we'll find much at the
Discovery Institute. And after that . . . "

"I have other leads I can show you when we get back. We're not
at a dead end," Dan said, thinking of Galileo and gaining access to
Stephen's work files. And there had to be something in those journals
that would point them in the right direction.

"What did you make of the discussions Stephen had?" Trish asked.

"It's hard for people here to relate to what he was working on.
They're good people doing important work, but they operate in a cul-
ture that, oddly enough, limits their own learning."

"You sound a bit like Stephen." She gave him a look he couldn't
interpret, then said, "That's not a bad thing."

Hearing that made Dan realize he wanted to keep rising in her esteem.

Back in the president's office, Trish said, "Thank you very much for your hospitality. It was a helpful visit. I think it's only a matter of time before we develop the necessary understanding of Stephen's work and are in a position to help resume it. At that time, we'd like to continue our discussion and see if there are opportunities to collaborate."

"By all means. Despite the tough initial reception he received, we're intrigued by Dr. Bishop's work on algorithmic gene expression," Chamberlain said.

"Great. Thank you again," Dan said as they left the office.

By the front doors, Dan motioned for Trish to stop. "Wait two minutes, then walk to the center of the plaza and stand there as though you are waiting impatiently for me. I'll join you a few minutes after that. I want to see if anyone hanging around the institute has something to say to us but has been too shy."

"What are you going to do? Nothing foolish, I hope," Trish said.

"Just making sure that if anyone is watching you, it's because they admire you," Dan said with a wink and a smile. He looked at his watch and walked down the hall toward the end of the building where he had last seen the flash.

After two and a half minutes, he eased out the door and peered toward the corner of the building that had a view of the center of plaza. Off to the edge was a woman holding binoculars to her eyes, facing Trish. Dan looked around for the other person but didn't see him. He walked slowly by the side of the building and Dan approached the woman. Dan tapped her right shoulder and said, "Mind if I borrow those and see what's so interesting?"

She smiled as though she was expecting him, though there was a chilling hardness in her eyes. Her green eyes were as murky as the ocean. Her frosted blond hair fluttered in the breeze. Without changing her expression, she shot her free hand toward Dan's throat. Before it got anywhere near its target, Dan grabbed her wrist. She swung the binoculars with her other hand, but Dan grabbed it and then twisted both her hands so she was turned away from him, immobilized.

"As much as I want to be a gentlemen, I really don't like being attacked. How about telling me what you're up to before I have security check you out?"

"You don't know what you're dealing with," she hissed.

"A lot of people say that. Maybe I don't care—" Before he finished speaking, a hand slammed against the back of his head, and another pulled on his left shoulder, spinning him around as he lost his grip on the woman. Slightly stunned, he stood face-to-face with Sergei.

Wrath crossed Dan's face as he looked at the man who was responsible for the Sarasovs' deaths, and also probably for Stephen's.

Sergei's initial expression of contempt turned to surprise when Dan said, "You killed the Sarasovs, you shot me as I carried their young son, and you were involved in Stephen Bishop's death. It ends now." As Sergei's eyes shot to Dan's left arm, Dan began to strike with his right hand. Before he could finish the blow, the woman slammed the binoculars on his head. Dan crashed down onto his knees. Slowly gathering himself, he looked up to see that Sergei and the woman were gone and Trish was approaching with institute security guards.

"I thought I told you not to do anything foolish," Trish said with worry in her voice.

Getting back to his feet, Dan said, "We're going to have to rethink our approach."

Chapter 53

After thirty minutes of searching online, Dan and Trish arrived at a location off the beaten path in San Diego to pick up a 1995 Mustang.

He paid for the car using a fake driver's license and prepaid credit card, and declined the use of an automated toll-collection device.

It was time to go dark. No electronic, visual, or monetary tracks. Travel as a ghost. No way for anyone to know where they were or that they were headed to Seattle. He hadn't booked any lodgings or flights in advance. They had already turned off their cell phones' location services and powered them down.

Dan held the car door for Trish as she lowered herself into the leather seats. After buckling his seat belt, Dan said, "You should nap whenever you can, since we'll be driving through the night."

"How many miles is it?" Trish asked.

"About twelve hundred and fifty using the fastest route. But we're going to avoid roads with bridges with license plate readers and facial recognition imaging. That'll add over a hundred miles. Since we have to watch our speed to avoid being stopped, and factoring in a few bathroom breaks, it'll take us almost twenty-two hours to get there."

"What happened back there? Who were they?" Trish asked.

"I don't know about the woman, but the big guy was Sergei. He was once a Soviet KGB agent but now is working for some other organization interested in Stephen's work," Dan said. He didn't want to worry Trish by telling her just how dangerous Sergei was. While she was with him, Dan would avoid Sergei. But eventually, on his own, Dan would go after him.

"You two have a history," Trish stated.

"What do you mean?"

"I saw it. You recognized each other. What was that about?"

"Eighteen years ago, as an intelligence field agent, I was helping an important scientist, and his wife and son, leave Russia. The mission failed. Sergei had the parents shot in front of their young boy. Evans was with me. Sergei got away," Dan said, looking off into the distance, beyond the horizon.

Placing her left hand on Dan's right shoulder, Trish asked, "What happened to the boy?"

"Evans brought him back to his home and we both searched for relatives. I found cousins in Israel and they raised him. I don't know what happened after that."

She watched him for a moment. "What aren't you telling me? I have a right to know."

"Two days ago, Evans showed me pictures of Sergei that placed him in Stephen's vicinity at the time of his death. My guess is that Sergei is working for people who were after Stephen's research. They must be following us, thinking we may lead them to one of Stephen's collaborators. Otherwise we'd already be in deep trouble. Either that or they just happened to be on the same trail. That's why we're traveling this way. Now no one will be able to find us," Dan said, still trying to understate the threat Sergei and his people posed.

"Will we run into them again in Seattle?"

"I don't think so. Where we're going next has very little to do with Stephen's known work. And this time, no one will be able to have any idea of where we're going."

"And?"

He figured it was no use denying it any further, and, as she'd said, she had a right to know. Dan said, "This has to stay between us. Stephen asked certain things of me, including secrecy. The night he died, he left me a message saying to be on the lookout for a collaborator of his who would use the code name Galileo. Everywhere we've been, I've been looking for that person. I think Sergei is looking for him, too. You are the only one who knows this. Please keep it that way."

"You shouldn't keep things from me."

Dan didn't answer.

Driving on the busy freeway, Dan felt strange without the technology he had in his own car. Yet, being off the grid, a quiet confidence surrounded him. Thinking back eighteen years to the fateful border encounter with Sergei, Dan felt sadness for young Mikhail Sarasov.

Though her head was tilted back and her eyes closed, Trish said, "It's okay to hurt, to feel sorrow. Just don't let it change you into something you shouldn't be."

"I'm not."

"Good. You have a lot you still need to do, and it will take the best of you."

"You speak as though you know more of me than you possibly can," Dan said.

"What I don't already know, I'm learning fast," Trish said softly.

Before she ever got to the point of really knowing him, Dan was determined to be a different person than he had been. Something had already changed within him, and he wanted the rest to follow.

The first hours of driving, though through several stretches of moderate traffic, had been deceptively tranquil. A smattering of small talk had interrupted their churning inner thoughts. Trish's, like his, probably revolved around what they needed to do, what had happened, and what lay ahead. His attention was also focused on the vehicles around him, and he was alert to the possibility that, despite his precautions, they could still be followed.

With Los Angeles behind them, and the road opening up, he decided to try to ease the atmosphere and also learn more about Trish.

"Mind if I put on some music? We have a long way to go and it helps pass the time," Dan said as he connected his smartphone to a tape cassette player adapter inserted in the car's radio.

"Go ahead," Trish said.

"I'll pick things that you might like."

"Don't worry about it. It'll be amusing to find out what you like," Trish said.

"I'm glad I'm a source of entertainment for you."

"Everyone has a positive contribution to make. Providing comic relief for others might be yours," Trish said laughingly.

"I had no idea you talked like this. You struck me as more respectful of people, especially those you don't really know."

"Just kidding around. I'll stop."

"Whatever suits you. I can deal with it," Dan said.

"Tell me what song or playlist you want and I'll put it on."

"Normally, I like to start long road trips with something rousing. How about 'Ramblin' Man'? It's in the Allman Brothers playlist."

"About what I expected," Trish said, smiling.

"Hey, my parents weren't outlaws, I wasn't born in a bus and it's a great sound."

"No need to be defensive."

As the song ended, Dan said, "Okay, you pick the next one."

The live version of Marshall Tucker's "24 Hours at a Time" began playing.

"Good choice. How come a half-Jewish girl from the Northeast knows so much about southern rock?"

"My father played lots of the music when I was growing up and still takes me to concerts."

"Sounds like a great dad. Aren't you young for parents who are probably in their sixties? Do you have older siblings?"

"No, it's just me. For a while, they got caught up in the whole 'world is too dangerous to have kids' thing. Eventually, they calmed down, got what they once called establishment jobs, and then had me."

"Lucky for Ava, and others, of course," Dan said trying to sound friendlier.

"What about you? What's your family like?" Trish said, ignoring his comment.

Despite trying to focus the conversation on Trish, Dan spent the next ten minutes talking about his deceased parents, moving from Brooklyn, his sister, growing up with Stephen, and the highlights of his career.

As the song ended, he said, "Let's make it interesting and take turns picking songs that we think fits the other."

"Are you always this presumptuous?" Trish said.

"Sometimes. And we have a long way to go and a lot to do. It would be good if we got to know each other better," Dan said.

"You think you can pick a song that reflects me? Go ahead," Trish said in a voice that was both amused and challenging.

"I can't decide. How about Cat Stevens, 'Moonshadow,' followed by 'Peace Train,'" Dan said.

As the music began, he said, "I've revealed a lot more about me than you have about yourself. That seems to happen a lot with you."

"What would you like to know? I'm not that interesting," Trish said.

"Humor me. What you were like growing up? Why did you became a doctor? What do you want out of life? You know, the little things that make a person who they are." What he didn't ask, and didn't want to know yet, was whether she had a boyfriend. No reason to place that barrier there prematurely if she had someone.

"I want the same things I think you do, only I haven't doubted or thought about them as much. My childhood started out unconventional and became more conventional as my parents became less counterculture."

"Funny how that works when people have to pay bills."

Trish ignored Dan's poor attempt at wit and said, "My father is even becoming religiously observant. I attended an alternative middle school that emphasized communal ideals. I spent parts of summers in Israel on a kibbutz and then later worked in medical clinics. That developed my interest in medicine. Though my parents had the means for high-end private schools, they insisted I attend public schools."

Feeling guilty about his prior comment, and genuinely impressed, Dan said, "The background they gave you is remarkable."

"Thank you. After high school, I went to a small college and then medical school. Though I am not Catholic, one of my idols is Dorothy Day. I admire what she did for those most in need. It led to me specializing in pediatric oncology because those patients and families need the most comforting. It's inspiring how much hope there can be in situations that call mostly for despair."

The previous song over, Trish selected another, and Van Morrison's "Enlightenment" began playing.

"Good choice. Is this what you believe?" Dan said.

"I've leaned toward Eastern philosophy, though I'm wondering if more than that will be needed. There are good messages in this, regardless."

"Yes there are."

The song over, Dan picked Michael Franti's "The Sound of Sunshine," a happy, upbeat, song.

"I like this. Thank you," Trish said. After that ended, she played Bruce Springsteen's "Growing Up" and then "No Surrender."

"A message as much as a commentary, I think," Dan said.

"Could be," Trish answered, a sly smile crossing her face that Dan liked.

Broaching the topic again, Trish asked, "You once mentioned something about it all started with Grace, but not in the religious sense. What was that about?"

Taking a deep breath, Dan began. "Grace was my next-door neighbor. We were born within weeks of each other. We were young enough that we could be good friends without boy-girl complications getting in the way. One day, when we were eleven, she was playing capture the flag at her house with some other friends. She thought the sliding door was open, and was running furiously from pursuit, and she ran straight through the closed door, shattering the glass and slicing her leg. A tourniquet barely kept her from bleeding to death on the way to the hospital. We all prayed intensely for her, especially me. The prayers seemed to work, but then an infection sprouted that led to sepsis and brought her near death. Once again, everyone's fervent prayers appeared to help lead to Grace's recovery. But when she was set for release, an undetected blood clot in her leg broke loose and made its way to her brain. The resulting stroke left her brain-dead until, several agonizing days later, the rest of her body's organs also failed. Prayers could do nothing. It was at that point that I decided that if God existed, He was malicious. At best human suffering meant nothing to Him. It took me years, but looking back, I finally realized it was futile to be angry at someone who didn't exist."

"I'm sorry. It must still hurt," Trish said.

"It was long ago. A different time and place," Dan said. But some things would never make sense, could never be made right.

"It's only been a few days, but so many things are challenging us. Why is it that so many people think they can be happy, believe that their own version of morality is objectively right? How can most of what people believe is right be the same, unless it is somehow true? Or do you believe God is an illusion that we just can't shake and common beliefs are coincidental or are shaped by the same society?" Trish asked.

"Either that, or God exists and we possess the nature He gave us, whether we acknowledge its existence and origin or not."

"Then perhaps our firm sense of morality is a form of evidence of God's existence."

"Many philosophers have said so. And since we call the few people who live truly as though objective morality is an illusion, we must think morality isn't a changeable, made-up thing. Though we sometimes think we get to define what moral standards apply to us, we're always quite certain when we've been wronged and that's another indication we think at least part of morality is objectively, universally, real."

· "You have a knack for getting into this type of discussion," Trish said.

"Simply trying to find a path forward, one that leads somewhere worth getting."

"You would think you might have some answers by now."

"I started looking late but think I'm getting there," Dan said, turning to glance at Trish then quickly back to the road.

With nothing more to say, they drove on in silence as each reflected on what lay ahead.

The sun was low in the sky, and they were on a stretch of the road close to the coast. Orange light danced off the ocean waves.

Looking over at an alert Trish, Dan thought of the remaining drive. "Though it's only early evening here, we're still on East Coast time, and it would be a good idea for you to rest. We'll need to take turns sleeping and driving. "

"You've been driving awhile. You could rest first."

"My mind is racing too much, trying to think about things I may have missed with Stephen, to do that now."

"Do you want music while you drive? I won't mind."

"I'll put an earbud in one ear and put something on."

"Wake me anytime you need me to take over," Trish said.

"Thanks, I will," Dan said, then put on Donovans's "Catch the Wind."

Feeling a bit forlorn over memories, and faintly longing for what he was coming to believe was an extraordinary person next to him; he thought the song was the perfect choice.

He wondered what she thought, if she was awake and could hear it.

Eight hours later, Trish was driving on a pitch-black road. Dan's eyes were closed, but he was awake. Every little twitch the car made caused him to sit up and open his eyes.

Eventually, he said, "I don't think I can sleep. How about we switch back?"

"You slept better than you thought."

"Good, then I'll drive."

"If you must," Trish said with a touch of criticism.

"I like feeling fully in control whenever I can. No offense, you drove well."

"All you need to dispel the notion that you can completely control your own life is struggling for your last breath."

"Now, that's a nice thought."

"You're the one hung up on reality. What's more real than that?"

Chapter 54

The singularity project must continue uninterrupted," Sarastro said over the secure video conference line to the rest of The Commission's governing council.

"The fusion event calls for different priorities. It upsets critical, international power balances and relationships. And there may be bigger things to come," said a titan of the tech industry.

"If we do not direct this to the proper outcomes, nothing else will matter," added a prominent European political figure.

Sarastro knew what they said was true, yet he was compelled by his own condition and interests to ensure that the project that had been The Commission's primary focus for two years continued unimpeded. He also knew that while he would ensure that The Commission carried out his wishes, he needed to let the council have its say, let them think they had reached his conclusion on their own.

"And we have to consider what minimizes human suffering," said a well-known spiritual figure.

"While maximizing the flourishing of the species," added a leading evolutionary philosopher.

Sarastro considered most of these people fools who spouted phrases and views they did not understand except in relation to their own interests. Yet the power and wealth they collectively wielded was important to the few real commission leaders, among whom he was first among equals, who sat quietly in the background shepherding the important decisions.

"Yes, this is all true," Sarastro said. "We have already reported to you the steps that are being taken and what they should achieve.

Unless something we haven't anticipated occurs, all efforts should proceed as planned. It is even possible that the efforts will converge."

A US senator on the Senate's Intelligence Committee asked, "Is that likely? Have you found out what caused the explosion at the MIT fusion reactor and how Viktor Weisman obtained the technology?"

"We're closing in on those who will answer these questions, and many more, for us," Sarastro answered.

"There are those that think the US has developed powerful new weapons that they are about to deploy as a step to US global dominance. We won't allow this," said the powerful Chinese politician.

Sarastro replied, "As the Senator can attest, the US government has no such programs or capabilities."

"Then what else can explain these striking discoveries? We won't wait for the answers to arrive via missiles on our soil," the Chinese politician proclaimed.

"We believe that Alex Robertson was the source of physics discoveries that John Welch and Viktor Weisman further developed and tested, using mostly existing technology," Sarastro answered.

"And that would mean that Stephen Bishop was the initial conduit between them, and probably shared all of his research with Dan Lawson. Why not grab Lawson, and extract everything he knows, right now, before the US government puts him outside our reach?"

"If he had the information we want, he'd have either already told his old colleague, Agent Evans, or tried to find others to help him with the technology—and he has done neither. Right now, he is searching for a treatment to save Ava Bishop's life. His search may lead us to a person who can provide us more information about Bishop's work," Sarastro said, pleased that his idea to cause a reoccurrence of Ava's cancer, while she was getting her checkup in the hospital, was turning out so well. It was with a strain that he possessed a treatment for; he could keep it under control. By substituting it for other treatments, he could control the disease's progression, at least for a while, to his advantage. If somehow the leukemia was eradicated unexpectedly, he could always introduce another strain to the girl's bloodstream. If at some point the treatment was no longer effective and she died, it would be an unfortunate necessity. For now, he had a fantastic tool for manipulating people, and its usefulness had survived Bishop's death. He wouldn't waste it by letting her die, at least not too quickly.

"And the fusion information?" the tech titan asked.

"We're working on that," Sarastro said.

"What do we do in the interim?" said the senator.

"Absolutely nothing," Sarastro directed. "The world is on a knife's edge, which is where we need to keep it until we are ready to direct what should be cut."

"Likewise, you need to consult with us once the people and information are in your possession," said the tech titan.

"I do not need to be reminded of that. I can accomplish nothing on my own. My interests are the same as The Commission's," Sarastro replied, though some of his interests went beyond theirs.

"We have had a disappointing run of events. Future outcomes must be better," said the Chinese leader.

"Appropriate steps have been taken, though better information from our US people would be helpful," Sarastro replied, a not so veiled criticism aimed at the US senator.

All understood that there was no more room for errors.

Sarastro was finding The Commission more and more tiresome. Once he alone possessed Stephen Bishop's work and Viktor Weisman's physics technology, he would finally bend the governing council completely to his will on his path to ultimate power and knowledge.

The singularity program was an important part of his, and the world's, future. Once the secrets of biology were revealed, he would be among the first humans to evolve to the new superspecies, a hybrid of man and machine. It was too late to reverse his physical condition, but not too late to become the first of a new species.

Then he would choose which Commission members would make the transition with him, though with important differences that would ensure their loyalty.

They would rule those they had left behind, for their benefit.

The unforeseen physics discoveries were a threat to his plans.

Things could disintegrate around him, and the knowledge he sought lost, before he was able to reach his goals. The clock was running out on him, too.

It was time to be more aggressive.

Sitting in a car by the airport with Elena, Sergei answered Sarastro's call. "We followed your instructions." Sergei thought that it had been a mistake for Sarastro to order them to let Lawson see them, even though the pace of things was forcing their hands, but knew better than to say so.

"Good. Continue following him," Sarastro replied.

"There's a problem. He's disappeared. Maybe he sought help from Evans."

"I don't think so. We'd already know if he had, and Lawson is a lone wolf foolishly trying to do things on his own. Perhaps he has made contact with the target. He knows we're onto him. Maybe he will act hastily, make a mistake, and lead us right to what we're after. All we need to do is stay on his tail," Sarastro said.

"We've been searching for hours without finding a trace. They've found a way to go dark," Sergei replied. It had gone against his judgment and nature to just frighten the quarry. They were paying the price for it. Alerted to their presence, Lawson had vanished like a ghost.

After several moments, Sarastro said, "Let's use this to our advantage. Forget Lawson for now. Go on to the next step in the plan. Others will look into Lawson's whereabouts."

"We'll leave immediately," Sergei replied, disappointed that, for now, there'd be no further contact with Lawson. He'd had enough of his meddling and had plans to put a permanent end to that. And while he had no prior history with the lady doctor traveling with Lawson, Sergei was disgusted by her innocence and would enjoy altering that radically.

Chapter 55

Day 13
Wednesday Morning

Three eggs over easy, a side of corn beef hash, two slices of buttered toast, a black-and-white milkshake, and two cups of strong coffee later, Dan was ready to go, feeling surprisingly optimistic. Trish was finishing her bowl of raisin oatmeal accompanied by fruit and a single cup of black tea.

Having forgone all but a few small snacks as they had driven through the night, Dan had developed a big hunger that he satisfied without restraint. They had stopped on the edge of Seattle at a place called the Brooklyn Diner. Pictures and memorabilia from that borough, from days gone by, hung on the walls. Dan, like most who had Brooklyn roots, felt strong ties to his old home. Yet as they had entered the restaurant, the Seattle skyline to the north, with its impressive Space Needle in the foreground of a blue, cloud-dotted sky, and Mount Rainier in the distance to the south, Dan understood what drew many people to the Pacific Northwest. Even now, looking west, the Olympic Mountains grabbed his attention.

"It's beautiful, isn't it?" Trish asked, noticing the direction of Dan's gaze.

"Yes," Dan replied, "even though it's often rainy and drab. There's a good reason depression is higher in the Northwest."

"Maybe you need to be your own sunshine, appreciate every day. You should think of days like today as gifts and enjoy this view now,"

Trish said, as if she was giving him advice for life, not just talking about the local weather.

Looking to avoid a serious discussion about states of minds, especially his, Dan said, "You're right." Then he glanced at his watch. "Well, we'll have to appreciate this one some other time. We have to get going." Waving to the server, he said, "Check please."

"I got it," Trish said, reaching for the check as it was placed on the table in front of Dan.

"Not a chance. I have an expense account for this," Dan said. He tried to grab the check before Trish did and instead wound up placing his hand on top of hers. After a long pause that he wanted to let continue, Dan released her hand and withdrew his.

"I'm here to contribute, too," Trish said, showing no acknowledgment of anything other than the check.

"If you insist, but—" Dan started to say, but stopped when he received a text. He glanced at the screen. "We have a meeting in ninety minutes at the Discovery Institute."

"That should be enough time to check into the motel, shower, and change into fresh clothes."

"You're fine the way you are," Dan said.

"I meant you, not me. You're tough to be around most times, especially after a night in a stuffy car."

"Thanks for appreciating for all the driving I did," Dan said with feigned exasperation.

"Just trying to help you be the best you can be," Trish said, with a pleasant smile. "It isn't easy."

Dan had chosen a small motel just south of Seattle's downtown, near entrances to two main highways, in case they needed a quick getaway. It was next to the sports stadiums and railroad tracks, between small business and industrial zone. Buildings were low and spread out, providing good visibility. The motel was walking distance to the Discovery Institute.

Their room was small, just big enough for separate beds.

Finished dressing after a quick shower, Trish said, "You know, being with you is exhausting. No rest. Dangerous situations. Always being in motion from one adrenaline rush to another. Nothing grounding you. Bad eating habits. It's impossible to tell if you are running toward or away from something. No wonder you've had all the troubles that you've had."

"I have no idea what you're talking about," Dan replied, refusing to acknowledge the truth of her words.

"That is exactly my point. You have no clue," Trish replied, exasperation in her voice.

"And you've got everything nailed down so well that you got stuck traveling with me?"

"I thought it would help Ava, though you continue to give me reasons to doubt that."

Before Dan could answer, his cell phone vibrated. He had set it up to receive messages posted to Stephen's blog in response to a message he had posted about Stephen's death. Quickly, Dan read, *Life is a journey with few guides. We are left to tour the past beneath the present while Discovering the future by ourselves. Without a good lens, everything is distant and fuzzy.*

It was signed *Bill S-30.*

With a rush of excitement, Dan reached for his tablet.

"What's going on?" Trish asked.

Dan handed her the phone, saying, "I not sure about the whole message, but I hope a heretical astronomer is trying to find me."

"Ah. I see. Because Galileo invented the telescope to see distant things. The telescope is the lens." Trish said after reading it. She lowered herself down and sat on the edge of a bed, looking down at the screen.

"That makes sense. Now we just have to figure out what the rest of it means."

"Maybe he knows we're in Seattle."

"The only way the could know that is through someone at the Discovery Institute." Dan thought about the implications of that for a moment. "That's probably why they typed 'Discovering' with a capital *D,*" Dan said. "To let us know."

Trish looked up from the screen. "But then wouldn't *they* just meet us there?"

"Maybe they thought it was too dangerous. "

"Then the rest of the message would be telling us when and where to meet," Trish said.

He thought for a moment about that before he answered, "Obviously, if we're right about the rest of the message, it has to be somewhere in Seattle." Now they just had to figure that out.

"But why post this message in such a public place? Couldn't someone else read the message and intercept us?" Trish said. "Wasn't there a more private way to contact you?"

"Not in a way that couldn't be traced. And anyone seeing this would have to know where we are to be able to figure the message out, and then they would have to be able to get to wherever we're going very quickly to do anything about it. Now, presuming Galileo is in Seattle, where could he be telling us to meet?"

"It's a city," Trish said. "There are hundreds of places to meet."

Dan moved over to the window and pushed aside the curtain. "He used the words *guide* and *tour,* right?"

Trish looked down at the screen and nodded. "'Life is a journey with few guides. We are left to tour the past beneath the present while Discovering the future by ourselves.'"

"Search on *Seattle, tour, guide, past, present,* and *Bill,*" Dan suggested. He turned back around and let the curtain fall closed.

She entered the terms on the tablet and searched. "That's fast and definite. There's a bunch of hits on Bill Speidel's Underground Tour of Seattle. It's only a few blocks from the Discovery Institute."

"Which means Bill S-30 is probably a half hour before our meeting time at the Discovery Institute."

"Isn't this all too obvious to anyone after us, or Galileo?"

"Only if someone is nearby, knows the message was just posted, and knows when we are meeting at the Discovery Institute. All together, highly unlikely. And given we didn't prearrange any form of communication, it would have to be a message we could decipher quickly enough to get there in time."

"What if it's a trap?"

"Unless someone else knows Stephen told me about Galileo, that's also highly unlikely. But we'll be careful anyway."

"If we're right, our rendezvous with Galileo is less than twenty minutes from now. Let's go," Trish commanded.

Dan shook his head. "Stay here for a half hour, then meet me at the Discovery Institute."

"You keep trying to go things alone. Forget it. I'm coming with you," Trish said. She started toward the door.

"You're not trained for this. Things get messy in the field," Dan said matter-of-factly, shuddering, thinking of the Sarasovs.

"Messy? Is that what you call what you did behind an analyst's desk?"

"I was in field operations before I became an intelligence analyst."

"And that turned out so well that you became an analyst?"

"Whatever deficiencies I might have had, that you really don't know anything about, don't translate into capabilities for *you*. You're not coming."

Trish faced off against Dan, took both his hands in hers, looked into his eyes, and said, "This isn't about you or me. We'll both do whatever enhances Ava's chances and us together does that. Now let's go. We'll have to walk fast."

Trish grabbed Dan's right elbow and pulled him outside.

He liked the sound of "us together" and wanted it to mean something to her, too.

Chapter 56

As they approached the tour location, near Pioneer Square, Dan handed his tablet to Trish and said, "Look at this."

On the screen was a map of the area around them. "See these," Dan said, pointing to small icons of cameras with gray-shaded regions projecting out from them. "They mark every security camera around here, along with their corresponding field of vision. The flashing ones are programmable, and I can send commands to shift their direction or shut them off. For now, all we need to do is follow this zigzag path and we'll be outside the view of the cameras. This gives us the means to enter and exit without images of our faces being run through automated facial recognition programs. Of course, some day everything will be in the field of vision, and with social media databases having already tagged every face—"

"Stop," Trish said. "You mean to tell me that right now, government surveillance programs are using facial recognition to track my every movement and put it in a database somewhere?"

"When you're in range of a camera with high enough resolution networked to the internet, they could be doing that. So could Facebook, Instagram, Snapchat, and so on. A retailer could be sending images to them and, with the technology and photos they already have, social media could send the name of the person back, along with a whole lot of other information. For a fee, of course. And all without violating their latest privacy agreement, which they retain the right to revise to their advantage at any time."

"And you helped develop these types of capabilities?" Trish said with indignation.

"For international, not domestic, purposes."

"You'd better not get caught tapping into this stuff. That wouldn't be too helpful to us right now," Trish said.

"I installed trip wires that will let me know if anyone is on to me."

"I don't know whether to be reassured or frightened by you."

"You know all too well what to think about me," Dan said, once again revealing more truth than he had intended. Though they had only been together a short while, and it *had* to be more his imagination than reality, Dan felt like whenever Trish focused her gaze on him, something new was being revealed to her. It did not bring him comfort. There was too much that wasn't the way it should be, and he didn't want others, especially her, to know it.

"I like it better when you're questioning yourself. It makes me think you're being properly cautious," Trish replied.

"Around you, I'm always cautious."

"Keep it that way," Trish said, handing the tablet back to Dan.

"We'll be there in a few blocks."

"Buy your tickets to Bill Speidel's Underground Tour. See Seattle as it once was," the tour guide barked as Dan and Trish approached. They stepped inside the old building that served as the tour starting point, and Dan purchased two tickets.

The large room looked like it had once been a saloon. Rows of benches faced a bar that still dispensed alcoholic beverages for those who wanted one after the tour.

About two dozen tourists were scattered across the benches. They were a mix of older couples, parents in their early forties with teen children, and twentysomething singles. Given the early summer cool weather, most wore long sleeves or light jackets. Standing near the bar was a woman in her early sixties, Dan guessed, with brown hair fading into gray, a friendly demeanor, and animated facial expressions. After a few minutes, she walked to the bar, faced the rows of people, and announced that she was their tour guide. Then she began telling them about Seattle's founding.

Dan was anxious. As best as he could tell, there was no Galileo here. And there was not much time. He'd gleaned from reading the brochure about the tour that they were going to explore remants of the old city of Seattle, now residing under the current city. Entering a confined underground space could be a trap. Once the introduction was over, they began descending steps to a level below, entering corridors underneath the present-day sidewalks. He half listened to the tour guide explain that Seattle had once been built in marshland and on steep hills that rose from them. That became a big problem as the city grew. A fire in the late 1800s burned everything in the low areas to the ground. Shop owners rushed to rebuild before the city could elevate the area. Later, ten-foot-high walls were built along the streets, the space in between filled in, and new roads paved above. What once had been ground-level storefronts became abandoned space as second floors were now at the new street level. Hollow spaces under the present-day sidewalks provided the walkways through which the past was toured beneath the present.

Dan didn't see any sign of Galileo. He followed the tour group, watching Trish carefully. There were lots of partial walls and doorways behind which someone could be lurking. After passing one recessed doorway, a man stepped out of the shadows.

Turning quickly, arms positioned for action, Dan stepped in front of Trish and faced the man. They were thirty feet behind the back of the tour group and hidden from their view. In the dim light, they sized each other up.

The man was average height, slightly pudgy, with rumpled clothes and wild, graying hair. He hardly looked like a threat. But when he moved his hand toward his coat pocket, Dan sprang forward, grabbed the arm, twisted it behind the man's back, and spun him a half turn, pinning him against the wall.

"There's no need for that. I'm the person Stephen called Galileo. In my right pocket is an envelope with a medical analysis of Ava in it and a USB thumb drive. I'm here to help *us* carry out Stephen's wishes, to finish his work."

"How can I be sure of that? Who are you?" Dan replied as he took the envelope and handed it to Trish.

"My name is Sam Abrams. Until a few months ago, I worked at

The Broad Institute, researching the human genome. Before that, I worked at HBC. Like Stephen, I've seen God's handwriting," he answered.

Looking at the bedraggled, frightened man in front of him, hearing the phrase Sam had said, Dan felt the odds were strong that Sam and Stephen's Galileo were one and the same.

"Octavio Romanov said you disappeared. What happened to you?"

"Outside Stephen, I couldn't trust anyone, though if we hadn't been able to find each other, I was considering seeking Romanov's assistance."

Meanwhile, Trish had opened the envelope and started reading. She exclaimed, "It's the same analysis of Ava's genome that I have!"

"We need to keep up with the group in front of us but keep out of earshot," said the skittish Sam Abrams. "Dreadful powers are aligning against us, and they have eyes everywhere."

At the words, shadows seemed to shift shape, and a chill passed over Dan, leaving him questioning his state of mind once again.

Without waiting for a response, Sam hurried after the tour with Dan and Trish in tow.

Dan whispered, "What was your relationship to Stephen and his work?"

"I was one of his first hires at HBC. When Stephen realized something extra was encoded *in* DNA, he had me leave HBC and join The Broad Institute. They're an endowed collaboration between Harvard and MIT that researches genomics. They have fantastic connections to all genome-related research. He thought it would be good to leverage their resources while splitting us up to avoid detection and reduce risk."

Trish looked quizzically at Dan when Sam said "encoded in DNA," then said to Sam, "You make it sound like he found more than genome information."

Both Dan and Sam shot Trish a look that said *Don't say anything more.*

Cautiously, recognizing he'd have to explain what he had withheld from Trish, Dan asked, "Why the cryptic name? Why didn't Stephen tell me about you?"

"He wanted to protect those around him by minimizing what and who they knew. He described it as each person being a spoke in the wheel. I focused on the biology side of things, including medical treatments," Sam said with a knowing look toward Trish. "Last December, right after Stephen's big breakthrough and Alex's death, we became aware of activity that made us very nervous, so I went into hiding. When Stephen died, I followed a plan that we had prearranged, came here, and waited for a safe way to contact you. I better have done a good enough job," Sam said solemnly.

"How did you know we were here?" Trish asked.

"I knew who Stephen had reached out to, thought you might think to reach out to them, too, and had a friend at the Discovery Institute keep an eye out for you. I wanted to meet in an out-of-the-way, but still public, place to make sure who you were, so I picked this."

Anxious to know, Dan cut to the chase and asked, "Do you have access to Stephen's work?"

"Together we will, but not here. We are going to see it all for the first time *together*. No more solo acts," Sam said. "Stephen gave me a security-protected thumb drive. There are buttons on it for entering codes. Once I enter the code I have, a prompt will appear asking for information only you can provide. Once you do that, we'll both have the other codes needed to access the information Stephen stored on your network."

Dan was frustrated. He wanted to unlock the encryption and see *now*, with his own eyes, what Stephen had claimed was scientific proof for the origin and meaning of human existence. He also didn't like sharing it with Sam, though he thought that Sam would probably be a good guide through Stephen's work. Still, Dan would find a way to control it. Too much was at stake.

"Yes, from here on out, we all have to be on the same page," Trish asserted, looking at Dan with an expression that reflected her displeasure with Dan for keeping things from her.

"Then let's go. We'll skip the Discovery Institute," Dan said.

"No. Go there. You may hear things that could turn out to be useful. And we should separate before regrouping to make sure none of us were followed," Sam said.

"Yes, let's do that," Trish said.

"Here is my motel key and the address," Dan said to Sam. "Meet us there in an hour. But first, turn off the location services of your phone, especially GPS, then power it down. Don't carry anything that can be tracked electronically."

"After traveling cross-country by bus, staying in odd hotels, always being on the lookout, using prepaid phones, and all the other precautions I've taken, I ought to be safe now," Sam said in voice that sounded as though he was trying to convince himself.

"Do it anyway," Dan said, thinking of all that had already happened.

With that, the man who had gone by the name Galileo dropped back out of sight.

As Dan and Trish left the tour and headed toward the Discovery Institute, Dan questioned whether they'd find friend or foe there.

Sam got out of the taxi a few blocks from the motel. He decided to walk the rest of the way, ducking in and out of shops and alleys, finally walking beneath a row of trees. Emerging into the open, he saw one of the few old-style motels left. After ascending the exterior stairs, he walked along the external walkway toward the room number printed on the sleeve that held the room key. As he approached the room, an attractive woman, with long black hair, approached from the other direction and said in what seemed like a slight eastern European accent, "Could you show me how the key works? I can't get into my room."

Chapter 57

So this is the place that causes such consternation and wrath," Trish said as they arrived at a two-story, block-long, sandstone building. An exercise club occupied the first floor and the Discovery Institute spanned the level above it.

After being buzzed in, Dan and Trish proceeded through a glass entranceway, then walked up a flight of stairs to the second floor.

"This place is further proof of the power of words and the importance of ideas. The people on the second floor are leaders in the intelligent design movement, proponents of the belief that the actions of an intelligent agent were required to explain human existence, in fact of many features of living things. This makes them the villain of the mainstream science community, which accuses them of hiding a religious agenda in the guise of science," Dan told her. As he explained the institute to Trish, he realized that his quest for truth was leading him to be more open and less judgmental of those also on the quest, whatever the answers turned out to be. One thing was for certain; Dan no longer saw it as an open-and-shut case in favor of materialistic Darwinism.

Reaching the lobby, they saw a small set of offices more befitting a small neighborhood business operating on a tight budget than an organization that had attracted the attention—and scorn—of most of the scientific establishment. "They hardly look like an establishment with the resources needed to challenge all the institutions and organizations they've upset. I don't see what Stephen could have gotten out of a place like this," Dan said as they pressed a second buzzer, anxious to be done with the visit and impatient to meet with Sam later.

"Good thing appearances don't always tell the whole story," Trish replied good-naturedly, lifting an eyebrow.

"I remember my discussion with Dr. Bishop quite well." The conversation with Dr. Peterson had begun after an exchange of regrets over Stephen's death. There was nothing about Peterson that would indicate the venom he conjured up in the halls of Darwinism. His books, when not ignored by the mainstream scientific community, were often vilified as antiscience. But that had been changing. A few in the scientific establishment, while not agreeing with the books' conclusions, were acknowledging legitimate scholarship within them.

Taking the lead in the discussion, Trish said, "We'd appreciate it if you could share with us what had Stephen discussed with you and your reaction to it."

"Certainly. His primary interest was what is commonly, but erroneously, referred to as junk DNA. He was looking for a relation between that and the human body plan, the genetic information that directs the shape, structure, and size of a person and everything within them. At present, the mechanism for the body plan is unknown," Dr. Peterson said.

Trish said, "Did Stephen mention anything about the amount of instructions required to direct human development and the need for an algorithm to take a small amount of DNA and expand it into a large amount of instructions, including for the body plan?"

Smiling, Peterson answered, "That's right."

"And what do people here think about that?" Dan asked.

"It makes sense to direct the body plan with what you described as algorithmic processing. This also presents a strong argument for intelligent design."

"Why?" Dan asked.

"Pretty simple, actually. If you make even the slightest change to a complex algorithm, you get radical changes, not the small changes that Darwinism posits. And for the algorithmic expression to work, you need a lot of things: the algorithm, a translation mechanism, DNA that means something when translated by the algorithm, and a mechanism to take the translated information and make something out of it. And that something has to work. All of this has to be there from the very origin of life. Taken as a whole, this is an example of irreducible complexity. If any one of these elements were missing, it wouldn't work. And an incremental path of small mutations, from a much simpler state to the present state, is extraordinary unlikely. More important, whatever algorithmic processing was there in the beginning couldn't change along the way as that would render everything else nonfunctional."

"The more I hear, the more I still don't get it," Trish said. "It seems so obvious that incredibly complex processing has to be going on, given the known amount of DNA versus all the instructions needed to make a person, yet nobody talks about it. I've never seen a scientific article about it."

"When you've decided beforehand, as I once did, that everything must be explained by natural causes, that there can't be an active God, then there is no reason to look for questions you can't answer or that lead away from what you want to believe," Dan said.

"A lot is acknowledged in pieces but not discussed as a whole," Peterson said. "Even Richard Dawkins recognizes that the code had to be there from the beginning."

"But ultimately it means that the code had to be able to lead to the creation of all species, even though they didn't exist yet," Trish said.

Peterson said, "Evolutionists would say that information got added later, though that leaves out all that is required to go from single-cell organisms to multicell organisms with distinct body plans. And the kicker—with or without algorithms—is the multilayered coding of the epigenome. Based on the setting, the epigenome takes the same area of DNA to mean different things, at different times, for different purposes. Epigenetic factors can even influence the genome for future generations."

"Why is that problematic with something working for one purpose layering on top another?" Trish asked.

"The thing is when one stretch of DNA codes for multiple things, if that area of DNA changes for one purpose, it changes for all its purposes. What might make one thing work better is highly likely to make others work less well, or not at all. The odds that all DNA coding came about through unguided, unplanned means are astronomical. What we see are indications of intentional design. We are the most complex creatures to ever exist, and rather than look at it objectively and deal with what that implies, some people, including many scientists, have decided beforehand that God can't exist, and therefore we have to be here by strictly 'natural,' material causes. That's bad theology leading to bad science."

"But just because the standard Darwinian theory might have flaws doesn't mean that 'God did it,'" Dan said.

"Intelligent design doesn't say anything about God's existence or the identity of the intelligent designer," Dr. Peterson replied.

Dan was confused and starting to get annoyed by what seemed like this man's evasiveness. Why wouldn't these people just come out and say what they must be thinking? Intelligent design had to be a euphemism for God. As much as Dan wanted to push things, he decided to hold back, both as a means to get as much out of Peterson as possible and to get out and see Sam sooner.

Trish wasn't that reluctant. "But isn't intelligent design being used to push the Genesis account of creation?"

"We're accused of that. But no, that's not our purpose. We're looking strictly at the science and not inferring anything about the intelligent designer, nor the means used to express that design," Peterson answered.

"Come on. If not God, then who or what?" Dan said, his thoughts drifting to a world where creationists used their science to impose their religious dogma on others. Yet, at the same time, he was seeking something for himself that would prove whether God existed or not.

"I'm sure everyone has their own ideas. We represent lots of different views and beliefs at this center—and some are without specific religious affiliations or spiritual desire. While there are definitely people out there who are looking to prove the Genesis account of creation, and use intelligent design as one of their arguments, that has nothing to do with us or our work. We don't have to prove the identity of a designer to show that we are the product of design," Peterson answered, a trace of agitation in his voice.

"Let's get back to the purpose of our visit," Trish said looking at Dan. Turning to Dr. Peterson, she asked, "What was Stephen looking for, and were you able to help him with it?"

"He wanted our help in decoding what he called the genome algorithm, but we weren't able to provide any. Dr. Bishop showed great interest in protein folds. We talked about the odds against functional proteins developing via undirected means, and that was the end of the discussion. We also discussed the evidence for gene regulation having multiple layers of controls to *prevent* genetic mutations from being expressed and propagating: in other words, biology working against Darwinian evolution. This led Stephen to speculate that providing different input parameters to genetic algorithms could generate new species rapidly, without requiring significant change to DNA. This would explain the Cambrian explosion."

Intrigued, Dan asked, "Where would these parameters come from and what would cause them to change? How could they change without producing nonfunctioning junk, given what Stephen described about the complexity of the genetic algorithms?"

"I have no idea. Stephen started to mention a connection to the soul but then wouldn't discuss it further. It was not something we'd research, given what we've already been accused of. Anyway, it was the last we spoke. I'm sorry again about his passing."

Lost in thought, Dan didn't acknowledge the condolences. Things were starting to add up, but only to lead to more questions. He felt like he was getting closer to Stephen's thinking. If all perceiving creatures had souls, and if there was a connection between mind and body, the attachment of a different type of soul, like one intended for a human versus an ape, to an existing species could conceivably change the input parameters of the genetic algorithms, via the epigenetic feedback mechanisms Stephen had described, and lead to new species. It would also mean that the algorithms were set up in advance for all the different parameters. And being able to generate new creatures by simply changing a small set of input parameters would support the simultaneous emergence of a large number of new species, in close proximity, in a short period of time, explaining the Cambrian explosion. It would also mean the active participation of a designer, at strategic points in time. It also implied that within each person now, awaiting a trigger, could be the information needed for whatever humanity could become next. What would happen if that information were activated?

"How come materialist Darwinism isn't questioned more in the mainstream press and academia?" Trish asked.

"You're instantly vilified, ridiculed, and shunned if you do," Peterson explained. "Eventually your funding is cut off, and you may lose your position. It would be funny if it wasn't pathetic, how wonderful scientific research papers that could easily be taken as evidence against materialistic Darwinism, have to say somewhere in the paper that in no way is it an argument against it."

"It's amazing how political science is," Trish said.

"It puts scientists with religious beliefs in the awkward position of saying the natural universe explains everything, even their own behavior, while they personally believe that God exists and has a meaningful role to play in our world."

"Isn't that where theistic evolution comes into play?" Trish asked.

"For some," Peterson said.

"The problem with that is it says evolution happened just as Darwin said, via purely naturalistic mechanism, not via intelligent design, yet God put evolution in motion with the explicit intent of producing us. That's quite a tightrope they're dancing on," Dan said.

"That's right," Peterson agreed.

"There are two major contradictions within it. First, if God intended it to turn out exactly as it did, that is a form of intelligent design whether there is visible evidence or not. Second, a person either has an immaterial soul or not. If they don't, theism doesn't make sense. If they do, materialist evolution can't explain its existence and the immaterial soul would play a role in a person's adaptability and selection, making it more than a strictly materialist process," Dan said.

"You may see it that clearly, but try and get the theistic evolutionists to understand it. You would think theists would remember the parables about not being able to serve two masters and the truth shall set you free." He leaned back in his chair. "How do you know so much about this? Why is it so important to you?" Peterson asked.

"I'm just looking for rational answers," Dan answered.

"He's having trouble figuring out whether his existence matters. I've been considering that question as well—about his existence, not mine," Trish joked.

"Have you come to any conclusions?" Peterson said.

"I am leaning toward believing that it does." She gave Dan a wry look.

Dan hesitated, but decided that, given where the discussion had led, he could ask one more question. Dan pulled up on his smartphone the image of the symbol Stephen had drawn and asked, "Have you seen this before? Do you know what it means?"

Peterson looked at it intently, then replied, "No, I haven't. I'm sorry."

Once again feeling anxious to get back to the motel and talk with Sam Abrams, Dan said, "Unless there is anything else you think we should know that would be helpful, I think we should be going."

"If I think of anything, I'll give you a call," Peterson said.

"Thank you very much for your time," Dan said, and Trish added her thanks.

The trip to the Discovery Institute had been worthwhile, though in ways they didn't fully understand, and in ways that were too fantastical. Could the origin of human life really be that bizarre? Could humanity really be on the verge of a major transformation? He had clearly veered into the territory of religious ideas intersecting with scientific ones, and it wasn't something he'd state publically nor seriously pursue, at least not without rock-solid evidence.

As Dan and Trish were headed out the door, Peterson yelled out after them, "Shapes. That's right. I had forgotten. Dr. Bishop said he thought protein shapes played a critical role in the decoding of the genetic algorithm. I don't know what he meant, but it was just one more thing that left my head spinning that day."

As Dan descended the steps to the first floor, his head was spinning as well. He was getting closer to believing what Stephen had told him, scientifically. But that would mean that he would have to believe that something like God existed, and our lives might actually make sense and have lasting value. He wasn't ready to take that leap yet.

He needed to get the codes from Sam and see Stephen's work for himself.

Chapter 58

Distracted by the sophisticated, beautiful woman, who appeared grossly out of place at the budget motel, Sam didn't notice that someone had crept up behind him until a solidly built, medium-height man with a square jaw and a military demeanor appeared at his side, showed him an official-looking badge, and said, "We'd like to have a word with you about aiding and abetting serious federal crimes. Please open the door and step inside."

The man's holstered weapon, revealed through a deliberately open jacket front, provided all the convincing Sam needed.

Whatever thoughts Sam had of escaping vanished when the door slammed shut behind him. With the room's thick curtains, and his sunlight-constricted pupils, he was plunged into darkness.

Seconds later, the woman flipped a switch, and a table lamp by the door shone dulled yellow light onto the main area of the room. Gesturing to a high-back cushioned chair in the corner of the room, the man said, "Please sit down, Dr. Abrams. My colleagues are on their way. When they arrive, we'll ask you a few questions, and then we'll leave."

Sam walked hesitantly to the chair, sat, and then asked, "What government agency are you with?"

"It's a special investigative unit not known to the general public," the man said. Without acknowledging Sam further, he walked to the window that faced the parking lot, pulled back the curtain slightly, peered outside, closed the curtain, then walked slowly back toward Sam.

"I'm not sure if I should feel good about that," Sam said in a low voice, briefly considering asking for a lawyer as a means to prove whether they were government agents. He decided against that. If it was a ruse, he didn't want to force the hands of ill-intentioned people.

The woman responded curtly, "We're not interested in how you feel. At least not yet."

More nervous than before, Sam tried to get comfortable in the chair, to little avail. His mind raced from one thought to another. Imagined visions of Stephen's last moments formed in his mind. He pictured Stephen in similar circumstances being forced to talk before dying. His thoughts turned to the thumb drive hidden in the heel of his right shoe where a firm stomp would destroy it. Torn between protecting its contents and preventing it from falling into the wrong hands, he pressed his toes down and raised the heel of his right foot.

His left hand began to twitch. To stop it, he moved it from his lap and grabbed the left armrest of the chair, trying not to think about whatever insects might inhabit the worn, grubby chair in a run-down, out-of-the way motel. He tried not thinking about the questions that he would be asked. Stephen had deliberately set things up so he couldn't answer many, and what he could, he wouldn't. He wondered how he'd been found. Had Dan Lawson been followed?

A train rumbled toward the motel, eventually passing so close that it felt like it was in the room, and then was gone. His left leg started to shake, and his eyes started to blink uncontrollably. He began to think these people had something to do with Stephen's death.

Several nerve-racking minutes later, there was a knock at the door. The woman opened it and two men entered. One was a blond version of the black-haired first man. The other looked very much like a Russian spymaster, like Karla from the old, cold-war, John le Carré thrillers. Why did Sam's mind work like this when he most needed his wits and calm?

Without saying a word, the Karla man pulled up a wooden chair and sat down in it a few feet from Sam. He stared at Sam coldly, as though debating what to do with someone who had committed a terrible infraction but still might be redeemed.

Finally, the Karla man spoke in an even, Russian-accented voice

meant to convey cool authority, but the menace behind it was clear.
"Dr. Abrams, my name is Sergei. You've already met Elena and
Peter." As Sergei said this, Elena removed the black wig she was
wearing to reveal her frosted hair. She smiled at Sam, a sinister, disturbing smile.

Looking at the man who had arrived with him, Sergei said, "And
that is Willy." Willy was setting up a camera and microphone on a
tripod, both aimed at Sam.

Sergei continued, "We know all about your involvement with Stephen Bishop and your own research. You will do your country, and
yourself, an important service by being as forthcoming as possible.
Do I make myself clear?"

Sam shuddered. He had never played sports as a kid. Instead, he
had read lots of books to escape teasing from the athletic boys, and
found his calling in science; he had always intended to use his mind,
not muscles. He knew more than he could handle was coming his
way, and it petrified him. In a shaky voice, he replied, "Who are you?
What organization do you represent?"

"Dr. Abrams, do not try my patience. You need to recognize the seriousness of the situation. Dr. Bishop violated the trust placed in him
by the government and by others, even you. He's placed this country
at grave risk by his unauthorized research, the biological weapons
his work was leading to, and by his association with Viktor Weisman,
whose work has now made the US a target of every regime in the
world. Do you understand?" Sergei said in a low voice that rumbled
with violence.

Sam nodded.

"Good. That's wise. Now, answer our questions with complete
honesty. Then we can come to a mutually beneficial arrangement,
and you will be allowed to leave. Is *that* clear?"

Sam nodded again. He thought the best approach would be to mix
in bits of truth, pretend to be uninformed in others, and mislead in
the remainder. After all, what could they really know? And therefore,
how could they tell if he was being truthful? And what he knew was
too important to disclose. Stephen had been emphatic about the danger of sharing information, had probably died trying to protect it, and

Sam understood the implications of what he knew too well to give it up now.

"Let's start from the beginning. What was the nature of your relationship with Stephen Bishop?"

"I knew him by reputation when he was at MIT. When he started at HBC, Viktor Weisman, who was in my synagogue, referred me to him. Stephen hired me, and we worked together on genome decoding for about nine months. Things didn't work out. The research went in directions different than I had signed up for, we had a disagreement, and so I left. We spoke once in a while after that, but that was it."

While Sam was being questioned, Elena and Willy searched the room.

After a long pause, during which he glared intently at Sam, Sergei said, "All right, then, tell me about Dr. Weisman's work. You are of course familiar with what took place at his MIT lab."

"I didn't know him well. His fusion research was more than a job or interest for Viktor; it was his life. He treated it like a vocation and believed that it could change the world. I don't know anything about what he was doing at the time of the explosion," Sam answered. That was absolutely true.

"What was Dr. Bishop's involvement with Weisman's work?"

"Absolutely none, of course. Why would you think they were related?" Sam answered.

"You are not complying with the terms I offered. There are penalties for that."

"I swear I'm telling you the truth," Sam pleaded.

Sergei, after listening to his earpiece, continued, "My superior, who is more temperate and forgiving than I am, thinks I should give you another chance. Let's try a different topic. How do you know Dan Lawson and the woman traveling with him?"

"I just met him. Stephen had arranged that. Did Lawson tell you I was here?"

Sergei laughed. "We'd lost him a day ago. Thank you for leading us back to him. Perhaps we'll talk with him next."

"Then how do you find me?"

"We've been keeping an eye on all of Bishop's relationships. You made contact with one here. That was all we needed. I tell you this so you know the power of our organization. Now, tell us about Stephen Bishop's research! We know it had strayed into dangerous territory, and that he had breakthroughs that can both revolutionize and devastate the world. He took things that weren't his and withheld what he owed others. This is your chance to redeem yourself for your part in this. We know you went into hiding for a reason. You want to be on the right side of this—and us, I can assure you," Sergei said, his face now inches from Sam's, his heated breath washing over Sam's face.

Sergei stood up and his shadow fell over Sam and blocked the light. "Tell me again about your work with Dr. Bishop. Do not leave anything out."

"I was hired by Stephen at HBC to analyze gene sequences to identify patterns. I found blocks of genetic code that seemed to function like subroutines in a computer program. Stephen surmised that if we could discover their functions, we could reassemble them to perform any task that we wanted. Our efforts failed. After his daughter got sick, he wanted to redirect his research toward stem cells. I didn't want to do that, so I left," Sam said, continuing to mislead.

"And you have had no contact with him since then?"

"Just an occasional hello, how are you doing type of thing," Sam said in a shaky voice.

"Then why did you just meet with his oldest friend, Dan Lawson, whom Dr. Bishop had recently sought out for assistance?"

Sam answered, "Stephen's daughter is sick again, and Lawson is searching for a treatment that he believes Stephen had found. It doesn't exist, and I told him that."

"And yet you decide to come to this motel, in the very room where Lawson and Ava Bishop's doctor are staying, to continue a conversation with someone you don't know about a man you say you weren't much in contact with, who died under mysterious circumstances, and about research you say you wanted nothing to do with."

Sam didn't answer. He started to move his mouth, then stopped.

Sergei stared at him. Sam tried to hold Sergei's gaze, to look like he had nothing to hide, but failed. Instead, Sam's eyes flicked nervously about the room. He felt sweat form on his brow and coalesce into drops as it worked its way down his face. The lack of reaction from Sergei began to give Sam hope. Maybe they were satisfied with his answers. Whoever they were, even if they were with the government, they were people who carried out their tasks with extreme seriousness. He just wanted to get out of there.

"Perhaps we'll wait for them to arrive and ask them? What do you think they'll say?" Sergei asked.

"I have no idea. Before today, I had never met them," Sam said, hoping this statement would ring as true as it was. "I don't think they would find your presence welcoming. In fact, you probably wouldn't get a lot of cooperation from them once they see how you are treating me," Sam added in an attempt to assert himself.

"Unfortunately for you, I think you are correct," Sergei said as he slammed his open hand across Sam's face, knocking him to the ground, pulled out an aerosol spray, and squirted it into Sam's mouth. Sam gasped for air, unable to yell. Sergei and Willy grabbed him by his armpits, yanked him up, and slammed him into the chair, then tied and gagged him. They searched through Sam's pockets and placed a wallet and a few coins on a table next to his chair. There was no doubting now what side of the law they were on or the danger he was in.

Peter looked suddenly uncomfortable. Sergei, noting this, said, "Go outside and look out for them if you don't have the stomach to do your job." Peter hesitated before slowly leaving the room and closing the door behind him.

Weak and fearful as he was, his face throbbing, Sam knew he had to summon the resolve to protect what Stephen had entrusted him with. He resumed his internal deliberations about what to do about the thumb drive.

Sergei's black eyes, the coldest Sam had ever seen, now glowered at him. Back in the chair across from Sam, Sergei moved closer. "Let me tell you how I view the world so you know what is about to happen. I think you will understand that you have no choice but to succumb, and that any hope of acting differently is an illusion that will be absolutely shattered."

Sergei continued. "I have no use for the weak or those who cling to superficial ideals. Life is simply a battle, and you either win or lose. It's about order and disorder. People can either be part of the superior order or join the mass of the lowly disorder. I hate disorder and weakness, and I will not allow it to prevail. I discipline myself in extraordinary ways to ensure I will win, that I will possess power, and that I will use it to obtain whatever I want. You are simply a pawn to me. What happens to you and those you profess to care about is no concern of mine. I cannot be appeased. You will be either useful to me or not. Do not doubt that I will extract everything from you. The only things in question here are the means that will be necessary to make you tell me the truth and whether you can convince me that you can provide further value once I am done."

Sergei turned toward Elena and directed her toward the brief-cases Willy had carried in. As Sam watched, working hard to breathe through the gag, Elena opened the cases and removed four speakers which she placed around the room. Then she pointed a microphone at Sam's mouth. She connected the speakers to an amplifier, the microphone to a laptop computer, and the computer to the amplifier. Finally, she started a program on the computer, and music began to play. Then she repeatedly and loudly clapped her hands in front of the microphone, adjusting settings on the computer, until the clapping was virtually impossible to hear.

Realization hit, followed quickly by terror.

With a calm expression that still conveyed menace, Sergei said, "I see you understand the purpose of this apparatus. It is a simple application of the same principles that are used in sound-damping headphones, only it will prevent the pathetic sounds you will make from escaping this room." Putting on the headphones, Sergei continued. "We will be able to hear you, but no one else will." He took off Sam's gag and said, "Go ahead and try it. Scream as loud as you can."

Even though Sam knew it was pointless, and wanted to control himself and maintain dignity, fear overcame him, and he yelled out for help. Instantly, he felt painful electric shocks on his arms and neck where electrodes had been attached. These only accentuated his pain and fear. He regained control and went silent. Whatever sound had escaped his mouth was barely audible within the room and certainly was not heard outside it. The sound-damping apparatus was too effective.

Sergei smiled thinly and said, "Allow me to put these on you so you can participate fully in our conversation." He put headphones on Sam, and then added, "Go ahead. Say something softly. You won't be shocked."

Struggling for thoughts, Sam heard himself via the headphones clearly say, "I don't believe that Stephen would have knowingly worked with people like you and your associates."

"That is an astute observation, though I am offended by the inference about my character," Sam heard a voice say. Sam recognized the voice, though its source was not in the room. "Stephen, for his own selfish reasons, made certain arrangements with us, perhaps naïve on his part, that he decided not to honor. You benefited from Stephen's arrangements, and now, by extension, must honor what he did not. My associates in the room with you will see to that. I offer you one last chance to influence the conditions under which that occurs and how you might endeavor to work with us enthusiastically, as part of a team that will transform itself and reshape the world. Your only choice is to decide what side of human history you want to be on. You cannot stop the inevitable. Now, describe in complete detail your knowledge of Stephen's work, leaving nothing out this time."

Sam's mouth went dry and he couldn't swallow.

Showing his first real emotion, a hint of pleasure, Sergei picked up a hot soldering iron and metal clamps.

Immediately, Sam drove the heel of his foot into the floor. Sergei heard the crunch of breaking plastic. He ripped off Sam's shoe, tore off the heel, and then tossed the broken components of the thumb drive onto the table.

In a barely controlled rage he said, "You will help us obtain what you just sought to withhold, and suffer doing it!"

Elena held up the medical kit she had found in Trish's luggage. She opened it with her gloved hand, withdrew a scalpel, and gave it to Sergei.

Twenty minutes later, Sam's battered, burned, and cut body slumped in the chair, held up only by the straps used to restrain him. Resolve almost gone, he had somehow managed to withhold the most significant information from his torturers. His headphones had gone silent as a disembodied voice now conferred with Sergei.

Sound back on, Sam heard the remote voice say, "No reason to hold anything back at this point."

Sergei set up a monitor on the computer. It was a webcam from the interior of a car parked outside Sam's brother's house.

Sergei picked up a syringe and two bottles. He drew fluid into the syringe and held it in front of Sam. "This first injection will revive and stimulate your physical condition and heighten your sensitivity to the pain you are already feeling. The second is a drug that will act as a truth serum. If they somehow prove ineffective, you can watch as one of your nephews suffers an unfortunate, prolonged, painful 'accident.' After that, you will have a short time before my associates enter your brother's home. Then you will see what happens from there. Is there anything you have to say to dissuade me?"

Sam heard the remote voice say, "Something worth fighting so hard to withhold must not be left to those not suited to using it. You've seen the failures of the world's governments and religions. Do you wish to hand over to them knowledge as powerful as you possess? Look at me and see who I am." A face appeared on the computer screen, one that Sam recognized and now feared. It continued to say, "You know that I am the right person to be entrusted with this knowledge, this power. I only use these means when important interests are at stake. And you must know that if I've revealed myself like this to you, your choices are gone. Now make the right decision for humanity, your family, and yourself. If Stephen hadn't foolishly tried to escape, he would have made the right decision eventually, without what you are going through. In the end, I will guide humanity to a new future."

With the effects of the drugs kicking in, Sam's pain increased, his heart raced, and the surprising mental strength he had found weakened. Something within him, not quite a prayer, called out to something outside of him. In response, he felt his chest tighten up, pain shoot through his right arm, and his peripheral vision narrow. He let out a big gasp and everything went black. His limp body sagged against the restraints.

Sergei cursed and checked Sam's pulse, then punched repeatedly on Sam's chest without response. He said to the remote voice, "He's dead."

"I pay you to succeed. This is twice you've failed," the voice roared.

"Something gave him unexpected resolve to resist but could not help his weak heart. You saw it. There was nothing to be done," Sergei said with a barely concealed hint of resentment.

"We can talk about your methods later. Leave the body and get out of there."

"I want Lawson. He'll tell us everything rather than watch his doctor friend face us," Sergei said with enthusiasm.

"No. He doesn't have what we need yet. If we act now, we'll blow our only shot with him. And try to remember that this is business, not personal. Sometimes you seem to enjoy your work too much."

"If it was personal, he'd be dead already."

"Search the room again before you go. Make it look like Lawson was involved," the remote voice ordered.

As Willy packed up and Elena resumed searching the room, Peter burst through the door and said, "They are on their way." Then he saw Sam's body, and a look of disgust crossed his face.

To Peter, Sergei said, "It was necessary." To everyone, he said, "Grab the equipment and get out of here, now!"

As they left, Sergei was concerned about Peter's reactions. How much longer could he trust him?

On her way out, Elena jabbed the scalpel into Sam's unfeeling right hand.

Back in their cars, they pulled out unobserved as Dan and Trish walked toward their motel room. Sergei called 911 and said, "A man and woman with a gun forced another man into room 211. You need to get someone over to the Ballpark Motel right away."

Chapter 59

For the first time since Stephen's death, Dan felt real optimism. He was on the verge of accessing all of Stephen's work, and with it, a cure for Ava appeared within reach. There was increasing reason to believe that life might have meaning. And in ways he didn't yet understand, he felt that the mysteries he perceived in Trish could help him become the person he now wanted to become, and perhaps more. There was a deep serenity in her that he was drawn to.

Still, he was cautious both in his hopes and security. Walking up the steps toward their room on the motel's second floor, he looked around constantly.

When he reached the room, he knocked, expecting Sam to be waiting inside. There was no response. Apprehensive, he knocked again. Optimism now replaced by concern, he waved Trish away, squatted down, put the plastic magnetic key in the lock, and opened the door partway. A wedge of light illuminated a portion of the room. Before he could make out everything inside, Trish pushed past him and rushed over to Sam. His body was motionless, slumped forward against the straps that bound him to the chair.

After closing the door, Dan threw open the curtains so he could see anyone approaching, then looked swiftly around the room while Trish examined Sam. She had her hand on Sam's wrist and her head against his chest. Dan picked up phone by the bed and called 911, only to be told by the operator that ambulances and police were already on their way. As he hung up, he realized that this meant whoever had done this to Sam had called 911, perhaps with the intent of making him and Trish the targets of suspicion.

Meanwhile, Trish saw her small doctor's kit open next to Sam and her scalpel stuck in his hand. Before Dan could caution her not to touch anything that could incriminate them, she withdrew the scalpel and used it to cut Sam's bonds. Dan grabbed Sam's body and gently lowered it to the floor. There were bruise marks on Sam's face and neck. His hands looked like they had been caught in a meat grinder. There were burn marks on his arms. Blood ran down one corner of his mouth. Whatever he had known, and probably the thumb drive as well, was undoubtedly in the hands of the people who had done this to him.

Distraught, Dan wanted to lash out in anger and frustration.

Opening Sam's shirt, empathy for Sam drawing pain on her own face, Trish put her stethoscope on Sam's carotid artery and with surprise said, "He's alive, but barely."

She grabbed the Epi-pen from her kit and gave him a shot of adrenaline. Then she placed an asthma inhaler in his mouth and gave it a short burst. A faint rasp of air escaped his lips. His face was drawn tight and racked with pain. His eyes fluttered and he tried to speak. Trish put the stethoscope to his throat, listened, and repeated what she'd heard: *I didn't crack. Stephen was right. You must finish his work.*

Dan bent over to Sam's ear and said, "Where's the thumb drive, and what's your code? I need to access Stephen's files."

Dan followed Sam's eyes to the broken fragments of the thumb drive that were left behind. Most, but not all, of the main circuit board was gone. Dan was frustrated and relieved that it was useless.

Struggling to form words, Sam mouthed something that Trish somehow picked up: *Remember, everything has a shape. Symbols have meaning. There is another . . . find them . . .*

Sam's right hand tried tracing something in the rug as he mouthed *code*. His bloody finger only left a smudge.

Dan asked, "What symbol? What meaning?"

With the sounds of sirens quickly approaching, Sam's eyes looked skyward, and he moved his mouth for the last time. Placing her left hand on his forehead, her right hand on his heart Trish whispered something into his ear. Sam's face relaxed. With a barely visible smile on his lips, he closed his eyes for the last time. His body lost all ani-mation.

"He's at peace now," Trish said.

"What did you say to him?"

"Those are just words, of no consequence now, that I say only to my dying patients. Don't ask me why I do that. They don't mean much," she replied.

"You won't tell me?"

"You're not dying," Trish said.

"This is going to be hard to explain to the police."

"It's not going to help that whoever did this used my surgical knife."

"Keep the story simple. We're here to find a treatment for Ava. A deranged man practically assaulted us in the underground city. We must have dropped the motel room key and he used it to come here. We don't know what happened, but he clearly had unsavory associ-ates who wanted something from him. Answer everything else exactly as it happened," Dan directed.

"They're going to press for a lot more than that. What about call-ing Agent Evans?"

"Already dialing," Dan said, raising the cell phone to his ear as the paramedics and police entered the room.

Chapter 60

The motel lobby had been transformed into a temporary investigation headquarters. Trish and Dan sat next to each other on the lobby couch, cups of coffee in front of them on the low, worn, fake-wood table. Sitting across from them were Police Chief Wilson and his lead investigator. Several other police officers stood around, while others walked in and out, stopping occasionally to talk to one another.

The chief was not happy. A man had been viciously tortured. Was it the work of a serial sadist who would continue to perpetrate his sick crimes? A targeted crime with a specific purpose? How were the two people in front of him involved? Chief Wilson didn't like the looks of the guy Lawson.

Dan's answers did not satisfy the chief. Another round of questioning was beginning.

"You're telling me that a complete stranger accosted you on a tour of the underground city, wound up in your motel room, where he was tortured, and that you arrived just as he was dying, and that he didn't tell you anything about who did it to him or why? I didn't get to my position by believing in extraordinary coincidences."

Dan looked the chief straight in the eyes. "I wish for both our sakes that I had more information. What happened in our room is extremely disturbing. Have you considered that we might have been the intended targets and perhaps the dead guy might have just stumbled in after taking off with our motel key?"

"You know, I was wondering about that. Why do you think some-one would target you?"

As the chief said this, a detective walked up and spoke privately with him.

In a serious tone, the chief said to Dan, "We have an ID on the victim. His name is Samuel Abrams."

Reading from a document on the tablet he held, the chief contin-ued, "A former employer of his was the Human Betterment Corpora-tion in Massachusetts. About a week ago, their director, a Stephen Bishop, also died under suspicious circumstances. Abrams recently worked at a place called The Broad Institute. He dropped out of sight about a month ago. You sure you don't know any of this that you *might have temporarily forgotten?*"

"No Chief Wilson. I would have told you if I did," Dan insisted, but not too strongly, lest he be viewed as protesting too much.

"The report also says you were long time friends with Bishop. I'm having a hard time believing that you didn't know Abrams. You're going to have to come down to the station where we'll take as long as we need to jog your memory."

Just then, the chief's phone rang. He answered it and mostly lis-tened, occasionally speaking. The expressions on his face ran from exasperation to indignation to resignation.

"Yes, I'm questioning them right now."

"No evidence yet."

"They appear to have alibis."

"I still have questions."

"It's what?"

"I don't like it but we'll arrange for it immediately."

Hanging up, the chief said to Dan and Trish, "It seems like your freedom, and well-being, are a matter of national security. I've been told to arrange for your lodgings tonight, provide security, and then see you safely placed on the first flight back to Boston tomorrow. An Agent Evans has bigger plans for you."

Chapter 61

Day 14
Thursday, 1 a.m.

Thanks to the police chief's influence, Dan and Trish were set up on the fourth floor of a desirable hotel near the center of the city, even though a large number of conventions were taking up almost all of the decent rooms in the area. For security reasons, they were staying in one room.

On the lower ten of the hotel's thirty floors, a rim of exterior facing rooms were bordered on the inside by hallways that were open, above waist-high railings, to an interior courtyard, providing a vertigo-inducing view of the lobby below. Two glass-enclosed elevators, busily ferrying tired guests up and down, were on the front-entrance corners of the building.

At Evans's request, a policeman in the lobby kept watch on Dan and Trish's room via security cameras and a line of sight to their door. Another was stationed nearby, out of sight.

Wary, Dan had taken his own precautions. Propped up on a table near the door, his cell phone camera was pointed at the door handle. An app that he had written used video from the camera to act as a motion detector. If the handle moved, the phone would beep. If the door opened even a sliver, the phone would blare out a high-pitched squeal. He had installed the same app on Trish's phone and aimed it at the window.

Keeping sentinel, Dan sat in a cushioned chair across from the door. The room was dark, save for the light that sliced out from the crack of the barely open bathroom door.

A few feet away, Trish lay on top of the quilted cover of the queen-sized bed, a row of pillows down the middle of it separating each side. Though she wasn't concerned, he wanted her to feel as comfortable as possible and had arranged the pillows.

In their short time together, he had grown to sense something special about her that he wanted to protect, that his first reaction to her looking at him had been real, but not about her. Somehow she had the ability to see into people, and what he had experienced with her was the reflection of the way he had been, as odd as this could be. It was one of the many bewildering things now filling his life that he had to find answers to.

After what happened to Sam, he wanted answers more than ever. Dan wanted to find out if there really was anything more to life than momentary existence; if there was a plan and purpose; if somehow each person's suffering was made right. First Stephen's and now Sam's death seemed to yell out a resounding *no*.

Even though it seemed like he was at a dead end, he would keep pushing on. Although his belief that his efforts would prove worthwhile was only an act of hope, not faith, the alternative was surrender. And whatever Stephen and Sam had known, it had proven strong enough to give them the will to persevere, to not surrender.

Dan wanted the strength to do the same.

Lying on her side of the bed, fully clothed, Trish glanced at Dan, motionless in the chair. Although he was in the shadows, she could see him clearly.

Trish was still shaken by what had happened to Sam. She was used to suffering and death in the course of her work. What sustained her through that, even gave her joy in her work, was the love she felt for her patients as she helped them through their treatments—and too often through to death. In the end, it wasn't death itself that bothered her, but how people treated each other while they lived. While suffering mattered, how people loved and lived mattered more and its pursuit was worth enduring hardship.

This made what happened to Sam all the more distressing to her, leading her to question her views on the nature of humanity.

How could people be so evil? How could they do that to Sam? What possible concept of good could they have had to justify it? If evil was an objective reality—and this was a new thought to her—then what else was, and what did that mean? What was the source of her love and joy?

She wanted to know what was so powerful that it motivated Sam and gave him the strength to endure what he had. Despite the intense pain he had experienced, he'd looked serene and comfortable in his last moments. How could that be?

She looked over at Dan, motionless except to periodically raise his beer to his mouth. She saw someone of both great strength and great weakness. He seemed to doubt almost everything, including his own purpose. That was good, for him. Awareness of ignorance could lead to wisdom. She also needed to find a way to be wiser herself. The things that were happening were out of any frame of reference she had known.

As she watched Dan sit there with his head in his hands, she heard a small sigh. After he finished his beer, he reached for a third one on the table next to him. Before he opened it, Trish got up and went over to him.

She kneeled to the side of the chair, put her right hand on Dan's left forearm, looked into his eyes, and said, "You have to lie down. Today was rough. There is no guarantee tomorrow won't be worse."

"I can rest here."

"You need to be strong and ready to face whatever comes next. While I was studying to become a doctor, I learned that you have to get rest whenever you can. You won't get that in this chair or with another beer."

"I'll be fine. Go back to bed."

"I will when you do," Trish said.

"You turning this into a contest of wills?"

"No, just good judgment. But if you won't rest, I won't, either," Trish said, getting up to sit on the end of the bed.

Dan didn't answer.

"What did Sam mean when he said something was encoded in DNA?" Trish asked. "I thought we'd discuss that with Sam. Now that he's dead, I think you should tell me."

With the risk they now shared, and the trust they were developing, Dan felt he owed Trish more explanations. He had gone over the room when they first arrived, but Dan was still cautious about listening devices, so he stood up, turned on the radio, sat next to Trish on the edge of the bed, and whispered into her ear.

"Stephen told me he had discovered remarkable things encoded within DNA, more than just matter-based genetics, that after he had conducted a big experiment he would show me proof of our origins, souls, and destinies. Despite my disbelief, I was searching for something to grab onto in life, so I agreed to set up a secure computer network for Stephen and his team to do their work and store their data. In exchange, he would tell me everything. I used encryption tools from my old work. He died before he could provide me what he had promised. Without the passcodes he used to encrypt his files, I can't access them. Something at the fusion center must have been part of the experiment he talked about. I need to find out what Stephen had discovered. I'm searching for a lot more than just a treatment for Ava," Dan said.

A look of wonder crossed Trish's face. "That's incredible. And Sam was going to tell you about Stephen's work and, with your help, obtain the passcodes?" she asked.

"That's right. Now that he's dead, I don't know where to look for them," Dan said.

"What type of things did Stephen say he found?"

"He only told me general stuff about genetics, human origin, and something about a relationship to physics."

"Sam said something about there being 'another,' like maybe someone else knows what he did," Trish said.

"I don't know what to make of that. I guess I'll have to look through Stephen's journals again. Maybe you can look, too, see if you can find something I haven't," Dan said.

"I'd like to do that. But first, we need to get some rest," Trish said.

Discouraged by the day, uncertain of what was coming next, he knew he needed all his resolve to face it. He wasn't going to use any of it to fight her further.

Dan stood up slowly and walked over to his side of the bed. He waited for Trish to settle herself, and then he lay down on his side.

Moments later, Dan said somberly, "I found Stephen's body, minutes too late."

Trish turned toward Dan, no pillows between their faces, sadness in hers, placed her hand on his shoulder, and said, "That must have been terrible," with an empathy that made Dan feel like she was completely embracing him.

"When I heard about the explosion at the fusion center, something told me that it might be related to Stephen's experiment. I immediately started searching for him. I got to his MIT biology building just as he was being driven away in the back of a truck. I tracked him to the site where he had been taken and saw people fleeing. Then I found his body. He had scrawled a small symbol in the dirt that I haven't been able to figure out. Maybe he died before finishing it. It's the one I've shown. I haven't told anyone any of this, not even Nancy, because I promised Stephen I would protect his work and his family. Afterward, I found a message he had left on his cell phone for me saying to look to be contacted by Galileo if anything should happen to him. There must be something to the choice of the name Galileo I need to figure out. I can't let Stephen down a second time—I have to find the medicine Ava needs. And there are still things I need to find out for myself."

"It's good you're telling me this. It must have been so hard to keep this inside you, unable to share it with anyone. As awful as you feel, you have to accept that none of it was your fault," Trish said softly.

"If I had been a better person, I would have been there for Stephen and been able to prevent all of this. I have a lot to make up for."

"You can't know that. Things are connected in ways none of us can understand. What you're going through now may be necessary for something more important later."

"Maybe, but it feels like everything I ever thought or did, all the choices I need to still make, are converging. I can't make sense of it. I'm really lost."

"No, you're not. Like everyone else, you're on a crooked path to a straight destination. But you're developing a good compass. You'll find your way. We can start again tomorrow."

"I wish I had your optimism, your confidence. But thank you for everything," Dan said, again embarrassed by all that he had said, but thinking it was the right thing to do. One more paradox to be understood.

"Go to sleep," Trish replied as she passed her hand gently across his face and then rolled onto her side, facing away from him.

He was still not ready to think of God as more than an intellectual possibility, but he silently asked for peace. A warm blanket seemed to descend on him. Whatever energy he had left drained from him, taking all his anxiety and fear with it as well. Before he drifted off, he thought of Trish. He imagined the scent of her hair, the touch of her hand, the softness of her soul. How far he had fallen that he had to resort to longing after another to keep him afloat. Without words, encouraged by the peaceful feeling, he issued an entreaty to whatever might be out there, yearning for something that could, and would, answer. He imagined a life with joy and meaning, with someone like Trish. But it had to be real. The illusions of his past had failed him for too long.

Dan woke in the middle of the night. He had moved into an awkward position. Trish had also shifted. While she was still on her side of the bed, the pillows were no longer between them. Long strands of her hair rested on Dan's face, and the fingers of her hand touched his forearm. Although he was physically uncomfortable in the position he was in, her touch was soothing, and he wasn't going to move. He made the decision to become more than he had ever been; to become someone that Trish would want him to be.

How strangely things had turned out. After living a life dedicated to self-satisfaction, where fun had passed for happiness, he now thought fulfillment might come through what he could do for others. The thought did not displease him.

PART 4

Chapter 62

9:30 A.M.

The announcement blared through the cabin, waking Dan. They were above ten thousand feet, climbing to cruising altitude.

Conditioned by years of flying early in the morning, Dan had fallen asleep as the plane, wheels rumbling rhythmically, engines racing, had started down the runway.

He and Trish were on their way back to Boston, where a difficult encounter with Evans no doubt awaited him. Ignoring government directives and needing to be extricated from a murder investigation would have consequences. There was even the possibility that Evans had found a link between Dan, Stephen, and Viktor, and that would be a real problem.

But Dan would have to wait to find out. With more than four hours to go on the flight, Dan retrieved his laptop computer while Trish gazed out the window at the nearby, snow-covered peak of Mount Rainier. They were in the last row of first class, with a bulkhead behind them, and, two rows further back in coach, a US Marshal, there to ensure their safe arrival.

Opening his computer, Dan placed his thumb on the biometric reader and then entered a series of complex passcodes. A scanned copy of Stephen's journals appeared on the computer's screen. He tapped Trish to get her attention, then placed the computer on her lap. Whispering, he said, "Place your thumb over the reader," while pointing to the thin slit at the lower right of the keypad. "Every three minutes, a prompt will appear on the screen instructing you to reverify your thumbprint. If you don't do that within twenty seconds, the computer will lock you out. If you try to connect to a Wi-Fi network, or insert any reader devices, the computer will also lock you out. I hope you find something."

"So do I," Trish said with a reserved expression, and then turned her attention to the images on the screen, scanning the words and paging through rapidly.

From his angle, Dan couldn't see what she was looking at. The computer's polarized screen guard prevented viewing from any angle but a direct one. He hoped he hadn't made a mistake by trusting her so completely, so quickly, knowing so little about her. He still didn't know why she seemed to be close to Stephen's work yet claimed to know so little about it.

While Trish worked her way through the documents, Dan looked around the cabin, thinking about what had happened. The knowledge of what Sam had endured hung over him.

The precautions Dan had taken when they left San Diego should have been enough to keep his and Trish's movements secret. Yet they had been found, and setting up Sam's death as a clumsy attempt to frame them had been meant as a warning. Had they led the killers to Sam, or was it the other way around? Was Sergei involved? What did the killers know, and what would they do next? They could have waited in the room and subjected Dan and Trish to the same treatment as Sam, but they had not. That probably meant that Sam had been the only target. With Sam gone, it might not be long before the killers turned their attention on Dan and perhaps Trish as well. He wouldn't let her face that risk. He'd go on alone, while making sure that Trish was well protected. He'd already had more than enough people dying around him, and he was convinced that she had something special of her own to do.

Beyond protecting her, he also wanted to avoid emotional complications. The evening before, he had said too much, indulged his emotions and exposed weakness, felt more intimacy than could be there, and longed for someone else to help make him feel whole. In the morning, embarrassed by his behavior, he had adopted a stoic approach and stronger demeanor. He'd have to make himself into whatever he needed to be before ever considering something real with her.

Trish, too, had been different since the moment they had woken up, reserved and distant, leaving Dan feeling that she also regretted the closeness of the evening before and wanted to restore emotional distance between them.

But this was extraneous now that he had gathered himself together and refocused his attention on what needed to be done. The remaining hours of the flight would be dedicated to figuring that out. Top of the list was determining what Sam had meant by *"another."*

Four hours and twenty-five hundred miles of silence later, they were below ten thousand feet, and Dan was stowing his computer. Twenty minutes to go until Logan.

Fighting the awkwardness he still felt, Dan asked Trish, "What do you think?"

"He surely believed everything you've said, and it had a profound effect on him," Trish said, her face showing no emotion. "And I have no idea what the symbol he drew means."

Disappointed but not surprised by the little she had found, Dan replied, "Even though I had been through the pages many times, I was still hoping you'd find something that I'd missed."

"His references to imaginary numbers were interesting," Trish said with what Dan thought was the appearance of a slight twinkle in her eyes.

"Where was that? All I saw were names of a few mathematicians that I couldn't make anything out of." How had Trish made a connection to imaginary numbers? He knew that imaginary numbers, now integral to mathematics, physics, and engineering, led to analyses that made possible all sorts of technologies and structures. As real as the results were, imaginary numbers themselves didn't exist. They were the square root of a negative number. Square roots were numbers that when multiplied by themselves yielded their squares. The problem with finding square roots of negative numbers is that a number times itself, whether positive or negative to begin with, always yields a positive number. The square of positive or negative 2 was 4. The square root of 4 was either 2 or negative 2. In reality, a negative square, and hence its square root, shouldn't exist. That was why square roots of negative numbers were called imaginary. You could never represent them with a physical quantity.

With her first full smile of the day, Trish said, "You did notice the small sketch of a bird with the squiggly *i* embedded in it on page eighty one?"

"The bird, but not the *i*. And what of the names? I researched the mathematicians in the journal—Descartes, Leibniz, Euler—but didn't find a connection." Dan answered.

"It probably would have helped if you'd seen the *i* and recognized the bird. It's a heron. And of course *i* is the symbol for the square root of negative one, and that should have tipped you off. While you were dozing—and by the way I had to elbow you a few times to stop your snoring—I used the internet connection on this screen since I couldn't use your laptop for that" —Trish pointed to the pop-up monitor on her seat's left armrest— "to research them. It turns out Heron of Alexandria was the first to make note of imaginary numbers in fifty AD, but didn't know what to do with them. They were considered an absurdity. This persisted through three Italian mathematicians, past Leibniz, until Euler first made the first real use of them. It was all easy to research and obvious once I found the initial connection. What do you think all this signifies?"

"I think that you figured a lot more out than I did," Dan replied, trying to determine what this new information meant.

"It's funny. So many brilliant minds were offended by the idea of square roots of negative numbers and thought they had no use, yet without them, quantum mechanics and a lot of modern technology would not exist. The products couldn't be designed without the math," Trish said.

"Well, whether it turns out to be useful or not for us, I'm *really* impressed," Dan said.

"Thank you. I like solving puzzles." Trish made a point to look at Dan as she said it. "And there is one more thing you'll find interesting. Leibniz said imaginary numbers are 'an elegant and wonderful resource of the divine intellect, an unnatural birth in the realm of thought, almost an amphibium between being and non-being.'"

Dan thought the words sounded like they could relate to evolution, though he didn't think Leibniz could have had that in mind. But what was Stephen thinking when he had made his notes? Was he linking imaginary numbers and human origin? Were they involved in the algorithms that were being used for genetic expression? That would mean all creatures were the result of deliberate thought, and therefore a designer.

"I was right to have you look at the journals," Dan said, refraining from adding that he was mad at himself for not seeing what she had.

"There's more," Trish said. "The heron and i were on page eighty-one. The square root Heron was trying to find was the result of eighty-one minus one hundred forty-four. Turning to that page, I saw a negative sign in front of the page number. The result is negative sixty-three. If you look carefully at the journal's page numbers, you'll see the page numbers skip from sixty-two to sixty-four. No sixty-three, as though its absence is a negative. Seems like a clue," Trish said.

Dan couldn't believe it. "I thought it was just a mistake. I'm going to have to take a closer look when we're back on the ground. Does it mean anything?"

"Only that maybe there was something that belonged there and its absence is a clue of its importance. Maybe it's a clue about the passcodes."

"When I first noticed that sixty-three was missing, I noticed that sixty-two seemed to have no connection to sixty-four, and I thought it was just a page-numbering error," Dan said. "Maybe some things on sixty-two and sixty-four are clues to what would have been on sixty-three. Did you look closely at those pages?"

"I tried. Sixty-two seemed odd. Whereas most of the journal was about Stephen's scientific work, a lot of this page was about his dad. Sixty-four had a lot of equations, with K as the main variable. One had a large arrow pointing away from K with a ribbon just to the right of that."

"Anything else?" Dan asked.

"Not in the journals. But I did find another interesting quote that I stumbled on while looking at Leibnitz's quote. It's from John Maynard Keynes, speaking of Isaac Newton: 'He regarded the universe as a cryptogram set by the Almighty . . . By pure thought, by concentration of mind, the riddle, he believed, would be revealed to the initiate.' Maybe Stephen thought so too and had set out to unravel it."

Dan could see that she was reveling in revealing the information bit by bit. "You have a knack for the remarkable today. And I like how you're enjoying being mysterious."

With a mischevious smile, Trish said, "So you think I'm mysterious? Why's that?"

"Sometimes you look at people in a way that is different from anything else I've ever seen, in a way that seems to almost physically affect them. There is a depth and magnetism that seems to lurk beyond your eyes, hinting at powers yet to be discovered. When you touch people, it seems to change them for a moment. People say things to you that they might not to others, as though you have a power to make them do that," Dan said, once again realizing, too late, that he had said more than he should. He was embarrassed by how his increased awareness of himself, a truthful interaction with reality, was being manifested in honesty that was unmanly, though no longer weak. In a sense, he was becoming stronger by being more aware, more in the world, and relating more directly with people, though he had to learn how to manage this new strength.

After a moment of almost solemn quiet, Trish asked, "You make me seem like a sorceress. That's not very nice."

"That's not at all what I meant. It's hard to explain," Dan said, trying to find a way to dig himself out without denying what he had said. "You just have a remarkable way of connecting with people that really comforts them, helps them through difficulties. It's amazing, really."

"Well, that sounds better," Trish said without a lot of conviction. It was as though she was aware of the truth of what he said but was bothered by it.

Dan decided to switch to small talk. "What do you do for fun when you're not working?"

In a flat and distant voice, she said, "I like hiking in the Catskills, where I vacationed as a kid, reading books, traveling, the usual stuff."

He worked up the nerve to broach the topic that had been on his mind since the prior night. "It must be hard to have a social life with medical school, residency, and now your position at the hospital."

"I have a full life. But if by that you mean am I romantically involved with anyone, I've had a boyfriend for a year and a half. We don't see each other as much as we'd like, but we try. What about you? I'm sure you have a busy social calendar," Trish said.

He shouldn't have been surprised that she had someone, but he was still taken aback. Dan tried to focus on his answer. "A pretty wonderful lady lived with me for two years. I don't know why, but it didn't work for me in the end. I kept telling myself she deserved better when I really meant that I didn't want to be responsible for someone else's happiness. Before I get involved with anyone else, I have to sort through a lot of things. I can't look to anyone else to make me who I need to be."

"That's more insight than most people have and a good plan. You should follow it."

Neither of them said anything for a few minutes. It seemed neither was in the mood for small talk. Dan decided her answer was an indication to keep his distance. He changed the topic again and said, "Going back to imaginary numbers, what I remember most about Descartes is his assertion of 'I think, therefore I am.' What do you think the connection is to Stephen, his work, and imaginary numbers?"

"I think the connection between imaginary numbers and Stephen's work is probably real," Trish replied, giving no indication she had intended a pun.

Dan was thinking the same thing. And he also thought that it was time to pay a visit to Kevin Collins. Stephen always referred to his dad as his Father. Maybe that is what page 62 meant. And the Ks on page 64 could represent a Kevin who became Father Michael. Priests wear collars that look like ribbons. Maybe pages 62 and 64 did flow together and the missing 63 pointed to Kevin Collins. Maybe the i in the symbol Stephen had drawn pointed to Father Michael. If so, what did the rest of the symbol mean?

There was only one way to find out.

Dan and Trish were followed off the plane by the US Marshal, and at baggage claim they were met by two other US government agents. The taller of the two said to the US Marshal, "We'll take it from here." Turning to Dan and Trish, he said, "Come with us. Cars outside will take you to your homes."

"What about Evans?" Dan said.

"He'll contact you when he returns from Washington. Until then, you're free to move about as long as you stay in the Boston area. An agent will be with you at all times to ensure your safety."

"No doubt Evans will have a lot to say when he returns," Dan replied.

"No doubt," the agent affirmed.

Chapter 63

Mid-afternoon

The government sedan pulled into a spot in front of Dan's brownstone, depositing him and Trish there while an armed agent remained in the car. They had come to together with the intent of regrouping, and contacting Father Michael, before Trish went to her own apartment.

A warm summer breeze rustled the leaves overhead. Patches of light and shade moved along the ground as the sun pushed through a partly cloudy sky.

"This is a nice neighborhood," Trish said as they walked up the steps.

"Thank you." Dan unlocked the door and held it open for Trish. "We're going to the third floor."

"Two flights of stairs isn't a bad way to exercise lightly. Who else lives here?"

"A young couple has the parlor floor. A British insurance executive has the second floor. The garden apartment is empty. I like having the backyard to myself."

"Not bad," Trish said as they entered Dan's apartment.

"It works for me. I'm making coffee. Would you like some?"

"Yes, please," Trish said, opening the refrigerator door. "You know, you're old enough to stock this better than if you were a frat-boy bachelor."

"I went through a stretch where I didn't eat much. Had I known you were coming, I would have stocked it properly."

"An impossible-to-test hypothesis. Therefore it's not a scientific statement and can't have real-world validity," Trish teased, returning to a more light-hearted mood.

"Not so. Once all of this is over, I can prove it by cooking you a nice dinner from a fully stocked refrigerator," Dan said, getting ambitious with her again.

"First things first," Trish answered. Looking out the living room window that faced Storrow Drive and the Charles River, she said, "You have a nice view."

"Especially on the Fourth of July. The Boston Pops and fireworks are straight across. That's part of the reason I bought this building. You're welcomed to watch them with me if you like. It's really nice sitting on the fire escape with a bottle of nice wine and good cheese."

She ignored his invitation and looked toward the flashing light on Dan's answering machine on the kitchen counter. "You're a techie and have an old answering machine? There is a message on it."

"When my father died, I transferred his number to my landline and attached his answering machine, with his greeting, to it. Don't ask me why I still have it. The only people who use it are old friends of my parents trying to get in touch, or my community-related things. I use my cell phone for everything else."

"Don't you want to listen to the message?"

"You can play it," Dan said, sure there wasn't anything that would be problematic for her to hear.

Trish pressed the playback button. The message was from one of Dan's neighborhood buddies, part of a group of guys who got together to play basketball once in a while. As soon as he heard the message, he regretted having Trish play it. "Dan, just reminding you of our upcoming dinner plans for Saturday night. Reservations are at seven. See you then."

"I forgot to cancel. I'll do that later."

"Sounds like you're good friends with them. Why cancel?"

"It's all married, or practically married, couples, all of whom will ask me what happened with my ex-girlfriend before grilling me on why I don't have someone else."

"I think there'll be lots of time to talk about more than that," Trish said.

Gesturing to the alcove, Dan said, "Come on. We've got things to take care of."

After turning on his computer, Dan unscrewed the end cap of the steam radiator and pulled out several loose wires. From a drawer, he took the end of an ethernet connection, also with loose wires and alligator clips at the end. He plugged the ethernet connection into the network connector on the side of his computer, then clipped the wires from it to the wires from the radiator and portions of the radiator itself.

As he sat down, he said, "I've set up my computer to use a wireless connection for activity that I want our government friends to think I'm engaged in. The connection I just set up is a practically untraceable wire system to a nearby building that uses a microwave connection to nearby radio tower, and that's where I do the things I don't want people to know I'm doing."

While he was talking, Trish had crouched down behind him, put her hands on his shoulders, leaned forward, looking at the computer screen, her cheek close to his. He wondered and hoped that there was more to it than just seeing better.

"Can't you use encryption to keep someone from eavesdropping?"

"Yes, but they will still be able to use IP addresses to track sites I've visited and people I've communicated with. Then later, via court order or other means, they could potentially access what I've done. Instead, I'll start this automated program that will make it look like I'm doing a bunch of things that they'll monitor while I'll use a special browser to communicate over my other channel. That's the one I'll use to contact Father Michael."

"Doesn't all this cloak-and-dagger privacy stuff get draining?" Trish said.

"Not nearly as much as not having privacy and enabling totalitarian-like government practices."

"Here I thought you were getting a better handle on things. I hope that is still true."

"Watch and see," Dan said as he brought up a special email program. Using the email address on Father Michael's card, Dan typed,

Need to talk, confidentially, ASAP. Don't contact me any other way than using the enclosed link to access a secure chat session. Thanks. Dan.

"Now what?"

"We wait."

Turning his head toward Trish, bringing their faces even closer, Dan tried to look into her eyes, but she stood up and walked over to the alcove wall.

Trish pointed to a photo of a seventy-year-old couple. "Is that your parents?"

Dan stood up and walked next to her. "Yes, before my mother's cancer changed things."

Next to that photo was a small picture of a young boy standing next to a young girl. Trish said, "That's so cute. Is that you and Grace?"

"Yes, a month before her accident." He turned toward Trish. "I have to let the past go and focus on the future."

As Dan raised his arms toward Trish, she placed her hands on his forearms, held them firmly there, and said, "We've got work to do. I need everything you've got focused on helping Ava and Nancy."

Feeling sheepish, but not entirely ashamed, Dan said, "I have a few other things I have to take care of as well. All I want is for things to be better for everyone."

"Good. Then let's get back to work." Trish walked back to the computer. "There's no response. Did he get the message?"

"He'll have to look at it. Something tells me priests aren't as tethered to email as the rest of us."

"I'll have to get to the hospital soon and check on Ava."

"Go now. I'll let you know when I hear something. The government guy downstairs will give you a ride. The other one will keep an eye on me, so there's not much I can do."

"If you try and pull a fast one on me, I'll clobber you."

"Relax. Go check on her. I'll met you at Nancy's later."

"Don't play any games and try and go it alone," Trish said strongly.

"You really have a low opinion of me."

"There might be some things I think highly of," Trish said, and headed out the door.

After she left, Dan sat back down, saw a message from Father Michael—*What's up?*—and activated the chat.

Dan typed, *I need to talk with you. I've found out things I need to share, and I think there are things you know that I need to find out.*

Moments later, a reply came, *It needs to be in person.*

Why?

You'll understand when you get here.

Five minutes later, the arrangements were complete. He would visit Father Michael in Italy and find out what required his presence.

Chapter 64

D an was loading the dishwasher while Nancy put away leftovers. Trish and Ava sat close together playing a game of Scrabble in the same kitchen seats Dan and Stephen had occupied two weeks ago. A lifetime earlier. Stephen's lifetime.

Despite all she was bearing, Nancy had insisted on cooking dinner. He thought that perhaps it was her way of seeking normalcy through the nightmarish reality of her husband's death and daughter's illness. She had even brought plates of food out to the two agents sitting in the unmarked, government cars in the driveway.

Once they were finished with the chores, Dan walked toward the study, followed by Nancy.

They too sat in the same seats they had two weeks ago, but now a more determined and purposeful Dan said, "How is Ava handling her treatment?"

"Wonderfully, so far. She's even more sprightly," Nancy answered. "Though it's only been a few days, the treatment looks unexpectedly promising."

"When will they know if it's effective?" Dan said. He wondered if Nancy was putting a positive spin on it in an attempt to deal with it.

"Not for a while. We still need to look for whatever treatment Stephen was working on. All of the Cambridge area research community is looking for it, has reached out to everyone they know, without finding a trace of it. Many labs, out of respect for Stephen, are trying to come up with new treatments. Octavio has a large HBC research team working practically around-the-clock. Her cancer is surprisingly widespread. Her doctors have never seen anything like it. Have you been able to find anything?" Nancy said in a drawn but steady voice.

"Not yet, though I won't stop looking."

"I know you won't give up," Nancy said.

"With all you have to deal with, I probably have no business saying this, but one thing has been bugging me since Stephen contacted me, and it's intensified since I began searching through his work. I've developed this weird sort of introspection that feels unmanly, if it's not sexist to say that. It's like I'm wallowing in past hurts, asking why, looking for a path to be happy. People don't think and feel as I have been."

"What you're doing now isn't weakness but strength. For some reason, you have been given a magnificent gift to see into yourself, to look deep into life. You need to make the most of it."

"If He exists, God help me for where this all leads."

"You are a funny guy at times, mostly lovable. Don't worry about it."

Dan got up and went to the bookshelves. "Have the investigators found anything new?"

"If they have, they haven't said anything. And they keep searching the house, each time taking more stuff. They spent a lot of time in the theater room, leaving it a mess. Some of the things are too heavy for me to put back by myself," Nancy said as she winked at Dan.

Picking up the cue, realizing that the house might be bugged, he said, "I can help you with that now if you like."

"Yes, that would be good," Nancy said, then stood up and walked toward the basement.

Dan followed and winked at Trish when he passed the kitchen door.

Trish ran her hand through Ava's hair said to her, "Go get ready for bed, and then I'll come up and read you a story."

Although she was almost past the age of story reading, and it was early, Ava smiled broadly and said, "Two chapters?"

Trish nodded yes with a warm smile.

As Ava headed upstairs, Trish joined Dan and Nancy downstairs in the theater room.

After putting a few of the heavy lounge seats back into place, Dan turned on the entertainment console and started Stephen's classical music playlist. Then he switched on the overhead light that also acted as an electromagnetic interference generator in case the room was bugged.

Nancy's eyes followed his every movement, seeming to plead for assurance.

Dan sat down next to her and gave a brief recap of his and Trish's visits to the Harvard Museum, Salk Institute, the Discovery Institute, and Stephen's apparent interest in the origin and use of imaginary numbers. He left out the encounter with Sergei and the details of Sam's death.

After she asked a few questions, Dan clasped her hand in his and said, "Nancy, how much do you know about Stephen's research and who he worked with?"

"You mean more than what he officially did at HBC," Nancy stated more than asked.

"That's right. He told me just enough to let me know that he thought it could revolutionize our understanding of life, the universe, and God, but not the what or how about that." In a deeper, quieter voice Dan added, "And that it could just as easily lead to the destruction of everything."

"I know he was consumed with research that he thought held incredible promise and was potentially dangerous, but I had no idea of the extent of it. But you know Stephen," Nancy said, again using the present tense, "he would never put his family at risk by involving us in anything dangerous. What have you found, and what was your involvement?"

Dan released Nancy's hand, sat back, and said, "Not nearly enough, and too much. I set up a secure computer network for his work. He encoded it using passcodes that I don't know. I can't get to it. I've been through all his journals and regular files and haven't been able to find the passcodes. Without them, we're stuck. Did he give them to you?"

"Not that I'm aware of," Nancy said.

"Did he tell you about a computer that had lost files on it? He wanted my help recovering them."

Somberly, Nancy shook her head no, then said, "What are you going to do? Stephen entrusted you for a reason."

"Not give up. And visit *another* old friend of mine," Dan said, looking at Trish. Then, turning to Nancy, he added, "It's been a long time since Kevin and I had a heart-to-heart talk."

"Yes, Stephen had talked with him recently. He could have confided in him," Nancy said with what seemed more like hopeful desire than knowing conviction.

"How are we going to get there," Trish asked, "given our escorts and Agent Evans's 'do not leave the vicinity' directive?"

"I have a few ideas I'm working on for *me*. You should remain with Ava," Dan said.

"It will be at least another week before Ava's next treatment. I'm coming with you," Trish said in an authoritative voice.

"It depends on what I need to do to get there. If Evans allows us to travel, you can come. Otherwise, no," Dan said. He'd probably have to break a bunch of laws, take a lot of risks, and he wanted Trish under the watchful protection of Evans's agents.

"What about Octavio? Can he arrange something?" Nancy asked.

"I think I've got something figured out. I don't want to say what, as that would make both of you legally culpable," Dan replied, though agreeing that he might need Octavio's help at some point.

"Is there anything I can do?" Nancy asked.

"Help me look around the house for anything that could be the passcodes Stephen used," Dan answered. "And keep thinking of anything he said that was meant to be remembered."

"He said a lot of memorable things. But I know what you mean and will try."

Standing up, Dan said, "Can we start in the study?"

"That does seem like a good spot," Nancy said.

"While you're doing that, I have a promise to Ava to keep," Trish said.

They had been looking through the books in the study for half an hour when Dan opened Benoit Mandelbrot's book on fractals. The book jacket said he had been born in Poland and had died in 2010 in nearby Cambridge. It was uncanny how so many things were converging around Dan.

Sitting down, he began quickly leafing through the pages. One page had a large illustration that explained the Mandelbrot set equation in detail. It was based on the complex numbers plane, a graphical area that had real numbers for the x axis and imaginary numbers for the y axis. He felt there was an important connection to Stephen's work, though he couldn't grasp it. Staring at the pages, it gnawed at him, though whatever it was hung tantalizingly just out of reach.

Nancy was opening and closing science books, looking for a scrap of paper that Stephen might have written the passcodes on.

Putting the last book back, she walked over to Dan and said, "Did something happen with you and Trish? You're keeping your distance from each other."

"We've been through a bunch of unsettling things. Nothing more complicated than that," Dan said, thinking that the closeness in the hotel, and his own issues that still needed to be resolved, might have pushed Trish away, especially since there was a boyfriend somewhere.

"What do you think Stephen was involved with?" Nancy asked, a trace of fear in her eyes.

"I don't know. He said things that were incredible. If it had been anyone else, I would never have believed what he said could conceivably be true. Even now, I don't know what to believe. I'm also confused by how it's veering off into the religious realm. I don't know if I'm just following the path he followed, and if that means anything for what we're looking for, and whether it's just my own confusion. Did he ever tell you that—"

Nancy raised her hand to his face to stop him from saying more. "Whatever Stephen said was meant for you. He kept some things from me on purpose. What we both need to do is keep our faith in him."

"I'll try," Dan answered as Trish walked down the stairs and into the study. Dan said to her, "I think it's time we go." Turning back to Nancy, he asked, "May I keep this book?"

"Of course, take whatever you want," Nancy answered.

As Dan walked toward the door, Nancy asked, "When do you think you'll go see Father Michael?"

"I'd like to go tomorrow night," Dan answered as Trish shot him a look. "Though I won't leave without telling Trish first," he said with a slight nod toward her.

At the door, Dan gave Nancy a long hug and said, "I'll do my best."

"I have faith in you."

Releasing her, he said, "Whatever I've got, you'll get."

"Have faith in yourself."

"I need a good basis for that."

"When the time comes, it will be there."

"I hope so, God willing," Dan was shocked to hear himself say, though it was more a figure of speech with a trace of hope than actual belief.

Separating, Dan walked outside, next to Trish, as Nancy closed the door.

"That's quite a knack you are developing," Trish said.

Confused, Dan asked, "What's that?"

"For getting people to believe in what they think you can be."

"I think it's more their needs than my promise," he answered.

"Still, you'll have to live up to it."

"Do you have any idea what that might mean?"

"I do. And soon you will, too."

Chapter 65

Day 15
Friday, 10 a.m.

Under a drab, overcast sky that seemed to press down on him, Dan ran along the northern flank of the Charles River on a narrow dirt pathway bordered by thin strips of grass and a paved bike lane. He was headed back toward Boston on the last few miles of a ten-mile run. To his right, the breeze-rolled water lapped softly against the embankment, while cars whizzed by on Memorial Drive. The shower-moistened ground cushioned his steps. Just ahead was what remained of the fusion lab. Though the fire was long extinguished, the memory still smoldered within him.

Any hope that the run would excise the tension within him, allowing him to get real rest, was long gone. The thoughts coursing through his mind had worked him up more than worked things out. The route he had taken, and everything it had brought him past, had, as he should have anticipated, disturbed him. But if he could have done it over, he still would have chosen the same course. It would be a long time before he would be ready to let the recent present become the distant past. He'd rather poke the wound, and feel the pain of the injury, then let it heal as though everything was all right, the damage not as bad as initially feared.

Yet he needed genuine rest, not fitful turning. The adrenaline and drive that had propelled him over the last week, while still enough to cut short his sleep, were waning in their ability to keep him going.

It had been difficult since he'd returned. He'd gotten no closer to finding the passcodes needed to access Stephen's work. Ava's prognosis disturbed him deeply. Nancy was holding together, but not by much. Dan and Trish were still under the watchful eyes of Evans's men, and there was no indication of when Evans would return, demanding answers. He had to go to meet Father Michael in Italy. Through it all, he was preparing for a confrontation, one that he looked forward to, even foolishly wanted to seek, with Sergei.

Focusing on his immediate goal, he pushed ahead and maintained his pace. There wasn't far to go before he reached the destination that was the main objective of the run.

Sweat formed thickly on his brow in the warm, humid air. Dan wiped it away before its stinging droplets reached his eyes, knocking askew the interactive video glasses he was wearing. After adjusting them, he issued a voice-activated command that triggered a display of a series of images showing his immediate surroundings and a map of security cameras on his route, including their blind spots. No one could approach him without being noticed. In case it was needed, a Taser, along with several other items, was tucked inside the pack on the back of his running belt. A tablet was strapped to his back, hidden underneath his shirt. An eighth of a mile ahead, one of Evans's agents rode on a bicycle. Another agent drove discreetly behind him, periodically pulling in and out of spots to allow traffic to pass while maintaining proximity with Dan. A tracking device was attached to Dan's wrist. The agents and tracking device were a condition of Dan's freedom, officially for his protection, though no doubt also meant for observation. While these things were "optional," Dan knew that declining Evans's requests would likely lead to more restrictive confinement, which, while not legally enforceable in the long term, could take time to challenge and overturn, time that Dan didn't have. However, he welcomed the protection for Trish.

The challenge now was how to make his prearranged rendezvous, away from the watchful eyes of his protectors and without raising alarm.

Despite his precautions and the agents' presence, he felt he was being stalked. He'd first noticed it the evening before, at Stephen's house. The suspicion had reappeared after breakfast and now was at the outskirts of his mind. Something made him feel as though he was being shadowed, as though something was biding its time before making itself known and demanding his full attention. It didn't feel like the paranoia he had experienced when he had isolated himself in his bedroom. It had a quality of reality, though no trace of it seemed to exist. With his sounder mind and sharper focus, he pushed the feeling of being stalked out of his consciousness.

Reaching a rightward bend in the river, Dan approached central Cambridge. Tall sycamores lined the left side of Memorial Drive, their long branches extending over the roadway, forming a partial arch. A single line of parked cars formed a continuous ribbon under the sycamores. Parking on the right side of the road wasn't permitted, and it was clear on that side. Across the water, the Harvard crew teams' green-roofed boathouse sat at the river's edge. The top of the distant, tall HBC building seemed to puncture the boathouse roof.

Turning his head backward, Dan raised two fingers, then tugged at his shorts and pointed at a building across the street, indicating he had to use the bathroom. He knew the agent on the bicycle ahead wouldn't see the gestures and the agent in the car behind would have to find a parking spot if he wanted to follow Dan inside.

With a rapid burst of speed, following a path in the security cameras' blind spots, Dan crossed the roadway and ducked down the alleyway of an apartment building. At the backside, he turned right into the monastic community of the Society of Saint John the Evangelist.

Entering the complex, Dan found the bathroom, took off the tracking device, and hid it in the paper towel dispenser. Dan exited the bathroom and found and entered the chapel, where a vision of old-world beauty greeted him. On the edge of Cambridge, the small-scale chapel was in the style of a European, early Christian basilica, with marble floors, limestone walls, and intricate stained glass. It seemed to transport him out of the Boston metropolis and into a different place.

Following the diagram he had received from Father Michael, Dan located and entered the confessional area. An Episcopal priest was waiting on a bench. Placing their conversation under what ought to be strict confidence, that could not be disclosed to anyone, under any conditions, Dan asked, "Are you hearing confessions now?" He was unwilling to say anything similar to what he had brought up to say: *'forgive me, for I have sinned.'*

"Yes, now is an acceptable time for whatever you have to say," the priest replied.

Dan compared the face of the priest with the mobile message he'd received from Kevin. A sixty-year old man, bald at the crown, thin, short dark hair on the sides of his head, with a bright and vital face looked back at Dan. He was part of the ecumenical community that Father Michael was spearheading in the US on behalf of the Vatican. While Dan had doubts about the wisdom of working through this group, it was the best means he had available.

Reusing the code phrase Stephen had set up with Father Michael, Dan asked, "What happens if an already fallen race eats from the Tree of Knowledge of Good and Evil?"

In response, the priest said, "May we never experience the consequences of such a thing as knowing fully that we are in a state that can't withstand it."

Satisfied, Dan said, "I have to be fast. Is everything ready?"

"I am told by our mutual friend that everything has been arranged as you requested."

"Good," Dan said. He took a small packet out of his running pouch and the tablet that was strapped to his back, and gave both to the priest. "As per his instructions, get this to our friend using his organization's fastest courier service. It must arrive before ten a.m."

"I'll do it immediately."

"Thank you."

As Dan started to leave, the priest asked, "Don't you want to confess and receive absolution?"

"I am not in a state to ask for it," Dan said.

"You're undertaking a perilous journey. May God be with you."

"Thank you," Dan said, as the feeling of being stalked returned.

Rushing out as fast as he could, he returned to the bathroom, put the tracking device back on, and started washing his hands, just as the agent who had been on the bicycle entered. Looking at the agent, Dan said with an awkward smile, "That was embarrassing. Sorry I had to run off like that."

"Maybe you should ride back in the car," the agent said severely.

"I'm fine now," Dan answered, half jogging out of the bathroom.

Dan resumed running and would soon pass near where Stephen had been abducted. Once again, Dan wondered whether he might have been there to save Stephen—if he had handled his life better, approached it with the optimism and resolve with which Trish approached it, not spent months deliberately withdrawing into himself? He'd have to live with that question for the rest of his life.

Meanwhile, Ava was very sick, in jeopardy of an outcome that Dan had to prevent at all costs. He would willingly sacrifice everything, including his own life, to save hers.

At the thought of this, he ran harder, almost desperately. He was in the last mile, approaching home, but he might as well have been Odysseus setting out from Troy for Greece, for all the closer it brought Dan to the destination he sought, a life with meaning and joy that made sense in its entirety.

He wondered how Trish did it. How did she handle what should have been desperation and suffering all around her? She wasn't just persevering but was actually joyful and happy. She wasn't religious in any overt way, yet he sensed a real spirituality within her. She wasn't hiding it. It was as though it was just so naturally a part of her, without organized religion, that it required no comment. Yet it hadn't been challenged by evil such as they were now encountering, and it could get far worse by the time everything was over. Would her spiritual sense remain intact, dissipate like his had, or transform into something even stronger, more explicit?

While he was now open to God in a manner he hadn't been for decades, it was a long way from that to belief. Yet he knew the claim that the materialist view of evolution was the most proven fact in all of science couldn't be more wrong. The theory still might be right, but there certainly were a lot of things that required more explanation that presently had none. The lack of complete proof for materialistic evolution didn't prove God's existence, nor explain his own, but it left open possibilities. Dan wanted something that gave meaning and hope yet didn't impose anyone else's view of God, or judgment, on him. A framework was emerging in his mind that might work. He finally was becoming a different person, someone better, someone he himself would like for the right reasons.

It all seemed to add up to a portent of change in atmosphere and fortunes. Not long ago, the low ceiling of clouds heavy with foul weather would have continued their descent, unleashed their torrents, and pressed him flat into the ground. Today, an opposing resolve kept the foulness at bay.

Almost in sync with his thoughts, a gentle rain began to fall, the drops soothing and massaging him as they lightly made contact with his skin, then rolled down along the rest of his body before disappearing into the ground. Though the sky was now filled with streaks, the clouds were breaking and the atmosphere was clearing up.

Finally drained of anxiety, his rhythm relaxed. Smooth strides covered the remaining distance. Turning onto Harvard Bridge, close to home, his taxed legs felt pleasantly tired. A sweet exhaustion spread within. The run had served its purpose after all. A restful nap awaited him at home. Afterward, refreshed, he'd start out on the next leg of the journey that he had already set in motion.

Springing lightly off the bridge, he covered the last halfmile and reached the entrance of his building.

A half dozen police vehicles, and several more from other agencies, crowded the street in front.

Dan approached the line of yellow tape that marked the boundaries of police activity, with the agents who had been accompanying him now talking on their cell phones behind him. He walked up to the officer that was controlling access to the site and said, "This is my building. What's going on?"

"Are you Dan Lawson?" the official said in reply.

"You know that I am."

Ignoring Dan's snarky response, the official said, "Please come with me. Under court order, we're searching your premises."

"For what? I'll happily provide you with whatever you like."

"Come inside with me."

"I'd like to see the warrant."

"You can't. It's sealed under special court order."

"I'd ask what court and judge authorized it, but I suppose even that is sealed."

"Now you're getting it. You've heard of a John Doe investigation?"

"Yes, in Wisconsin. They're a gross violation of the Bill of Rights, and are the express things the founders of our government wanted to protect against and prohibit without exception."

"Then you know you cannot acknowledge the existence of this investigation, cannot tell anyone about it, cannot contact a lawyer, nor see any documents or orders that we have, under penalty of a felony charge."

"Including seeing anything that even confirms that this invasion of privacy and violation of rights, characteristic of a fascist government, is in fact a John Doe investigation."

"With that understanding, you should come upstairs."

"Gladly. It's getting very chilly," Dan said with an edge that implied the issue wasn't the weather but the activities underway and the loss of civil liberties they reflected. Halfway up the stairs to his apartment, he asked, "Where's Evans?"

"Tending to other matters," the lead official said.

"As everyone here should be," Dan replied, earning a visual rebuke from the official.

Of course the agents found nothing of consequence during their painstakingly thorough search of the apartment. Everything important was stored on well-hidden cloud servers. Accessing or viewing the files was virtually impossible to anyone who didn't know the access paths. Stephen's original journals were kept elsewhere. Dan's apartment was devoid of anything that he didn't want to be found. In case of a situation like this, he had deliberately left, in places where they could be discovered, but not too easily, questionable technology and information so that a determined searcher would not come away empty-handed. He'd let them find enough to feel they had succeeded, and therefore would believe Dan wasn't hiding anything else, though what he gave them would not prove detrimental to him.

Still, the time the search took had been enough for Dan to take a quick shower and rest for a short while. While he could have used more rest, at least the vise of fatigue around his head had dissipated, and his mind was sharp.

Now it was time to head downtown to finally meet with Evans. Certainly they both had a lot to say to each other. He had to make sure that it didn't take so long that it would interfere with the plans he had confirmed back at the monastery.

In five hours, he needed to board a commercial flight, alone, using false identification.

Chapter 66

Evans's stone-cold face chilled the air over the bare metal table as he glowered at Dan in a small, windowless, concrete room located deep inside Boston's FBI offices. Two hulks, sidearms in full view, flanked Evans.

Tired of waiting for Evans to speak, and wanting to convey both innocence and confidence, Dan spoke. "I presume you brought me here for reasons other than staring. I'm not that good-looking, nor your type."

"Did you already forget what took place in Seattle and at your apartment?"

"I'm sorry, if an investigation is underway, I'm not allowed to comment on it," Dan answered curtly.

A flash of real anger flashed across Evans's eyes. Evidently, whatever latitude Dan had previously enjoyed was gone.

Without altering his gaze, Evans said in a slow, emphatic voice, "You need to listen *very, very* carefully and, for a change, weigh your course of action wisely *before* you do or say anything. The well-being of one young girl, or of you or your traveling companion, is of no consideration *whatsoever* in comparison to what is at stake."

After a pause meant to allow Dan to absorb the words, Evans continued. "Lawson, I don't know what you know, but it's time you stopped screwing around and started cooperating. Events of the highest importance are unfolding. You have no idea what steps people in Washington want to take with you. The only reason I'm here, and you're not there, is that *our* leadership views my relationship with you as an asset, and I negotiated a deal on your behalf, presuming you're wise enough to take it. Otherwise, well, things work a bit differently these days. Indefinite custody in a location where we'd have the autonomy to gain your cooperation, while leaving your new friend to fend for herself, would be the least of it."

Dan's mind raced through questions and possibilities. What led Evans to speak to him this way? The explosion at the physics lab was catastrophic but localized. The fusion technology, while revolutionary, shouldn't lead to international conflict. Stephen's and Sam's deaths were terrible, but hardly rose to the level of a national security concern.

On the other hand, Sergei's involvement didn't bode well. Had others somehow gained access to Stephen's work, despite Dan's precautions? How much of what Evans was saying was real, and how much was just a bluff? He looked as serious as Dan had ever seen him. Surely that was part of the intent of having Evans face him now—that Dan would recognize it. But what if Evans was being bluffed as well? Evans could be sincere while nonetheless being misled. Dan had to choose his response prudently. If Evans's arms were being twisted, if Dan made it clear to Evans he was playing the expected part for the benefit of the broader audience that was undoubtedly monitoring their interaction, Evans might recognize Dan's unspoken thoughts, and help guide him, with communication only they would recognize.

Referring back to their conversation at Stephen's MIT office, Dan replied, "I don't understand why the government is treating Stephen's death as a national security issue by trying to connect it to an explosion at a research laboratory that worked on unclassified, nondefense-related physics technology, and then trying to connect that to me. Whoever was after Stephen's genetics work went after Sam Abrams in Seattle . . . not me. Isn't it obvious they had reason to do that?"

Evans's face first tightened then softened just slightly into a knowing exasperation, as though Dan had answered exactly as Evans had expected.

Continuing, Dan said, "And I'm confused by your saying 'our leadership.' I'm retired."

Evans withdraw a sheet of paper and pushed it across the table to Dan. "Actually, you were on temporary leave. Fortunately for you, we recently discovered a 'clerical error' that prevented the final processing of your retirement papers. Otherwise the agency technology you've been using—including accessing classified databases, using government protocols to access private consumer data, such as cell phone tower usage, misdirecting Chinese hackers to NSA resources to bring them to the attention of US government cybersecurity investigators—would all be viewed as serious crimes, with potential sentences of several lifetimes. But as the paper in front of you states, that you *will* sign, you've been reinstated to active duty, and all of the aforementioned activities were legal and at our behest. The agreement also includes a confidentiality clause. Only a handful of people will know you are an active agent. You are not permitted to disclose this to anyone other than me."

Dan tried to stifle his surprise and anger.

Noting this, Evans said, "Save the outrage. You were very good. It took a number of our absolute best, and increased capabilities that were developed since you left—I mean, went on leave—to identify your activities. Now, take a few moments to read the agreement, but not too long, before signing it."

Dan was relieved to note that Evans had mentioned nothing of Dan's private, encrypted storage, both cloud-based and using other servers. The techniques Dan had used for that should have still been beyond the best detection methods, unless someone knew what it was and where to look for it. Plus the trip wires he had installed would have signaled him had anyone attempted to breach his security. Reading the agreement, he noted a clause stating he was required to disclose all information, of any nature, on any subject, that was requested. That was something he was not going to do until he knew more of what was going on, including exactly what it was that he had. And that required that he get to Italy to meet with Father Michael, without government oversight.

Evans noticed Dan's eyes lingering on the clause and said, "Forget about whatever the agreement says. It means whatever we want it to, whenever we want it to, until we want it to mean something else.

Just sign it so no one doubts your cooperation. If time wasn't critical, more than your signature would be required. Of course, there is always the John Doe investigation, if you prefer a different course. There are no time limits or constraints on that, as long as we get a judge to sign off on our activities, and you can be certain only judges that grant our requests actually get appointed to their positions."

"That's a hell of a system."

"It's what the nation needs," Evans replied, his voice flat.

Something in Evans's now matter-of-fact manner, indifferent to rights, struck Dan as odd, something that someone who didn't know Evans so well would miss. Evans was a true fighter for the America he believed in. He wouldn't abuse core liberties without showing significant remorse, and there was nothing like that in his expression. Dan wondered if Evans was opening a side door for both of them to walk through that no one else would notice. He'd have to play it through to find out.

"You know how illegal this is, don't you?" Dan said, testing his theory.

"And you know you're appealing to the wrong guy," Evans said with an exaggerated, dismissive shake of his head.

Dan signed the paper and shoved it back to Evans saying, "Now I'm authorized to know everything you do—that is, if you want to get the most out of me."

"Need-to-know basis only," Evans replied, withdrawing a folder from his secure briefcase and placing it on the table in front of him. Looking at the two agents flanking Dan, Evans said to them, "You guys aren't cleared for this. Have a seat outside the door until I call you back in."

Once the agents had left the room, Evans said, "You're a real piece of work. You happen to resume contact with your estranged friend just as he has lots of interaction with the head of a fusion research lab that blows up from something that wasn't supposed to be possible. I tell you to stay out of trouble, and a security camera in San Diego records you in a confrontation with Sergei that, lucky for you, he wanted to avoid. You go dark, and we have no idea where you are. You show up in Seattle and find someone you say you never met before, tortured and dying in your room. Then you ditch my guy for a few minutes for a *'bathroom break'* during a run they shouldn't have let you go on."

"Still nothing that warrants this treatment," Dan replied.

"We don't have time to play cat and mouse with each other. And my knee has 'accidently' turned off the recorder, so you'd best talk freely," Evans said, opening the folder on the table. Passing the top image to Dan, Evans said, "Here's the situation. The fusion explosion, as much tension it caused with other countries and interests, is an afterthought compared to what you are looking at right now. Each colored dot on the geographical image represents the location, type, and relative quantity of significant amounts of nuclear material. Somehow, not only did Viktor Weismann figure out fusion power, but he developed the means to produce the image in front of you. You understand what this means? Imagine if a country knew where everyone else's nuclear weapons and submarines were. Even worse, what if a country didn't have this technology but knew another country did? Rogue nations would be in a 'use it or lose it' situation. Major powers might think they had enough of an advantage to act."

Dan didn't bother trying to restrain his surprise and concern.

Noting this, Evans said quietly, "I see that you do understand the extremely dangerous implications. Where did Viktor get this technology, and what was Stephen's involvement?"

Unprepared for the revelations he'd heard, uncertain of the right course of action, still clinging to trusting Stephen, Dan struggled with what to say to Evans. On the one hand, Dan wanted to help avoid global catastrophe. On the other, he might also have knowledge that could be even deadlier than anything that might be unleashed by the images. And there was also a good chance that as well-intentioned Evans probably was, higher-ups, with far less noble intentions, could misuse whatever Dan provided. And Dan still needed to continue his pursuit for Ava's treatment, wherever that may lie.

Deciding on a middle course, Dan said, "Stephen believed he had decoded the human genome and how it directs human development. Incredibly, he said it utilized a form of algorithmic processing that begged the question of its origin. Somehow, the processing takes a small amount of DNA and turns it into a much larger set of instructions. He wanted my help in setting up a highly secure environment where he could store his work. I did that. Then Stephen was going to show me everything he had discovered, but he died first. I'll give you what Stephen gave me," Dan said, intending only to give the encrypted files of the raw data, the only ones he had he passcodes for, that would be useless without the rest of Stephen's work.

"As for Viktor, I don't know of any relation in their work, can't see how there could have been." While Dan was prepared to turn over the fusion files to appease the government, he wanted to hang onto them for leverage he might need in the future.

Evans showed no emotion during Dan's revelations and remained silent afterward. A faint breeze from the HVAC system chilled Dan. Slowly, Evans pulled another page from the folder, then said, "This is Stephen's autopsy report. The real one, not the sanitized version we gave his widow. Stephen was injected with a powerful drug that was starting to take effect when he died. It acts as a high-powered truth serum while also weakening resistance to pain. Had Stephen not died then, it was likely that he would have been subjected to the same treatment that Sam Abrams was in your Seattle motel room. An analysis of the area found broken glass from a medical vial in an area were he was likely held before trying to escape. Whatever had been in the vial had been tainted from the dust, dried cleaning fluids, and other compounds on the basement floor, although we did identify traces of unusual chemical compounds and a broken vial of blood that was also too contaminated to trace."

Dan was reeling from the information. What had Stephen been doing in a search of a cure for Ava? Composing himself, Dan asked, "Who did this to him?"

"You mean you don't know? You were there," Evans answered.

Not bothering to ask how Evans knew, Dan answered, "I arrived after he was dead and the people who had taken him were gone. I didn't get a close look at them. Who did this?" With anger, Dan added, "Was it Sergei?"

"He probably was there, but he is just the lieutenant for a shadowy figure who goes by the name of Sarastro, one of the leaders of an organization that calls itself The Commission. We've only become aware of both recently and haven't been unable to learn much about them. Its members are rumored to be some of the most powerful people in the world, in places of great influence," Evans answered.

"What did they want with Stephen?"

"Stephen was involved in espionage, trading technology he obtained from others, including Viktor, for foreign experimental treatments for his daughter. He must have known she would get sick again. Stephen had an arrangement with The Commission for the treatment, but they got wind of Viktor's work and went after Stephen. After he died, they went after his associate Abrams, probably to get the same information that you now hold. Turning it over to us is the safest thing you could do for yourself and others."

"I don't believe Stephen would do that, no matter how sick Ava is and how desperate he was to save her," Dan asserted.

"There is no way Viktor came up with the physics breakthroughs by himself. Stephen had introduced him to another physicist, John Welch. Both had accessed technology within various government facilities. If you have a better answer, now is the time to share it. Who knows whom Viktor shared his information with. Also, we believe that Sousan Ghardi had something to do with getting the tritium that caused the explosion. You can bet, if she has any of Viktor's information, she's going to do something with it that won't be in the best interests of any of us."

Dan, realizing just how precarious everything truly was, said, "Stephen asked me to set up the same computer security for Viktor's work." He left out the real reason he had found and copied the files. "We hadn't finished copying the files over before the explosion. I'll give you whatever I got," Dan said. In fact he had copied all the files but would turn over only the fusion information, and hang on to rest of Viktor's files. That would be tricky, since he wasn't certain of the contents of the various data directories. The imaging technology, if it existed, sounded too dangerous to give even to the US.

"Where are the files?" Evans asked.

"On different cloud servers. But there's a condition."

"You're in no position to negotiate. What I told you was true. I'm the reason you're not in a bad situation, partially because I think you can do more free than in custody. You might even be good bait," Evans said, only partially in jest.

"I appreciate what you've done. But here's the deal. I give you Stephen's files; I get to travel to Italy to meet with Father Michael. When I return, I'll give you access to Viktor's files. I'm still after treatment for Ava Bishop. Sam Abrams said something about 'another' before he died, and I have reason to believe that Father Michael may know something about the source of the treatment. And, if what you say about Stephen is right, then Father Michael may know something that will be beneficial to both of us with regard to Stephen's work and what you described as his espionage with Viktor. I would think you would want to learn as much as possible about that."

"I don't like it, even though I understand your concern for the girl and do want to know more about Stephen's activities," Evans replied.

"Liking it has nothing to do with anything. It's your only option, since if I can't continue looking, I don't care where I am. And I don't much like turning over such powerful technology, so none of us will be happy, not that feelings matter here."

"It will have to be under my strict supervision, with no more 'bathroom breaks.'"

"I expected nothing less," Dan said. "And Trish Alighieri comes along to evaluate any medical treatments we may find."

"You're operating well out of your league. This time, you could get burned badly." Evans's tone left Dan wondering whether he was talking about the deal he had just struck, traveling to Father Michael, Trish, or all three.

"Get me access to a secure computer, and I'll get you Stephen's files right away. I have to be in Milan by ten a.m. tomorrow."

"If you go down, don't bring others with you—especially me," Evans said.

"I wonder how this will end for us. Will we get to enjoy our retirements?"

"Let's try while keeping anyone else from dying," Evans answered.

"People always die," Dan said. "Usually the wrong ones."

Chapter 67

After giving Viktor's fusion files to Evans, and an uncomfortable flight on a military aircraft, Dan and Trish were crossing the expanse of Milan's Piazza del Duomo, headed toward the massive cathedral, Duomo di Milano.

A handful of US government agents were sprinkled about, keeping an eye on them, attempting to blend in with the myriad tourists always about, even early in the day.

Before leaving, Dan had told Evans that he had arranged to meet Father Michael in front of the cathedral's main doors. Now there, with no sign of Father Michael, a none-too-happy-to-be-up-at-3-a.m.-US-Eastern-time Agent Evans said, via the earpiece Dan was wearing, "He reconfirmed the time and location with you?"

"Yes, we agreed to meet right in front of the doors at nine" Dan replied.

"You better not be trying to pull anything on us," Evans said.

In fact, that was exactly what Dan intended to do. He needed to continue his search for Stephen's passcodes and Ava's treatment unencumbered by US agents, so he had worked out a plan with Father Michael.

Fifteen minutes later, Father Michael was still nowhere to be found, despite the efforts of Evans's agents. After watching a guided tour of twenty people enter the cathedral, Dan looked at Trish and said to Evans, "I was sure I said in front of the main doors. But maybe he thinks it was in front of them, *inside* the church."

"I don't like it. Don't go anywhere until an agent is with you," Evans said.

Nodding to one who was thirty feet away, Dan replied, "One is just behind me. I'm going in now in case Father Michael's inside, wondering where we are."

"Move slow, and don't stray from the door," Evans directed Dan.

"Got it," Dan replied as he and Trish entered the church. Mouthing *Let's go* to Trish, Dan grabbed her left elbow and guided her toward the tour group as it rounded the back, right side of the cathedral.

Trish, looking confused and alarmed, whispered in Dan's ear that didn't have an earpiece, "What's going on?"

Dan covered the microphone hidden in his shirt with his hand and whispered back, "We need to ditch these guys."

With widening eyes, Trish mouthed, "Are you sure you know what you're doing?"

Dan shook his head "no" as the agent who had been closest to them outside entered the cathedral and looked around for them. Dan's earpiece crackled as Evans said, "Where the hell are you?"

"I think I see him sitting in a pew on the middle of the left side. And that's not a way to talk to someone inside a church," Dan answered.

"Never mind that. Don't go anywhere until my agents are in place," Evans commanded.

Continuing to hide behind the tour group, Dan noticed the petite nun standing a little further up the right side. As two more of Evans's agents entered the cathedral searching for them, Dan and Trish followed the nun through a small doorway hidden behind a large column.

Closing and locking the door behind them, the nun descended steps and beckoned for them to follow. They were now in the crypts below the cathedral's main floor.

Evans voice bellowed in Dan's ear, "Whatever you're up to, cut it out. The guys accompanying you have strict orders, from up on high, to do *anything* needed to secure your physical whereabouts. Even you shouldn't mess with orders like that."

"I know what I'm doing," Dan said as he removed the earpiece, microphone, and transmitter, dumping all into the basin of holy water carved in the wall next to him.

After passing the crypts, they ducked into a short, narrow tunnel that ended at an iron door. Using a skeleton key, the nun opened the door and motioned for them to go outside.

A black Mercedes, with a man dressed as a priest in the driver's seat, was right by the door waiting for them.

Dan held the door open for Trish, then turned to the Nun and said, "Thank you."

In reply, she said, "God bless you on your journeys. The car will take you to Father Michael in Bergamo, as arranged."

They were now on their own, in a foreign country not known for its national security, under the guidance and protection of someone known as a Vatican fixer, whatever that meant. And they were doing all this knowing that a man going by the name Galileo had been recently tortured to death.

It would be a cosmic irony if Dan's undoing came from putting his faith in someone associated with a church for the first time since he was a naïve kid.

Chapter 68

BERGAMO
10:30 A.M.

Ascending the last of the steep streets, the warm day already growing hotter, Dan and Trish approached the Basilica di Santa Maria Maggiore in the historic Città Alta, the upper town of Bergamo, nestled in the foothills of the Alps. The area straddled the past and present. More than a few of the stone edifices in the Città Alta had been constructed nearly a thousand years earlier. In the center of the vehicle-less streets, blue rectangular stone slabs formed a path bordered by strips of small, rounded rocks embedded in gray mortar. Pedestrians ambled at a pace suited to the age in which the streets had first been laid.

Focused solely on the present, with a mind on humanity's, and their own, fragile prospects, Dan and Trish moved rapidly.

Dan's feeling of being stalked had returned in Milan and was intensifying now. Torn between fitting in and looking out for pursuers, he took quick glances, as though he was just a sightseer admiring his surroundings. No one appeared to be a threat. But, as dangerous as Sergei was, Dan felt a presence that was more ominous than anything Sergei posed. All around, the air seemed to thicken, and his breathing felt labored.

Trish continued along without apparent concern.

Together they covered the remaining distance to the basilica's entrance and slipped by the tourists who were slowly passing through the large open door.

Within, an abundance of natural light, airy and joyful, illuminated the many ornate tapestries, finely carved sculptures, intricate wood-work, vivid paintings, and frescoes. The atmosphere seemed almost worthy of what the church's builders had aspired to glorify.

For a brief moment, the church's beauty nearly made Dan for-get why they were there. Seeing the look of wonder on Trish's face, he saw that the basilica had the same effect on her. The sense of being stalked had been pushed to the back of his mind, but then he remembered that, as of an hour ago, they were major international fugitives on an urgent mission. There was no time to admire human handiwork. They were on an accelerating train already moving too fast for its rickety tracks.

Refocused, Dan looked around. With a slight movement of his wrist, he motioned for Trish to come with him as he walked over to four short rows of pews in the open center of the basilica. The pews were empty, save for Father Michael, kneeling, apparently in prayer.

Dan glanced around, and then sat down to the left of him while Trish sat down on his right.

Father Michael sat up and said, "Everything go well?"

Dan answered, "Yes. Thank you for getting us out of Milan. Do you have the pouch?"

With a small nod, Father Michael stood up and walked slowly to the organ console on his right, lifted the corner of the red leather cov-ering closest to the altar, and retrieved a brown, foam-rubber pouch. Returning to the pew, he handed it to Dan, saying, "I could pay a high price for this. I'm still an American citizen and don't want to have to depend on my Vatican diplomatic status."

Dan opened the pouch that he had given the priest in Cambridge so that it could be transported to Father Michael without being searched by Evans. He verified that the encrypted tablet was still inside. He said, "Let's make sure all of us come out of this in good shape. How about telling me, *this time*, everything you know about Stephen and his work? It's a question I've been asked a lot of times, and I'd like to know myself."

"I have done what I have done because you told me that you were in grave danger and had information about Stephen's work and death that could shake the foundation of humanity, including the Church. With words like these, you owe me an explanation before I go any further," Father Michael replied.

Dan said, "Right before Stephen died, he left me a message saying that if anything happened to him, I should watch out for someone going by the name of Galileo. He would provide important information about Stephen's work. Galileo contacted us in Seattle. His real name was Sam Abrams, and he had worked with Stephen. Before we could talk, we found him tied up and tortured in my motel room. Dying, he told us to find an 'other.' I think that's you. Why else would Stephen have chosen the code name Galileo? His research was a threat to the Church's existence and power."

"Absolutely not. The Church knows nothing of Stephen's work. What little I knew, I did not, nor could have, opposed," Father Michael said emphatically.

"If you are not the 'other,' then why does a page in Stephen's journals refer to you?"

"I'm not anybody's 'other.' And I don't know anything about Stephen's journals, so I can't comment on anything in them. But now that you mention it, as we agreed, I get to see them. Only then will I know if I have anything of value for you."

"Do you mean you need to see them before you know if you can tell me what you already know, or you need to take a look in case you find something worth telling me?"

"Let me see and then I'll know," Father Michael replied firmly.

With things at an impasse, Trish leaned across Father Michael and grabbed his and Dan's hands. A moment of silence ensued before she released them and said, "We don't have time for distrust and conflict. We're all on the same team. Stephen's team."

Turning toward Father Michael, Trish quickly recapped all that had happened to them, what Dan had told her about his meeting with Agent Evans, the images Dan had been shown, and the grave threats they posed.

While Trish was speaking, Dan watched Father Michael's expressions and body language. Whether it was from years of hearing confessions or well-developed guile, Father Michael registered the reactions of someone hearing shocking things for the first time. If he knew more than he had let on, it wasn't outwardly apparent.

After Trish finished speaking, Dan waited a moment for Father Michael to think about what he'd heard and then said, "Now you know why I was reluctant to talk about this. Things are headed in a bad direction. I need to know if Stephen was honest with me. Did he discover the fantastic things he said he did, or was it all a ruse to cover up espionage and use me to protect his materials?"

With a troubled sigh, Father Michael said, "I have no reason to doubt Stephen's integrity, though I can't say what he discovered. I am not a scientist. But if what you two have said about his work is true, you, Dan, may soon bear the extraordinary responsibility of being the only one with access to Stephen's discoveries, the only one who will get to decide what to do with them. That would make you the only one who can use them to prevent the catastrophes that appear headed humanity's way. Are you prepared to be the caretaker of all of this, by yourself?"

Startled, Dan replied gravely, "No one can be prepared for that. But I am not going to give it up. Though I don't know why Stephen gave it to me, I will honor the judgment of the only person who knew the truth."

"What made it Stephen's to give and withhold?" Father Michael exclaimed.

"Something he saw led him to think that."

Turning back to Trish, but speaking to Dan, Father Michael said, "I'm glad to see that despite your oft-practiced desire to go it alone, Stephen was smart enough to provide you with someone with the wisdom, compassion, and strength to help guide you, in spite of yourself."

Now looking at Dan, Father Michael added, "I see by the look of surprise on your face that the thought hadn't occurred to you. There's probably a lot more to Trish than you see."

Though Dan did know there was much to be discovered about Trish, he ignored what seemed a reference to his shortcomings. "You still haven't said anything about Stephen's work. Did he tell you the passcodes he used to encrypt it? Without them, I can't access his research, and Ava, and many, many more, may be doomed."

Solemnly, Father Michael replied, "The last time I spoke with Stephen was early May. He was very excited and deeply troubled. We talked about the implications of his genetics work; you already know them. This was all before you helped him with computer security."

"Is that it? Was there anything else? Anything that sounded like it could be a passcode?"

"There are two things that I am able to say," Father Michael answered, pausing long enough for an unfathomable idea to occur to Dan. "Stephen told me that if the time ever came, I was to help you in every way possible."

"*Possible* meaning everything outside of the confessional?" Dan asked.

Father Michael did not answer.

Trish asked, "You mean, if Stephen told you something in confession, no matter how terrible, that you could prevent by telling people or acting on it, you couldn't do it?"

Dan answered, "That's right. Even if Stephen had confessed to espionage, discussed the passcodes, or described mass murder he was about to commit, a priest cannot break the seal of the confession without triggering automatic excommunication. So when Father Michael here says he doesn't know anything else, it doesn't mean he doesn't know anything else. Only that he can't acknowledge it if he does. And they call that a sacrament!"

"You know the Church considers the state of the soul more important than anything corporeal. The seal of confession is needed for absolving penitents of sins they would not otherwise confess. What is more important? Temporary suffering or the eternal disposition of the soul?" Father Michael replied.

The thought that Father Michael might actually have and know everything Dan sought, but couldn't acknowledge it, couldn't steer him in the right direction or even give him the smallest hint, was too much to handle. Rage boiled within him. His vision narrowed on Father Michael, to the exclusion of everything else. A firm, cool grip on Dan's right wrist pulled him in another direction. For the first time in a long time, he sought to turn away from Trish's gaze, but then awareness of her goodness took over. Looking down at his arm, he saw that

Trish's left hand held his arm firmly, then slowly released its grip. A sense of peace descended upon him.

Now calm, Dan said quietly to Father Michael, "Stephen said that he had found the human soul, had proof of its existence, that it was part of each and every moment of our lives, and that without it we could not be present to each other."

"He told me something similar," Father Michael said.

"I could use the proof he spoke of," Dan said

"Then keep looking. Who knows what you may find?" Father Michael said.

After another pause, during which Dan thought about what it would mean to always feel, if it existed, the presence of his soul, he said, "What's the other thing you can share with us? Were you able to help with my other request? Does that fall under the umbrella of helping me in every way possible?"

"Yes it does, and I have," Father Michael said.

Before he could say more, a man dressed as a Franciscan brother approached Father Michael. A startled look crossed Father Michael's face, and he stood up in an alarmed posture. Sensing something amiss, Dan moved quickly, placing himself between the approaching Franciscan and Father Michael. The Franciscan's right hand began to move from the fold of his cassock. Immediately, Dan took a step forward and prepared to strike. Before Dan did anything, Father Michael grabbed Dan's right shoulder and said, "It's all right. Brother Cletus is a member of my staff."

After motioning Brother Cletus toward a nearby pulpit, a pensive Father Michael spoke quietly with him for a few minutes, after which Brother Cletus hurried off.

Returning slowly to the pews, Father Michael, obviously disturbed, said, "A member of my organization has been acting suspiciously. There is a lot of unusual activity in the lower city. We may not have much time."

"We better get a move on it," Dan said.

"In fifteen minutes, after it's cleared out, we'll walk a short way to the Colleoni Chapel. There are items stashed there that may help answer some of your questions."

"What are they?"

"Relax. You'll know soon enough. Now may I see the journals?"

Removing the tablet from the brown pouch, Dan handed it to Father Michael, saying, "There is too much to go through now. I've highlighted the pages and sections that will interest you the most. They pertain to implications of Stephen's work on human origin and existence."

Father Michael sat down and began to skim the scanned journal pages, while Trish, drawn by the artistry around her, walked around, not straying far.

Ten minutes later, Father Michael handed the tablet back to Dan and said, "I understand our predicament better. And there is more. But we should not discuss that here." Spying Trish studying a fresco to their right, he added, "Most interesting that's the one capturing her attention."

"Why's that?" Dan asked.

"Come and see," Father Michael said as he walked toward the fresco. It depicted a structure based on a tree. Floors of a dwelling branched off the trunk. Within the floors, separate rooms held people.

Reaching Trish, Father Michael asked, "What fascinates you so much?"

Trish responded slowly, as though things were gradually coming to her. "The center structure is meant to look like a tree. Within the tree are different representations of what seems like Jesus, Mary, and some others. Around the tree, people are holding up numbered pages. And the image is incomplete. Something is missing at the top."

Father Michael responded, "It's interesting that you said 'the image *is* incomplete.' Something *is* missing. You didn't say *seems*, you spoke as though you *knew*. How did you *know* the top of the fresco had been painted over? Have you seen this before?"

"Never. It just feels that way to me."

Dan took pictures of the fresco with his tablet, though he felt like he was missing something important. "What is it? What's so odd?"

Father Michael said, "This fresco also intrigued Stephen. It is based on Saint Bonaventure's work called *The Tree of Life*. He was known as a great mystic"—he raised his eyebrows, looking at Trish— "and I studied it in the seminary.

"Numbers in Stephen's journals correspond to the biblical passages, from both the Old and New Testaments, that St. Bonaventure cited in the text that forms the basis for this fresco." Pointing to the lower right of the fresco, he added, "This one is from the Book of Revelation and refers to the healing waters of a new Jerusalem."

Immediately, Dan thought the fresco could lead him to Stephen's passcodes. He couldn't wait to find out.

Trish asked, "What do healing waters and new Jerusalem mean?"

Father Michael answered, "The Book of Revelation is attributed to Jesus's disciple John, based on a heavenly revelation John was said to have received and was instructed to write down. It is about the end of times. After great tribulations, a new Jerusalem descends from heaven. Healing waters flow in a river from God's sanctuary. On each side of the river is the Tree of Life." Speaking more slowly, and quietly, nearly stopping before getting the last words out, he continued, "Its leaves are medicine for healing."

A truly awful thought struck Dan, "No. it couldn't be."

Trish and Father Michael looked at him.

A fantastical thought came to Dan and he said, "Stephen would never have been so distraught over Ava's illness, so religiously fanatical, that he would have tried to bring on the apocalypse to get healing water and leaves for her. He never would have tried anything like that, never would have lost his mind that way, right?"

Hesitantly, Father Michael said, "I never saw anything like that in him. And it would have reflected a serious misunderstanding of the symbolism in the book and the meaning of the apocalypse or last days."

"I don't understand," Dan answered, reassured that Stephen never would have, or could have, done anything to try and bring on an apocalypse.

"There are three main things that are confusing about the book of Revelation. First, what are the last days? Second, what does the symbolism mean? Third, when will the events take place? According to Saint Peter, we've been in the last days since his time. The symbolism is hard to understand and needs to be considered in the context of the people of the times in which the book was written."

"That's one of the few things I remember from my religious education," Dan said.

"Did you know there are four views of when the events will take place?"

"No. What are they?"

"Didn't think so. Idealists believe the book is allegorical and does not foretell actual events. Preterists believe the book was intended for the people undergoing Roman persecution in the first century and that most of the events took place then. Futurists believe that most of the events have yet to take place. Historicists believe the events have been transpiring throughout the last two thousand years. One thing we know for certain: God's view of time is different than ours, and we have to be careful how we interpret things."

"It would be truly, truly terrible if Stephen's actions inadvertently help bring on terrible events, apocalyptic or not," Dan said.

"Why? Everyone has to die sometime. Why does it matter if everyone dies at once or death is spread out over time? Wouldn't there be less suffering if no one was left behind to mourn or feel sorrow?" Father Michael asked.

The words struck home. Dan answered slowly, "To many, an eternal void is terrifying, and meeting God even more so."

"Just seek a pure heart and make the best decisions you can. Then, if there is such a thing as an apocalypse, it won't matter to you when it comes. We all have a personal apocalypse whenever and however we die, anyway. You can't get out of here alive," Father Michael said with a sardonic smile.

"What do you think Stephen thought?" Dan asked.

"I think he looked at it the way I do. Events that seem to foretell the end times have been happening since the book of Revelation was written. The Black Death alone took over a third of the population. Plenty of other things that could qualify for what's written in the book have happened. I don't think Stephen thought of the apocalypse as single moment of time that he could influence."

"But that doesn't mean others aren't going to try and use Stephen's work to bring on terrible events. Every time I start to think God could exist, almost want Him to, I get turned away by what religions, and religious people, do in His name," Dan said.

"But they are not doing it with His spirit. It is their own will, not His," Father Michael responded.

"That's easy to say. But it doesn't explain why a God wouldn't do something about it."

Still looking at the fresco, Trish said quizzically, "I've always had a positive, naturalistic view of life. For me, it was simple. Just be good to others. Was that enough?"

"You mean, just being good, without reference to the soul and conscience that God gives you? That objectively good things would exist in what would otherwise be a subjective and temporal existence?" Father Michael asked.

"All I know is that it will be absolutely wrong if don't try to stop whatever Stephen may have started, whether he meant to do so or not," Dan said.

Trish didn't acknowledge his words. She pointed to the upper right of the fresco. "What Bible passages does that refer to?"

Father Michael said, "It's from the book of Daniel. 'God shall awake some unto life ever lasting and others unto reproach in death.'"

"I'm afraid I'm not in good shape if that is true. I'm no Daniel," Dan said.

Father Michael quickly replied, "Woe to that man who did not return to the fountain of mercy out of hope of forgiveness but, terrified by the enormity of his crime, despaired. That's also in this Tree of Life and refers to Judas. His great sin was not betraying Jesus. It was believing that God was not merciful and loving enough to forgive him. The only thing God's forgiveness does not overcome is unrepentance, for forgiveness must be freely received. You should keep that in mind."

Father Michael looked at his watch, and with a faint smile, said, "Time to get going on your path to either help bring on or prevent whatever might happen next."

Trish looked one last time at the fresco. "If you turn the fresco upside down, the tree looks like a truncated pyramid, the same shape that led Heron of Alexandria to discover imaginary numbers. This similarity to what's in Stephen's journal seems too unlikely to be a coincidence. What do imaginary numbers have to do with everything?"

"Let's go and see what we can find out," said Father Michael.

Chapter 69

Father Michael halted at the back of the basilica. After a single bell chimed, he looked around intently and then hurried Dan and Trish out the door and toward the main entrance of the Cappella Colleoni. A sign on the door stated that it was closed. As they approached it, the door opened and Brother Cletus stepped out, holding the door open for them. Once they entered the chapel, Brother Cletus nodded toward Father Michael, then closed the door and left.

The three of them stood in eerie silence until Father Michael spoke. "This is the funeral chapel of Bartolomeo Colleoni, an influential military leader who became wealthy defending numerous ruling factions in the fifteenth century, including the Republic of Venice. Such was his power that he had the sacristy of the basilica torn down to make room for this. It is often described as a 'jewel box' because of its shape and the mix of ornate pink and white marble in its façade."

The sixty-foot-square marble interior was as ornate and impressive as the that of the basilica. Yet again they had no time to admire this magnificent example of Renaissance art. Father Michael walked toward a funeral monument embedded in the marble-clad wall. Underneath it were oak panels and a single pew.

After looking back over his shoulder at Dan, Father Michael pushed a hidden clasp on the outer side of the leftmost panel. It swung open on a center axis, with half the panel recessed into an opening in the wall, while the other half protruded outward.

Moving with haste, Father Michael reached in and pulled out a slim envelope and handed it to Dan.

Seeing *For my friend Dan* written in a familiar hand on the front, Dan felt the scab ripped off his wound yet again.

Duty took over, and he pushed aside his feelings and examined the sealed letter. He took pictures with his phone of its exterior. He didn't want to miss or destroy something important. With deliberate care, he used his thin drivers license to detach the lightly attached flap.

Unfolding the single sheet of tightly creased paper, Dan saw a dozen tables mapping DNA base pair triplets to the alphabet. In the first table, the triplet GCT corresponded to A, and so on.

While the mappings were clear, he wasn't certain of their purpose. Was it meant to translate DNA triplets into letters or the other way around?

He couldn't believe that human DNA, simply translated using the paper he held, would produce anything other than gibberish or a short word that was nothing more than a random outcome. Otherwise, it would mean life was completely designed, in every aspect, and that the designer had enough foreknowledge of what humans would become that he knew the language to use to communicate whatever was intended to be discovered at a far-off date.

The other possibility, that the table was meant to translate letters into DNA triplets for human purposes, was confirmed when Father Michael said, "Stephen said you might need this someday to access his work."

That meant the paper was the means to the passcode Stephen had used to encrypt his work on the computer environment Dan had set up for him. That also meant the first possibility for the use of the translation tables was as far-fetched as Dan had thought.

Yet, without a key phrase to translate with the tables, Dan was still stuck. He needed to know what word or phrase would lead him to enter the right set of DNA triplet letters to unlock Stephen's research. It would also help if he knew which of the tables to use for the translating but, worst case, he'd try each. It would just take more time.

With a quizzical expression, Dan looked at Father Michael and asked, "Is there anything else?" In a voice tinged with urgency, he added, "This is useless without something to translate."

A small smile formed on Father Michael's face as he said, "Stephen said to ask you what were the first eleven words he said to you, letters only. I guess he thought it was memorable enough that you'd remember."

Indeed, Dan did. Stephen made it impossible to forget. Throughout the years, Stephen repeated the last three words whenever he wanted to prod Dan into doing something. "Take a swing" was short for "Don't just stand there. Grab a bat and take a swing."

"When did you get this?" Dan asked.

"Steven had it delivered to me days before his death," Father Michael said.

So Father Michael had withheld it from him. "Why didn't you give this to me right after Stephen died? One person died and many more are at risk because of the delay."

"You said you didn't know his work. You were in a lousy state of mind. Stephen was dead and I needed reasons to believe in you and in what you'd do with Stephen's work. I don't think you realize how far you'd fallen and how much you've changed for the better in a really short time. Whatever has happened has clearly benefited you. And how could any of us know how our actions would have impacted others? Things might even be worse if I had given this to you at Stephen's wake. I did the best I could with what I knew."

"What if I had never sought you out? What if we hadn't figured out that Stephen's journals pointed us to you?" Dan said solemnly, reflecting on the meaning of how he'd been and the path he was on.

"I would have reached out to you."

Suddenly, Dan wasn't sure if he could trust Father Michael after all. "A little more trust still would have been nice." He watched for Father Michael's reaction to the word *trust*.

Father Michael shrugged slightly, then said, "I got a message from Stephen the night he died. You should use one table, in sequence, for each word in the phrase."

"Great. And now that you're being more forthright, do you know anything about a treatment for Ava?"

"Nothing. I certainly wouldn't have withheld anything that could help her."

Dan sat down in the pew and glanced once at Father Michael. Then he turned on his tablet and began entering the DNA triplet characters that corresponded to the letters of Stephen's long ago words. Eleven words became 39 letters that formed a 117-character string of Gs, Ts, As, and Cs.

With trepidation, he entered the last character and hit enter. The screen went momentarily blank, then was replaced by a list all of his failed attempts to gain access. He was in.

A flood of thoughts filled his mind. Finally, he held Stephen's work in his hands. But now that he had access to it, Dan was as apprehensive as much about what he might find as what he might not. One of Stephen's mottos had always been, Don't ask a question if you don't want to hear the answer. Dan had asked a lot of big questions lately, and he definitely feared some of the answers.

But he didn't have the luxury of time to prepare himself for what might come next. "I'm in!" he exclaimed.

"What do you see?" Trish asked eagerly.

"It's going to take time to figure that out," Dan replied.

"The chapel reopens in forty-five minutes," said Father Michael.

Instead of responding, Dan buried his face in the tablet and began typing, swiping, and reading as quickly as he could. It was essential for him to understand the nature of Stephen's work, and its relation to Viktor's, as quickly as possible.

The first order of business was finding any evidence of whether Stephen had been involved in any sort of espionage or exchange of secrets. From there, he'd look for indications of revolutionary discoveries in biology that could lead to the next stage in human evolution, provide a cure for Ava, or reveal evidence for the human soul and God.

Fortunately, Stephen had organized his work well. Four main directories were titled Source Data, Processors, Converted Data, and Notes. Dan would focus on the notes and converted data. For now, he was far more interested in Stephen's results than how he'd got to them.

Within each of the main directories were three subdirectories, labeled Biological Sciences, Physical Sciences, and Other. The last, while probably least helpful for what he needed now, grabbed his immediate attention. Both the notes and converted data directories were empty. The source data, whatever it was, was in a format that made it impossible to understand.

Father Michael hovered nearby, looking back and forth at the tablet, seemingly in an internal struggle between trying to see and avoid seeing what it would disclose. After a few minutes, Trish grabbed his arm and tugged him toward the altar on the other side of the chapel, away from Dan.

Focusing on the biological sciences notes, with occasional peeks at the converted data, he got an overview of what was there, but very little about what the detailed contents meant. That would take days, if not weeks or months, to understand, and he would need the right knowledge even to attempt it.

Then he began examining the connection between biology and physics, searching for how anything Stephen had discovered could have impacted Viktor's work.

Minutes later, an alarm on Father Michael's smartphone chirped and he said, "Fifteen minutes left. If you want privacy, you should wrap up what you are doing until later."

Dan had to decide what to do. His initial excitement at gaining access to Stephen's work had been damped by the confirmation of what it would take to understand it. The desire for definitive answers would not be satisfied on this day or any other in the near future.

Yet what he had seen was promising. Every indication was that a lot of Stephen's work was indeed based on actual DNA. Stephen's notes pointed to data and programs that could model anatomy and physiological development. There were numerous references to a symbolic language, or at least processing that mimicked it, derived from DNA. And, most fascinating of all, there was mention of a code within DNA. Whatever the truth turned out to be, there was nothing yet to cause Dan to question Stephen's beliefs. There was still reason to have faith in his friend and hope of finding something worth knowing, as far-fetched as Stephen's claims had been.

The physics side of things was more challenging. In the little time he had spent on it, Dan had seen things in Stephen's notes based on pure physics, but he didn't understand them, nor was there a clear link to their origin or relationship to biology.

The good news was that there was nothing that pointed to espionage.

Sadly, he had not found anything that referred to a treatment for Ava. Still, there was a lot more of Stephen's files to work through. Until he could do that, it was premature to say there was nothing that could help her.

That left the immediate issue of deciding whether to turn over the remainder of Viktor's files to Evans. Dan feared what they could trigger more than what they could prevent.

While lost in thought, from across the chapel, he heard Trish ask, "Father Michael, with all that is going on, maybe you can answer a question I have had for a long time. If God exists, why are there so many different religions?"

"Exactly, why should anyone think religion is anything more than man-made?" Dan yelled out before returning his full attention to the contents of his tablet.

Father Michael said, "Think what it would take for there to be one religion, throughout the whole world, throughout all of human existence. God would either have to have implanted that one religion so deeply into everyone's mind, or appeared so frequently during all of human history, that we would not have free will nor have a right relationship with Him."

"But then how can anyone know what is 'right' to believe? And what happens to those who weren't fortunate enough to born into the 'right' faith?" Trish added.

"I think our conscience still guides us, and enough has been revealed to know what God wants from all of us, no matter what we believe or practice. Then, at some point in our lives, maybe even immediately thereafter, we are presented with the ultimate truth about God, whatever that is, which we either accept or reject of our own free, fully informed will. Until then, we try as best we can to practice the religion that we believe is closest to God, recognizing there are things we'll be wrong about—not about Him, but in our understanding of our relationship to Him."

"That's all well and good," a distracted Dan said, looking up briefly, "but what about religious people who say they're rightly killing in God's name, or carrying out His judgments?"

"I think it's a pretty safe bet that if God wasn't going to impose His will on us to make us believe the same religion, He doesn't want highly flawed people to think we need to do that for Him. Ironically, when people force their religion on others, they're opposing God's will by impeding peoples' ability to come to Him freely. They're also contradicting their stated belief that God is all-powerful, by assuming He can't act on His own."

"Try telling that to the not so small number of people who think God has told them they should kill those who don't believe as they do."

"That's their will, not God's, and replacing His with theirs is a terrible mistake. You can see it on their faces. There is no love of God in them, just the hatred that comes from the devil."

"Get rid of one and you get rid of the other," Dan replied.

"Shouldn't you be concentrating on what we've been after?" Trish said.

"I've got this not so small problem of deciding what to do with technology that could tip the balance among people and governments who take their religious and political differences very seriously. Given that, I thought there might be some relevance," Dan said sarcastically.

"You found something in Stephen's files that could do that?" Trish said. "What is it?" she asked, while Father Michael focused his gaze on Dan.

Dan wasn't sure how to answer. Silence prevailed until he turned toward Father Michael and said solemnly, "Stephen told me that his genetics research revealed a teleology in physics that contributed to the formation of life. In other words, the properties of physics were established in such a way as to guide the formation of life. Consequently, learning more about biology also revealed something about physics. He was researching this with Viktor Weisman. And I may have the only copies of his files left. That means what I do with them has to be dead right."

"And you hoped Stephen's files would have information on this that would help you decide what to do?" Father Michael said.

Quiet again prevailed as Trish looked at Dan. She looked disappointed. Although she didn't say anything, she didn't have to. Dan knew what she was thinking. With all the danger they had faced together, he still hadn't been completely honest with her.

Avoiding her gaze, Dan turned to Father Michael and said, "Stephen also said that he believed that science, as deadly as it can be, progressed in a manner that kept history on track, kept humanity from destroying itself even while horrific things were happening, and that his discoveries could do that, too. What do you think of that?"

"It does seem that just as everything could collapse, something comes about to prevent it. Fate's hidden hand, or something more than that, applies the right touch at the right time," Father Michael answered.

"Only I don't get the luxury of being just an observer to it this time."

"No, you don't. How does it feel to be the potential caretaker for humanity after wanting to withdraw from it for so long?"

"About as crappy as you would think," Dan answered.

"Now what will you do?" Trish asked softly in a voice that sought to reassure.

"I'm not sure. Definitely try not to repeat the errors of my past," Dan said.

Looking at Father Michael, Dan said, "Can I talk privately with you for a moment?"

"In the confessional?"

"The end of the pew over there is good," Dan said.

"Go ahead," Trish said to both of them.

"What's on your mind?" Father Michael said once they were seated.

Dan was tempted to reply, *You mean other than all the other little stuff we've discussed?* but said instead, "I don't want to sound crazy, but I've had this halting feeling lately of being stalked, but not by anything human. It feels powerful and threatening. I can consider the possibility of believing in God and definitely don't believe in the devil. What do you think's going on in my mind? Is stress getting to me? Without breaking confidentiality of others, have others said things like this to you, and what do you advise them? I need to know what to think about myself as I decide whether I can trust my judgment."

"Well, each situation is different. In your case, for a long time, your beliefs seemed settled. Now they are apparently in play. Perhaps the bystanders have decided to get involved and what you're experiencing is a battle for your soul. If so, you might want to think about the consequences of that and what you can do to influence the outcome," Father Michael said solemnly.

Dan was thunderstruck by the idea. Perhaps the isolation and separation from the world he had felt weeks earlier had been way more than he had thought; perhaps he'd been losing a battle he didn't know he was in, his humanity was diminishing, his soul really had been at risk, and now he had a chance to win once and for all. Too much to fathom, too much to risk.

All Dan could say in reply was, "Then pray for me."

"I have been, ardently, for a long time," Father Michael said.

"Thank you. I hope that means something."

In the void of the silence that followed Dan's words, Brother Cletus burst through the door saying, "Brother Vincent ran off after we caught him going through your office again!"

Chapter 70

Who's Brother Vincent?" Dan asked, springing to his feet and thinking that they might need to get out of there, fast.

"He's a new administrative aide, a transfer from Rome," Father Michael said. Addressing Brother Cletus, he asked, "What was he was looking for?"

Interrupting, Dan said, "I think we have to assume the worst—that he is working with someone that we don't want to find us."

"Who could be waiting out front for us at this moment," Trish added.

"What about the passageway below?" Father Michael said to Brother Cletus.

"I have the keys. The alley is usually empty," said Brother Cletus.

"Where did you plan to go after this?" Father Michael asked Dan.

"I hadn't decided," Dan replied. He didn't want to say more in front of Brother Cletus, uncertain of what to make of him, and even of Father Michael.

"They could wait in the old parish house," Brother Cletus suggested.

Nodding, Father Michael said, "Yes, that would be good."

"To throw off anyone watching out for us, we'll need to make it seem like we came out the main entrance," Dan said. "Can you find two people that we could pass off as us?"

"There's a couple that works the souvenir stand. Brother Cletus could tell them what we want them do," Father Michael said.

"Let's do that," Dan replied.

After Brother Cletus left, Dan said, "I have to talk with Evans about helping us get out of here." He exited Stephen's files and initiated a secure video conference call.

On the small screen of the tablet, an enraged Agent Evans said, "Lawson, this time you nailed us both with that prank. What are you up to? It'd better be worth a cut in my pension and years in a cell for you, that is if the bad guys don't get you first. There happen to be a lot of them after you, not to mention my guys, who have instructions to be forceful with *both* of you."

"Never mind that. I got what I came for and would like an escort back. Once home, I'm sure we can work something out," Dan said implying that he still had Viktor's fusion files as leverage.

"That may be a little harder than getting you there. It actually may have been good that you gave my guys the slip. The Commission must have a mole here and found out you were headed over there. After we tried tracking you, we reviewed video and spotted a bunch of their people getting ready to make a play for you. It could have really cost you and your lady friend, not to mention my agents," Evans said.

Upon hearing those words, Trish leaned into view of the webcam on Dan's tablet and said, "My name is Trish, and I'd appreciate you'd remembering that. I'm not just an attractive travel companion and have important interests at stake as well."

"Just making sure you understand your predicament hanging out with that guy. No disrespect intended," Evans answered.

"He's proving more capable than you may have thought," Trish said, turning slightly to wink at Dan.

"That's good, for all of us. Now, about getting you back," Evans said.

"We're in Bergamo, in a chapel in the old part of the city. That's a forty-five-minute drive from Milan. We can't stay here. Your guys can meet us in the basilica's old parish house. What about your mole?"

"I'll only tell the two agents who are going to pick you up. They can drive you to the airport and fly back with you. I have an idea where the mole may be and will keep that area in the dark about the plans."

Father Michael tapped Dan's shoulder and pointed to his watch.

"We have to go," Dan said to Evans.

"Good luck," Evans replied.

"You, too," Dan said, ending the call.

"Now what?" he asked Father Michael.

"As soon as Brother Cletus sneaks back in with the couple covering for us, we can go."

Chapter 71

Brother Cletus entered the chapel with the confused-looking shopkeepers.

Speaking in Italian, he instructed the couple to put on the hats and cloaks that were in the shopping bags they carried, to make it seem like Dan and Trish were sneaking out in disguise. Hesitantly, they did as requested.

Pointing to a small door, he began walking toward it. Father Michael, Trish, and Dan followed him through it and then down a narrow stone staircase to the basement crypt. On the far end was another door that creaked noisily as Father Michael opened it. An arched, gray-stoned passageway extended fifty feet to iron gates that stood between them and the outside.

"Once I signal, Brother Cletus will escort you to the old parish house. It's about to undergo renovations and is vacant. You should be safe there until Evans's agents arrive. Now go. I have to get upstairs and pretend I'm smuggling you out of the front of the chapel," Father Michael said.

With an appreciative look and a handshake, Dan said, "Thank you. I'll find a way to repay you for this, someday."

"Doubtful, even if you live, but that's okay. I mean the repayment part, not living," Father Michael answered with a poignant smile.

Surprising himself, Dan gave him a hug, saying, "That crazy Kevin guy turned out pretty well."

"You're becoming someone good yourself."

"Better late than never."

Before the priest left, Trish said, "Thank you. I hope we get to meet again."

"Me, too," he said with a smile. Gesturing to the outside gate, he added, "Better hurry. There's evil about," then stepped back inside as the door swung closed with a loud click as the latch reengaged.

Very quickly, the passageway felt problematic. It was the perfect place for a trap. Thick stone walls surrounded them through which no sound could escape. A locked door behind them. An iron gate ahead, and beyond it, anything could await.

Out of the blue, a battle he thought was already over was re-forming for a last stand. Was existence manifestly good or futile? Could humanity be trusted to use Stephen's work well or were people so flawed that the only way there'd be a future worth having was if a select, wise, few ruled magnanimously?

The dank cylinder seemed to be closing in on him. Shadows appeared to move as if the absence of light allowed something manifestly dark, yet not inert, to fill the void.

Doubt reigned. Rather than accepting Evans's protection, should he seek out those who would use technology and power to prevent suffering, even if it cost freedom and the illusion of meaning? Wasn't that a worthy exchange? Was The Commission as bad as Evans said, or should Dan see if he could trade Stephen's work for a cure for Ava? Or, instead of following Brother Cletus to a rendezvous with a future he couldn't control, should he strike out on his own, even if it meant Ava would not get a treatment that could save her?

Seconds later, Brother Cletus's watch beeped as a text from Father Michael indicated that he was headed out the main entrance with the decoys. After checking the mirror mounted outside the passageway's gate to be sure the narrow alley was clear, Brother Cletus unlocked the gate. The heavy metal groaned as it opened slowly outward.

Dan only had a moment left to decide what he'd do; continue on the path he'd set with Evans or strike out on his own.

Without hesitation, Trish followed Brother Cletus into the alley. Dan went after her. Once again in the light, his doubts vanished.

He glanced around as they skirted the buildings on the left and descended the alley, trying to stay out of sight. Soon they approached a small intersection and turned right onto a narrow street opposite a three-story, stone building. A set of two tall windows, blocked from the inside by tapestry-like drapes, were to the right of the solid wood door.

Leading the way, Brother Cletus pushed the door inward and crossed the threshold. Watching their back, Dan entered after Trish into a dimly lit vestibule.

Immediately, the door slammed closed as the butt of a gun struck Brother Cletus's head and sent him crashing to the ground.

Chapter 72

The rope around Dan's hands was uncomfortably tight but not painful. The slight strain in Trish's face suggested the same.

They were both tied to straight-backed chairs in what had been the living room of the old parish house. Brother Cletus was hogtied on a couch, out cold.

Microphones and speakers had been placed around the room in an odd arrangement.

The room was fifteen feet wide by twenty long, and bare save for the two chairs, couch, table, large oval rug, and several floor lamps that dimly lit the area. A door, opposite the hallway through which they had been marched in, provided access to the exterior. A fire extinguisher hung on the wall, close to the door.

The man who had struck Brother Cletus sat on table top near Dan. Another, wearing a sinister, gleeful smirk, blocked the door to the hallway that led to the vestibule where they had been ambushed.

The woman he'd encountered with Sergei outside the Salk Institute stood before him. Dan strongly suspected that a third encounter with Sergei, perhaps including the shadowy Sarastro, was imminent. Whatever came next, their situation was dire.

Thinking through the possibilities, he figured The Commission was after Stephen's work and thought Dan could provide access to it. That meant they would be aggressive with him and the others but wouldn't seriously hurt him until they either obtained what they wanted or were convinced they couldn't get it. Then things could get very nasty for all of them. Their best option was to play things out until Evans's agents arrived, hopefully before Sergei or any others showed up. If in the process he could find out whatever The Commission knew about a treatment for Ava, so much the better.

Any doubts about whether the woman held a grudge from their prior encounter were erased when she began tapping the barrel of her gun against the left side of his head.

Dan looked into her eyes and saw a burning beauty, borne of exquisite features and a heart full of hate. He could see that it was a hate capable of scorching everything within its range and that it would eventually consume her. Until that time came, she was every bit as lethal as Sergei.

She returned his stare, tapped the gun against his head again, turning the barrel so that the sight dug sharply into his scalp. Then she finally spoke. "Willy, go up front and keep watch."

With a guttural grunt as acknowledgment, the brute by the door walked down the hall.

The woman grabbed Dan's hair with her left hand, pushed his head back, and placed the barrel of her gun against his lips. Dan realized immediately that he had seriously miscalculated what could take place.

Trish's eyes opened wide in terror.

Agitated, the man sitting on the table exclaimed, "Elena! You know our orders. He's to remain unharmed until Sergei arrives and Sarastro talks with him."

"He hasn't been damaged. Not yet," Elena said with a smile that could crack steel with its fierce coldness.

Walking over to the table, Elena picked up Dan's tablet, then asked him, "What's the password?"

Dan didn't answer.

Turning to Trish, Elena said, "Sergei didn't say anything about the girl, Peter," as she raised her gun, apparently preparing to pistol whip Trish.

Peter stood up and took a step toward Trish.

Dan yelled out the code: "Alpha*689!Beta?Omega&&&787."

Elena lowered her arm, turned on the tablet, then said, "Again, slowly."

"Don't tell her," Trish urged. "They're going to kill us anyway. Remember, Sam died protecting it. We can't let them have it."

"Whether you die or not is up to your friend. He has to convince Sarastro that he can be useful and trusted. Sergei and I don't think that will happen," Elena said with a look that made it clear she looked forward to what would come next if it turned out that way.

"They can't—" Trish started to say before Dan cut her off.

"Trish, it's useless. As bad as their tactics, and people, are, Stephen's work shows that their organization's objectives are right. Humanity will evolve and we either adapt or vanish," Dan said, trying to buy time.

Trish looked crestfallen, injured by how easily he had acquiesced.

Dan wasn't sure if it was an act on her part or if she genuinely thought he felt that way. Slowly, he repeated the password.

"I'm disappointed. I get excited playing with men who aren't afraid of getting physical. You are softer than I thought," Elena said dismissively as she typed.

Before she hit Enter, Elena's face turned grim as a thought occurred to her. "It will go very badly for you if the code is a trigger to erase what's on here."

"It's the right code," Dan replied.

Pressing Enter, Elena smiled, looking self-satisfied, when it worked.

As she scrolled around, looking at things that she could not possibly comprehend, Brother Cletus groaned and shifted.

Concerned for him, Dan said, "He needs a doctor."

"You shouldn't worry about someone who betrayed you," Elena said. Smiling at the shocked look on Dan's and Trish's faces, she said, "That's right. He brought you to us."

"We don't have time for this. You need to rendezvous with Sergei," Peter said, suddenly more assertive with Elena.

She bristled. "While I am gone, you can have a little fun with the girl, before Willy does. After he's through with her, there won't be anything left for anyone else." Pointing at Dan, she added, "Leave the guy alone. The only one who gets to mess with him is Sergei or me."

Peter watched Elena leave, taking the tablet with her. When he heard the front door close, he quietly closed the door to the hallway, then walked over to Trish.

Dan's mind worked frantically, trying to figure out what he could do to protect Trish and forestall anything from happening until Evans's people arrived. Even then, he'd need a way to ensure his and Trish's safety through any ensuing conflict.

"I didn't want things to turn out this way," Peter said softly to Trish.

Trish looked at him, meeting his eyes, and something in his manner seemed to change.

"How did you end up here?" she asked gently.

"I served in the Special Forces for twenty years. I was forced out by what I had experienced in defense of our country, only to be treated by the VA and our government like a decrepit, embarrassing relative. I needed work, and there was only one thing people were going to pay me to do."

Alarmed, Dan began working on his bonds. They were strong. The narrow cords cut into his wrists as he strained against them. He shifted his weight, seeing if he might be able to break the chair and free himself, but it was metal and well made.

Trish kept her eyes on their captor.

"I have a young boy to support," Peter said as he reached out and stroked Trish's face. She didn't pull away from his hand. Pain briefly crossed his face, replaced by an eerie calm.

Dan went ballistic, trying with all his might to stand and break free, but he just crashed to the floor, helpless, squirming.

Peter pointed his finger at him and said, "Don't try that again if you want to get out of here in one piece."

Chapter 73

After righting Dan's chair, Peter said, "I needed to feel innocence one more time. I'm sorry," Peter said.

"I know you are," Trish replied quietly.

After a pause, he pulled a knife from a belt holder. "Do you think it is too late for me?" he beseeched, more than asked, Trish.

"It's never too late. You are free to be who you were always meant to be," Trish answered with a strong yet incredibly soft voice.

"What are you going to do?" Dan said to Peter, loud enough to be forceful but quiet enough that Willy wouldn't hear it. He didn't know what to make of what was going on. The guy who was supposed to be keeping them captive seemed to be turning. Was Trish somehow causing this?

Ignoring Dan, Peter said, "I've been thinking about this for a long time. Something in me broke when I saw what they had done to the guy in Seattle. I was repulsed—I felt damned. There was a voice in me urging me not to let go of my last bit of humanity, to stay horrified at everything, and myself. But I've felt that slipping away, like this is my last chance to decide my fate."

"How did it get to this point?" Trish asked.

"I was broke, applying for private security jobs. One of them must have been a front. Someone saw something in me they liked. An ambiguous organization I had never heard of called. I had doubts from the beginning, but the pay was high and promised to be even better. Slowly, over time, feeling less and less human, I found myself following progressively worse orders, doing things that I never would have imagined doing just months before." He broke off and took a deep breath.

"It's never too late," Trish said.

"Even now, I say 'found myself' instead of 'choose to do.' A long series of small non-decisions were adding up to one big, wrong decision. They planned it that way. They enjoy corrupting people instead of picking those who are already depraved."

"You can choose a different path," Trish said.

"Not anymore. I've been thinking about this a long time. "

Throughout this exchange, Dan was mesmerized by what was taking place, reluctant to say anything lest he cause it to go awry.

"I helped abduct Stephen Bishop. I was outside the building. I didn't know what they had planned to do."

"And you hated what happened. You didn't know how bad it was going to be," Trish said.

"Yes, but I knew it wasn't going to be good. I can't be forgiven for that."

Remembering what she heard earlier, Trish said, "The only thing that can't be forgiven is unrepentance. And you *are* very contrite. Someday, when he is old enough, your son will be proud of you."

"I won't be around for him."

"You can be. You don't belong with these people. Let's all go," Trish said.

"They'll kill my son if I leave," Peter said sadly.

"I can get government protection for both of you," Dan said.

"They've infiltrated the government so deeply that it wouldn't be long before we were found and my son killed before my eyes."

"There must be something you can do to save you and your son," Trish said.

There was a pause, and Peter seemed to be deliberating. Then, slowly, he stood. "There's only one thing I can do. End it now," Peter said as he approached Trish with his knife drawn, then cut her free.

Peter looked down at Dan. "As Elena said, they plan to give you a final choice. If you reject their offer, they'll do preliminary 'work' on you here, and then take you somewhere else to finish things off. They'll do to you what they did to the guy in Seattle, and worse. It has to end now, do you understand!"

Dan nodded. As Peter cut his bonds, Dan looked toward Brother Cletus and asked, "Is he really working with them?"

Peter nodded, "They get to people everywhere. They knew you're friends with the priest and turned this guy." Peter gestured to Brother Cletus.

Dan was still confused by the apparent conversion of the mercenary. Had it really happened, just like that? Or was he lying to them, a ruse to gain their confidence? "If you're telling the truth, why did you stay with them till now?"

"He's telling the truth," Trish said.

Peter looked at Trish and nodded, and then turned back to Dan. "I decided to stay and look for a chance to take them down. When I heard about their plan for you, and what they were after, I thought maybe I could save you." He looked down at the knife in his hands. "I need an act of redemption that can earn grace for my son," he said.

A low moan indicated that Brother Cletus was waking. Dan walked over to him, gestured for him to be quiet and then demanded, "Why did you do it?"

To his surprise, the priest answered right away. "I didn't want you to use Stephen Bishop's work to undermine the Church," Brother Cletus said in a weak, pained voice.

"Why would Father Michael help me if I was going to do that?" Dan said.

"I was shown evidence that you were misleading him and were behind Stephen Bishop's death. You hate God and religion so much that you are committed to destroying it."

"O ye of little faith. There's a reason he's called the Prince of Lies," Dan said harshly. He freed Brother Cletus and helped him sit up.

"What good is your belief in God if science threatens it?" Dan asked.

Brother Cletus bowed his head.

Dan added, "I don't want to make a martyr of you. Sit down and don't dare move. I'll crucify you if you pull anything further."

Ignoring Trish's *Oh, really* look, Dan faced Peter and asked warily, "You do have a plan, don't you?"

Chapter 74

Peter walked down the narrow hall to the front vestibule. Willy, simple, eager, and depraved, stood by the door, peering out through a crack between the curtain and the side of the window.

Seeing Peter approach, Willy tightened up and said, "You're supposed to be watching them."

"They're not going anywhere. The religious guy is going into convulsions. He may die."

"That's his problem. We don't need him anymore."

Peter looked at a text displayed on his smartphone. "They're almost here."

"It'll be fun watching Sergei work. He said something about unfinished business with the guy. I get to *talk* with the *lady* at the same time," Willy said with obvious relish.

"You really know how to have a blast. You must be a hit with the ladies," Peter said.

"Got a problem with that?" Willy said, in rising anger. "Maybe *we* should have a *conversation*."

"We *definitely* should. But not now, unless you want to answer to Sergei. You know how *those* conversations turn out."

"You'd better get back to our guests before Sergei gets here."

Taking a sideways step, Peter said, "They'll be gone by then."

Willy looked confused, then his face twisted when he saw Dan walking up the hallway, pointing Peter's gun at him.

As Willy started to raise his own gun, Peter Tasered him, grabbed his gun, then used plastic ties to bind his hands behind his writhing back.

Peter pointed Willy's gun at him and said, "Get up."

Willy stood shakily, then snarled, "Sergei's going to cut you into little pieces, slowly, and I am going to love every second of it."

Jabbing the gun into Willy's back, Peter said, "Walk if you want to keep breathing. And don't try anything. I'm doing my best to find a reason to take care of you right now. You don't want me to succeed."

Willy snorted, then began walking, with Peter behind and Dan in front, both with guns drawn.

They entered the living room and Peter tightly tied and gagged the seething Willy on the floor. Then he pointed to the back door and said to Dan, Trish, and Brother Cletus, "Now get of here. I'll take care of Sergei so you won't have to worry about him anymore."

"Sergei won't be alone." Looking at Brother Cletus, Dan said, "Take her to safety until Evans's agents get here. That can be the start of your penance."

"I'm not leaving without you," Trish said.

"You can't stay," Peter said to them.

"I won't let you sacrifice yourself for me," Dan said to Peter. "Sergei is my problem, too. And I have a longer history and bigger score to settle with him."

"I have no intention of dying. I still have my son to take care of. I need to make sure he makes better choices than I did. I want him to have the father I never had," Peter said.

Before anyone could say anything further, there was a sequence of knocks on the front door.

It was too early to be Evans's agents.

Chapter 75

Dan and Peter raced to the vestibule. Dan hid behind the long curtain next to the entrance.

Peter opened the door.

"We have a problem," Peter said as Sergei and Elena entered cautiously.

Trish moaned loudly from the living room.

Peter continued, "Willy started playing with the woman. The guy got upset and tried to break free. Willy started slamming him, and I had to intervene. The guy's hurt. Willy's watching both, worried about what he's done and what you'll do to him."

Sergei and Elena looked at Peter and then each other, angry, confused, and wary.

Sergei pulled his gun and started down the hallway saying, "Sarastro is not going to be happy about this."

Elena gestured for Peter to go next, then pulled her gun, carrying Dan's tablet in her other hand. Elena took a step to follow, but Dan stepped out and jammed his gun in her back.

"Drop it. I don't get my kicks getting physical with women, but for you I could make an exception," he said.

Hearing Dan's voice, Sergei started to turn, but stopped when he felt the barrel of Peter's gun against his head.

Elena dropped her gun, which Dan picked up as Peter grabbed Sergei's gun.

"Keep walking," Peter said.

Sergei's eyes met Willy's as he entered the room, delivering an unmistakable message: it wasn't going to go well for him no matter how things turned out.

Pointing at the chairs, Peter said, "Sit."

Elena sat in the chair by the couch where Brother Cletus and Trish were. Sergei took the chair by the back door. There was nothing to tie them up with.

Peter emptied the clips and chambers of Sergei's and Elena's guns.

"Leave now and your son will be spared," Sergei said to Peter in a businesslike voice, leaving unsaid that the same would not hold true for him.

"That's right. Threaten the innocent instead of being man enough to deal with the difficult things yourself," Dan said with derision.

"What you call innocence is nothing more than weakness unfit for survival. But it does have value for one thing: the enjoyment in despoiling it." said Sergei.

"Shouldn't you be worried about what's going to happen to you?" Dan said.

"What, this from a guy who lacks the stomach to do his job and another who isn't man enough to face the world? We know all about you, Lawson. You failed once, you'll fail again. Go ahead. Turn us in. We'll get right out, have fun with the 'innocence' of a boy, girl, and a woman doctor." Sergei looked at Trish. "After we've given you time to watch what happens to them, then we'll see how manly you are. Peter knows what he has to do to save his son, despite whatever you told him."

"You're making a very good case for why we should finish you off right here, right now," Dan said with deadly intent.

"You should hear what Sarastro has to say before you make any more foolish decisions. He thought, given the right information, you might want to help him build a new society based on science, reason, and strength. One where things like this aren't necessary, the type of place our analysis says you've always wanted."

The idea of finding out more about The Commission, Stephen's involvement with it, and the possibility of treatment for Ava, appealed to Dan but not at the cost they'd have to pay.

"We can set up a simple phone conversation," Elena said.

"If I talk with him, you'll leave the others alone?" Dan asked.

"Yes," Sergei answered.

Peter said, "Don't do it. They'll never let you live once you know Sarastro's identity. Your family will always be at risk to guarantee your loyalty."

"All you'd hear is lies and deception," Trish said. "They have nothing for you. They want what you have, including your soul."

"Who else is on the way here?" Dan asked.

"Wait and see," Sergei taunted.

Turning to Peter, Dan said, "US agents will be here in twenty minutes. Can we hold them until then?"

"Sarastro will be disappointed to find out that I was right about you," Sergei sneered at Dan.

Dan and Peter exchanged glances.

Dan said, "Trish and Brother Cletus, go to the basilica and wait for Evans's agents. We've got these low-lifes under control."

"We'll all wait here for them. There'll be no 'unfortunate accidents' while we're gone," Trish said, looking at Peter.

Sergei snickered at the idea that Peter and Dan would execute them.

Elena's eyes did their best to burn holes into Dan.

"Please go. If they behave, nothing will happen to them," Peter said. "I promise."

Trish and Brother Cletus headed toward the vestibule. As they reached the hallway, a man holding a gun burst through the back door. He tripped over Willy's prone body and lost his balance.

Mayhem broke out.

Dan knocked the gun out of the man's hand. It flew out the door and into a storm drain.

Trish yelled to Brother Cletus, "Get help. Quickly!"

He ran to the vestibule and out the front door.

The new man reached for Dan's gun and they struggled for control of it.

Elena stood up and walked toward Trish, followed by Peter's eyes.

Taking advantage of the distraction, Sergei kicked the gun out of

Peter's hand. It slid past Elena to Trish. She picked it up, pointed it at Elena, and said, "Sit."

Elena hesitated, then took another step toward Trish.

"Sit now!" Trish said, raising the gun and pointing it at Elena's chest.

Elena sat, eyes riveted, catlike, on Trish, waiting for a moment to pounce. She was clearly wondering if Trish was the type of person who could actually pull the trigger. Many could not.

On the floor, Willy squirmed, trying to free himself.

Driving the barrel of his gun into the man's chest, Dan said, "Stop or I'll blow a hole through where your heart should be."

The man stopped struggling. Dan shoved him back a few steps. "Turn around," Dan said, then clocked him on the back of the head with the butt of the gun, knocking him out.

The fight raged between Sergei and Peter. Superhuman strength seemed to radiate from Peter, until at last he drove Sergei to the ground with one dreadful blow, the sickening crack of it echoing in the room.

Trish winced at the sound. Elena kicked the empty chair next to her into Trish and then jumped up, grabbing at the gun.

Seeing that, Peter turned and pulled Elena back.

Staggering, Sergei found the strength to withdraw a knife from his jacket, plunge it deep into Peter's back, and pull it out. Dan attacked Sergei before he could stab Peter again, slamming the side of his head with the butt of the gun and causing Sergei to drop the knife.

Sergei grabbed Dan's wrist and twisted it until his gun fell to the floor. Sergei, unsteady from the effects of Dan's strike, faltered momentarily, giving Dan just enough reach to kick the gun out the door.

Peter slumped to the floor, gasping for breath, blood flowing from his mouth.

Now empty-handed, against a weakened Sergei, Dan delivered a crushing blow that sent him sprawling.

Seeing that Sergei was about to be defeated, Elena no longer deterred, rushed Trish, and grabbed her gun.

Elena pointed the gun at Dan and yelled, "Stop!"

No one moved.

"You don't have everything you need from me. I'm indispensible to The Commission. None of the rest of you are," Dan said.

"You are, but she's not," Elena said, turning toward Trish, only to be on the receiving end of a blast from the fire extinguisher that used to be hanging by the door. Elena dropped the gun and fell to the floor.

Sergei scrambled and picked up the gun.

Dan grabbed Sergei's knife from the floor and threw it at him, driving it deep into the center of Sergei's chest.

With the little strength Sergei had left, he pointed his gun at Dan.

Before he could pull the trigger, Trish blasted the fire extinguisher at Sergei, leaving him gasping and blind. The gun tumbled from his hand.

Dan recovered it as Elena, clutching his tablet, rushed past Trish and out of the house.

Trish yelled, "She's getting away!"

Chapter 76

Go after her. I've got these guys," Trish said.

"No. I'll explain later," Dan said.

Sergei's breathing was rapid and shallow, his eyes closed.

Peter was slumped against the wall and Trish was kneeling beside him, tending to him with a tenderness that seemed almost sacred.

She looked at Dan and shook her head slightly. Peter raised his eyes in Dan's direction.

Dan bent over and heard Peter whisper, "My son will be safe."

Dan thought, not again. Another young boy orphaned by Sergei. Another father Dan couldn't save.

To Trish, Peter faintly said, "Thank you," then, slowly, his breathing ceased. Serenity settled over him.

A gasp from Sergei caught their attention. Despite who he was and all that had happened, Trish went over to him and touched his wrist.

Immediately, his eyes opened, dark with fury. He flung her hand off. Full of defiance, he spat skyward, then fell facedown into the ground, knife twisting further in his chest, as he died.

Trish looked at Sergei with pity, then sat back down next to Peter.

Dan secured the man who started the chaos when he came in through the back door, and who was still unconscious, with Sergei's belt, then collected weapons.

Sitting down next to Trish, Dan said, "I'm sorry you had to go through all this. As tremendous as you've been, I never should have allowed you to get involved."

"You're still under the mistaken belief that you're in control of things."

"That illusion used to be comforting. As you've said, it doesn't take much for reality to shatter it."

She nodded, the stress of what had taken place showing on her drawn face. "Why did you let her get away with the tablet?"

"Before I sent it over here, I set it up with facial recognition. If anyone other than me accessed it, key files would be deleted, leaving only decoys behind. It would look real enough, causing people to spend lots of time on things that wouldn't get them anywhere, without letting them know they should be looking for something else, including us." Dan added with a wistful smile, "Stephen had helped me select the right data sets for that."

"Once in a while, you do have almost as much control over things as you think you do."

"That might be the biggest compliment you've given me."

"It wasn't," she said.

He stood, and reached out a hand to help her to her feet. "Let's get to the chapel and wait for Evans's men. We don't want to hang around here in case the wrong reinforcements arrive first."

Chapter 77

The Colleoni Chapel had been emptied of visitors, and it felt every bit the crypt that it was. Though it was the warmer part of the day, the chapel felt cooler, the air heavier, the stone colder, than when they had first been there.

Brother Cletus knelt prostrate before the altar, his fingers rapidly rubbing the rosary beads as he prayed fervently. Father Michael had already heard his confession, and it took a big effort by Trish and Dan not to hear it as well. Even though he knew that it wasn't very charitable, Dan hoped that the beads would wear out before Brother Cletus's penance was finished.

A drawn-looking Trish sat slumped in a back pew.

Father Michael walked back and forth between the doors, continually checking that they were still locked. Security guards were posted outside them and, barring a heavily armed assault, they were safe.

Dan looked behind the recessed panel again, even though the opening behind it was empty.

They had been there fifteen minutes, and the wait for Evans's men was draining. There wasn't much to do before the men arrived and took them to the airport for a flight back to the US—hopefully well before the Italian authorities decided to hold them indefinitely.

Dan saw Trish lean back and look upward. He walked over and sat down next to her. Gently, he placed her right hand between his, leaned over, and said quietly, "I'm sorry I got you into this. You should never have had to do what you did, though it saved our lives."

With a calmness that was as deep as her enormous soul, Trish said, "Now that you have Stephen's work, what will you do with it? Is there something there for Ava?"

"I don't know. It will take time to find out. I'd like to do that before I turn anything over to Evans. What do you think?" Dan said, asking a question when he had already made up his mind.

"Your secrets are safe with me. Even the ones you don't yet know about," Trish said with a smile that brought warmth back to her, and to him.

"You always seem to act like you have a special insight into people, know more about me than I do myself."

"I wouldn't rule it out."

Father Michael walked over and stood in the aisle by the pew.

"That was a bad ordeal you went through. Are you sure you're okay?" he said.

"We'll recover," Dan answered.

"What about Stephen's files? Are there things that will help Ava? Did he actually find what he claimed he did?" Father Michael asked.

"You really want to know?" Dan asked.

"Yes."

"Then let's go find a confessional and I'll unburden myself," Dan said, a faint, amused, smile crossing his face as he said it.

"You know that's not entirely fair. I won't be able to tell anyone or act on the information."

"Exactly."

"We can go to that pew," Father Michael said, pointing to the other side of the chapel.

"Wait a second. You have to tell me, too," Trish insisted.

"Then it will have to be a confession that you listen in on. If I am correct, that places the seal of confidentiality on you, too. Is that correct, Father Michael?" Dan said.

"Yes, absolutely, to the extent she honors the restrictions of confession. Trish, that means you're not allowed even to acknowledge to Dan that you heard anything from him," Father Michael said.

"Although I'm not Catholic, I'll honor it," Trish said. "Not that I couldn't get him to tell me anyway."

"Now we don't have to move. Dan?" Father Michael said.

"I'll begin with the easy part. Forgive me Father, for I have sinned," Dan said.

"Easy? For most of your life you would have choked trying to say those words."

"I'm a little more aware, not convinced in their meaning, but willing to say them for the sake of the confessional. Where they'll lead, we'll see. Now shut up if you want to hear what I have to say."

"A good priest will do what's needed to hear a confession. Go ahead."

Dan proceeded to tell them everything he'd found in Stephen's files, what he still suspected was there, how he was going to keep looking through the files, and his plans for what to do with them.

When he was done, Father Michael said, "You haven't said anything that requires absolution. Do you want to finish this privately?"

"That wasn't by accident. I won't do what I don't earnestly believe. That said, to retain the seal of confession, is it permissible for me to reflect on this and come back, if things change and I so desire? The one thing I cannot do now is confess to an entity I don't fully believe in. That would be worse than not confessing at all."

"You can reflect and come back later," Father Michael said.

"Good."

"Now I get to say what I've longed to for a long time. Dan, say two Our Fathers, two Hail Marys, and two Glory Bes, with a special intention for Stephen," Father Michael said.

"I can do that," Dan said.

"You Catholics get off easy," Trish said.

"He didn't absolve me of anything since I did not complete a full and sincere confession. I didn't get let off of anything," Dan said.

"Reflect on what your conscience says and consider coming back. God bless you and go in peace," Father Michael said.

"Thank you," Dan said, then walked over to the pews, where he quietly completed his penance for his nonconfession.

After he was done, he sat down next to Trish again.

"Aren't you worried that Elena and her organization will find a way to crack your tablet, despite your precautions, or that you'll need it?" Trish asked, steering clear of anything Dan had said to Father Michael.

"No. When I sent a message to Evans after we got back to the chapel, I also sent a command to wipe the tablet, just in case. A few minutes later, I received a signal back that it had successfully completed. And everything on it, I have back home. As I still have Stephen's coded files, I can resume where I left off."

Trish started to say something, then bit her lip in frustration, realizing the restrictions she'd agreed to were more problematic than she anticipated.

"Were you going to say something?" Dan teased.

Trish swung her right arm sideways and her fist rammed Dan's biceps.

Rubbing it, he laughed a little. "Okay, I release you from the seal of confession that you know I confessed something in your presence to Father Michael."

"If you don't trust me enough to completely release me, there will be nothing for us to discuss, ever," Trish said firmly.

"You win. I release you completely, though I request, outside the seal of confession, that you not discuss any of this with anyone else, without first discussing that with me. That doesn't mean you can't discuss it with others, only talk with me beforehand."

"I want you to promise that you'll tell me whatever else you find."

"What if I think it will endanger you?"

"As long as you are genuinely following a pure conscience, I will leave it up to you."

"That's fair," Dan said. "I'm not looking forward to talking with Evans."

"I wouldn't either if I were you," Trish said. In a more serious voice, she added, "Borrowing from Churchill, do you think this is the end of everything Stephen stirred up, or just the end of the beginning?"

"I don't think it's over, and I hope it doesn't become our end someday."

Chapter 78

DAY 17
SUNDAY

After an eight-hour flight in first class, almost all of it spent sleeping, a subdued Dan stood with Evans at a northeast-facing window. The Potomac was on the left, and the White House on the right. They were in Evans's temporary office, chosen for its proximity to Secretary Robbins.

"That was reasonably convincing, even though you still haven't explained all you know of Stephen Bishop's work," Evans said, referring to the debrief Dan had just given to a large number of senior US intelligence and other government leaders.

"That's because I don't know much about it," Dan said. He was anxious to get to a place where he could resume his review.

"Both of us could still be in serious trouble for what you did in Italy."

"Look how badly that turned out," Dan said, gesturing to the beautiful view. "We live in a more secure world, thanks to my copying Viktor's fusion files. What are you going to do with them?"

"Research it further. Find out what went wrong. With luck, make it a commercial technology."

"Did you find out more about the images of nuclear material that Viktor had?"

"The copies of Viktor's files you gave us contained no evidence that he ever developed a technology that produced the images.

Our intelligence analysts think he accessed a Nuclear Regulatory Commission database and used a graphing program to produce the images, but we were able to contain the damage before they felt compelled to act."

"What about Stephen's research? The files are rather cryptic," Dan said, knowing he had only turned over the raw data translated into symbolic code, useless without the rest of Stephen's files.

"I think they'll keep a large number of people busy for a long time, presuming he really did discover something."

"Any luck tracking down the rest of The Commission?"

"They've receded into the mist. We have some people trying to locate them, but most of our attention is focused elsewhere. But at least you got Sergei. That was no small achievement."

"It didn't provide the satisfaction that I thought it would."

"It never does for good people," Evans said as he patted Dan on the back.

"Elena is as bad as he was. I'm sure she knows how to survive and will turn up again when she wants to."

"Yup, I agree. Haven't found Sousan, either, though our analysts think, after looking at more detailed images after the blast, there's a good chance she's dead."

"What about your retirement, and *mine*?" Dan said.

"I should be able to phase out in a few weeks. As for you, they'll keep you on active status until they're sure you've given them everything. You'll get paid for it, of course. You got anything else up your sleeve?"

"You always think I do," Dan said, giving him a wide smile, one he hoped looked trustworthy. He was antsy to get back to the rest of Stephen's files.

"It seems to work out that way," Evans said. "I suppose you want to get to Boston. We have a plane waiting to fly you up there."

"With accompaniment?" Dan asked.

"For a little while, until we're sure things have settled down."

"I don't need the security, but if it is really only for a little while, that's fine," Dan said. "And no more John Doe investigation crap."

"No."

"Good, because that is the type of thing I'd get myself in trouble going after."

"I didn't see much of her, but it seems like Dr. Alighieri is a re-markable person," Agent Evans said.

"That and more," Dan said wistfully, wondering what Trish was doing. She had left an hour earlier, headed toward Ava.

"Maybe something will work out."

"I've got other stuff to deal with. And sometimes, in circum-stances like we've been through, things seem more significant than they are," Dan replied. He knew that once things change back to normal, artificial closeness was often replaced by awkwardness, as seemed to have happened with them on the flight back to DC.

"Still . . ."

"My mind is on other things now," Dan lied.

"What are you going to do next?"

"Help with Ava."

"I'm sorry about Stephen Bishop. It must be painful to accept that he manipulated so many people to get technology to exchange for medicine to save his daughter's life. He probably didn't understand what he was trading."

Dan didn't answer. While Evans's explanation of Stephen and Vik-tor surreptitiously obtaining classified US technology made far more sense than his finding the keys to the universe encoded in DNA, Dan still had trouble believing that Stephen acted in that manner. While he believed that Stephen had found things in DNA, he still had doubts whether he had done other things that he shouldn't have. For the sake of secrecy and freedom to find out on his own, he'd play along with the government's view.

Filling the silence, Evans said, "You ever get the feeling the uni-verse is laughing at us?"

"All the time," Dan answered.

Chapter 79

Groggy from a lack of sleep and too many hours spent at the computer screen, Dan poured himself another cup of strong coffee.

He walked from the kitchen to his bedroom window to stretch his legs. A brisk wind whipped the trees and water. Long, thin, white clouds raced across the mostly blue sky.

None of it registered.

He was completely fixated on Stephen's files.

Except for a brief visit with Nancy, he'd spent all of his waking time since his meeting with Evans trying to understand Stephen's work.

What he had been able to figure out from Stephen's notes was mind-boggling.

DNA was indeed coded multiple ways. A section read one way, or through one translation mechanism, directed one outcome. Read another way, or interpreted with a different translator, it led to a different outcome, for a different purpose.

Cell processing was based on something that could be considered analogous to a computer operating system utilizing hierarchical storage systems, only it was for biological processes.

How all of this could have come about was inconceivable.

How it led to one species becoming another, through a myriad of small steps, was also challenging to understand, as redundant regulatory mechanisms operated to prevent, not enable, changes in the genetic code.

And what a code it was.

Algorithmic gene processing used input parameters, from a source yet to be determined, to drive physical development and body plans.

The odds of developing a single, simple protein, as astronomical as they were, were nothing in comparison to the specificity of neural arrangements in the brain. No learning could have taken place in utero that would allow a pony to be able to stand, see, and walk so soon after birth. That knowledge had to be either included in the genetic code or supplied by something else. As with the body plan, there simply wasn't enough DNA to specify all those neural connections without algorithmic processing. There was no conceivable path, without guidance provided at the time of its origin, to produce what DNA did.

Sitting back down at his computer, using instructions Stephen left in one file, Dan began to operate a program that apparently used information from DNA to illustrate the full cycle of human development *and* decline. If this was right, aging was programmed in, though to what end, Dan didn't know. Perhaps it was intended to keep the generations apart. Society wouldn't do too well if the older people, in the same physical condition as the younger, competed with them for companions and other resources. There wouldn't be much of a family structure, and things like love would be hard to develop and sustain. Biology reeked of purpose.

A variation of the human development programs also appeared to show humans' relationship to, and evolution from, their physical ancestors. A sequence of key parameters drove the representation of each species. The next in the series was blank. With the right input parameters, would they show what humanity was to become next?

All of what Dan had been viewing was driven by Stephen's converted data. He still hadn't been able to use symbolic code created from DNA to generate Stephen's data. That appeared to require passcodes that Dan did not possess and could not find. Perhaps it didn't exist and everything he was looking at was just a simulation Stephen had created. It was possible it wasn't really from DNA.

Yet everything in Stephen's files indicated that *he thought* it was real.

The physical sciences portion of Stephen's files, while smaller, was equally astounding, pointing to a physics more radical than previously imagined, though it meant nothing to Dan. Maybe the symbol that Stephen had drawn was a clue to something Dan was still missing. Probably Stephen hadn't had time to complete it, and maybe that was the way things were meant to be.

Everything screamed design, yet direct proof remained elusive. There was no signature with a name. It still came down to a degree of faith.

Whether there was a third set of data, he might never know. He had been unable to find the files and programs needed to re-create the processing environment that would generate it, if it existed. Perhaps that, too, was best.

What he already had, as far as he understood it, could be devastating in the wrong hands. That was responsibility enough for him.

And then there were the rest of Viktor's files. Although Dan didn't have the knowledge to comprehend most of what was in them, he found more copies of nuclear images. If Viktor did develop the technology to produce them, it was way too dangerous to be entrusted to any one nation, even the US. Just trying to find out if the technology was real could trigger terrible outcomes.

He had a decision to make. As long as organizations like The Commission existed, as long as human nature remained unchanged, could he seek out others to work with him on Stephen's files, or should he destroy them? It might only be putting off the inevitable, until someone else discovered, or was led, to what Stephen had, but that might be enough time to ensure the world's future.

His finger hovered over the delete command, rising and lowering in unison with his thoughts.

Instead, he displayed the symbolic code Stephen had created from DNA. Something about it drew him in, tugged at his mind, as if he had seen portions of it before.

Father Michael's words came back to him. Somehow, if what he was looking at was more than random in origin, he was its caretaker. That was not a responsibility to be tossed aside.

Since he could not re-create all of Stephen's work, he had not found the near-absolute, scientific proof of God that he sought. But he could not deny what science and reason were showing him. There was more to life, and human origin, than randomness. If he didn't keep searching, it would be because he didn't want to know. And he might not get a free pass, from whatever existed, for that.

Chapter 80

I t was odd to be in Stephen's HBC office later that afternoon, and sitting at his desk. He felt like he was intruding on the space of the spirit of his friend.

Dan had finally accepted Octavio Romanoff's request, and was conducting a thorough review of HBC's computer and network security. Also at Octavio's request, and for his own interest as well, he was searching the network for any remnants of Stephen's work files that had been missed. So far, he had found none.

He looked up as he saw Octavio passing by the open door. Octavio caught his eyes, pivoted back, entered, and sat down.

"Thank you for agreeing to do this. How is it going?" Octavio said in a cultivated voice full of quiet authority.

"I'm only partway through. Except for the usual smattering of minor vulnerabilities, I haven't found serious issues or evidence of any successful intrusions. HBC has done a good job mitigating its vulnerabilities."

"Excellent! Were you able to find out anything about the attempted intrusions? They were disturbing, especially in today's world of aggressive theft of corporate secrets."

"Not yet," Dan said, omitting what he experienced before Stephen's death.

Octavio's eyebrows arched slightly before he said, "Do you think it was related to what the government investigators have described as Stephen's participation in espionage?"

A pained look crossed Dan's face. After an extended pause, he said, "I don't know."

"You don't think he was involved in anything like that, either, do you?"

"No, I don't."

"The investigators claimed that he was trying to trade government secrets for foreign, experimental medicine to treat his daughter's cancer. You were his close friend and went looking for that medicine. What do you think he was up to?" Octavio said, eyes focused like lasers on Dan.

"I believe that Stephen sincerely believed that DNA used advanced algorithms, and a code within a code, to generate the large amount of information needed to direct human development. He once showed me a program—he said it was based on actual DNA—to generate images of the human body." Dan wanted to see Octavio's reaction, and what he was telling him was too general to be of use to anyone anyway.

"What do you mean, a code within a code?" Octavio asked, leaning forward.

"That beyond the basic role of genome encoding for proteins and other known purposes, the same DNA base pairs can be translated into what appears to be another code, for other purposes, using what appears to be sophisticated encryption-like translation to do it."

Even though Dan had heard and thought about this before, hearing himself say it aloud sucked the air out of room, much as it had when Stephen first said it to him.

It was also clear that Octavio was genuinely stunned, his mouth agape.

"How could something like that come to be by chance, from the beginning of life?" Octavio said in a near stammer.

"I don't see how it could. It suggests that God exists and created it that way. Or some ancient aliens designed it and started life going on earth—and then made no future contact."

"Which do you think it is?"

"I don't know. I'm predisposed to think of God as the creator, but that raises a lot of troubling questions for the way things are. If we're alien in origin, it would have helped having an owner's manual or something else like that." Dan remembered the third set of information, the one that Stephen never completed translating—if in fact there was a third set and something to translate.

"We have to find all of Stephen's work!" Octavio exclaimed.

"Perhaps we have. We've both been looking for more. If it existed, we'd probably have found it."

"Yet you believe that Stephen found something. Therefore, more has to exist."

"Maybe it once did. It might have been lost in the MIT explosion. It could have died with a collaborator of his, Sam Abrams, in Seattle. Or it may still be here. Or perhaps someone has to find a way to re-create it. I don't know. I'm not a biologist and Stephen and I were estranged for years. Most of what I learned was after he died."

Dan shared details he didn't have to, mixing in some misdirection, in an effort to gauge Octavio's reaction and see if there was something worth pursuing further with him.

"Who else knows this?"

"I'm not sure. A few. Not many. Certainly the organization Agent Evans called The Commission thought Stephen had found things worth obtaining. I bet the government investigators have that idea, too."

"That explains the problems you've faced. You were fortunate to come out unharmed."

"If you consider losing a close friend and having every aspect of your life exposed, unharmed, then yes."

"Are you safe now?"

"Since everyone who was after Stephen's work knows I don't have it, I ought to be."

"I've heard rumors about The Commission for years, though I didn't realize they'd go to such extremes. I thought they were nonviolent, a think tank. Supposedly, their main interest is transhumanism."

"If that's all they're about, they're in for a big surprise," Dan said.

"Why's that?" Octavio said blandly.

"Transhumanism is the merging of humans and machines. It treats the human mind as a supercomputer whose contents can be transferred from a biological existence to another, stronger, faster repository. Stephen claimed he found evidence that the brain wasn't enough to produce consciousness—that we have immaterial minds, or souls. If he was right, unless people find the soul, and find a way to confer it on to other things, true artificial intelligence and transhumanism can never come about. We poor humans will remain imperfect mortals."

"Dan, it's too much to believe that Stephen, mostly by himself, discovered this."

"And yet we do exist, and something has to explain that, whether Stephen discovered any of the answers or not."

"I think copies of Stephen's work must be somewhere."

"I'd like to think so, but if you haven't found it here, where could it be?" Dan said.

"It's too important to the world to be lost. Imagine if there is more to it. That inside of us is the way to find our true origin and whatever that means about our purpose," Octavio said.

"Yes, I want to know that, too. Forgive me for saying so, but your secular views are well known. Does that mean you believe that we're alien in origin?"

"I have no idea. Yet the universe is enormous. Life has to be throughout all of it. Some of it could be very advanced. I'd like to find out."

"Right now, I'd settle for medicine that Ava might need someday."

"Then let us both keep looking and see what we can find."

"Agreed," Dan said, extending his hand and shaking Octavio's.

Chapter 81

The mid-June sun hung over the horizon, just barely over the tree tops, casting its last rays into the western windows of Stephen's study.

Nancy sat on the window seat while Dan poked along the bookshelves, looking for clues—anything Stephen might have hidden.

"You're not going to give up?" Nancy asked.

"Not anymore," Dan answered. He knew she meant both his outlook on the future and finding out the full truth about Stephen. She apparently had no idea of the extent of Stephen's work—what Dan already knew, and what might remain to be discovered—but it was better that way. Of that, Dan was confident. She already had enough to deal with.

"I knew that without asking," Nancy said, smiling. "I have faith in you."

"What did Trish say about Ava?" Dan said.

Both gazed toward the backyard, admiring the day's waning light as it slowly retreated from the sky. In the time she'd been back, Trish had stopped by the hospital several times, talked with all of Ava's doctors, reviewed medical reports, and visited her many other patients. Remarkably, and wonderfully, a treatment for which they initially had low expectations was proving highly effective for Ava.

"She's doing very well. While it's too early to know for certain, Trish is optimistic."

"That's really great," Dan said. Whatever treatment Stephen had once sought, it wasn't needed now and hopefully never would be, at least for Ava, though he'd keep looking in case it was ever needed, for her or for others. "And her energy's coming back?"

Ava walked into the study and sat down at the piano. "See for yourself," Nancy said. Trish followed and sat next to Nancy after a brief glance at Dan.

Ava began playing an instrumental version of "Thunder Road" with vigor, filling it with passion and life. Dan hummed softly to himself as she played, thinking of Stephen.

After she finished, Dan said, "That was beautiful, and so are you."

Beaming, Ava came over and gave him a hug. "I know that you and Daddy liked that song."

Dan picked her up, hugged her back, then lowered her slowly.

"Is it okay if I go downstairs?" Dan asked Nancy.

"Of course," Nancy answered.

"I'll come along," Trish said.

Together, Dan and Trish walked in silence down the stairs and into the theater room.

As Dan began to reassemble the wires and components of the theater system the investigators had taken apart, Trish said, "You were tremendous. It was amazing what you did in Italy."

"You give me too much credit."

"I don't think so," Trish replied matter-of-factly. "What are you going to do with Stephen's work?"

Dan shrugged and replied simply, "Try to understand it."

"What we've been through taught me a lot. Thank you."

Their conversation's formal tone, and the lack of that full immediacy of her presence that he had felt during their travels, caused a sinking feeling in Dan that he fought to suppress.

"I can't imagine what you could have learned from me," Dan said, trying to keep a light tone.

"What'd I learn? As someone who never really questioned myself, who felt secure in my views, it was an education to see and experience you and your incredible courage as you struggled with your place in the world. You were looking for honest answers and, without

flinching, you followed where you thought they led. It got me thinking as well."

"It wasn't courage. It was the fear of what would happen to me if
I didn't do it. And I did flinch. You just weren't looking when I did."

"Lots of people get paralyzed by fear and lack the courage to try to
become what they need to be. You didn't. Keep it up," Trish said with
words that clearly intended that he still, as he knew, had a ways to go.

She continued, "I'm sorry I can't spend more time with you now.
There are things I need to get back to, things I've neglected. And I
have to focus on Ava's treatment. But we should keep in touch. Ava
will need us both. And you need space to continue your journey."

Dan understood the full meaning of her words. Though they
didn't surprise him, hearing them was like feeling a void in himself
once more, though it passed quickly. They also reminded him that
he still had to figure out who he needed to become, who he wanted
to become, before he could truly be one with another, especially her.

Smiling, Trish put her arms around him, kissed him warmly on
the check, and left.

Chapter 82

Dan leaned back in a chair on his balcony, facing the deepening evening sky. Just slightly to his left, behind a row of buildings along the north edge of the Charles River, a cone of light shone upward at the site of the MIT fusion reactor remains. While looking at it was still difficult, it no longer enraged or embittered him.

He sipped a beer that tasted better than any he had in years, feeling the sweetness of being more in the world, and less into himself, than he ever had been before. Hope enlivened him. It was borne of an optimism that something good was yet to come—exactly what, he didn't know but he was going to seek it.

There was only one thing that could justify new hope, make it more than a fleeting feeling based on illusion. Despite the many reservations and unanswered questions he still had, he believed that life had true meaning and that he would someday come to know it.

Stephen's work certainly had revealed profound things that Dan could not ignore. The algorithmic processing DNA used to create body plans was based on fractals. This required the expression of imaginary numbers. While thinking beings could use imaginary numbers to describe physical behavior, these numbers could not exist physically themselves. That meant they were coded in DNA as a concept, not as a physical arrangement or a behavior of physical properties. And that meant they came to be as an expression of a thought. And that required a thinker!

Yet if something like God existed, why did He leave people—leave Dan—so alone when they faced terrible things? Though there had been times where Dan had thought that he had felt a presence, it hadn't lasted.

Still, Dan knew there was only one way that life and love had meaning, that people were more than biological robots and had inherent worth. That was if people were categorically more than physical matter, and had a real spiritual existence.

Stepping out on the balcony, he wondered if the proof he sought was actually all around him. The sights that pleased him, the cool breeze that refreshed him, the sounds that were like music, the thoughts that lifted him—might all these be evidence of his soul in action? Could the brain alone produce the perceptions he was experiencing? Was every moment, of every life, indication of a spiritual existence?

Would people live differently if they believed that?

He wished he could share what he had discovered in Stephen's work with the world. But unless he could find out more about it, know more about its origins and purpose—divine or something else—he couldn't do that. There were too many aspects of it, extremely dangerous aspects, that could lead to the end of humanity well before other aspects could be used to elevate humanity beyond the failings of the present.

The world was on a dangerous precipice between the past and future. Ancient battles, at times seemingly dormant, but never ended, were ratcheting up.

Right before the fateful explosion, Stephen had told him that he thought God planned for scientific discoveries to emerge when they did to keep humanity on track, that God wrote history with broad, faint strokes that could only be seen from a great vantage point.

What if Dan really was the caretaker of what he possessed? What if he had a role to play in the next stage in human evolution? How would he know what to do?

All he knew for certain was that he'd have to persevere and keep trying to find out. He'd have faith that there were answers that mattered. In his heart, he knew life was worth it; that it wasn't only an illusion that would be dispelled by the scattering of atoms.

The answers were out there for those who sought them.

Author's Note

This novel features a lot of science talk. Some of the science is considered well-established, some I consider probable, a portion is pure speculation on my part, and the rest is fanciful for the purposes of interesting fiction. Though I trust readers recognize which is which, for the sake of clarity I am providing this short section to delineate the well established from the less proven science. Note that in some cases in this book, I challenge established science, and I hope that too is clear.

In the realm of generally accepted science, fall the:

- Importance of the relative strength of the four fundamental forces of nature;
- Requirements for fusion reactions to take place and for commercially viable fusion energy;
- Basics of DNA and biology, including epigenetics;
- Core tenets of neo-Darwinian evolution;
- Present lack of conclusive evidence for how the first life originated;
- Present lack of knowledge about body plans;
- Possibility of multiverses. Although several different kinds of multiverses have been proposed by physicists, for this book I have focused only on the many-worlds version;
- Sorry to say, almost every surveillance or cyber technology Dan uses or refers to.

In the area of what I consider probable:

- The ratio of individual instructions needed to direct human development, on a one-for-one instruction basis, is far greater than the amount of DNA.

- Complex algorithmic processing is involved in human development
- All perceiving species have some degree of consciousness (though not equivalent).
- Consciousness requires an immaterial mind (more to follow in the next book).
- The immaterial mind falsifies a strictly materialistic origin of life, including strictly materialistic evolution (I do not assert that evolution didn't happen, but rather am challenging the exclusively materialistic mechanisms for it).
- The immaterial mind turns natural selection into intelligent selection.
- All that I described of what's required, at a minimum, process-wise, for the origin of the first life.
- We are the product of intelligent design.

I've speculated what might be true with no direct evidence to support it:

- That aging is designed into us.
- The implications of what would happen if DNA didn't use algorithmic processing (I recognize that the consequences might not be as I stated, but I wanted to illustrate consequences would be significant).

Lastly, for the purposes of sheer entertainment, I included fanciful ideas:

- That information on the physical laws of the universe, or any other type of conceptual information, is encoded in our DNA.
- That there is a means to alter electromagnetic repulsion to enable fusion energy.

I may well be proven wrong in some aspects of the above, but I expect the core assertions to stand up. This is, after all, a work of fiction written by a nonscientist. Of course if I am fundamentally wrong, then we're only matter and it won't matter! Time will tell.

Acknowledgments

Of all the words I've written for this book—both those that made it in and the many that did not—the words in this acknowledgments have come the easiest. Writing them gave me a chance not only to enjoy the fact that the book really is completed but, more important, to reflect on all it took for that to happen and, especially, on all those who helped me on the way.

Of course, acknowledgments and thanks begin with my parents, Bruce Buff and Ann Buff. These two have consistently loved and supported me throughout my life, always thinking the best of me and what I could accomplish—although novel writing is definitely outside the realm of anything they thought I would attempt.

The forbearance of my wife, Claire, and children, Maggie, Julia, Susanna, Timothy, and Patrick, as they accepted the many weekends and "free time" I spent on this book was gratifying. Even more so was their gradual change of view from "couldn't you being doing better things with your time?" to mild acceptance, to outright pleasure with the accomplishment. In fact, I appreciate the former attitude (accepting, however resignedly, what seemed like a fool's errand) even more than the latter, which I am nonetheless thrilled to have.

My agent, Roger Freet, guided me, providing strong counsel and support, for which I am very thankful. His expertise, enthusiasm and efforts were indispensable. My Howard Books editor, Beth Adams, skillfully shepherded the initial manuscript to become a far better novel than I could ever have accomplished on my own, one that I am honored to have the opportunity to have published. Her hard work and patience never flagged. Both Roger and Beth were fun to work with.

ACKNOWLEDGMENTS

Years before I had an agent or publisher, Pat LoBrutto believed in my story and me, and provided valuable editorial assistance and encouragement along the way. Likewise, former publishing executive Marjorie Braman provided another set of eyes, and perspective, to shape and sharpen my story. Tragically, she passed away before she could see the finished product, although she still left her mark on the novel.

Numerous people read my manuscript as it progressed and provided important contributions, in particular Nick Gentile and Mariah Macias (via Penn's Kelly Writers House). Casey Connor was generous with his time, skillfully helping me with early publicity copy assistance.

Other early readers and commenters included my daughter Julia, David Polinchock, JoAnn Marvin, Richard Scurry, Joe Battagalia, Eugene Kelly, Paul Kocourek, Mike Jones, Kristen Ulfsparre, David Ryan, Tom Gallagher, Mike Ghelardi, Wilma Jordan, Jeannie Carr, and John Ronan. Their willingness to read the early manuscript of a novice novelist helped me editorially, but even more important provided terrific reassurance of the value of this project.

I am grateful to Dr. Richard Temkin, associate director of MIT's Plasma Research and Fusion Center; Dr. Robert Kaita, deputy head of research operations at Princeton's Plasma Physics Laboratory; and Dr. Leland Ellison, computational physicist at Lawrence Livermore National Laboratory. Sharing their valuable fusion and physics expertise with me, as well as giving me tours of MIT's and Princeton's fusion research centers, was important to the book in obvious ways.

I appreciate the feedback I received on my arguments for the immaterial mind from Dr. Kaita (again!); physicist and philosopher Dr. Stephen Barr of the University of Delaware; philosopher Dr. J.P. Moreland of Biola Univesity; Fran Maier, special advisor to Archbishop Chaput; and author George Sim Johnston.

Dr. Peter Kreeft of Boston College kindly provided feedback on some of the religious related arguments.

I consulted Ann Gauger and Jonathan Wells from the Discovery Institute, and biology professor Thomas Reilly, PhD (my brother-in-law), regarding the accuracy of what I present as biological science, and am grateful for their numerous corrections. Though I am sympathetic to the concept of intelligent design, and find many of the arguments for it compelling, this book is not an ID apology. That topic, as well as others in this book, would require far more space to discuss their merits, by people better equipped to do it. Rather, my intent was to bring up a few ideas that were new to me and see what I could do with them. In the end, this book is solely the product of the story I wanted to tell and was not conceived by any particular interests other than my own, though I certainly do rely on the work and knowledge of others. That said, I do appreciate the support and encouragement I received from Steve Meyer, Casey Luskin, and John West, also of the Discovery Institute.

To anyone I neglected to mention, it is not for lack of appreciation.

Please note that I do not mean to imply that any of the people who reviewed all or part of my arguments in the manuscript agreed with every aspect of them, or in some cases, even most of them. Some people were fine with some aspects of the ideas in the book but not with others. Some were ID supporters and others objected strenuously to any doubts about Darwinian evolution. However, all were generously willing to share their knowledge and opinions with me.

In a similar vein, any errors of science or reason in this book are solely mine.

Finally, and not in the least, least, I would like to thank everyone at Howard Books and Simon & Schuster who contributed to the publication of this book, including the production, art, marketing and publicity, and sales teams. Their creativity and professionalism were outstanding.